raise for William Ryan's Captai

THE TWELFTH DEPA

*isted for the CWA Ellis Peters Historical Dagger for Best
Historical Crime Novel of the Year and the Ireland AM
Irish Crime Novel of the Year Award*

'... satisfying as its two predecessors . . . Ryan's achievement is
... his characters and their milieu so tangibly immediate that
... you're actually in their presence' *Irish Independent*

'... the time the talented Ryan has been among the very best
... novelists working in a period setting and if your taste is for
... fare by Martin Cruz Smith or Philip Kerr, in which an
... sleuth tries to do his best in a corrupt foreign regime, you
... not hesitate . . . Once again the balance of pungent period
... and increasingly tense plotting are handled with total author-
... Korolev remains one of the most persuasively conflicted
... characters in crime fiction' *Daily Express*

'The third outing for William Ryan's increasingly impressive Captain
... series . . . The geographical setting and political backdrop
... compelling enough, but Korolev is a fascinating character in his
... right' *Irish Times*

'... fetid and suffocating atmosphere created by Ryan is brilliantly
... realized . . . As a crime story this is excellent, but as a historical crime
... novel, it is outstanding' **Historical Novel Society**

'... uly magnificent book: addictive, interesting, well-written and full
of interesting characters' *Eurocrime*

'Ryan's tense, tightly plotted whodunnits feel gloriously plausible'
Guardian

THE HOLY THIEF

Shortlisted for the CWA John Creasey (New Blood) Dagger, the Theakston's Crime Novel of the Year Award and the Irish Fiction Award

'A first novel written with all the narrative assurance of someone who'd been perfecting his art for years . . . it was persuasive in all its local and historical details, told its tense story with style and aplomb and had an engagingly troubled hero'

Books of the Year, *Irish Independent*

'Impressive . . . The Great Terror's atmosphere of fear and paranoia is well portrayed, and Korolev is an appealing hero'

Marcel Berlins, *The Times*

'A subtle, superb mystery, a wonderful central character and with a sense of place and period to rival even the greatest of the Russian masters. More please!'   **Kate Mosse, author of *Labyrinth***

'Ryan's novel has an authority that belies his first-novel status . . . Ryan demonstrates considerable skill in evoking this benighted period, along with a deftness at ringing the changes on familiar crime plotting moves. The auguries for a series are very promising indeed'   **Barry Forshaw, *Daily Express***

'Fans of Phillip Kerr, Tom Rob Smith, and Olen Steinhauer have a treat in store'   ***Booklist***

'An inspired choice of setting . . . vividly imagined'

***Metro* Crime Books of the Year**

'Ryan's first detective novel confidently recreates a paranoid society where mutual suspicion is the norm . . . An absorbing and assured debut'   ***Sunday Times***

THE BLOODY MEADOW

Shortlisted for the Ireland AM Irish Crime Novel of the Year Award

'An outstanding thriller . . . Ryan is so alert to the psychology of his characters'
Irish Independent

'Every bit as darkly compelling as its predecessor with all the elements that made *The Holy Thief* so successful: razor-sharp plotting, an evocative sense of location in a vividly realized Ukraine and most winning of all the vulnerably human Alexei Korolev making a nuisance of himself'
Daily Express

'*The Holy Thief*, set in Stalin's Russia, was one of last year's most impressive crime fiction debuts. *The Bloody Meadow*, William Ryan's follow-up, does not disappoint. Ryan has obviously done much research into that sinister period of Russian history and manages to convey its claustrophobic atmosphere brilliantly'
The Times

'A novel that confirms Ryan's talent'
Sunday Times

'Ryan's unrolling of the mental gymnastics required to survive this upside-down world where the morning's hero is the evening's victim is both thrillerishly pacey while also allowing his characters to grow in moral stature'
Spectator

THE TWELFTH DEPARTMENT

William Ryan was called to the English bar after
university in Dublin, then worked as a lawyer in the City.
His Captain Korolev series – *The Holy Thief*, *The Bloody Meadow*
and *The Twelfth Department* – set in 1930s Stalinist Russia, has
been shortlisted for the Theakston's Crime Novel of the Year
Award, the CWA New Blood Dagger, the Irish Fiction Award,
the Ireland AM Irish Crime Novel of the Year Award and
the CWA Ellis Peters Historical Dagger Award.
William is married and lives in West London.

Discover more at
facebook.com/WilliamRyanAuthor
www.william-ryan.com
@WilliamRyan_

Also by William Ryan

THE HOLY THIEF

THE BLOODY MEADOW

WILLIAM RYAN

THE TWELFTH DEPARTMENT

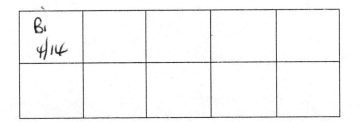

Bi
4/14

PAN BOOKS

First published 2013 by Mantle

This edition published 2014 by Pan Books
an imprint of Pan Macmillan, a division of Macmillan Publishers Limited
Pan Macmillan, 20 New Wharf Road, London N1 9RR
Basingstoke and Oxford
Associated companies throughout the world
www.panmacmillan.com

ISBN 978-0-330-50848-3

1 3 5 7 9 8 6 4 2

A CIP catalogue record for this book is available from the British Library.

Typeset by SetSystems Ltd, Saffron Walden, Essex
Printed and bound by CPI Group (UK) Ltd, Croydon, CR0 4YY

Visit www.panmacmillan.com to read more about all our books
and to buy them. You will also find features, author interviews and
news of any author events, and you can sign up for e-newsletters
so that you're always first to hear about our new releases.

For Charlie

Characters

Dr Irina Azarova – Professor Azarov's wife

Isaac Babel – famous author and also Korolev's neighbour

Sergeant Belinsky – Militiaman in charge of the investigating uniforms (uniformed police) at Leadership House

Blanter – State Security operative working for the NKVD's Twelfth Department

Dr Zinaida Petrovna Chestnova – pathologist and friend of Korolev

Danilov – foreman in charge of the removals at the Azarov Institute

The Deacon – one of Count Kolya's men

Dubinkin – a lieutenant with the NKVD

Nikolai Ezhov – General Commissar of State Security and head of the NKVD

Monsieur Hubert – a representative of the French embassy in Moscow

Count Kolya – leader of the Moscow Thieves

Captain Alexei Korolev – a detective with the Moscow Criminal Investigation Division

Yuri Korolev – Captain Korolev's son

Valentina Nikolayevna Koltsova – Korolev's friend and neighbour

Natasha Koltsova – Valentina Koltsova's daughter

Kuznetsky – Militiaman assisting Korolev

Levschinsky – forensics specialist for Moscow CID

Lilova – maid to Dr Shtange

Maria Lobkovskaya – Korolev's elderly downstairs neighbour

Galina Matkina – maid to Professor Azarov

Menchikova – resident of Leadership House

Mishka – Count Kolya's right-hand man

Pavel Morozov – responsible for the car pool at Militia headquarters and a friend of Korolev

Petya the Persuader – an informant

First Inspector Popov – Korolev's boss

Priudski – original doorman at Leadership House

Colonel Rodinov – a senior NKVD officer

Semyon Shabalin – a bank robber and gangster

Dr Arkady Shtange – Deputy Director of the Azarov Institute

Anna Shtange – Dr Shtange's wife

Shura – maid to Babel and a friend to Korolev

Nadezhda Slivka – a junior detective with the Odessa CID

Spinsky – Director of the Vitsin Street Orphanage

Svalov – State Security operative working for the NKVD's Twelfth Department

Tambova – also known as 'Little Barrel', attendant at the Vitsin Street Orphanage

Timinov – replacement doorman at Leadership House

Sergei Ushakov – forensics specialist for Moscow CID

Vera – Valentina's friend and a worker at Moscow Z

Dr Weiss – neighbour and colleague of Professor Azarov

Captain Dmitry Yasimov – Korolev's fellow detective with Moscow CID

Colonel Zaitsev – head of the NKVD's Twelfth Department

Prologue

PATRIARCH'S PONDS was one of Korolev's favourite corners of Moscow – a small park with a square-shaped lake around which, especially on a hot summer's day like this, white-shirted men and their befrocked womenfolk strolled with slow steps. At the southern end a white colonnaded pavilion stood where, for a reasonable price, a citizen could sip a glass of tea and sit and watch the ducks. Alternatively, in the eastern corner of the park, there stood a wooden kiosk where beer and kvass could be purchased and, if you knew how to ask for them, stronger beverages as well. If they'd had time to spare and a less pressing matter to attend to, Korolev thought to himself, a sip of vodka mightn't have been such a bad idea. But not today and not now. Not with a certain gangster he'd been after for six months about to walk into a trap of Korolev's making.

Anyway, he decided, he'd need all his wits about him. Semyon Shabalin was as slippery as an eel dipped in oil, and clever with it. Korolev and his comrades had managed to catch up with most of his Grey Fox gang and put them where they belonged – but Shabalin had wriggled free each time they'd thought they had him, even when escape had seemed an impossibility. And while most of Moscow's underworld had certain standards – which, it had to be said, they often seemed to forget about – the Grey Foxes had none. With each robbery they'd committed, they'd set new standards in brutality and viciousness – so that now even the Thieves, the organized clans that ran crime in Moscow, were shaking their heads in disapproval. Whatever else happened today, Korolev was determined Shabalin wasn't leaving this park a free man.

Korolev walked outside the park's railings while Petya the Persuader, their informant, followed the tree-covered path that ran alongside the sky-reflecting blue water. Slivka was a few paces behind Petya, wearing a pretty white dress, her short blonde hair looking almost golden in the dappled sunlight. Her lips might be a little thin and her expression grave, but she was a good-looking woman and he watched men's heads turn one after the other to follow her procession through the park. He wondered if they'd be so keen if they knew the hand nonchalantly resting inside her open purse was wrapped around the butt of a service-issue revolver.

Korolev glanced at his watch. If Petya was to be believed, Shabalin would meet him on the fourth bench to the left of the pavilion – in just a few minutes' time. He adjusted the ticket machine he had slung over his shoulder – part of his disguise as a tram conductor on a break – and found himself, to his surprise, wishing there was a sandwich in the tin lunchbox he was carrying – as opposed to his Walther.

Korolev kept his eyes moving – examining each of the pedestrians who passed him, watching for anyone or anything that seemed out of place. If things went as he hoped, there'd be a small scuffle and Shabalin would be in the bag. If things didn't go to plan? Well, if he had to shoot Shabalin's legs from him, then so be it.

Korolev took a seat beside an elderly lady ten metres from the bench Petya now occupied. Slivka found herself a spot a little further along the path on Petya's other side and, two minutes later, a familiar-looking balloon seller began hawking his wares in their general vicinity. From where Korolev was sitting, Yasimov's disguise looked less than convincing – it seemed one end of the detective's moustache was slightly higher than the other. But it was too late to do anything about that now.

Korolev sighed, took his newspaper from the pocket of his coat and opened it, scanning his surroundings one more time as he did so. All was peaceful – a toy sailing boat moved slowly across the water, leaving a v-shaped wake behind it, the only disturbance on the pond's surface. It was a sweltering afternoon and the heat seemed to be pressing down on everything – making even the noises of the city that surrounded them seem distant. He found himself yawning as he opened the latch on the lunchbox so that his Walther would be easily accessible. It wasn't much good having a gun if you couldn't get to it quickly. The toy yacht moved onwards and Korolev had no idea where it was picking up a breeze from. He could feel nothing – just the remorseless weight of the heat. It occurred to him that if he couldn't have a sandwich, then an ice cream would be just the thing on a day like this.

He yawned again. He could feel his eyes growing heavy and put a hand to his ear to twist it – hard. The pain woke him up a little – just as a gaggle of *besprizorniki* came ambling into the park and caught his attention. Most of the street children were barefoot and wearing nothing but short trousers, their shirts tucked into belts or slung over their bare shoulders – skin dark as oiled wood from the long summer. They walked with chests out and shoulders back and it seemed that if they didn't own the place, then no one had told them.

Korolev didn't like the look of them – the thing was, they looked in the mood for wickedness, staring impudently into the faces of the citizens they passed and sharing jokes amongst themselves that seemed to have more than a hint of malice about them. They were out for trouble, no doubt about it. And, in a moment of complete clarity, Korolev realized that the target they'd choose for their mischief would inevitably be the odd-looking balloon seller with the unbalanced moustache.

'Twenty kopecks for a big red balloon,' Yasimov called out and his voice sounded like the sad bleat of a lambless sheep. The *besprizorniki* turned as one, like hounds catching a scent. And, without anyone needing to say a word, they fanned out around the unhappy detective.

'Twenty kopecks? Twenty? For a balloon that you filled with your own gas?'

This from the leader – a ratty-looking rascal and one Korolev didn't doubt would be a long-standing future acquaintance of the Moscow Militia.

'Get lost, puppy, or you'll feel the toe of my boot,' Yasimov said, whipping around as another of the youngsters pulled at the striped sailor's shirt he'd thought, for some unknown reason, would make him look the part.

'Two for ten would be more like it, damned speculator.'

A stunted, dark-haired boy, this one, with a prematurely lined forehead and a nose that had been bent sideways somewhere along the way. A cigarette jutted out of the corner of his mouth and the runt blew a cloud of smoke up into Yasimov's indignant face to make his point.

'I'd say he's more than a speculator, Comrades,' their leader drawled. 'I'd say he's an enemy. He's got that look about him.'

'Get out of here, fleas, or you'll regret waking up this morning.'

That was when the first balloon popped – the runt stabbing it with a glowing cigarette end. And simultaneously, as if the balloon had been a signal, from further down the pathway came a rapid series of explosions not unlike machine-gun fire, as a separate group of children let off a belt of firecrackers.

From complete calm, the scene around him had changed in an instant to chaos, but strangely Korolev found that for him everything was slowing down. This turmoil was no damned coincidence, he was thinking. It was a diversion, or he was a Bolshoi ballerina.

Where was Shabalin?

Once he looked, it wasn't hard to find him – he'd already climbed over the park railings not twenty metres behind him. And once inside the park, Shabalin was heading for Petya at a brisk walk, one hand in his pocket. And Korolev was pretty sure it wasn't a comb that Shabalin was holding in there.

Petya saw Shabalin and the big man jumped to his feet, lifting his hands up to fend him off. Korolev was running now and, just as the silver flash of Shabalin's blade began to slice towards Petya's chest, he found that he'd swung the solid weight of the ticket machine on its leather strap over his head and down towards Shabalin's shoulder, where it hit with a solid blow, knocking the arm down just before the knife connected – and sending it skittering away across the path.

'You damned traitor, Petya,' Shabalin cried out as he ducked, clutching his shoulder and twisting himself out of Korolev's attempt to hold him.

'Stay where you are, Shabalin,' Korolev shouted, but the gang leader was already two steps away and moving along the pathway fast. Yasimov's whistle was shrieking somewhere close and someone was shouting for the police.

'Stop,' Korolev called out. 'Or I shoot.'

Shabalin turned to look back and so never saw the white dress coming towards him like an express train. Slivka drove her right shoulder into the killer's midriff – every ounce of her weight behind it – and Shabalin hit the ground like lead, his head bouncing off the tarmac path. He lay where he fell, completely still – a bundle of clothes and limbs – while Slivka scrambled to her knees, turned him and handcuffed his arms behind his back.

'Sit down,' Yasimov was shouting and Korolev turned to see Petya slump back onto the bench, putting his hands on his head – a penitent look on his face. Balloons were floating through the branches above, while the last of the *besprizorniki* were scattering as uniforms flooded into the park.

'Good work, Comrades,' Korolev said, kneeling down to examine the unconscious Shabalin. It seemed it was all over – the battle was won. He put his hand to the gangster's neck, feeling for a pulse – relieved to find one. In the circumstances, the fact that no one had been killed seemed a miracle.

Korolev took a packet of cigarettes from his pocket, offering one to Slivka and lighting one for himself. It was just coming up to four o'clock – plenty of time to make it to the station. And what happier omen could there be for young Yuri's visit to Moscow than to have put Semyon Shabalin behind bars?

Chapter One

YAROSLAVSKY STATION was crowded and unpleasant – but Korolev breathed in the hot, muggy air and allowed himself a smile. What did it matter, when Yuri, his 12-year-old son, would be stepping down from the Zagorsk train in a matter of minutes?

It *was* hot though. Even in the relative cool of the ticket hall, Korolev could feel sweat pooling under his arms and running down his back in what seemed to be a constant stream – but he still couldn't help the joy bubbling up through him. Anyway, it couldn't stay this hot for much longer – the weather would turn more comfortable in the next few days. It had to.

Ideally, he'd take off his jacket, which felt heavy as a fur coat in this heat. But if he did take it off then he'd have every citizen in the place looking at the Walther in its holster and wondering if he was a Chekist come to arrest somebody – and whether that somebody might just be them. He could do without that kind of attention.

He just hoped that the train would be on time – or at least not too late.

There was one niggling concern at the back of his mind about this visit though, and that was its unexpectedness – it had come completely out of the blue. His ex-wife Zhenia had called him just a few days before to ask if he could take Yuri – she hadn't explained why and he hadn't asked. At the time, it had been enough for him that he'd be seeing the boy for a whole week – just the two of them. But afterwards, when he'd thought it through, he couldn't help but have a more complex reaction to the news. After all, he'd loved Zhenia back when they'd still been man and wife – and love left its mark on a man's soul and that was all there was to it. And even if it wasn't any of his business what Zhenia was up to, he couldn't help but feel a little low at the thought that, likely as not, she'd be spending a week with some other member of the male species, and in a place where their son wouldn't be welcome. He bore her no ill will, of course, and she was within her rights – but still.

His thoughts were diverted from their glum turn by two shrill blasts of a whistle from somewhere far down the tracks and, as if in response, the station speakers announced the arrival of the Zagorsk train. Not a minute passed before it came into view, steam billowing out behind and around it – eventually coming to a halt just short of the buffers with a loud grinding of brakes. In no time at all, the empty platform was full of passengers and a surge of baggage and humanity flooded towards him.

Korolev took up position just beside the engine's coal tender, keeping his eyes peeled for a mop of blonde hair and a smiling face, hardly able to contain his own excitement – but there was no sign of Yuri. The people kept coming but still his son didn't appear, and now he was looking only at stragglers and railway workers. Where was he? There'd been youngsters amongst the crowd right enough, but they'd had parents and family in tow. Zhenia had sent the boy on his own, saying he'd be fine, that the journey wasn't very long; but Korolev knew things he'd never tell Zhenia about what could happen on a Soviet train – even in the middle of the day with the sun shining. He found his hands had balled into fists and that dread was seeping through his veins.

Korolev moved forward along the length of train, his pace

increasing with each step, checking each compartment and pushing aside anyone who got in his way. By the time he'd reached the fourth carriage he was almost certain something had happened to the boy. And by the time he'd checked the fifth carriage, and found it empty as well, he was convinced of it. It wasn't until the very last carriage – by which time guards were shutting doors further up the train – that he found what he'd been looking for. A small head. Blonde hair pressed against a window.

Korolev swallowed hard and opened the door, fearing the worst. The young boy sat slumped in the corner of a bench seat, a suitcase on his knees nearly as big as he was. Deathly pale, his eyes shut. Yuri. Korolev reached forward to touch his son's cheek, bracing himself; but the skin was warm. Korolev hadn't even been aware he was holding his breath until he let it go.

The boy was fast asleep.

Korolev took the seat opposite, not sure quite what to do. Should he wake him? He examined him – a little over five feet tall now, he'd say – a good-looking child with a strong mouth and a firm chin. His hair was cut short at the sides but had a little length on top so his curls showed. Around his neck, above the white sleeveless shirt, hung a red Pioneer's scarf – the brass ring that gathered it together underneath the boy's chin looking as though it had been polished for the trip.

He'd changed was the truth of the matter, his face was leaner and he'd grown an inch or two, but it was more than that. It seemed to Korolev almost as if he was looking at a version of the son he remembered. He'd only seen Yuri once in two years, for three days back in March, and even then they'd only been together in the evenings. Of course, he would have changed – he was young, it was what they did. Only middle-aged men like him stayed more or less the same.

Eventually he leant forward and shook Yuri's shoulder till his blue eyes opened in surprise. The boy shifted his focus rapidly from Korolev to the carriage, to the station he found himself in – sitting up as he did so.

Korolev heard him murmur a single word – 'Moscow' – before he leant back against the seat.

'Yuri,' Korolev said, softly, and expected to see the boy's face break into a smile, for the suitcase to be tossed aside and for arms to reach around his neck, but instead his son's expression remained melancholy, and he said nothing. Korolev leant forward once again to ruffle the boy's hair – careful to be gentle with him.

'Are you all right?'

Yuri nodded but it seemed to be an effort for him. Korolev looked at him for a long moment – there was something not right, that was certain. But like as not, tiredness was mostly what it was – that and the heat. He took the bag from the boy's unresisting grip then slipped his arm around him.

'Come here, Yurochka,' he said and scooped the boy up to his shoulder, turning to climb down from the carriage and place Yuri on his unsteady feet.

'We'll have to walk for a while, can you manage?'

The boy nodded.

'I'll carry the suitcase then.'

They made their way along the platform in silence, Yuri's eyes fixed on the ground in front of his feet, not once looking up at him. And Korolev felt almost as lost as the boy looked.

§

They travelled by tram back to Bolshoi Nikolo-Vorobinsky. Korolev managed to squeeze Yuri onto a seat and stood over him, protecting the boy from the late-afternoon crush. Yuri didn't look at him or the other passengers, or even out the window at the city passing by. His stare was blank and seemed fixed on nothing. Korolev felt his hand instinctively reach forward to touch him, but he held it back. He'd take it slowly –

there was time. They needed to get to know each other again was all.

It was only five minutes from the tram stop to the street Korolev lived in, but Yuri still hadn't spoken – or even properly acknowledged him. Korolev stopped at the door to the apartment and crouched down in front of Yuri so that the boy couldn't avoid looking at him. Even in the gloom of the stairwell, the boy's blue eyes seemed unnaturally bright.

'Listen, Yuri. I know you're tired, I can see that, but these are your neighbours for the next week and you'll make an effort, yes? The woman is called Koltsova – Valentina Nikolayevna.' Korolev spoke distinctly – until the boy was better acquainted, it would be polite for him to use both Valentina's name and patronymic. Yuri nodded to show he had it memorized.

'Her husband was that famous engineer I told you about, the one who died in the Metro accident.'

'I remember.' Yuri's voice, when it came, was little better than a croak.

'Good. Now her daughter is Natasha – she's a bit younger than you and a good person as well. A Pioneer, same as you are. They're the best of people, both of them – I couldn't ask for better. So I want you to speak up and speak strongly, as Comrade Stalin would expect from such a fine young specimen of socialist youth, and treat them as the good comrades they are.'

Yuri seemed to wake at that, and give Korolev his full attention for the first time.

'Of course.'

'Good.'

Korolev stood and put his key in the lock, knocking once on the door as he opened it.

'We're here,' he called in.

'Come in, come in,' Valentina bustled out from the small kitchen area, wiping her hands on an apron, her cheeks rosy from the heat. It occurred to Korolev that he'd never seen her wear an apron before.

'We made a cake,' she said. 'We wanted to do something nice for Yuri.'

'An apricot cake,' Natasha said, appearing beside her mother, a smile on her face. 'I queued for them. The apricots that is.'

'We didn't get everything we needed,' Valentina put a finger to her chin as she considered this. 'But it worked out, I think.'

'It smells good.'

'It does smell good,' Yuri agreed, and Korolev was pleased to see his son was smiling along with everyone else.

'Yuri,' Valentina stepped forward to embrace him. 'We're pleased to have you here.'

'Thank you. I'm pleased to be here.'

Yuri looked up towards Korolev, who nodded his approval.

'Yes, Comrade Yuri — fellow Pioneer.' Natasha took Yuri's hand in hers, shaking it vigorously. 'Welcome to Moscow.'

Chapter Two

IT WAS STRANGE to spend a night with another human being so close by – and periodically Korolev found himself waking, just about, and listening – though for what, he couldn't quite remember at first. A dark silence surrounded him. Then, his ears attuning, he might hear a car's engine a few streets away, or perhaps some mysterious metallic grinding from down near the river, or a late-night walker's footsteps. Nothing unusual, in other words. It was like that, Moscow – it moved around in its sleep.

Finally, however, Korolev would detect the quiet rhythm of Yuri's breathing only feet away. The boy was sleeping on a borrowed couch on the other side of the bedroom and Korolev felt a warm happiness at his proximity. But even in his half-awake state, he remembered that all wasn't well. Yuri had cheered up when they'd come back to the apartment, but until then – well – he'd been strange and silent. And, remembering that, worry would gnaw away at Korolev – until he slipped back into unconsciousness once again.

How he found himself lying beside Valentina Nikolayevna, looking across at her sleeping face, he wasn't sure. Her hair was spread across the pillow like an angel's halo – never had she looked so beautiful. Her lips opened slightly as she stirred, the blanket slipping down from her bare neck, lower and lower. Then lower still . . .

'Papa?'

The voice was clear, very clear, but it didn't fit – he decided to ignore it.

'Papa?'

That voice again. He wished it would *go away*. If this was a dream then it was a damned good one – one he wanted to wrap tight around him like a blanket. Even now, as it seemed in danger of slipping away. But she was still there – just. Valentina, the woman with whom he shared his apartment – the woman he secretly admired. And now this perfect dream. It was hard to hold onto it, with that gentle tapping on his chest.

'Papa?'

A boy's voice – close enough for him to feel the breath against his cheek. If he shut his eyes very tightly it would go away, no doubt of it. The important thing was to stay asleep and hold onto the dream.

'Papa, wake up.'

And it was gone. Such a dream, as well. He opened his eyes to find his son looking down at him, frowning.

'Yuri?' he said, rubbing his fingers over his eyes. 'What time is it?'

Early, to judge by the flat sunlight coming through the curtains. He'd half-hoped to lounge in his bed for a change, but it seemed that wasn't to be.

'You were groaning.'

'Was I?' Korolev said, feeling his cheeks redden.

'I thought you might be ill.'

'No, just a dream.'

'You were talking to yourself.'

Damn, he'd been talking to himself. What had he said?

'What did I say?' Korolev asked, deciding it was best he knew.

'I couldn't make it out. You sounded in pain, though.'

'Probably just a bad dream.' Or a good one, of course. 'How did you find the couch?'

'Good, I think.' Yuri looked unsure. 'How did I end up in here?'

'You fell asleep while you were eating so I brought you in.'

Yuri considered this.

'I was tired from the journey.'

'You were,' Korolev said, pushing down the sheet and sitting up. He thought about that niggling worry of his and whether he should bring it up – and decided not to. There was time enough. He yawned and stretched his arms above his head. He should be fully awake for such a subject.

'Let's get some breakfast then, and plan our day.'

'Mother said you might have to work.' Yuri's eyes slid sideways. 'She said I shouldn't expect to see much of you.'

Korolev sat on the side of the bed and regarded his son, smiling as he did so.

'As it happens, I've your whole visit off. I need to go in to Petrovka and sign some papers this morning but that won't take more than a few minutes. And I happen to know there's a jazz band playing in Hermitage Park, which is just across the street – we can kill two birds with one stone.'

§

By the time Korolev had done his morning exercises and they'd dressed, Valentina and Natasha were also up and about in the bedroom they occupied on the other side of the shared sitting room.

'Good morning,' Korolev said, the memory of his dream making him feel more than a little shifty in Valentina Nikolay-evna's presence.

'Yurochka,' Valentina said, embracing his son – the diminutive of Yuri's name sounding surprisingly natural to Korolev, even though they'd only met the night before. 'You're awake. We were worried about you last night. You just fell forward – you'd have a bruise if your father hadn't caught you.'

Yuri gave her a shy smile.

'I thought it might have been the apricot cake,' Natasha said, gravely, coming into the room. 'I thought Mother might have poisoned you.'

Valentina reached out a swift hand as though to cuff her only child, who giggled as she danced away.

'I'll poison *you*, one of these days.'

'I thought the cake was very good,' Yuri said, 'I liked it very much.'

'At last, a polite child in the house.'

'Have you been to the zoo, Yuri?' Natasha asked, clambering onto the heavy wooden table in the shared room and sitting there in the morning light, her legs swinging. She was ten – a couple of years younger than Yuri – but if he hadn't known this to be the case, Korolev would have guessed she was the older of the two.

'Never.'

'You see, Mama. I told you. We have to take him. You must call your friend. If Yuri went back to Zagorsk without going to the greatest zoo in the world – well.'

It was clear that, in Natasha's opinion, this would be a source of bitter shame for everyone involved

'Can I come?' Korolev asked.

'If you're not working, of course you can,' Natasha said. 'But you work all the time. Which is good, of course. The State needs hard workers.'

'I have the next six days off.'

'Six days?' Valentina said, raising her eyebrows. 'Six days with no work at all?'

'I've got to sign some paperwork this morning – on the Grey Fox investigation. But apart from that – I'm free as a bird.'

Yuri's eyes widened.

'The Grey Fox investigation?'

'A serious business – we captured the leader yesterday.'

'He was a murderer,' Natasha told Yuri, lowering her voice. 'And a bank robber. They called him "Needle" because he killed seven men with an ice pick.'

'A bank robber?' Yuri asked, looking to Korolev for confirmation.

'Only one bank. Mostly post offices and factory safes. A tough customer – we were glad to catch up with him. I'll tell you about it on the way to Petrovka, don't you worry.'

'You're taking Yuri to Petrovka?' Natasha asked. 'To Militia headquarters?'

'I wasn't going to,' Korolev said. 'But I could do that. Shura said she might come up with us – there's a concert in Hermitage Park. A jazz concert. I was going to drop Yuri and Shura off there, do my business, and join them later.'

Shura was maid to their famous neighbour, Babel the writer, and a maternal figure to many of the children in the building, as well as, strangely, Korolev. Natasha's face was a picture of longing and Korolev was detective enough to know it wasn't the concert she was interested in.

'Would you like to come as well?'

'To Petrovka? To visit the Moscow Criminal Investigation Division?' Natasha asked, doing her best to sound offhand – and failing. 'Yes, that could be interesting. Very interesting. Will there be criminals?'

'Probably, but I'll steer you clear of them,' Korolev said, looking to Valentina Nikolayevna – who looked amused.

'And afterwards, seeing as it's such hot weather, we could go swimming.'

'Swimming?' two young voices said in unison.

'All Pioneers have to be able to swim long and fast. I wouldn't want you falling behind in such a thing.'

Yuri and Natasha agreed that this was something that should be avoided.

'How about tomorrow morning for the zoo?' Valentina asked, making her way towards the small kitchen. 'I'll call Vera. First thing?'

'Vera works at the zoo,' Natasha explained. 'No one else is there in the morning, Yuri. We'll see things no one else has ever seen. Animals eating other animals.'

Yuri looked impressed and Korolev felt relief – the children would get on, Yuri's visit would be a great success. 'Tomorrow sounds good,' he said. 'First thing.'

Chapter Three

'I'M SORRY, KOROLEV, I heard you were in the building and I'm afraid I need you. Urgently. Bring Slivka with you.'

Korolev placed the receiver back in its cradle, raised his eyes to the ceiling and considered asking it, or the Lord who resided some way above it, why he hadn't cut his visit shorter. That was the thing about places of work – if you spent too long hanging about them there was always the chance someone would ask you to do something. His sigh drew Slivka's attention. Even his old friend Yasimov looked up from the report he was working on.

'The boss wants us,' Korolev said in answer to Slivka's quizzical look. He attempted a smile – a poor attempt, he didn't doubt. 'Something's come up. Something urgent, it seems.'

His mood wasn't improved by Slivka's evident sympathy – or Yasimov's, for that matter. The worst thing was it had been his own fault – he'd spent too long introducing Yuri and Natasha to his colleagues, taking them around the small internal museum, telling them about famous cases that Moscow CID had solved. He'd even shown them the cells and one of the interrogation rooms. By the time he'd sent them off to Hermitage Park with Shura, the best part of an hour had passed. Too long for papers that had only needed a signature.

He reached into the bottom drawer of his desk and retrieved the Walther he'd just placed there, pulling the leather strap of the holster over his shoulder and fitting the gun snugly under his armpit. He patted the gun for luck and prayed it wasn't a murder Popov wanted to talk about. If it was, that would be the week gone. He'd be lucky if he saw Yuri at all. Still, there wasn't any use complaining about such things. And with a bit of luck, Popov just wanted to ask them about the Grey Fox business. With a lot of luck.

'Mitya?' Korolev asked Yasimov, standing, 'Can you spare five minutes to go up to the park and tell the little ones the good news?' He handed him a five-rouble note. 'Give this to Shura in case she needs it and tell her I'll send her a message when I know what's what. And kiss Yuri for me.'

'Of course, brother. Consider him kissed.'

'Thank you.'

Korolev's face must have still been showing his disappointment when, two minutes later, he and Slivka entered Popov's office, because the first inspector looked at him kindly as he waved them towards the empty chairs in front of his desk.

'Sit down, sit down – it mightn't be as bad as all that.'

'At your orders, Comrade First Inspector,' Korolev said. The seat he chose gave out a creak that was close enough to an animal's squeal of pain to leave a moment's awkward silence behind it.

'Well,' Popov said and reached for his pipe, filling it with tobacco as he considered his detectives. He took his time and Korolev and Slivka, used to Popov's ways, waited patiently. They knew he liked to think things through before he opened his mouth, and then he liked to think them through once again. And he never much liked talking unless his pipe was lit. Sure enough, once the tobacco was glowing orange and Popov's head was surrounded with an aromatic cloud of smoke, the first inspector tapped the notepad in front of him.

'There's a man sitting in his apartment over in Bersenevka with a bullet in his head. It seems he didn't put it there himself.'

'I see,' Korolev said, concerned. Bersenevka was just across the river from the Kremlin and Popov hadn't said the body was in a *kommunalka*: the shared housing that most citizens had to put up with. No, he'd said 'his apartment', and anyone who lived in that part of Moscow and had their own apartment was fortunate indeed. Fortunate and important.

'You know the place – that new building across the river from the Kremlin. What's it called again?'

'You mean Leadership House,' Korolev said, fearing it could be no other. He caught Slivka looking across at him. She was fresh from the wilds of the Ukraine – well, Odessa – and new to Moscow, so Slivka probably hadn't heard of the building before – but she was a smart girl and, to judge from her expression, was putting two and two together. She was right – Leadership House, as its name and location implied, was home to generals, important officials, senior Party members, directors of vital State concerns – in short, the type of people who needed to be inside the Kremlin five minutes after the phone rang.

'You do know the place,' Popov said, having the good grace to appear a little guilty. 'Good, that makes things easier.' The first inspector considered his pipe for a moment or two. 'Needless to say, it's not somewhere I can send just *any* detective. It has to be someone who has experience in such . . .'

Popov hesitated, as if considering how best to acknowledge the fact that Korolev had found himself handling more than one investigation involving senior Party members, foreign spies, State Security and the like – investigations that had damned nearly left Moscow CID with one less detective on its books.

'Well, I suppose whoever I send has to be able to deal with *delicate* matters. As the saying goes, Alexei Dmitriyevich – no good deed goes unpunished. You've done some good deeds in the past and here's your punishment – the chance to do another good deed.'

Popov's use of Korolev's patronymic was strange – things

were usually more informal between them. But perhaps Slivka's presence accounted for it – and not some other, more worrying, reason.

'I'm always ready to do my duty,' Korolev said – there wasn't much point in saying anything else. 'What do we know about the dead man?'

'He was called Azarov. A medical man – a professor, I believe. I don't know much more but I'll see if I can get his Party file, information as to where he works and so on for you. Anyway, his maid found him half an hour ago and the sergeant at the local Militia station knew enough to call us in straight away. Given where it is, there isn't a moment to lose – Morozov has a car waiting for you in the courtyard.'

Slivka's frown deepened another millimetre or two.

'Comrades, I won't pull the wool over your eyes on this,' Popov continued. 'It won't be too long before important neighbours with nervous wives start calling me asking why we haven't arrested the murderer. In fact, the building management have already been on the phone, very keen to do anything they can to ensure the matter is resolved "as soon as possible". And maybe it won't just be them who'll want this tidied up quickly. There are other people who won't like blood being spilled that close to the Kremlin.'

'Of course,' Korolev said, thinking that the 'other people' would be his old friends in State Security. You could throw a stone from the roof of Leadership House and land it in the Kremlin's gardens. More or less. Of course they'd take an interest in a killing that close to where Stalin laid his head.

'Forensics?' Korolev asked, doing his best to ignore the dread swilling round his innards. He wouldn't be going to the zoo with Yuri tomorrow – that much seemed certain.

'Ushakov and Levschinsky. They might even be there already,' Popov said, sucking on his pipe. 'And Dr Chestnova will look at the body for you.'

Popov's thin smile revealed a certain satisfaction that he'd pre-empted Korolev's next request.

'Well then,' Korolev said, rising. Slivka did the same and Popov nodded his approval.

'With luck, it will be easy enough,' Popov said, nodding in the vague direction of Bersenevka. 'Maybe the wife did it. Or the maid. The sergeant is called Belinsky – he'll give you all necessary assistance. If you need anything – call me.'

Chapter Four

SLIVKA DROVE down Neglinaya Street until it ended opposite the Metropol Hotel, where she turned right. In Teatralnaya Square, the white facade of the Bolshoi was vivid against the purple sky. The weather had turned humid that morning and now dark clouds were rolling across the city from the west. They looked heavy with rain and, unless he was mistaken, they'd be dropping it on Moscow in the not-too-distant future.

'How do you want to handle it, Chief?'

Somehow Slivka managed to speak quietly yet still be heard over the rattling engine.

'We'd better take it easy until we know the lie of the land. I'll do the talking, you take notes and keep your eyes and ears open. This is the kind of place where you have to have your wits about you. So I'll be counting on you for that.'

Slivka nodded her agreement and then they were passing the hole in the skyline where the cathedral of Christ the Saviour had stood until it had been blown to smithereens back in thirty-two – all to make way for a skyscraper that had yet to appear and, recent rumour had it, never would.

And here was another structure due for replacement – the Bolshoi Kamenny Most. The 'Great Stone Bridge' had linked Balchug island to the Kremlin side of the Moskva river since long before Korolev's time – but now a wider, higher replacement was under construction not fifty metres to the east. They said the new bridge would be finished in a couple of months and then – well, the old Bolshoi Kamenny Bridge would go the way of Christ the Saviour, he supposed. Another piece of old Moscow disappearing in a cloud of dust.

'Here we are, Slivka.'

Korolev pointed to the massive construction ahead of them – ten storeys of grey concrete that stretched from the end of the old Kamenny Bridge right along the embankment as far as the chocolate factory – and then back all the way to the Vodootvodny Canal. Of course, some might say it looked more like a prison than home to two or three thousand of the most important citizens in the Soviet Union – but no one could deny it was impressive.

'Leadership House, Slivka. I'll bet you've nothing like it in Odessa.'

'No,' she said drily. 'Truly, a person hasn't seen beauty till they've seen Moscow.'

Korolev laughed. Slivka liked her proverbs and that one hit the nail on the head. Within its forbidding exterior, Leadership House contained a theatre, a cinema, a post office, shops and the Lord knew what else – the leaders who gained the right to live there were well looked after – but Slivka was right, it wasn't beautiful. It was functional – a straightforward building for hard-working citizens. In due course everyone in the Soviet Union would live in constructions such as this, so they said – protected from the elements by thick concrete and warmed by electricity from the new power stations. It might be only intended for important personages at the moment, but a building like this told the people that things were getting better – just as Comrade Stalin had promised. And it told the State's enemies that the Soviet Union was becoming a force to be reckoned with.

§

Slivka pulled in behind a row of black motorcars, their drivers gathered together at one end of the rank. How many vehicles were there? Fifteen? Each of them belonged to someone senior enough to have a car and driver at his constant disposal – and this was in the middle of the day.

'That must be it.'

Slivka pointed to a cluster of people being kept waiting outside one of the entrances by two solid-looking uniforms in their summer whites. Behind them stood an older sergeant, who looked as if he might be waiting for someone, his blue peaked cap held in his hand.

'Comrade Captain Korolev,' the sergeant said when Korolev showed him his identity card. The fellow had to shout to be heard above a sudden hammering from the bridge works. 'I'm Belinsky.'

'Good to meet you. This is Sergeant Slivka, she works with me. Well?'

The sergeant pulled out his notebook, leafing through its pages.

'We received a call at 11.05 from the apartment of Boris Vadimovich Azarov, forty-nine years of age, medical professor. The call was from his maid, informing us Professor Azarov had been shot. I immediately called the nearest post, just down by the bridge, and ordered Militiaman Startsev to hotfoot it up here, which he did. I didn't like the sound of it, so I came directly with Militiaman Kruger – we arrived at 11.12. Startsev was waiting for us in the apartment and confirmed the professor was dead. I looked in – it was clearly a violent death, so I called for more men from the station and told my boss what was up. He said call Moscow CID.'

'We must thank him for that,' Slivka said, but the irony seemed to go over Belinsky's head. 'What then?'

'The chief said to ensure the crime scene was preserved and

wait for your instructions – so we've prevented entry to the apartment. We've also ascertained from the doorman that access to this part of Leadership House is only possible via the front door or a door to the courtyard – which is fully enclosed. He signs guests in and out – but not residents. My men have just finished checking floor to floor in case the murderer was still on the premises but we found no one who shouldn't be here. Everyone we've identified is a resident or a guest of a resident. I've one of my men compiling a list for you.'

'Good work, Belinsky.' Korolev was beginning to cheer up – if all uniforms were as organized as this fellow they wouldn't need a Criminal Investigation Division. 'How about a murder weapon? He was shot, wasn't he?'

'Yes Comrade Captain,' Belinsky struggled for a moment to hide a proud smile at Korolev's compliment, before continuing, solemn once again. 'We didn't find anything, but we didn't search thoroughly either – I wanted to make sure we didn't mess it up for forensics.'

'Good work again, Belinsky – let them poke around first. A murder investigation is like a good meal, it shouldn't be rushed. Are they here?'

'They arrived about ten minutes ago.'

'Good,' Korolev said, 'very good. What do you know about the body?'

Belinsky appeared confused, looking between Slivka and Korolev for an explanation.

'The dead man,' Slivka said patiently. 'What do we know about him as a person?'

'Ah, yes. Of course.' Belinsky flicked forward a couple of pages in his notebook. 'Professor Azarov lived in the apartment with his wife, Irina Ivanovna Azarova, forty-seven – no children. And their maid, Galina Matkina – I don't know her age, sorry, but she's young enough – anyway, she was the one who discovered the corpse. She told me the professor got up early this morning and he left the house at about 7.30. She made him coffee before he left so she's pretty sure of the timing.'

'Go on.'

Belinsky turned another page of his notebook.

'He asked her for coffee when he came back at about nine – she doesn't know where he went in the meantime but he seemed distracted. She last saw him alive at approximately 9.30 when she brought him more coffee at his request. Then she went out to shop, visiting the store on the building premises, entry to which is restricted to residents, and a nearby bakery. She returned just before eleven. She didn't notice anything unusual on her return, but that might be because she went straight to the kitchen. It was only when she went to the deceased's study to offer him another cup of coffee that she discovered the condition he unfortunately found himself in.'

'Dead, you mean?'

The sergeant nodded. 'Definitely dead. Bullet-in-the-head dead.'

'He really liked coffee,' Slivka said.

Belinsky turned to look at her – his expression was difficult to read.

'It would seem so.'

'And the wife?' Korolev asked, giving Slivka a warning glance. She shrugged.

'According to Matkina she was at an orphanage on Vitsin Street. She works there in the mornings. She returned at 11.48. I took note of the time, of course.'

'Slivka – you'll call this orphanage?'

'Yes, Chief.'

'Belinsky, you've met the wife and the maid – your impression?' Korolev asked, looking up at the grey building, wondering if it might be possible to tell, just from looking at it, behind which window a murder had been committed.

'I don't think the maid had anything to do with it. She's a simple country girl, very young. Also she dropped a pot of coffee on the study floor when she found him. I don't think she's bright enough to have done it to cover something up.'

'We'll see. Have someone bring her up to the apartment – we'll talk to her there. And the wife?'

'We had to restrain her from entering the apartment and viewing the body – I felt it necessary in case she contaminated the crime scene. She's with a neighbour at present, a doctor. He had to sedate her.'

'Can she be questioned?'

'You'd have to ask the doctor.'

'Any corroboration of their movements?'

'The doorkeeper's name is Priudski – he's verified that Madame Azarova left the building at 7.50 this morning. I was here when she came back, so we know when she returned for certain. Where she was in the meantime, we haven't established as yet. Priudski confirms the maid left the building at around 9.30 and returned about fifteen minutes before the body was discovered. He's over there if you'd like to speak to him.'

The sergeant pointed to a grey-skinned man in his early fifties, wearing a brown suit and an off-white shirt buttoned to the neck. He looked more like an office clerk than a doorman.

'Comrade Priudski?' Korolev said, approaching him.

'That's me,' the doorkeeper said, extending his hand. Priudski's teeth were yellow and uneven but he smiled with them anyway, a smile that seemed to come too easily to be genuine.

'You're the detective, are you? Captain Korolev?'

'Yes.' Korolev shook the man's hand – it felt like taking hold of a two-day-old fish. 'And this is Sergeant Slivka. You were listening then?'

Priudski looked momentarily uncomfortable.

'Only in order to assist in any way I can, of course.'

'That's kind of you,' Korolev replied, allowing a little menace to slip into his tone. 'Everyone visiting the apartments via this entrance has to pass by you, is that right?'

'Yes, each entrance serves a separate part of the building so we know our tenants well. They pass freely but if there are guests or deliveries we call up to the apartments. I keep a record of the comings and goings. '

'And today?'

'No deliveries or guests for the Azarovs.'

'We'll need that record – and a list of all the residents in the building. I'll want you to go through it with Sergeant Slivka here and tell me if and when you saw each one of the residents today.'

'I'd be happy to, Comrade Captain.'

'Well, what do you think about this killing? Any suspicions?'

'The professor works at the Azarov Institute on Yakimanka – it's named for him. All I've ever heard is he was a good Party man – and a respected scientist. My guess is it was counter-revolutionary terrorists.'

'Counter-revolutionary terrorists?'

'Seeing as he was an important scientist.'

'Did you see anyone resembling a counter-revolutionary terrorist pass by your office today?'

Korolev was careful to ask the question completely straight. It wasn't the kind of thing you could joke about, no matter how ridiculous it might seem.

'They're sly dogs. They probably slipped in some other way.' Priudski's gaze moved away from his as he spoke. A shifty character, it seemed to Korolev.

'Thank you, Comrade, we'll consider all possibilities, of course. And if you can think which "other way" they could have slipped in, let us know. What did the professor do at this institute of his that might have attracted such people?'

'Brains.'

'Brains?'

'Research into brains. Secret research, I believe.'

'Secret research?' Korolev wondered if this case could get any worse. 'I see. Did you hear anything unusual today? It's likely there was a gunshot.'

'If there was, like as not I wouldn't have heard it, Comrade Captain. The work on the bridge starts first thing and continues till dark.'

Priudski indicated the new bridge being built further along the embankment. And as he did so a pile-driver began to hammer once again. Bang, bang, bang. A gunshot would have as much chance of being heard as a whisper in a gale. All the same.

'Sergeant Slivka will take your statement – I want you to try and recall every single thing about this morning for her, no matter how insignificant. And every person you saw.' Korolev paused and looked up at the darkening sky.

'Belinsky, let the residents back in – there's no point in them getting soaked. Which floor is Professor Azarov's apartment on?'

'The fifth,' Priudski said.

Korolev nodded and turned back to the sergeant.

'Just ask them to stay away from the fifth floor, Belinsky. And get your men to take their names and ask what they saw, on the way in.'

The sergeant nodded.

'Comrade Priudski, can you take me to the professor's apartment?'

The doorkeeper opened the door that led into the small entrance hall.

'We've a lift,' he said.

'I'll take the stairs, thanks.' Korolev didn't trust lifts – he didn't like the idea of plummeting ten floors in a tin box without anything to grab hold of. Not at all. Priudski could keep his lift.

'It's a long way up,' the doorman said, 'it would be quicker.'

'I want to see the layout of the building before I see the

apartment – you can't see anything in a lift.' Korolev knew damned well it was a long way up – just as he knew it was a long way back down when some rusty cable went snap.

While they climbed the stairs, Korolev considered Priudski. If Korolev knew one thing about Moscow doormen, it was that they were acquisitive when it came to information. Most of them shared that information with anyone they thought might provide them with more of the same – nobody liked to gossip more than doormen. But it was also widely suspected that a smaller, but not insignificant, number shared their information with State Security – on an exclusive basis. In an apartment complex like this, full of bigwigs, and with the way this fellow was dressed and his whole demeanour – well, Korolev had little doubt he was one of that kind.

They'd reached the third landing now, two floors below the Azarovs' apartment, and, as if to confirm Korolev's suspicions about Priudski, one of the doors was sealed with string and red wax. Korolev walked over to it, peering closer to read the stamp that had been applied to the seal. 'By Order of the Ministry of State Security'.

He sighed. Another arrest – the inhabitants carted away in a black van, no doubt, and the apartment closed up until the Chekists had finished searching it for evidence.

Korolev looked over to Priudski and the doorman looked away.

Chapter Five

'FOUND ANYTHING YET?' Korolev said, nodding to Ushakov's colleague, Levschinsky. The forensics man was on one knee in the internal hallway, dusting the handle of the door to the apartment.

'No signed confession, if that's what you mean. We haven't been here long though.'

'Can I come in?'

'Just don't touch anything.'

Korolev put his hands in his pockets to keep them out of temptation's way. Many a mysterious fingerprint had turned out to belong to a Militiaman who'd wandered into a crime scene with his mind on other matters.

'We found the body though.' Levschinsky pointed over his shoulder to an open doorway.

'That's something then.'

'All right, someone else found it.' Levschinsky looked up from the doorknob and smiled. 'This doorknob is a waste of time, by the way. But we're thorough, if nothing else.'

Korolev nodded his appreciation and decided to take a quick look around before he introduced himself to the corpse. The place was a palace by modern Moscow standards – a dining room, two bedrooms, a small kitchen – they even had their own private bathroom. Korolev stepped into the professor's sitting room and could only imagine the satisfaction the dead man must have taken from the view – the Kremlin, the river and most of central Moscow were visible from the windows. You could leave aside Lenin Prizes, appointments to the Academy of Red Professors and any other accolade the State might throw in the direction of a deserving scientific fellow – this view and the size and number of the rooms told anyone who needed to know that Professor Azarov had been at the pinnacle of his profession. Korolev thought he was lucky having a room all to himself in Kitai Gorod – but this was something else again.

'Anything for me, old friend?' Korolev said, entering the study with reluctance. The truth was, having to deal with dead bodies was the thing he enjoyed least about the job. If murders could be committed without producing corpses then he'd be a happier detective.

The burly, silver-haired Ushakov looked up from his examination of the windowsill and nodded towards the corpse.

'A bullet to the back of the head – a big calibre, by the look of it. Possibly a nervous shooter.'

'Why do you say that?' Korolev said, forcing himself to step closer to the body. The dead man was slumped forward onto the papers that covered the desk, white hair spilling over his bent arms, his forehead pushed up against his right hand – the fingers of which still held a pen.

'Well they missed him once. There's a spare bullet hole in the desktop.'

Korolev walked around the table to look at the Professor's face – bearded, a high forehead, a long nose and a square jaw. Someone had thought to close Azarov's eyes but there was a silky fineness to the hair that wasn't stiff with blood that suggested to him the professor had been blonde in his youth – so they'd probably be blue or grey. It looked as if he'd been working on a document of some sort when he'd been shot, but now its pages were caked with blood. A photographer's lamp had been raised above the corpse and a camera and tripod stood beside it – artificial white light making the motionless body look as though it existed in a different time to the rest of the room, which was true in some ways. He found the gouge in the desk just beside the large black telephone. Another sign of Azarov's importance – very few people had their own telephone.

'You're sure it was a miss?' Korolev said, knowing that bullets could take strange meandering routes through a body.

'Seems so.'

'And we're sure a bullet was the cause of death?' he asked – questions with obvious answers being something Korolev had never shied away from.

'Well, I don't think it was poison,' Ushakov said, 'but Chestnova will tell you for sure.'

'Yes, she's on her way I'm told.'

Korolev looked at the hole in the back of the professor's head and cursed under his breath. If it wasn't the wife or the maid, and Belinsky thought it wasn't, then this could be a long investigation. And important people getting themselves murdered in important places was never good news for detectives. He'd be working and sleeping and not doing much else until this matter was tidied up. Poor Yuri.

'Captain Korolev?'

He turned to see Belinsky standing in the doorway.

'The maid, Matkina, is waiting in the kitchen.'

'Thanks, Comrade Sergeant. I'll talk to her straight away – but if you see Sergeant Slivka, send her up please.'

§

Galina Matkina, the Azarovs' maid, was wide-shouldered and round-waisted, and might have spent the morning driving a tractor on a *kolkhoz* farm – if her sun-reddened face and the white kerchief over her blonde hair were anything to go by. She sat on a chair in the kitchen while Korolev leant against a small table. He was tempted to turn on the light – the moody sky was darkening by the minute – but secrets were sometimes easier told in the shadows.

'Are you the policeman?' she asked in a quiet voice, before he could open his mouth. She seemed to be struggling to regulate her breathing. More nervous than he would have expected.

'I am.'

'I should wait until Comrade Madame Azarova is here. She won't like that I'm speaking to you without her.'

'Comrade Madame?'

A strange combination of the bourgeois and the Bolshevik. *Bourgevik*, perhaps.

'It's what she likes to be called. By me, anyway. She'll be unhappy if I talk to you when she isn't here.'

Korolev didn't have time to argue.

'Let's start by having a look at your papers, Citizeness Matkina – and your residency permit, while we're at it. You know residency permits can be revoked by the Militia. Just like that.'

Korolev clicked his fingers. It wasn't a threat he'd ever carry out, of course, and Korolev felt guilt as the girl's face lost all its colour. He was about to reassure her, when the kopeck dropped and he realized she probably didn't have a residency permit to be revoked. Not that this was unusual – although he'd have thought the Azarovs would have been able to fix the problem if they'd wanted to.

'Residency permit?' The girl said eventually and Korolev held up his hand.

'Provided you're straight with me, we can forget I asked that question. I don't have time to be chasing round after pretty young girls who don't have their Moscow papers. Not today anyway.'

Matkina nodded, attempting to smile. Korolev's hopes for a

quick resolution were receding however. A girl like this, with no residency permit, wouldn't want trouble with the law.

'We'd best start at the beginning – surname, name, patronymic.'

'Matkina, Galina Andreyevna, Comrade Captain.'

She straightened herself as she spoke, as if making an oath.

'There's no need to be too formal, Galina Andreyevna. You certainly don't have to stand to attention – next thing you'll be saluting me or something. That wouldn't do at all.'

She smiled, a little bit more confident now – there was a flash of white teeth in the gloom.

'Where do you sleep?'

'In here – I've a mattress I roll out. It's comfortable enough.'

'Good for you. How long have you worked here?'

'Here? Since last summer, Comrade Captain. They only moved in then, before that they were in a smaller apartment upstairs – I was with them there as well, but not for long.'

'When did you come to Moscow?'

'November of thirty-five, Comrade Captain. There wasn't much of a choice, where I was.'

The worst of the famines in the countryside had been in thirty-two and thirty-three, when the push towards collectivization had been at its height, but everyone knew that peasants were still heading for the cities if they could – it was one of the reasons you had to have a residency permit to live in Moscow these days.

'Enough of the "Comrade Captain",' Korolev said. 'You can call me Alexei Dmitriyevich; it's less of a mouthful. Do you smoke?' He took one for himself and extended the packet to the girl, who looked at the door with a hunted expression.

'Have one – my sergeant tells me your mistress is sleeping. Some doctor gave her a sedative. And don't worry about her smelling anything – there'll be half a dozen of us puffing away in here by the time we're done – one more won't make any difference.'

With a nod of gratitude, the girl helped herself.

'Good girl. So tell me everything that happened in this apartment from, say, six o'clock last night. I mean everything. How many spoons you washed, what you served for supper, how many glasses of tea were drunk and by who. Everything.'

And she did. The professor, it turned out, didn't like tea – but then Korolev already knew that. He liked coffee himself, but he'd need a few promotions before he could afford to drink as much as the professor had. By the time Matkina had finished, Korolev had a pretty good insight into the domestic life of the Azarovs. The professor, it would seem, worked, ate, slept and did nothing much else. And his wife wasn't much different. She was also a doctor, it seemed, but not a surgical one. More of a psychiatrist. Not bad people, it seemed, they treated the maid well enough and better than many others would. They got on well, the Azarovs, in her opinion, although they'd had few social friends – not enough time, it seemed. Interestingly she thought the professor wasn't much liked in the building.

'Why not?' Korolev asked, giving her another cigarette and lighting it for her.

'The other residents were nervous of him. He was, well, political.'

'Political?' Korolev asked, considering the slight emphasis she'd placed on the word. 'Do you mean he denounced people?'

She nodded, looking to the door once again.

'Did he have anything to do with that sealed apartment on the third floor?'

'They say he did. The other girls in the building. I've heard him on the telephone asking for people to be investigated, arrested, that kind of thing.'

The girl exhaled a perfect smoke ring. Not a casual smoker then, for all her initial nervousness.

'But I don't know about the Golovkins. You'd better ask the doorman about that kind of thing.'

'The Golovkins?'

'That's the couple who lived on the third floor.'

'I see – and why should I ask the doorman?'

'They call him up when they need a witness – State Security – even for the other buildings in the block. He knows all about that kind of thing.' There was an edge to her voice that confirmed Korolev's own suspicions about Comrade Priudski. A willing ear for the Chekists, at the very least. Maybe more.

'When were they arrested?'

'Last week, Monday, I think. There were three arrests last week.'

'In this part of the building alone?'

'In the whole building.'

Korolev thought it through, three arrests out of five hundred apartments – quite a high number all the same.

'Is that unusual?'

'No,' she said. 'Ever since I came here there have been arrests. But it's not people like me – it's people like the Golovkins. Girls like me just go and work for someone else. Unless they get caught without a residency permit.'

She gave him a look that said, I'm being honest with you, *Ment*, you'd better be honest with me.

'I won't be bothering you about your permit, I've said as much already. Now, what about this morning?'

The professor, it seemed, had left the house at 7.30, as Belinsky had told him, to go to his institute – a short walk away on Yakimanka – then he'd returned at about nine. He'd had some meeting, she thought, but about what she didn't know, and when he came back he'd seemed distracted, maybe even worried. Again, consistent with what she'd told Belinsky. He'd made a phone call – but to who, she couldn't say. She'd brought him a pot of coffee at 9.30, as usual – just before she'd left to do the shopping. The only strange thing was that the professor had complained about rats, or mice perhaps. In the walls. He told her he'd been hearing them all morning.

'Rats?'

'I didn't hear them,' the girl said, helping herself to another cigarette. 'But he could be a bit like that. He liked everything just so. You couldn't have a dog in the building, in case it might bark and the professor be disturbed. Then you'd be in trouble. Big trouble.'

The professor had drunk most of the coffee she'd brought him by the time she returned, and left the pot and the dirty cup in the kitchen.

'What size pot?'

She pointed at a coffee pot drying beside the sink – it wasn't small.

'So a few cups?'

'He finished most of it, so I'd say yes.'

If she'd left just after she'd brought him the pot of coffee it would have taken the professor some time to drink so much – at least fifteen minutes, would be Korolev's guess. Which narrowed the period in which the death must have occurred, he supposed.

'So you washed the cup and the coffee pot?'

'And I began to make their lunch.' She pointed to a pile of chopped vegetables. 'And then. Well, Comrade Captain, then I found him.'

And she looked away from him, chewing on her lip – her eyes wet.

Chapter Six

KOROLEV AND SLIVKA stood on the landing one flight up from the dead man's apartment, looking out the open window down onto the street far below, watching the traffic pass over the soon-to-be-destroyed Bolshoi Kamenny Bridge and sucking the smoke out of a pair of Belomorkanals. Korolev could see lightning flicker over the northern suburbs and the shadow of rain underneath the low clouds as they approached. He hoped Yuri wouldn't be caught outside when the bad weather came.

'What we need is a motive, Slivka,' he said, flicking the papirosa tube out the window and resisting the temptation to light up another. 'If we can find one, then like as not we'll find a murderer attached to it. But the only thing we've got to go on so far is that the sealed apartment on the third floor might have been the victim's doing. It seems he liked to tell tales.'

'I see.' Slivka didn't seem keen on it as a motive – but, then again, nor was he.

'I know. We'll have to look into it all the same – I'll ask Popov for the best way to go about it. What did this doctor say about Comrade Madame Azarova?'

'He said she should be awake soon. We can speak to her about half an hour after that, he thinks.'

'Good, we talk to her as soon as we can. What else?'

Slivka looked down at her notebook.

'The doorman has gone through the list of residents – who

was here this morning and what their movements were. Belinsky's men are going door to door through this part of the building – so we'll soon add detail to that. No one we've questioned so far has heard or seen anything directly related to the murder, but we have two people who say they saw the professor leaving the building early in the morning, which confirms what the maid told you. We've also got a list of people who were visiting the building – Belinsky's men are working their way through them. And they're also trying to make contact with residents who left for work earlier in the day, in case they might have seen anything.'

Korolev considered this, and found that somehow another Belomorkanal had ended up in his mouth. He lit it.

'Talk to the widow when she surfaces – I'm going to take the car and drive to this institute of his and find out what he was up to there this morning and why it might have upset him. Oh, and I got one more thing out of Matkina – she could smell gunpowder when she went into the study. That – and all the coffee he drank after nine-thirty – suggests he wasn't shot long before she found the body. Something to bear in mind.'

He turned to lead the way down the staircase and found Priudski, the doorman, standing on the landing below – his ears no doubt having been tuned in to their conversation like a radio receiver.

'Comrade,' Korolev said drily. Priudski returned the greeting without the slightest trace of embarrassment. Well, Korolev thought, the fellow's probably just doing his job – the same as he was. Not that this made him any happier.

§

Inside the Azarovs' apartment the forensics men were standing back, watching the burly figure of Zinaida Chestnova carefully lift the dead man's head in her small plump hands. Gouts of semi-coagulated blood were providing some resistance and her assistant was holding down the paperwork on which the head had rested while Chestnova moved it from side to side. She was careful, almost gentle, but Korolev knew she'd be less gentle when the autopsy proper began. She was looking for hypostasis on the dead man's face, unless Korolev was mistaken – one of the indicators that might tell her when he'd died.

'Let me guess, Korolev,' Chestnova said, without looking up. 'You want me to tell you to the minute, as usual.'

Despite the fug of cigarette smoke, he could smell the corpse's sweet stench now. The summer heat was having its effect.

'I wouldn't be so unreasonable. We've some ideas, but if you tell us something different then we'll have to think again.'

'I see,' Chestnova said, pressing a thumb to the dead man's eye. The elasticity would give her another clue as to the time of death.

'No more than two or three hours ago, I'd say. I doubt his body temperature will indicate much different. It wasn't yesterday, that's for sure. Does that tally with your ideas?'

'It does.'

Korolev looked down at the body and had the sense that everything around him was receding, leaving just him – and the corpse.

'Chief?'

Korolev started, aware that he had somehow become the centre of attention. He sighed. That was the thing about death – it had a way of slipping into your thoughts and taking them over, leaving you forgetting where you were.

'Yes, Slivka, yes. I hear you.' Korolev rubbed the palm of his hand across his jaw once or twice, savouring the bristly scrape. He had to focus on the job in hand.

He turned to regard Chestnova.

'Zinaida Petrovna, we can see the bullet hole in the back of his head, and we can draw our own conclusions. The question is, is there anything else you'd like to bring to our attention?'

'No. The bullet killed him, if that's what you're asking. I doubt the autopsy will tell us otherwise.'

'Nothing that might indicate a struggle of any kind? Or resistance?'

'Not that I can see.' Chestnova said, placing the head gently back on the desk. 'I studied under him at university. An ambitious man – not pleasant about it, either. Have you any idea who killed him?'

'None,' Korolev said. 'So he wasn't well-liked?'

'Not at all,' Chestnova said. 'Not by his colleagues and certainly not by the students. Feared, perhaps.'

'Feared? Well that's useful to know.'

Korolev examined the dead man's face. It was difficult to deduce a corpse's personality just from looking at it. Death rubbed away much of a person's character – and left only a misleading impression at best. But Chestnova was someone whose opinion he could attach some weight to. If she said Azarov wasn't a pleasant man, then he believed it. Especially since the maid had given a hint or two along the same lines.

'Well, he must have trusted whoever shot him,' Korolev said. 'Why else would a man sit at his desk calmly while his killer stood behind him?'

'Just because he wasn't afraid of the killer, doesn't mean he didn't know they despised him,' Slivka said, with a shrug of her shoulders.

'Perhaps. Ushakov, I'd like to have a look at what he was working on at the time of the murder. Can you clean the blood off these?'

Korolev pointed to the blood-caked papers.

'We'll do our best – I'll let you know how we get on. In the meantime, I've extracted your bullet from the desk.' He held up a small brown paper bag. 'It looks like a .45 calibre – big, in other words. It must have been fired from close range but it barely made a dent, really – for its size.'

There was something in Ushakov's tone that suggested he had some thoughts on this.

'Go on.'

'It's just a hunch, but I'm thinking a very small pistol. One of those waistcoat weapons, you know the kind. We've asked the local Militia station to pull all the firearms certificates for the building. The bullet's a bit battered but we should have enough to match it to a weapon. If we locate the weapon, that is.'

Korolev glanced towards Slivka.

'We'll go through the place atom by atom.'

'Well, I'd better go and meet the late professor's colleagues.'

Korolev said his farewells. On his way out, he wasn't surprised to find Priudski the doorman still loitering on the landing, barely visible in the gloomy light.

'Comrade Priudski?' Korolev asked.

'Yes?'

'I need to call Petrovka. Can I use your phone?'

'Of course, Comrade Korolev. Of course.'

Priudski led him down the staircase and, when they reached the bottom, ushered Korolev into his small office. The doorman picked up the receiver, tapping three times for the operator.

'I need to call Moscow CID,' Priudski said. 'Petrovka.'

'Thank you,' Korolev said, taking the receiver from the smaller man and holding the door open for him.

The doorman left the room with an expression that reminded Korolev of a scolded schoolboy – but if Korolev was going to make a report to Popov on a case like this, he'd rather it wasn't overheard by a fellow like Priudski.

Chapter Seven

KOROLEV HAD NEVER heard of the Azarov Institute before but he often travelled along Bolshaya Yakimanka and knew the building well enough from the outside. At one time, long before the Revolution, it must have been the residence of someone who'd had money to burn – and had decided to burn a good portion of it on a large and ornate mansion. Since then a revolution, the Moscow winter and the passage of time had worked on it, turning once bright-red bricks to brown, and white marble to grey. And what time and weather hadn't managed to alter, man had. Bars and barbed wire guarded each window and ledge – and the high wall that surrounded the grounds was topped with spikes.

Korolev parked the car and got out, first walking to the heavy oak front door, conscious that large raindrops were beginning to spot the pavement around him, and then, following the directions on a hand-written sign, around the corner and down a narrow lane, his mood darkening with each step. Two men in black hooded rain cloaks stood waiting for him in front of a small sentry box that guarded the side entrance. They watched him approach with apparent indifference.

'I'm from Petrovka,' he said, showing his identification card to the nearest of the two – a heavyset man with blank blue eyes and a hard face. 'I'm—'

'From Moscow CID. Korolev.' The guard said this without bothering to look at his papers. He sounded bored.

'You're expected, Comrade Captain,' the second guard said.

'You knew I was coming?'

'Please come with me, Comrade Captain.' The second guard spoke as if he were persuading a temperamental child to perform an unpleasant task. 'The deputy director will answer your questions.'

He stepped aside so that Korolev could pass and, after a brief pause, Korolev did just that. After all, the rain was beginning to come down fatter and faster – pittering and pattering around him on the lane's cobbles.

It was unsettling, of course, that they'd been expecting him, but perhaps Popov had thought it wise to call ahead. Or Priudski. Anyway, he was a senior detective from Petrovka – it wasn't likely that entering the place on his own would be dangerous. These were just ordinary guards, doing their duty – same as he was.

But as he followed the guard along the gravel path, he caught sight of two concrete buildings. They were invisible from the street because of the institute's high perimeter walls – they were only two storeys and set well back – and at first glance they looked like ordinary office buildings or some such. A second glance, however, revealed the heavy metal doors and the shuttered windows, the thick walls and the regular lampposts that surrounded them. And it occurred to him that these were buildings designed not to keep people out – but to keep them in.

§

The man behind the large desk stood as he entered, giving him a smile that seemed genuine enough.

'Captain Korolev, I'm pleased to meet you.'

The deputy director was young, not yet forty, broad-shouldered and in good shape. In fact he had the sort of rude health that suggested he'd be more comfortable working in a field than sitting in an office.

'Thank you for seeing me at such short notice,' Korolev began, before a roll of thunder seemed to rattle the very building itself. A simultaneous gust of wind sent splashes of rain through an open window onto the wooden floor. The deputy director stood up and, with an incongruous half-bow, moved quickly to close it.

'The storm has come at last,' he said. 'Let's hope it means the air will be cleaner – cooler too, with luck. I'm Shtange. The deputy director.'

'Korolev,' he said, still feeling the strength of Shtange's grip, 'but you know that.'

Korolev was surprised at how rough Shtange's hands were – they didn't feel like a doctor's hands, far from it.

'Yes, they told us you'd be coming. I've been instructed to be as cooperative as possible.'

'Thank you.'

'We're all shocked by the news, of course.'

For an instant Shtange was silhouetted against the window by lightning, which was followed almost immediately by a deafening blast of thunder – even closer now, it seemed. A real summer tempest, Korolev thought, not without some satisfaction.

'Professor Azarov was a tireless striver for Socialism, a Stakhanovite worker of the highest productivity. With more like him, the State would be completing Five Year Plans in two years not four.'

Shtange had to shout to be heard over the wind and rain lashing at the windows, but even so, his words sounded formulaic, almost as if he were embarrassed by what he was saying.

'We'll investigate his death with every resource available to us, of course.'

'I don't doubt it, Comrade Korolev, I don't doubt it. Such

an important figure in Soviet science – well, the State will expect nothing less.'

Shtange extracted a metal cigarette case from the pocket of his dark jacket, took one out and tapped it on the table. Korolev noticed with interest the engraved propeller design on the case's lid – wondering to himself what Shtange's connection with aeroplanes might be. Shtange caught the glance and, misreading his interest, offered Korolev a cigarette.

'I have my own,' Korolev said, embarrassed, and pulled his Belomorkanals from his pocket.

Shtange shrugged and closed the case with a snap. Korolev could see there was an inscription beneath the propeller, but it was illegible from this distance. Maybe he should have taken a cigarette after all.

'I presume Azarov's death will have a serious effect on the institute's work?' Korolev asked.

'We operate as a collective, Comrade Korolev, like all Soviet organizations. The institute bears Comrade Azarov's name, of course, but whoever of our number falls away, there will always be another ready to step forward to replace them.'

'You, perhaps?' Korolev said, feeling his bait being taken. 'I mean to say – will you be appointed the new director of the institute?'

'Comrade Korolev, if I'm appointed director it will be because someone higher up decides I should be – not because I ask for it. As it happens, I think they'll find someone else. Unless I'm wrong, my remaining time here will be very short.'

He spoke with a certain satisfaction and Korolev had the impression the fellow wouldn't miss the place at all.

'Anyway,' Shtange continued. 'You're here to investigate Comrade Azarov's death – what can I do to assist?'

Korolev looked around him – it was a large room, over-looking the garden. The desk that Shtange sat behind was also large and on it two wooden trays sat either side of a wide

leather-cornered blotter. The trays were marked 'in' and 'out' –
the 'in' tray was almost empty, whereas the 'out' tray was piled
high.

'You've been busy,' Korolev said.

'Not me, Comrade. The director attended to these papers
himself this morning.'

'The director?' Korolev asked and then worked it out. 'This
is his office, then?'

Korolev let his eyes wander round the wooden panelling
that covered the walls, the obligatory portraits of Stalin and
Lenin, Marx and Engels, the filing cabinets ranked along one
wall – but this time with a different eye. So this was where the
dead man had worked. He turned his attention back to Shtange.

'You've moved in quickly.'

The deputy director laughed, a genuine laugh – rich and
good-humoured. It was unusual to come across such a laugh
during a murder investigation.

'Look, Korolev – I'd nothing to do with Professor Azarov's
death, nothing whatsoever. I've been asked to take over in the
short-term, at least until a decision is made as to the institute's
future – so here I sit. There are aspects of the institute's work I
simply don't know about and this is the place to find out about
them.'

'Of course, you serve Socialism in whichever capacity you're
asked to.'

Shtange raised an eyebrow but otherwise didn't react.

Korolev, disappointed, let the conversation go silent. But it
soon became clear that the silence didn't bother Shtange at all.
In fact the deputy director sat back in his chair and began to
give every appearance of enjoying it.

'I'd like to look through this paperwork of his,' Korolev
said, feeling a little irritated at the fellow's calm reaction. 'If
that's all right, of course?'

'I'm afraid you can't,' Shtange said, leaning forward to stub out his cigarette.

'I can't?'

'I'm afraid not. The professor's work was, and remains, strictly confidential. If you'd like to get access to his correspondence or anything similar, you'll have to ask permission from the organization that the Azarov Institute forms part of. And thirty minutes ago the responsible person at that organization informed me that such permission will be refused.'

Korolev had a fair idea what organization that might be – his encounter with the guards at the front gate should have made it clear to him that this visit was a waste of time. But he dutifully scratched his head and pretended to look puzzled.

'I'm sorry, Comrade Shtange, I don't understand. You said you would be cooperating with the investigation.'

'Only as far as is possible. I think I was clear about that.'

'I see,' Korolev said, understanding all too well. 'So you'll be helpful to the extent you're able to – which is not at all.'

'I wouldn't put it that way – I can't discuss the work carried out by the institute. Or the identities of any of my colleagues working here. Or any information of any sort concerning the institute. That's all true.'

Shtange smiled.

'But then, even I don't know everything that goes on here – it's nothing to do with wanting to obstruct your investigation. Our research would lose its value if we went around telling everyone about it.'

Korolev found himself scratching his head again.

'So what *can* you tell me?' he asked.

'I can tell you that I met with the professor this morning – he came into the institute first thing. I wrote a report which he . . .' Shtange paused, seeming to consider his words carefully, 'which he wanted to discuss.'

'He seemed normal, to you?'

'His normal self,' Shtange said, and Korolev wondered whether the careful way the answer was phrased was deliberate. Shtange smiled, as if acknowledging Korolev's observation.

'How shall I put it, Comrade Korolev?' he continued. 'The professor could be forceful and direct. We didn't always see eye to eye – and certainly not on this matter.'

'I see – an argument?'

'You could call it that.'

'About your report?'

'Yes.'

'But you can't tell me what was in the report.'

The deputy director gave him a wry smile.

'No. But I *can* tell you that the guards at the gate keep a record of everyone who enters and leaves and they can confirm I've been here since seven. I'm sure, if you ask them, they can also tell you precisely when the professor arrived and left this morning.'

'Will they be allowed to tell me though?'

'They will be. I requested it. I don't want my time taken up by your investigation any more than it has to be. I thought you'd inevitably want to – how shall I put it? – ensure yourself of my innocence. I anticipated your frustration, Captain Korolev, and so, at my further request, I'm allowed to give you some assurances.'

'Assurances?'

'Yes, and impressions.'

'Impressions? Well, I'd be grateful.'

Korolev decided to light the cigarette that had been hanging forgotten from his mouth since he'd put it there. Shtange took a sheet of paper from a drawer.

'Firstly,' he said, looking to the page for guidance, it seemed, 'I'm instructed to assure you that Director Azarov's death did not arise from any connection he might have had to this institute, to any of its staff or to the work he performed here.'

'I see,' Korolev said. 'That's reassuring.'

Shtange smiled once again.

'I'm also instructed to assure you that, notwithstanding the previous assurance, a separate investigation will be undertaken as a matter of course into Comrade Azarov's death – in so far as it might possibly relate to his connection with this institute, its staff and the work he carried out here. In fact it's already begun. I'm further permitted to tell you that if any such connection emerges and such connection indicates any culpability in relation to his death – then it will be dealt with as part of that investigation.'

Korolev frowned. Here he was, being assured Azarov's death had nothing to do with the institute, but at the same time that someone would be investigating whether there was in fact a connection between the murder and the institute. And, if by any chance there was, then that would be dealt with separately, thank you very much for your interest. It was confusing.

'Who?'

'I beg your pardon,' Shtange said.

'Who'll be investigating it?'

'I'm afraid that information is classified.'

'You surprise me.'

'It couldn't possibly be in safer hands, however.'

If Shtange wasn't talking about Korolev's old friends in State Security then he'd be even more surprised.

'Could you pass me the ashtray?' Korolev asked, and Shtange gave it a quick push so that it slid across the desk's polished surface towards him. Korolev stopped it just before it reached the edge and tapped his papirosa into it twice. Then he took one more drag from it and stubbed it out altogether.

'Thanks for your time, Comrade Shtange,' he said and stood.

This was, after all, a conversation that had probably gone on for far too long already.

'Wait one moment, Comrade Captain. I mentioned I was also authorized to give you my impressions.'

Korolev pushed his hands into the pockets of his jacket and waited.

'While Comrade Azarov was all the things I've mentioned, in terms of his qualities as a worker, he was not someone who dealt with those around him in an amicable way. I doubt he was any different in his personal life – in fact, I know he wasn't. I thought you'd like to know that. My impression of his character, that is. You'll find plenty of people inside and outside this institute that share my opinion, I'm sure of it. And as for his contributions to science? Well, perhaps they didn't reflect the amount of work he put into achieving them.'

'And you've been authorized to tell me that?' Korolev asked, in complete disbelief.

'I've been instructed to tell you that,' Shtange said and shrugged his shoulders, as if to say the reasons were beyond him as well. Shtange seemed to consider something for a moment, then put his fingers together to make a small pyramid with his hands. There was something mischievous in his expression.

'Although perhaps with my comment about his contributions to science I went a little further than I should have.'

Chapter Eight

BY THE TIME Korolev reached the car his clothes were soaked through and still the rain kept coming down, rattling on the roof like a battalion of military drummers. He sat there on the bench seat, rainwater pooling around him, wondering what the hell he'd got himself into. Thankfully someone had left a box of matches on the dashboard and Korolev used them to light a damp cigarette, the smoke scraping his throat as he inhaled. He thought about leaving the matches for the next detective but then decided to hold on to them – they weren't always easy to find these days.

A truck drove past, its engine like a rolling explosion, and flung a great wave of water up onto the car, rocking it. Korolev rubbed at the fogged glass. Even though it wasn't much past three o'clock, it was black as night – and the few dark figures making their way along the street looked like refugees from a war.

He glanced up at the institute and swore under his breath. Whatever they were up to in there was no business of his – that was for certain. There might be cleverer men than him around – plenty of them – but he was no fool. He smoked the last of the cigarette, stubbed it out on the floor and started the car – just as the first patch of blue sky appeared to the west and the rain, without warning, stopped.

§

'Well?' Korolev said when he found Slivka sitting in the dead man's study, her notebook open and a pencil in her hand. The forensics men had gone and all that was left of the professor was a damp patch on the desk where his blood had been washed away.

'Forensics are finished. Ushakov says they've found a number of possible fingerprints – but it will take them a while to go through them.'

'I'll call him. We can't wait around on this, believe me.'

Korolev found that he was looking at the gouged-out hole in Azarov's desk and, not for the first time, wondering how one of the bullets could have missed at such close range.

'Did you speak to Comrade Madame Azarova?' he asked.

'No, but I've confirmed her alibi. She was at the orphanage all right. And the maid's story stacks up as well. There was a queue at the bakery and she was standing in it for at least an hour. Two of the other maids confirmed it. Everyone has a maid in this place, did you know that?'

'It's a place for important people. Important people have maids.'

'That must be it. Anyway, that doorman fellow remembers her leaving at nine-thirty and coming back not long before eleven. So that's still more confirmation of her story.'

'He'd remember, right enough.'

There was something about Priudski that suggested to Korolev that he'd be the type who'd keep a particular eye out for pretty young things like Matkina.

'Still, she could have killed him when she came back,' Korolev said, not convincing himself or, it seemed, Slivka.

'Assuredly. But you've met her, and now so have I. I don't see it.'

'Stranger people have committed murder.'

'True.'

'She's the obvious suspect and she had the opportunity.'

Slivka said nothing and Korolev found himself nodding in agreement.

'All right, I agree. She doesn't strike me as a killer either, on top of which she doesn't seem to have a motive – on the contrary, in fact. What else did you find out? Anything from the other residents?'

Slivka looked through her notebook.

'The upstairs neighbour thought she heard something not long before eleven o'clock. At the time she thought it was noise from the bridge-building but, whatever she heard, she heard it twice. And no one told her there were two bullets. And, yes, thinking back, she agreed the noises could have been gunshots.'

'Before eleven would rule out Matkina,' Korolev said.

'If what the neighbour heard was a gun.'

'Matkina said she could smell gunpowder when she entered the room. That would tie in with the neighbour's story nicely. Of course, if Matkina did it the gun should still be here. If it was one of those little pocket pistols, you could almost fit it inside a packet of cigarettes. Have we been through the place thoroughly?'

'Not a speck of dust hasn't been lifted and looked under. I'm sure as I can be that it's not here. What's more, Levschinsky checked the wife and the maid's hands for gunpowder residue – nothing.'

There was a cough from behind Korolev, and Slivka, looking up to see who it was, stood so quickly that Korolev had to take a step back to avoid being knocked into.

Korolev turned to see who could have had such an effect on his normally unflappable sergeant – and found a full NKVD colonel standing in the doorway, dressed in his summer uniform, the golden sword and shield badge gleaming on his chest – alongside the Order of the Red Star, the Red Banner and several others. He was smiling at them benignly.

'Comrade Captain Korolev, isn't it? My name's Zaitsev.'

The colonel looked around the room and took his time doing it. He was a tall man, over six foot, and broad in a way that not many Muscovites could manage to be these days. Not exactly fat, was Korolev's impression, more muscle gone soft. The Chekist's round, pale face was decorated with a small triangular moustache that only covered the middle of his upper lip, and his scalp had been shaved down to a grey shadow that left his ears sticking out like jug-handles and revealed an interesting collection of scars; as if someone had given the colonel a savage beating sometime in the past.

There was something almost dreamy about the colonel's expression, but there was also an absolute authority. He turned his attention to Korolev, his thumbs hooked into the waist strap of his Sam Browne belt – the colonel's forefingers beating time on its buckle to a tune only he could hear.

'What progress have you made, Korolev?' the colonel said eventually, and Korolev, as succinctly as possible, filled him in. Meanwhile it sounded as if other men were moving into the apartment, fanning out through the rooms, but it was difficult to see if this was indeed the case as it would involve breaking eye-contact, which was something Korolev was loath to do.

'So, in summary,' Zaitsev said when he'd finished, 'you've no idea who the killer is, except that he has escaped and may even now be planning his next crime.'

'We've only just begun the investigation,' Korolev began – but the colonel's eyes narrowed with menace.

'I'm not interested in excuses, Korolev, and nor is the Party. We only care for results. Professor Azarov was engaged in work vital to the State and, through his death, a blow has been struck that may threaten the security of the Revolution itself. It seems to me we'll have to take a different approach to catching this killer – a more direct one. You could be blundering around for weeks at this rate. I'm sure First Inspector Popov will assign you to something more worthy of your talents. You may go.'

Korolev must have looked confused because the colonel leant forward so that his face was only a few inches away.

'You understand what I'm telling you, don't you, Korolev?'

'Yes, Comrade Colonel. You want us to go.'

'That's right, Korolev. Look at you, you're leaving puddles on the floor. You can't even look after yourself, let alone a matter like this. So go on, Korolev, go.'

'At your command, Comrade Colonel.'

Three Chekists slouched in the corridor behind Zaitsev, and Korolev found his cheeks warming as he and Slivka passed them. It wasn't just shame he felt, there was anger too – a rage that flickered in his stomach like fire.

'Well, that's that then,' Slivka said, when they'd made their way down the stairs and out of the building.

'It seems so,' Korolev said, conscious that his hands had bunched into fists.

'Back to Petrovka?'

'Why not?'

§

Pugnacious black clouds still scudded across the brightening sky as Slivka drove them across the Bolshoi Kamenny Bridge, but they were only camp followers to what had preceded them. The sudden storm had more or less passed and, despite the battering it had received, Moscow looked much the same as it always had – as it always would, Korolev supposed. People might come and go and regimes might change back and forth, but Moscow would remain – the city was a constant, even when everything else turned to dust. Slivka opened her mouth to speak but Korolev shook his head – there wasn't any point in talking about it, she must know that. So they travelled in silence, listening to the car's engine, until they reached Teatralnaya.

'Chief,' she said finally, reaching across to feel the arm of his jacket, 'he really wasn't wrong about you being wet.'

And perhaps it was just the way the sun was bathing the wet Moscow streets, turning them a brighter gold than the eye could bear, but Korolev found he was smiling.

Back at Petrovka, Popov had left instructions for them to come up straight away and Korolev wasn't surprised to find the first inspector pacing his office when they entered.

'What happened to you?' he asked Korolev.

Korolev looked down at his clothes.

'I got caught in the storm – over in Bersenevka.'

Popov sighed. 'You look like you went swimming, that's what you look like. Over there in Bersenevka.'

Korolev looked down at himself, hearing an echo of the colonel's rebuke in Popov's words.

'It's not as bad as it looks.'

He caught Slivka's sideways glance out of the corner of his eye.

'That's just as well – a drowned rat couldn't look more drowned than you do at the moment.' Popov paused to smile. 'Be sure to get yourself dry when we've finished here. It wouldn't do for you to catch a summer cold.'

'I will, Comrade First Inspector.'

Popov waved for them to sit down. He walked to the window, taking his unlit pipe from his pocket as he did so and chewing on its stem. Then he turned and walked slowly back towards the desk, placing his left hand on the back of his chair as he considered them.

'Investigations don't usually come and go this quickly,' Popov said. 'But we weren't to know the responsibility for it lay elsewhere.'

Slivka opened her mouth to speak but a glance from Popov closed it.

'You're back on holiday, Korolev. And Slivka, you're back chasing Grey Foxes.'

Popov pulled his chair back and sat down, taking reading glasses from the breast-pocket of his jacket and picking up a handwritten sheet of paper from the desk – precise instructions would now follow, it seemed.

'Any notes you took or other evidence collected must be given to me – I'll see they reach the right place. If any file was opened with regard to the matter it is to be immediately closed and its contents passed to me, as before. You will not discuss or refer to the investigation into Professor Azarov's murder – not even amongst yourselves. In fact, you're to forget it ever happened. I think that's all pretty straightforward. Understood?'

They nodded.

'Good. Off you go then.'

Korolev stood up and left the first inspector's office with Slivka in tow.

'Are we in trouble of some sort, Chief?' she said out of the corner of her mouth as they descended the stairs.

'I don't think so,' Korolev said, 'as long as we do as we're told we should be fine. The whole business never happened, is all.'

Korolev located the last of his cigarettes in his damp pocket, along with the matches from the car – and was pleasantly surprised when he managed to get them both to light.

Well,' he said when they reached the second floor, where their office was. 'I'd best leave you to it. Good luck with Shabalin.'

'Thanks,' Slivka said, nodding. 'Good luck with your holiday.'

What else was there to say? They certainly couldn't discuss the matter in question. So instead Korolev nodded once again and squelched off down the staircase, across Petrovka's cobbled courtyard before making straight for the Sandunovsky bathhouse on Neglinaya Street. And there he soaked in a long bath while a white-coated attendant with a boxer's ears took his clothes from him and promised he'd have them back dry as a bone within the hour.

So Korolev emptied his mind, allowed his feet to float up till his toes broke the surface and ignored the conversations going on around him. He focused on the ornate ceiling, on the gilded knots and twirls, on the occasional damp patch that marred the decoration, and squinted away the sweat that rolled down into his eyes. It occurred to him that this was as good a way as any to forget all about the day he'd just had. And, after half an hour of floating, a long stretch in the sauna and a few pages of the newspaper, he found he felt more like a human being again. In fact, by the time he come back out onto the street, his clothes dry and ironed, and looking better than they had for some time, he felt as relaxed as anyone had any right to expect these days. The evening sky was a deep blue and the light that the low sun cast flattered the older Moscow buildings and burnished the newer ones. His son was at home waiting for him and nothing more could be desired from life, really.

It was only because Korolev happened to be walking past the Lubyanka's side-entrance that he allowed himself to even think of anything to do with State Security. They were doing more work on the building, he saw. More cells, he supposed, or more offices for more Chekists. The comrades from State Security were busier than ever these days.

Chapter Nine

'PAPA?'

Yuri's voice came from the other side of the bedroom. Two streets away a cockerel crowed, as it did every morning, and Korolev, as he did every morning, wondered how the bird had managed to survive this long. There were plenty of people in Moscow who'd happily eat a cockerel given half a chance, cooked or uncooked. Its owner must guard it well.

'Yuri?' Korolev said. His voice sounded like the creak of a barn door.

'You're sure you won't have to go to work today?'

'As I told you,' Korolev said, his eyes still firmly shut, 'they've assigned the investigation to someone else. Which means we can do anything we want.'

'Anything?'

'Yes,' Korolev said, but he didn't fully trust his answer. Who knew what a 12-year-old boy might want to do?

He heard Yuri get out of bed and pad over to him.

'We could go to the zoo then, couldn't we?'

Korolev opened his left eye to see Yuri looking down at him. Weak sunlight was streaming in through the gap in the curtains and footsteps were moving back and forth above his head as the people upstairs prepared to face the day. They wouldn't be so loud if they put down a carpet. He should mention it to them.

'The zoo?' Korolev looked at his watch. A quarter past six already. 'Isn't it a bit early for the zoo?'

'Natasha says they feed the lions at eight.' Yuri crossed his arms and turned his face towards the window, avoiding Korolev's gaze as if expecting a refusal. 'With red meat.'

Something about the thought of the red meat seemed to cheer Yuri up, however, and he smiled slowly. No doubt he was imagining the gore.

'Red meat, you say?' Korolev allowed his open eye to close naturally.

'Blood red. She says sometimes they give them a goat. A whole goat. But not alive – at least I don't think so anyway. Although Natasha says sometimes the goats *are* alive, but I'm sure that can't be right.' Yuri paused, his mouth twisting sideways as he considered this.

'That Natasha says a lot.' Korolev turned onto his side so that now he was facing his son.

'Well,' Yuri said, 'I suppose the goats might be alive – every now and then. You know, for authenticity – what good would a lion be if it didn't remember what it was to hunt?'

'That's a good question.' Korolev made the effort to open both his eyes now, look at his son fondly and smile. He even managed to push himself up onto his elbow. This was what it was to be young, he supposed – to think that anything was possible.

Yuri, after a moment, smiled back.

'Torn to pieces?' Korolev continued, fighting a yawn. 'Now that would be a sight to see.'

Moscow's zoo was located only a few streets from where Korolev had lived when he was Yuri's age. And sometimes back then – not often, but occasionally – a boy might hear a lion roar – a strange and marvellous sound in the middle of a Moscow winter. The memory persuaded Korolev to push down the sheet and get out of bed.

'But I thought the zoo didn't open until nine?'

'That's the best thing of all, Valentina Nikolayevna called her friend there yesterday evening and she can give us a tour before it even opens. A whole zoo just for us.'

Korolev remembered something about this friend of Valentina's from the morning before.

'So she called her, did she?' Korolev looked down at his son – the boy looked a little unsure, apprehensive even. And it occurred to Korolev that he must seem a remote figure to Yuri. They barely saw each other these days. Well, if Zhenia was going to pair up with some fellow back in Zagorsk, then it would be no bad thing if the boy took away a memory or two worth savouring from this trip.

'They could be alive, I suppose – the goats.' Korolev stretched his arms above his head. 'It would be a shame to miss it if they were.'

Yuri said nothing – but his smile was so broad that Korolev wondered whether the youngster's face was wide enough to hold it all in.

§

From then on, things moved quickly – not least because Natasha and Yuri nipped around the adults' heels like sheepdogs, urging them here and there. Natasha and Yuri seemed to be engaged in some kind of competition as to who could have their parent ready first. As a result, washing and dressing were brisker than Korolev might have liked, while breakfast was a rushed but hearty affair. In no time at all, it seemed, they were boarding a tram which then hurtled around the Boulevard Ring. And by 7.50 they were exchanging comradely greetings with the famous Vera beside the zoo's newly colonnaded entrance.

Korolev's last visit had been his only visit, even though he'd grown up not five minutes' walk along what was now Barrikadnaya Street – back then there hadn't been enough spare money to come to places such as this. The exception, however, had been the day before Korolev had departed for the German War – he'd had a month's pay in his pocket and he'd decided to treat his mother while he still could.

'Is there something on your mind?' Valentina asked him. They were following Vera, who, at the children's insistence, was taking them straight to the lion enclosure. Valentina's voice was gentle and she took his elbow as if to reassure him that whatever he was thinking of, it was nothing to worry about.

'I was just recalling the last time I was here.'

He looked around him and thought it was strange that he could remember, as though it were yesterday, the weight and feel of the uniform he'd been wearing, the heat of the day, the sound of church bells somewhere near and, oddly, the smell of a woman's perfume – and yet he couldn't recall anything about the place itself. It was as if he'd never been here before. Oddest of all was that he'd no recollection of his mother – and that afternoon had been the last time he'd seen her.

'Dead,' Yuri said and Korolev looked down at him in surprise, wondering if he'd been talking aloud. But Yuri only had eyes for the lions and the creature they were devouring. Korolev followed his gaze and couldn't tell what animal the carcass might have been.

'A sheep,' Vera said, as if reading his mind.

'We must have come on the wrong day,' Natasha whispered. 'Or perhaps it had a heart attack when it saw the lions.'

'I hope you're not suggesting we'd ever feed a live animal to them, Natasha. That would be barbaric.'

Vera spoke firmly but Korolev saw Natasha exchange a glance with Yuri that seemed to say: 'That's what she *wants* you to believe. The truth is something else again.'

'When was that?' Valentina asked Korolev. 'The last time you were here?'

'Before the Revolution – a long time ago.'

'We've made many improvements since then,' Vera said. 'Now we have an area devoted to the animals that underpin the fur industry – so that we can demonstrate nature within its socialist and industrial context.'

Korolev couldn't help but exchange a glance with Valentina, who looked away quickly and covered her mouth as if she might be about to cough.

Not far along from the lions were the elephants – four of them. The huge creatures used their trunks to pick up carrots, two and three at a time, and place them in their mouths – all with a dexterity that had Yuri rubbing his nose in speculation.

'So much food,' Valentina said, in a quiet voice – not for the children's ears, nor Vera's either. No one must have told the elephants that belts needed to be tightened if they were to complete the Five Year Plan in record time. Or maybe elephants weren't subject to the Five Year Plan. Perhaps they worked to a completely different schedule of industrial development – one that allowed them to guzzle as many carrots as they wanted to.

At Vera's suggestion a young keeper, a bit of an athlete it seemed, persuaded the largest of the beasts to rear its head back and took a hold of its tusks, before using them to do chin-ups. The keeper looked over to the children, proud of his bulging biceps no doubt, and Korolev found that his mouth had curled with disdain of its own accord. He rearranged it into what he hoped might be a polite smile.

'Look, Mama – look,' Natasha squealed, delighted by the buffoon.

'Do you see him?' Yuri said, turning to Korolev to point him out as well. Korolev nodded approvingly, although his instinct was to go over and give the fellow a good shake. Not least because it seemed to him that the rascal wasn't performing for the children, but rather for Valentina. And that sly smile he'd pasted on his handsome face had more than a suggestion of charming sweet-nothings about it, damn him.

'Fifteen, sixteen, seventeen,' the children counted and with each number Korolev's mood darkened further. It was a shame elephants weren't carnivorous, really – it would be upsetting for the children, of course, but they'd recover in time. Children were surprisingly resilient to that kind of thing.

Korolev decided it was best to turn away before he said something unfortunate and, as he did so, he spotted none other than Count Kolya, Chief Authority of the Moscow Thieves, standing on the other side of the small square, looking as if he hadn't a care in the world.

Korolev couldn't believe his eyes for a moment – but it was Kolya all right, and the Thief wasn't only looking right back at him, he was waving him over.

It occurred to Korolev that it would be unusual for Kolya to be out on his own and, sure enough, a quick glance around the environs revealed little Mishka, Kolya's right-hand man, sitting in companionable silence with an outsized fellow, just past the polar bears. There'd be others nearby as well, he didn't doubt – Kolya wasn't a man who liked to take unnecessary risks.

Korolev said nothing to Valentina and the children, who anyway were all still beaming at the damned elephant keeper, and took a stroll over to Kolya, taking his time about it and allowing his gaze to wander over the surroundings – just in case.

The Thief nodded as he approached and Korolev was struck by how much older Kolya looked than when he'd last seen him – but the dark eyes were as intense as ever, and his presence just as menacing. Kolya might pretend gregariousness when it suited him, but he hadn't become overlord of the criminal clans through charm alone.

'Korolev, it's nice to see you in the company of friends. I worry about your solitary existence sometimes.'

Kolya spoke quietly, almost as if he were sincere.

'I worry about you too, Kolya. I worry about how you'll fare in the Zone.'

'In the Zone? I think you know how I'll fare,' Kolya said, shrugging. 'I'll do just fine – a prison camp is like a holiday for me.'

Korolev took the opportunity to scan the area around them once again – it wouldn't be healthy for him if he was seen chatting away to a man wanted for any number of criminal acts. It was just the kind of meeting that could be misconstrued these days.

'How did you get in here, anyway?'

'I have acquaintances in strange places, Korolev – and not only you, either. Don't worry, we were careful. I wanted to talk to you and when it turned out you were coming here, I made my way over. I wasn't far away.'

Korolev glanced over at Mishka. He hadn't looked for a tail earlier, but it was doubtful he'd have seen Mishka even if he had.

'Well,' he said, 'I'm listening.'

'This investigation of yours – into the Azarov killing. I've some things to tell you about it.'

Korolev felt the muscles in his shoulders tense at the mere mention of the Azarov business – he'd almost forgotten about the aborted investigation, not without effort, and yet here it was, rearing its ugly head again already.

'I'm off the case, Kolya – it's nothing to do with me.'

'Really?' Kolya said. 'Is that how it is with you, these days?'

'What do you mean?'

'It's not the Korolev I know, is all. You're the *Ment* who always gets his man, come hell or high water.'

'I'm also the *Ment* who keeps my nose out of anything to do with State Security.'

That made Kolya smile, understandably – his thick moustache

curving upwards in what Korolev suspected was something close to mockery. It struck Korolev, not for the first time, how similar Kolya was in appearance to Stalin. It made him wonder, sometimes.

'Really, Korolev? Every time I meet you you're up to your neck in Chekists.'

'Well, I've learned my lesson.'

Kolya came closer, his voice dropping to a whisper. 'Listen Korolev, if you knew what went on at that institute – believe me, it would interest you.'

'You think so, do you?'

'I'm certain of it, or I've misjudged you. And I don't misjudge men often.'

Kolya pulled at his moustache with his tattooed hand. Korolev saw the circled crown of a ranking Thief on one of the fingers and remembered who he was dealing with.

'Kolya, even if I did give a damn about this institute – I'd have to ask myself why you of all people would come and tell me about it. In my experience you've never done anything that hasn't been for your own benefit – in some way or another.'

'You see, I knew you'd be interested. And why shouldn't I assist the forces of law and order when we both seek the same thing?'

'The forces of law and order are looking into the matter, believe me – I've seen them at it.'

'No they're not, Korolev. The men who've taken over your investigation have no interest in law or order, and certainly not in justice. You, on the other hand? You there's hope for.'

Korolev shrugged his shoulders.

'There's nothing I can do, Kolya. Even if I hadn't been ordered off that investigation, I'd still avoid it. That case is trouble.'

'Oh – it's trouble all right. I don't deny that – but a man like you doesn't mind such things. You've a son, Korolev –

other men do too. And men's sons have died there. Don't you owe something to them? What if your son ended up in such a place?'

'I owe no one anything when it comes to Professor Azarov and his institute, and even if I did I couldn't do anything about it, Kolya. That's all there is to it.' Korolev nodded a farewell and turned away. 'Put Mishka in with the wolves before you go.'

Kolya said something in response that sounded like it might be a threat, or perhaps a curse. Korolev wasn't sure which and didn't much care – it was true what he'd said. There was nothing Korolev could do. Nothing at all.

§

'Someone you know?' Valentina looked at him enquiringly as he rejoined the others.

'Unfortunately,' Korolev said, deciding to forget about the conversation, even as another part of his brain couldn't help but wonder what it might have been that Kolya had gone to such lengths to try to tell him.

'You're worried about something.' Valentina slipped her hand inside his elbow again, as naturally as if they'd been together for a lifetime. He felt his whole being fizz at her touch and he was sure he was blushing. He must be.

'I was worried the elephant would lose his tusks the way that idiot kept tugging on them,' he said, coming out with the first thing that came to mind.

Valentina's peal of laughter made everyone turn to look at her.

'Korolev, you make me laugh sometimes.'

'I make myself laugh sometimes as well,' he said, his voice gruff with embarrassment. How was it that here he was, well past forty and a hardened cop of long standing, and this woman could make him feel like a schoolboy once again?

He turned to find his son examining him carefully, and he

wasn't the only one – Natasha wasn't hiding her interest either. He summoned all his courage and returned their gaze with what he hoped was a calm demeanour.

He had the impression neither of them was fooled.

Chapter Ten

KOROLEV SAT in companionable silence with Valentina, a bottle of Georgian wine on the table between them. The good news was it lacked its cork and some of its contents. The bad news was they only had the one bottle – and it had a spicy, pleasing taste to it that made Korolev wish for more than just a couple of glasses.

The last of the sun coloured the room orange as it dipped below the house on the other side of the street, and what sounded like a church bell was ringing somewhere close. But that must be his imagination. They'd banned the ringing of church bells years ago. He sighed – thinking another bottle would be a good thing. It had been a long day with the children, but he felt he'd done well – they were both still alive and, when Valentina had left them to go to her workplace, he'd marched them around Moscow for most of the day with no more moaning than was to be expected. In fact, they'd seemed to enjoy themselves. In the morning he'd take Yuri out to Babel's dacha for a few days and, with luck, the weather would stay as pleasant as it had been today.

'Korolev,' Valentina said and it sounded as if she was checking that he was still there. She had a point, his mind had wandered.

'Valentina Nikolayevna.'

She smiled at him.

'Isn't it time for Valentina?'

'Valentina,' he tried it out and it sounded comfortable to him. 'Yes, I think you're right.'

There was another pause in the conversation but Korolev knew he didn't have to say anything – Valentina's calm smile told him as much. And the truth was, he was tired – it had been a long time since he'd had sole charge of his son for an entire day. Even when he'd visited him earlier in the year, Zhenia had been around – which reminded him he must call her. She'd enjoy how Yuri's elbow had dug into Korolev's side during a talk at the Planetarium – outraged that his father had snorted at the speaker's suggestion that men would be walking on the moon within twenty years.

But, then again, maybe Yuri was right – maybe they would be growing wheat beside the Sea of Tranquillity by the time Korolev was drawing his pension. Maybe it was possible after all.

Korolev found his glass had made its way to his mouth. He looked over and was concerned to find that Valentina was frowning.

'Is there something the matter?'

'Yuri,' she began and she seemed to be thinking how to approach what she wanted to say. Korolev, his feeling of contentment slipping away as her frown deepened, wondered what the boy had done.

Valentina toyed with her glass, swirling the wine, before she continued.

'He was upset yesterday – it seems his mother has some troubles at the moment.'

'Troubles?' Korolev asked.

'He wasn't clear about them, I'm not sure he knows all of it. But it seems their apartment was searched last week.'

'Searched?' Korolev said and everything slotted into place – Yuri's last-minute visit to Moscow, his strange behaviour since he'd arrived – even the fact he hadn't been able to get hold of Zhenia when he'd called her the night before. He found he'd stood up, his hand to his head as he tried to work out what to do. But, of course, there was nothing he could do. Not for the first time in the last few days he found that he was powerless.

'I'd no idea, Valentina. None at all.'

'I know that,' she reassured him. 'I know you would have said if you'd known.'

'Perhaps it's nothing – a boy's imagination.' His words sounded optimistic, even to himself.

'And if it isn't? What will you do about Yuri if something happens to her?'

'Yuri?' Korolev asked, and slowly but surely it became clear to him that Zhenia's troubles could have ramifications.

'He can stay here, of course.' She spoke firmly, as if there was no question in the matter. 'We can manage between us. The four of us.'

'I . . .' Korolev began to put his thoughts in some kind of order but it seemed Valentina had done enough thinking for both of them. She stood and faced him, putting a hand against his chest.

'Of course,' she said, 'we'll pray his mother will come through this safely – but you should know that Yuri can come and live here and that we'll manage. Together.'

Chapter Eleven

THEY LEFT FOR Babel's dacha first thing, before Yuri was even properly awake. Babel was in the south for a month and had told Korolev to use it in his absence, and now Korolev intended to. He needed to spend some time with his son and he couldn't think of a better place than his good friend's summer house. And he also needed some time to think. He was still struggling to come to grips with Valentina's news about Zhenia. And his worry wasn't helped by the fact that, yet again, he hadn't been able to get through to her the night before.

Korolev had to use his bulk to make a space on the tram for Yuri and their suitcase. Even though it was still early in the morning, the city was full of citizens making their way to work. But the boy didn't seem to mind that they were jammed in so close – all he was interested in was the view outside and discovering which building this might be and whose statue that was. It seemed he didn't remember Moscow at all from when he'd lived here – although, Korolev supposed, it was three or four years ago now.

'Where are we now?'

'Dzerzhinsky Square.'

'And that building?'

Yuri pointed to the Lubyanka, the headquarters of State Security and Korolev felt his mind go blank for a moment, then he pointed at the corner the tram was just about to turn.

'And this takes us down towards Teatralnaya Square, where the Bolshoi is. And the Metropol as well – now that's a place. Luxury like you could hardly imagine.'

Yuri looked up at him, a question in his eyes, and Korolev returned his gaze with what he hoped was a completely neutral expression – so neutral it might even work as a warning. It did.

'The Metropol?' Yuri asked. 'What's that?'

Korolev could see him looking back at the Lubyanka, his curiosity no doubt piqued. Perhaps he'd tell him about the place when they were safely out in Peredelkino, where they wouldn't be overheard by a tram full of who knew who.

'It's the big hotel, on the left. You should see inside it – they've a pool with beautiful girls swimming in it, a bar with white-jacketed waiters and a band that plays music all day long. And past it, on the other side of the square, is the Hotel Moskva. They say it's even grander still.'

'A pool full of beautiful girls?' Yuri wrinkled his nose in amused disbelief.

'I didn't believe it either but I've seen it with my own eyes,' Korolev said, and ruffled the boy's hair. 'Anyway, you're too young for that sort of thing.'

'Better than being too old,' Yuri responded and Korolev felt obliged to give his ear a gentle clip.

§

They carried on like that all the way to Kievsky Station – sparring. They were getting to know each other. There had been awkward moments the day before – when Yuri had treated him almost as if he were a stranger – but they'd got past them and Korolev was relieved. After all, if something happened to Zhenia, Yuri would have to come to Moscow – and if they were to live together, they'd better find a way of getting on. And that thought, mixed with his nagging concern for Zhenia, stayed with him throughout the train journey.

It took forty minutes or so to get out to Peredelkino and Korolev was surprised, as always, by how soon Moscow turned into countryside and the contrast between Peredelkino and the bustle and hustle they'd left behind. When they descended from the train, they took their time as they walked slowly along the platform towards the waiting ticket collector, looking around at the forest that surrounded them.

'Is it far,' Yuri asked, 'this dacha?'

'Not too far.'

The station building was tiny, a white cube with a tiled roof, painted green. Each carriage of the departing train was reflected in its single window as it pulled away. The ticket collector, a young woman who didn't look much older than Yuri, sat on a stool beside the arched entrance. When the last of the train disappeared, it left silence behind it.

At first Korolev thought they'd been the only passengers to descend but, as he reached for their tickets, he caught a glimpse in his peripheral vision of two men strolling behind them. He hadn't heard any other doors opening and shutting when they'd got off the train but then he hadn't been listening. There was something about these men though – something in the way they held themselves – that drew Korolev's attention now. He made a show of emptying his pockets for the train tickets and used the opportunity to allow his gaze to wander back towards the strollers.

The two men were young – late twenties would be his guess. The taller of the two had tousled brown hair, a dark complexion and a fighter's fist-flattened face – he looked like he could handle himself. The other was softer-looking, with a round chin and a physique to match, but when he saw Korolev looking he didn't avoid his gaze. Instead he seemed amused by it.

Korolev turned to hand the tickets to the collector, and made the effort to smile, even though, if the truth were told, he was unsettled by the two men behind them.

'Will we go swimming straight away?' Yuri asked. Korolev took back the clipped tickets and pushed him forward gently.

'As soon as we've unpacked. Not a moment later.'

'Good, after we've unpacked then.' Yuri looked up at him and Korolev nodded to confirm his agreement. He was jumping at shadows – he had to be. The men couldn't be who he thought they might be. After all, why follow him? If State Security wanted to know what he was up to they could just demand he tell them. And if they were worried about what he might do – well they could stop him doing anything ever again whenever they chose. And if the men were from State Security, they'd been surprisingly visible – almost as if they'd wanted to be seen. Why on earth would they want that? That wasn't the way they did things.

Korolev risked another look back as they neared the old monastery, where the road turned to the left – but the men had gone. Probably they'd just been ordinary citizens after all, coming back from a night out with friends in Moscow, likely as not. That was it. That might make sense.

He wasn't so reassured, however, that he didn't keep looking behind them from time to time – just in case.

§

Babel's dacha was fifteen minutes' walk from the station – a fine house: a red-painted corrugated-iron roof topping the white-planked walls, and a solid concrete base for it all to stand on. It was only a couple of years old and sat in a small clearing in the forest. Behind the house was a garage that Babel had no car for, and a small cottage for Lipski, the caretaker, an old comrade of Babel's from the writer's years with the Red Cavalry. Korolev could think of worse places to spend a few days with his son, and he told himself to put all his irrational concerns aside. All was well, he was sure of it.

Korolev stopped on the driveway and squeezed his son's shoulder.

'Hear that?' he asked.

'What?' Yuri asked, looking around him.

'The wind in the trees, Yuri. If we were in Moscow now, think of the hundred different noises there might be now – cars, trams, people, building work. Here it's only the wind in the trees.'

Yuri looked up at him and then at the house.

'Your friend lives *here*?'

'He's away in the south. He told me to use it while he was away.'

'He has a whole house to live in – on his own?'

'No – he lives upstairs from us in Moscow. This is just his summer house. I told you about him – Babel. The writer.'

'His *summer* house?' Yuri seemed to consider such luxury a mathematical problem. 'And he has an apartment as well?'

Korolev resisted the temptation to explain to the boy how some people were more equal than others in this socialist society of theirs.

'Come on, let's go inside.'

Korolev directed the boy towards the side of the dacha where steps led up to a covered porch that ran around two sides of the house. The hollow sound of their footsteps on the wooden boards brought a twinkle-eyed old man to the doorway – Lipski. When Babel had been allocated the house, he'd managed to wangle a job for the old Cossack.

'Korolev? I wasn't expecting you till later. So this is the boy? Let me look at him.'

Lipski leant forward so as to be able to examine Yuri on an equal level, his rosy cheeks seeming to glow with pleasure above his thick white beard.

'So you're the famous Yuri Korolev?' he said.

Yuri considered the question for a moment before nodding his agreement.

'A Pioneer as well, are you?' Lipski reached out to touch the red scarf tied around the boy's neck. Yuri took a step backwards to avoid the caretaker's hand, but Lipski's smile didn't dim.

'I never heard of a shy Pioneer. Did you, Korolev?'

'I'm not shy,' Yuri said, looking at the caretaker's boots.

'That's good to hear. Do you swim at all?'

'I swim.'

'Well, you've come to the right place. That's the best riverbank this side of Moscow, not a hundred metres away. What do you make of that?'

Yuri said nothing.

'We're going for a swim later on,' Korolev said – deciding some kind of intervention was necessary, unsure why Yuri had decided to clam up all of a sudden.

'Good, good,' Lipski said, pushing himself up to his full height, no longer smiling so much as grimacing. He was still fit, the old cavalryman, Korolev could see, but age caught up with everyone's bones in the end.

'I've made up the beds for you and aired the place. If there's anything else you need, you know where to find me.' Lipski glanced down at Yuri with a thoughtful expression. 'I can pick up food from the shop for you if you need it – I'm going that way.'

'We brought some,' Korolev began, but then he looked at Yuri and wondered if he'd brought enough. 'But if you're passing, we could probably do with more.'

He found his wallet and handed him two five-rouble notes. There was no point in asking for anything in particular – Lipski would get them what was there. That was the way things worked in village shops.

'I'll bring you change, don't worry about that.' Lipski nodded over his shoulder in the general direction of the river. 'They've turned the old monastery into some sort of summer camp for children and they've been bringing orphanage kids out from Moscow the last few weeks. Not many of them Pioneers,

I can tell you – as rough a bunch as I ever saw. A lot of people avoid the river when they bring them down to swim, just so you know.'

Korolev thanked him for the tip and they said their farewells.

'What was all that about?' Korolev asked Yuri, when they'd walked inside.

'What do you mean?'

'You went very quiet.'

'I don't know him.'

Yuri's expression seemed to be a mixture of stubbornness and uncertainty.

'He was being friendly. Don't they teach you to respect your elders at school?'

Yuri considered this for a moment. 'They teach us to respect those who strive for socialism and to judge each citizen on their merits. For all I know, that fellow could be a Fascist spy.'

'A Fascist spy? I know him, Yuri. He fought for four years with the Red Cavalry. He's a good comrade. He's sure as hell no Fascist.'

'Pavel Anatoliyevich says that the older comrades have to be watched no matter what they say they did.' Yuri spoke as if reciting something learned by heart. 'He says that some of the old comrades were never real socialists. He says they just fought on our side to save their skins.'

Korolev didn't speak for a moment. When he did allow himself to say something he kept his voice low and even. 'Who is this Pavel Anatoliyevich?' Korolev had to admit he didn't like the sound of the fellow.

'He's the teacher who leads our school's Pioneer detachment.'

'And this Pavel Anatoliyevich – where did he fight? Back when fellows like Lipski and me were spilling our blood for the Revolution.'

Yuri looked embarrassed on behalf of his teacher.

'He didn't fight – he was too young. But he's a glider pilot.'

'I see – a glider pilot.' Korolev didn't mean to sound as dismissive as he did – but it was some sorry state of affairs when young whippersnappers with an aeronautical interest were allowed to criticize men who'd fought with Budyenny against all comers and lived to tell the tale.

'He says many of the old comrades are contaminated by their past,' Yuri said, a stubborn look about him now. 'He says they can never become real socialists. He says Soviet youth, who've grown up in a socialist society, will protect the Revolution in the future.'

'You think I'm contaminated by my past, perhaps?'

Yuri didn't seem to hear the irritation in his voice, which was probably just as well. The boy shook his head.

'They don't give the Order of the Red Star to just anyone. Pavel Anatoliyevich said so.'

A teacher, Korolev thought to himself, should teach – not express opinions on their students' parents, even positive ones.

'Whoever he is,' Korolev said, 'you weren't supposed to tell anyone about the medal, were you?'

Yuri shook his head to indicate it hadn't been a disclosure he'd made lightly.

'I'm sorry – but I'm not allowed to keep secrets from Pavel Anatoliyevich. A Pioneer must always be honest with the leadership. And he wanted to know about you.'

Korolev felt his attention sharpen.

'When was this, Yuri? When was he asking you these questions?'

'In March – after you visited. He wanted to know all about you. To make sure I came from a good Socialist background. When I told him you were a captain with the Moscow Militia and had been awarded the Order of the Red Star, he thought I was lying – but he must have investigated it, because later on he apologized to me in front of the whole class. He said you'd done the State a great service and promoted me to Team Leader on the spot.'

'He did, did he?' Korolev wondered how a teacher of primary-school children from Zagorsk was able to find out what he'd done to earn the medal. Particularly when most of Moscow CID didn't know – and didn't dare ask either. 'What other questions did he ask, when he was asking them?'

'The same he asks all of us – about the loyalty of our parents. If our parents express opinions against Soviet Power. Whether our parents engage in antisocial behaviour – whether they are cultists. We have to give a list of the books we have at home before we can even join.'

It seemed that to Yuri this was as commonplace as being asked what your favourite colour was. Not that Korolev was surprised – everyone knew that Pioneers were told their first loyalty was to the State, rather than their family. It was why adults were careful what they discussed in front of children – in case something might be misinterpreted by young ears or, even worse, not misinterpreted at all.

'You had to give them a list of Zhenia's books?'

'Every single one. Some of the kids' folks have no books at all – they're the lucky ones.'

It occurred to Korolev that they weren't just lucky, but sensible as well. Who knew which writers might be out of favour at any one time – these things weren't always announced. He sighed and Yuri looked up at him, his eyes wide and his mouth curving downwards.

'Is it because of the list that Mother's in trouble?'

Korolev had been waiting for an opportunity to discuss Zhenia's situation, and this, it seemed, was it. He put a hand on the boy's shoulder.

'What trouble, Yuri?'

'I don't know,' Yuri said, his face a picture of misery. Two fat tears rolled down his cheeks.

'You probably know more than you think – tell me why you think she's in trouble for a start.'

Yuri pushed a hand across his face and looked up to meet Korolev's gaze.

'Some men came last week. They took away Mother's papers and some of her books.'

It came out little louder than a whisper. Korolev leant forward.

'These men, Yuri,' Korolev asked. 'Who were they?'

'They didn't say – they only said they had a warrant. They brought the house manager and the old woman from the bakery with them, but they just sat around.'

'Did the men have uniforms?'

'No.'

'I see.' The house manager and the old woman would be witnesses, required by Soviet law to be there during the search – which meant it was a formal investigation of some kind. The men had almost certainly been Chekists.

'Tell me everything they did and said, Yuri. From the beginning. And everything about this Pavel Anatoliyevich fellow as well.'

And, in between the sobs and the tears, Yuri did as he was asked, and Korolev liked little of what he heard. The search itself wasn't likely to have come up with anything much – not in the papers anyway. Zhenia was no counter-revolutionary – on the contrary, she was a loyal Party member of twenty-odd years standing. But books could produce unforeseen problems – for all he knew, Lenin would end up on a forbidden list one of these days. Babel said there were librarians whose fulltime jobs it was to burn banned works, and others who spent their days erasing references to the arrested and exiled from the books that were left.

'And after they went,' Yuri said, finishing his story. 'After they went, Grechko – the house manager – he spat on the floor.

On *our* floor. He said we were saboteurs and Trotskyists – all of us. And Mother said nothing – just cleaned it up and carried on as if nothing had happened. And then Grandfather made tea.'

Korolev took a deep breath. 'Don't worry about that fellow Grechko – he knows nothing. He's like a dog barking to show he's there.'

No, Grechko was no threat – just another citizen keen to make sure he was the one spitting and not been spat on. The bigger worry was this damned teacher and what Yuri might have said to him – but the boy was in enough of a state without asking him further questions. At least for the moment.

'I'll bet he told stories, to those men – Grechko, I mean. I'll bet he did.'

There was a bitterness in Yuri's voice that didn't seem entirely natural and Korolev found that he was examining his son very carefully, an uncomfortable suspicion growing.

What if Yuri had been the one telling the stories?

Chapter Twelve

OF COURSE, KOROLEV reminded Yuri that Zhenia was a Party member of long standing, and that everyone knew she was as true a comrade as ever breathed – that there was no possibility she could be considered disloyal to the State. What else was he supposed to do? Tell the boy his mother was, likely as not, in great danger?

Perhaps Yuri believed him – he hoped so – but when the boy had dried his tears, it seemed as if he'd lost the power of speech. Maybe he was exhausted by the journey or their conversation, or both, or it could be he was embarrassed for having cried in front of him, or it might even have been something else altogether – Korolev couldn't be sure and Yuri wasn't telling. The boy just sat on the veranda steps, carving a stick he'd found lying on the grass, and showing no interest in anything else whatever.

Korolev left him to it and tried to place another call to Zhenia in Zagorsk, but the operator told him a line was down somewhere between here and there, and that it would be the evening at least before he could get through. It made him feel like punching the wall but what was the point in that? He'd only add bruised knuckles to his troubles.

§

Korolev had a lot on his mind as they walked through the trees towards the river. The more he thought about it the more it seemed a worrying coincidence that this news about Zhenia should arrive at the same time as the two men on the station platform. If they *were* State Security, then might they be following him because of Zhenia? They often worked like that – if suspicion fell on an individual it wasn't long before it fell on their friends and family, their co-workers and even neighbours. Even if he hadn't been with Zhenia for some time now, he could still be at risk. He needed to talk to her, yet he knew that might increase the risk. It was a dilemma.

At least Yuri had revived enough to now be whistling. He was walking beside Korolev and, even if he was avoiding his eye as he whittled his damned stick with that little pearl-handled pocket knife of his, he seemed cheerier. Maybe he'd believed him after all.

Was his behaviour normal though? It seemed odd to be so upset and then, not an hour later, to be whistling tunelessly as if nothing had ever happened. Korolev scratched his head – he didn't know much about small boys except what he remembered from his own youth. And since he'd left school at ten to work for a butcher in Khitrovka, he wasn't sure his memories were that useful – boys grew up quickly in those days. Perhaps there was a book he could read.

They stepped out from the trees onto a grassy expanse that stretched down to the slow-moving river – the slope dotted with sunbathers and picnickers. There was a workers' rest home on the other side of the bridge – at least some of them must be from there – and the lean youths gathered around the volleyball net by the far trees would be from the Komsomol camp past the cemetery. It was a complete cross-section of Soviet society, in any event. Some of the citizens had the trappings of relative prosperity – a crisp white shirt or a summer dress of a quality that couldn't be bought in an ordinary store – while others looked as though they might be factory workers or the like. Children ran backwards and forwards, wet hair shining in the summer sun and watched over by women in white headscarves.

It occurred to him that most other people seemed part of a larger grouping, while Yuri and he were relatively unusual in their isolation amongst the hullabaloo. But Korolev was used to standing apart from things and, anyway, there were two of them – that was all he cared about.

Korolev picked a spot on a slight rise so that he could keep an eye on Yuri if he went swimming, and under a tree so that he wouldn't be burned to a crisp. He spread out the blanket he'd brought from the house, rolled up his sleeves like all the other men, and eyed the curve of the tree's trunk with the anticipation of a man who'd had an early start to a day that had turned out to be, well, not an easy one. He doubted he'd sleep but he might be able to empty his mind for a few minutes. And that would be as good as a holiday in itself, after the last couple of days.

'Off you go, Yuri. No need to wait around for me.' Korolev settled himself down. 'Don't swim out too far – there might be a current.'

In fact, the water looked sluggish as engine oil, and if Korolev hadn't known better he'd have suspected it of being a long, meandering pond rather than a river. Still, he was sure this kind of caution was expected of fathers.

'I'll just finish this off first,' Yuri said, looking at the group of youngsters who were splashing in the shallows, before resuming scraping at his stick.

'Go on,' Korolev said, moving his back from side to side to find the perfect spot. 'They won't bite.'

Yuri looked sceptical about that, and Korolev took a second look at the boys in the water – and had to admit Yuri might have a point. And now that he glanced around, he could see the other citizens were keeping a safe distance between themselves and this particular bathing spot and he couldn't blame them – it was temporary home to as evil a gathering of rascally youth as he'd ever seen, certainly in the same place anyway. The orphans had hard thin faces and sharp yellow teeth and, on second thoughts, he wouldn't put it past any of them not to bite – and probably infect you with something nasty when they did so.

Korolev was about to turn his attention back to his tree trunk when he realized one of the boys was showing just as much interest in him and, not believing it could be who he thought it was, he stood to get a better view. There, in amongst the mayhem, was the red-haired Kim Goldstein, onetime leader of the Razin Street Irregulars and now, it seemed, the ringmaster of a much hardier crew. He'd filled out a little and grown an inch or two – but there was no mistaking him.

With a word to some of his fellows, Goldstein swiped water backwards over his skull and stepped up onto the pebble beach. He walked slowly over to where they were sitting – taking his time, confident and purposeful.

'Goldstein. I never thought they'd get you into an orphanage – I'm surprised.'

'Me too, Korolev – but it was a hard winter. I looked for you but you were off somewhere in the south – I thought you might have found us a better class of establishment.'

'I'd have done what I could,' Korolev said.

'I know it. Still, we made it through the winter alive – most of us anyway. That's what's important.'

Korolev had absent-mindedly taken out his cigarettes when he caught Goldstein's meaningful glance. He offered the packet without thinking, then became aware of Yuri, the boy's expression caught somewhere between disapproval and fascination.

'This is my son, Yuri.'

Goldstein raised a finger to his forehead in a laconic salute to which Yuri responded in kind. For some reason, this amused Goldstein.

'Well, Yuri – your dad's all right for a *Ment*. Straight and reliable – can't ask much more.'

'Yes,' Yuri said, raising himself to stand. He held out his hand and Goldstein took it, shaking it firmly.

'The winter's over,' Korolev said, nodding towards the other kids. 'Not planning to move on?'

Goldstein smiled and Korolev noticed he'd lost one of his front teeth since the last time they'd met. He'd also picked up a raw-looking scar on his left cheek.

'We'll go soon enough,' Goldstein said, 'but some things can't be rushed.'

Korolev sensed there was some secret irony in what the boy was saying but, whatever it might be, it wasn't his business. He was on holiday.

Goldstein lifted the cigarette he'd given him to his mouth and Korolev lit it for him. Korolev turned to Yuri and offered him the packet as well. It seemed only fair.

'I'll be honest with you, Yuri – they taste like old boots soaked in petrol and they make you smell like a crematorium. But, if you want one, you can have it. There's no need to tell your mother, though.'

Yuri and Goldstein exchanged a glance and Korolev could have sworn some sort of challenge was made and accepted. The result was that Yuri picked out a cigarette, Korolev held up his lighter and the next moment his son was doing his best not to cough up his lungs. Korolev cursed and patted his back, immediately regretting having given him the damned cigarette, while Goldstein dropped his tough facade enough to giggle. Korolev scowled at him.

'You weren't lying about the taste,' Yuri said, spitting on the grass. Korolev leant forward to take back the cigarette – but

Yuri took a step back, taking another puff on it, this time managing to do so without coughing. He made a wry face. 'But it just takes getting used to.'

'Come on,' Goldstein said, smiling widely and putting an arm around Yuri's shoulder. 'Come and meet the guys. Don't worry, Comrade Captain – they'll behave themselves. I'll make sure of it.'

Korolev watched his son walk down to the river with Goldstein then sat down once again underneath the tree. Well, that had been interesting. He felt a glow of pride in the way the boy had behaved. Good for him. He found himself smiling and all seemed well with the world – for the moment, at least. The day was hot, but not too humid. The sun was shining and the people nearby were happy and laughing. He thought about opening the book he'd brought with him and then found his eyes were closing whether he liked it or not – and his thoughts slowly spiralled towards something that seemed like oblivion.

How long he slept he couldn't tell – and when he woke he wasn't entirely sure he wasn't still dreaming because the first people he saw were the two men from the train station, standing in amongst the far trees, half hidden by branches. They were talking together in a serious manner. And it wasn't him they were looking at – but Yuri.

Chapter Thirteen

KOROLEV TOOK YURI back to the dacha shortly afterwards – he didn't feel safe down by the river after he'd seen
the men. At first he was sorely tempted to head straight back
to Moscow – but when he thought about it, he realized that
wasn't the sensible thing to do. If he was being watched, then
running back to Bolshoi Nikolo-Vorobinsky might be seen as
an admission of guilt – even if he'd no idea what it was he
could be guilty of. And anyway – if those men *were* State
Security there was nowhere he'd be safe. The thing to do was
not panic.

Lipski, meanwhile, had found them some eggs, two fish that
were still cold from the ice they'd been packed in, a small bag
of potatoes, half a watermelon and a piece of butter. It was
enough, with what he'd brought from Moscow, for a good
lunch – though Yuri only picked at it, his gaze drifting to the
open window from time to time. Korolev wondered if he'd seen
the men as well.

'Aren't you hungry?' he asked, after several minutes during
which neither of them spoke.

'No,' Yuri said. 'I think I'll just go upstairs and read for a
while – is that all right?'

'Of course – your brain is a stomach too, you know. Except
you have to feed it with books.'

Korolev thought about that for a moment – not sure if he'd

expressed himself remotely well. Yuri glanced up at him, looking a little confused.

'What I meant to say was—' Korolev began.

'I know,' Yuri said. 'Don't worry, Papa. I like books. I read as much as I can.'

'That's good, very good.'

When Yuri left the room, Korolev waited a moment or two before reaching across the table for the boy's plate. He'd learnt early in life that you never knew for sure when you might be able to eat again.

He'd barely finished the last mouthful when the phone rang, much louder than he'd been expecting – it was as if there were a fire engine in the room with him. He picked the receiver up carefully, a part of him wanting to let it ring and not answer it at all. He'd tried to get through to Zhenia again when they'd come back to the house and this must be the operator calling back.

'Hello?'

'Your call to Zagorsk. The line's clear – I can put you through now.'

'Thank you.'

He listened to the phone ringing at Zhenia's end. Once, twice, five times. The phone was in the communal hallway and sometimes it took a while for someone to answer. After all, answering might mean climbing four flights to find the person the call was intended for – no fun in the middle of a hot summer. Eight times now.

'Hello?'

A man's voice, elderly would be his guess – and annoyed at having been the one to answer, if he wasn't mistaken.

'I'm calling for Citizeness Koroleva. Apartment 3 on the second floor.'

'Koroleva, you say?'

The voice sounded half-amused.

'That's the one.'

'She won't be answering phones today, I don't think. No, my guess is she won't be answering phones for a while.'

The man chuckled and before Korolev had a chance to question him, there came the click of the phone being hung up.

Korolev stood there, listening to the monotone hum of the empty line in his ear. He heard a floorboard creak behind him and turned to find Yuri standing in the doorway, his face pale. Korolev smiled.

'I see,' he said, speaking into the phone. 'Well, I'll call back tomorrow then. Can you tell her Alexei called? Thanks.'

He hung the receiver back onto the phone and shrugged.

'She's out, it seems. We'll try again tomorrow.'

Yuri nodded and Korolev listened to his footsteps retreating back up the stairs to the first floor.

It might be nothing – some people made dark humour from other people's misfortune these days. And the whole house would know Chekists had come to visit, that was certain. It could just be a neighbour who wanted to make a call of his own or someone who couldn't be bothered to go and find her. It was unnerving – but it was probably nothing unusual. Neighbours were like that sometimes. He should just remain calm – that was the sensible thing to do.

§

Later they searched for mushrooms in the woods around the dacha and turned it into a game. Yuri was soon scampering around, his eyes roaming the ground in front of him and his nose pointing forward as if he might sniff their quarry out.

'Yuri,' Korolev had said, in what he hoped was an offhand way, 'if I should suddenly be called away, do you think you could remember how to get back to Moscow – to the apartment?'

Yuri, whose feet had been making their careful way across the sunshine-dappled forest floor, looked up at the question.

'You think you might be called away?'

'It's possible. I'm a detective, sometimes these things happen. Like the other day, if you remember.'

Yuri considered this. 'You'd want me to get the train on my own?'

'I don't see why not – you made it all the way from Zagorsk on your own.'

'I'm only twelve.'

'I was only ten when I started work for the butcher Lytkin – and you're a brighter spark than I was.'

Yuri looked pleased at the compliment.

'I'd need money for the train and the tram.'

'You're right – and I should have given you money before, anyway. A young man needs a rouble or two on his person, or so I've always found.'

Korolev reached in his pocket and Yuri rubbed the notes he handed him between his finger and thumb. He looked suspicious.

'It's just in case,' Korolev said. 'But if I have to go – make your way to Valentina, she'll look after you till I get back.'

§

In the evening they played chess and then listened to a football game on the radio, an important match between Spartak and Lokomotiv, and then, when Yuri fell asleep in his chair, Korolev carried him to bed.

He looked down at the boy in the half-light of the dusk and saw Zhenia in his features, but also some of himself. He couldn't help but feel frightened for the boy, and leant forward to kiss his forehead before he left the room.

Korolev stayed up for a while pretending to himself he was reading, knowing he wouldn't sleep while his brain kept going over the little he knew and trying to make sense of it. And when he did go to bed he found himself shifting around, unable to relax or get himself comfortable, turning over possibilities and probabilities in his head; wide awake – no matter how much he wished he wasn't.

So when the silence was shattered by someone hammering on the door downstairs, Korolev was on his feet and reaching for his clothes before he'd even thought who it might be. He went straight to Yuri's room and found the boy sitting up in his bed, his eyes dark and round in his moonlit face. Korolev tried to keep the fear out of his voice.

'I'll go and see who it is – but if I'm called away, remember what I told you. Valentina will look after you and I'll come as soon as I can.'

He turned and went down the staircase, his feet hitting the steps with the same rhythm as whoever was still banging at the door. Whoever? Well, no thief ever knocked and no honest citizen battered another's door in the middle of the night.

'I'm coming, I'm coming,' he called out as he passed through the kitchen – and the knocking stopped.

He turned on the light in the small winter hallway and opened the door. Two men were outside, their faces yellow in the glow that spilled from the doorway. They were wide-bodied, slab-shouldered professionals – one a dark-skinned, black-haired fellow with the look of the Caucasus about him, and the other a blonde, unseasonably pale Slav. They examined him without speaking and he wondered if they were deciding whether he'd come easily or whether he'd be trouble.

'Comrades,' Korolev said.

'We'll see about that,' the paler of the two answered, with a curl of his lip that didn't bode well.

'Korolev, Alexei Dmitriyevich?' The dark one's cheeks were round and might have been jolly with another man's eyes. This one's had seen too much.

'That's me.'

'Do we need to introduce ourselves?' the pale one asked.

From behind them came the sound of a door closing and Lipski appeared from the caretaker's hut. The men turned quickly and Lipski had the good sense to come to a halt, putting his hands on his head as he did so. By then the dark one had a pistol pointing at the old man's chest and the other was aiming his weapon at Korolev.

'It's Lipski, the caretaker,' Korolev said in what he hoped was a calm voice. 'He must have heard the noise. This is nothing to do with him.'

'That's the truth,' the pale one said, an ominous tone colouring his voice.

Lipski looked at the Chekists for a moment, then seemed to decide this was the worst possible thing to do and shut his eyes altogether.

'I've seen nothing, Comrades, and I've heard nothing. Nothing whatsoever.'

'Remember the orders; the matter's to be handled quietly.' The darker of the men spoke softly, with a Georgian accent. 'Citizen Lipski here will oblige us by keeping his mouth shut, I'm sure.'

'Of course, Comrade,' Lipski said, his eyes still closed and his shoulders hunched over as if to make himself a smaller target.

'Good. So we'll all be very calm, won't we? And then we'll be on our way all the quicker.'

The Georgian was speaking as much to his colleague as to them, and the pale Chekist nodded his agreement.

'Korolev? You're coming with us.'

Korolev nodded, looking down at his feet.

'I'll need some shoes.'

'We'll come with you to get them, don't worry.' The dark one spoke softly. 'And you'll need to wake the boy while you're at it. He's coming too.'

Korolev felt his stomach turn so violently that he thought he must vomit.

'The boy?'

'He's coming too,' the pale one repeated.

As he spoke, he took a step forward so that Korolev found himself staring down the barrel of his gun from a distance of no more than a few inches. Korolev prayed the fellow had the safety catch on.

'You can't arrest a twelve year old,' Korolev managed to whisper, mastering his fear. 'He's too young.'

The pale Chekist's eyes narrowed and Korolev braced himself for a blow.

'We're not arresting anyone, Citizen Korolev,' the Georgian said in his calm voice. 'We're just taking you to see someone. Your presence is requested. No one's forcing you; but, of course, you'll be coming with us just the same.'

The Georgian's eyes were unreadable, but if he wasn't being arrested that was a good sign, surely?

'Do we have a few minutes to pack?' he asked, hoping to extract a little bit more information.

'We're wasting time here. We should be back in the car by now.'

'Cover Citizen Lipski here,' the Georgian said to his colleague. 'I'll get things moving quickly enough.'

'Yuri isn't well,' Korolev began to say, but the Georgian interrupted him by taking his elbow and pushing him through the door to the house.

'I don't care if he's got two broken legs, he's coming with us.'

Korolev felt the pressure of the gun barrel digging into his spine as the Chekist pushed him through the kitchen and into the dining room.

'Where is he?'

'Upstairs.'

Korolev was about to suggest he just call the boy down, but one look at the Georgian and he changed his mind. They climbed the stairs.

'Which room?'

'The one on the left.'

'In you go.'

Korolev opened the door and stepped in, turned on the light and found – no one.

'He's gone,' Korolev said, mystified. He'd meant Yuri to go to Moscow if he was taken away – not for him to run off into the forest.

The Chekist pushed past him, saw the open window and cursed.

'Where?'

'I don't know. He was here two minutes ago.'

Before he even saw the fellow's hand move, the Chekist's gun had hit the side of his head, knocking him to his knees.

'Where's the damned boy, Korolev?'

Chapter Fourteen

'WHY DID HE RUN?' Colonel Rodinov asked him, making another note on the file he was reading. It was the first time he'd spoken. In fact, in the five minutes Korolev had been sitting in front of him, Rodinov had yet to raise his eyes from his paperwork.

'He knows I deal with hardened criminals – maybe he thought men coming to the door with guns in the middle of the night were bandits.'

Korolev wasn't surprised to find his voice was a little distorted – he rolled his jaw around. He didn't think it was broken. Just bruised – like most of his body. But the fat lip that went with it probably wasn't helping his pronunciation.

'Are you suggesting the operatives that went to collect you from Babel's dacha looked like bandits? Respected members of State Security?' Rodinov said, finally lifting his gaze to examine Korolev.

'Well they certainly didn't look like ballerinas, Comrade Colonel.'

Rodinov considered him for a moment, his face impassive. Korolev had a suspicion he looked as if he'd been used as a punchbag by a pair of heavyweight boxers – and it wasn't far from the truth. A nurse had cleaned him up when he'd arrived but even so he'd a fat lip, plenty of cuts, bumps and grazes, his shirt was splattered with dried blood and he could barely see out of his left eye. At least he hadn't lost any teeth.

'I see,' Rodinov said. 'Their orders were just to bring you in. Still, it says here you resisted our people.'

'I didn't want to leave my twelve-year-old son wandering around the woods in the middle of the night. I wanted to find him before we left. If that counts as resisting, then I resisted.'

Korolev spoke in a monotone – he was tired, it was just past two in the morning and there wasn't much of him that didn't hurt.

'He shouldn't have run,' Rodinov said. 'You knew who they were, after all.'

'I've met members of State Security before. He's only a boy.'

'And now he's a missing boy.'

Korolev had nothing to say to that. Yuri had been with him for three days and somehow he'd managed to lose him *and* end up in the Lubyanka.

'Well, I'll ask Popov to make sure the local Militia start looking for him first thing,' Rodinov said, signing a page that was stapled to the inside of the file's cardboard cover. 'I'm sure they'll track him down soon enough. Anyway, it's time we got to the point.'

Rodinov closed the file and placed his pen down on top of it, turning his full attention to Korolev.

'We'll start with you telling me why you carried on with your investigation into Professor Azarov's death when you were given explicit orders not to.'

Korolev could feel his mouth go slack with astonishment. Or as slack as it could go, given the damage that had been inflicted on it.

'But I didn't. As soon as we were told to drop the matter, we dropped it. Like a hot potato, believe me. I wanted nothing to do with the investigation once I knew it was State Security, I swear it on my mother's grave.'

Rodinov had had a hard year by the look of him. Korolev had first met him not twelve months before, and back then he'd had a healthy sheen to his skin and seemed solid and full of energy. Now, despite a summer that had turned most Muscovites dark as Abyssinians, the colonel had the grey pallor of a prisoner – his cheeks were drawn and his tunic seemed too big for him. Whatever kind of work he was doing these days, and Korolev most certainly didn't want to know what that might be, it looked as if it didn't take him outside very often.

'It's known what you were up to in Peredelkino, Korolev. What did you think? That you could go around questioning people without State Security hearing about it? And what did you hope to achieve by it? You knew this was a secret matter. Did you hope to pass information to the State's enemies?'

Korolev ran his tongue over his fat lip and shook his head, both in disagreement and in bewilderment.

'I spoke to no one in Peredelkino, Comrade Colonel. The caretaker, Lipski, of course – but, apart from him, no one.'

'No one, is it?' Rodinov said. 'No one? I have on my desk a report, submitted only a matter of hours ago, that says differently.'

Rodinov opened a thick green folder and extracted a typed piece of paper.

'It says here you were seen talking to a number of people who have a clear connection with Professor Azarov's work. I'd like to know why.'

Korolev thought back – he'd spoken to the ticket collector at the station. Apart from her, he couldn't remember anyone else. Except for Kim Goldstein, of course. He frowned.

'There was one of the boys at the river – they were out from some orphanage in the city for a few days, I think. A youngster by the name of Goldstein – but I knew him from before.'

Rodinov said nothing, giving Korolev the distinct impression that Goldstein was exactly who he'd been referring to.

'I spoke to him,' Korolev said. 'But I'd no idea he was connected with Azarov.'

'And the others?'

'I spoke to no one else.'

'Your son did.'

'He went swimming with Goldstein is all. But Goldstein was the boy who assisted on that matter last year – the icon affair. You'll recall he provided useful information.'

Rodinov considered this, tapping his pencil against his chin as he did so.

'And what did you speak to him about this time? Did he provide you with more useful information? Or was it his friends who told your son what you wanted to know?'

'Have those orphans got something to do with the professor's murder?'

'You don't ask questions here,' the colonel said and Korolev looked around at the chipped blue walls and the stained parquet flooring – and saw his point.

'I apologize, Comrade Colonel. Goldstein just happened to be there at the riverbank and so were we. It was a chance meeting – no more than that. If anyone has informed you to the contrary, they're mistaken.'

'And the zoo? Who were you talking to there?'

'The zoo? Count Kolya? But he came to me – I didn't go looking for him.'

'So that was Count Kolya? The Thief?'

Korolev nodded.

'I see, the report doesn't mention that fact – perhaps they didn't know who he was.'

Rodinov looked pleased – which struck Korolev as odd. The colonel wrote a quick note.

'And what did Count Kolya want to talk to you about?'

'He told me if I was investigating Azarov's murder, I should find out what he was up to at the institute. I explained I wasn't involved with the matter any more. That it was State Security business. And that was that.'

'And you didn't think to report this to someone here?'

Korolev shrugged his shoulders.

'It was made clear to me that the institute was run under the auspices of the NKVD – so I thought they'd know what was going on there better than anyone. My orders were very specific, Comrade Colonel – I was to have no further involvement in the case whatsoever or there would be consequences.'

In his youth he'd been to more than one livestock market with the butcher he'd worked for. Back then he'd seen men weigh cattle with their eyes, and Korolev felt as though a similar kind of assessment were taking place now – only this time he was the bullock in the ring.

'Very well,' the colonel said, after what seemed like several hours but probably wasn't more than a few seconds, then pushed a cigarette case across the desk to Korolev.

'Help yourself,' he said and Korolev did, thinking he'd never needed a smoke more in his entire life. 'There's been another murder,' the colonel said, lighting his cigarette and then leaning across to light Korolev's. 'Which, as it happens, is good news for you.'

'I see,' Korolev said and had to stop himself from laughing out loud, so great was the release of tension. For a moment the colonel seemed about to say something, then appeared to think better of it. Instead he opened one of the files on his desk and passed a photograph across the table. Korolev recognized the man in the picture – what was his name again?

'Dr Shtange – Professor Azarov's deputy,' Rodinov said, and Korolev had the oddest thought. What if Azarov had invented some way of reading people's minds? What if Rodinov was able to hear his thoughts as clearly as if he were speaking them aloud? Was that what he'd been up to?

'What's wrong?' Rodinov asked, frowning, and Korolev

cursed himself. He had to concentrate, remember where he was – not allow his mind to wander.

'Nothing – it's just, I met the man, that's all. Only a day or two ago.'

'Someone stabbed him to death the same morning you went to the zoo.'

Korolev inhaled a lungful of smoke and held it there, before releasing it slowly.

'Well?' the colonel asked.

'The director and deputy director of the same scientific institute murdered within a day of each other? It's unlikely to be a coincidence.'

Rodinov smiled and picked up the photograph, putting it back into the folder.

'I agree.'

'The NKVD is investigating the matter though,' Korolev said, and despite his best intentions it came out as more of a question than a statement.

'Yes. A different department has been handling the matter but it was transferred to this department – where it should have been all along – a few hours ago. The file, which isn't much use otherwise, it has to be said, contained a series of reports from operatives that were, curiously, ordered to keep track of your activities. Perhaps there was some suspicion that you'd carry on your own investigation. You do have a reputation for doing things a little differently to other detectives, I suppose.'

'But—' Korolev began.

'Fortunately for you, I know that your methods are successful and, most importantly, accurate. Our men are stretched thin and have a tendency to adopt – well – imprecise solutions.' Rodinov gestured with his cigarette to indicate the bruises and bumps certain State Security men had left Korolev with.

'The more I think about it, the more I like the idea of you taking up the investigation once again. With you in charge, we're more likely to find out who actually killed the scientists and why. With our people – well, they'll find someone who'll admit to the crime, certainly.'

Rodinov smiled – it seemed the thought amused him – before becoming serious once again.

'But these two were important to the State – so an accurate understanding of the situation is necessary. And you seem the ideal candidate for that job.'

'I'm ready to do my duty, of course,' Korolev began and didn't know quite where to go from there.

'You don't sound very enthusiastic, Korolev.'

'You'll forgive me, Comrade Colonel, but it was made clear to me this was a case involving State secrets. I'm an ordinary Militia detective – I just don't have the authority to investigate such matters.'

The colonel picked up a piece of paper and handed it across the table to him. It had an NKVD letterhead and Korolev could see his name in the text, beneath which had been applied three signatures and three ink stamps. One he didn't recognize, another was Rodinov's and the third belonged to Nikolai Ezhov – the People's Commissar for Internal Affairs and, some said, the most powerful man in the Soviet Union after Stalin.

'It's been decided that you'll work, temporarily, for this department. As you can see, this letter gives you all the authority you need.'

Korolev didn't dare ask which department of State Security this might be, and anyway he was struggling to come to terms with the idea that he was about to become a temporary Chekist. It wasn't an outcome he'd foreseen when that blonde oaf had been kicking him in the guts.

'Have you any further questions? You may speak freely, there should be openness between us – now that we are colleagues.'

It was a statement that invited Korolev to put his cards on the table – and there was something in the colonel's demeanour that told him it was safe to do so – perhaps safer than not doing so anyway.

'Comrade Colonel, I only know the work Azarov did was related to the brain. Kolya suggested to me that some of his research was on humans and I got the impression he thought things didn't go well for the men involved. Of course, I don't believe that – I'm only repeating a Thief's slander of the State. But if it *were* true . . .'

'My understanding is Professor Azarov applied scientific methodology to our interrogation techniques,' Rodinov said in a neutral voice. 'And that his research was successful – our effectiveness had improved immeasurably as a result. But Azarov's research wasn't limited to that. I've heard he worked with various pharmaceutical substances, examining how they might affect the human mind; and I believe he also carried out a series of experiments into attitude alteration – turning enemies into friends, if you will. Telepathy was another area he may have investigated. The truth is I don't know as much as a person in my position would expect to know. In my opinion the institute's activities have been – well – a little *too* secret. But I do know that, yes, people died as a result of his research.'

'I see,' Korolev said and wished he didn't.

'The ends sometimes justify the means, Korolev.'

'I understand that, Comrade Colonel – of course I do.'

Rodinov's gaze felt like it was looking inside Korolev's very skull, peering into every nook and cranny of his mind. It made him nervous, that gaze.

'Telepathy?' Korolev said – picking out, much to his own surprise, the word he'd decided was most worrying in the colonel's description of the institute's activities. After all, if men like Rodinov were able to read men's thoughts then – well – the world would be a lot less safe.

'You know what it is?'

'I've heard of it,' Korolev said, recovering. 'I understood it wasn't possible.'

'It would make my job much easier if it were,' Rodinov said. 'But I don't think anything came of it – or, at least, that's my understanding.'

The colonel paused, put his pen down on the table and seemed to consider what he should say next.

'You see, if my department were to directly investigate this matter,' he said finally, choosing his words carefully, it seemed to Korolev, 'it might be difficult. People would begin to take sides. There would be different versions of the truth – there always are. And, as you of all people should know, truth can be manipulated to suit certain agendas – and hidden if it suits certain persons. In other words the case would become a political matter – and, as a result, whatever truth would finally be chosen would be based on politics. With you looking into it, there's a chance things may be a little different. Korolev, let's be clear – I want to know who killed these men and I want to know why. But I also want to know what was going on at this institute – and it occurs to me that while you're investigating this murder, you may uncover things that could be of interest to me.'

He looked at Korolev expectantly and Korolev frowned. Was Rodinov really suggesting what he thought he might be?

'Comrade Colonel, forgive me, but are you asking me to spy on a department of the NKVD?'

The colonel smiled.

'Of course not, Korolev. You misunderstand me. I want you to keep your ears and eyes open – no more than that. You're under my orders, so you should be safe enough if that's what you're worried about. Safer than if you don't do what I suggest, let's put it that way.'

When the colonel put it like that, of course, everything became clearer for Korolev – he took a deep breath.

'I'm always ready to do my duty, Comrade Colonel, as I said.'

'Good.'

'And the evidence we gathered?'

'Will be made available to you. This will be an ordinary investigation, to all intents and purposes, but without involving the procurator's office. You'll have the same team assigned to you as before, along with Lieutenant Dubinkin, who works for me. He'll assist you and your colleagues in getting hold of any information which might otherwise prove difficult to obtain. You shouldn't have any problems, however – as you've seen, this investigation and your involvement have been authorized at the highest levels. Comrade Ezhov remembers you, you'll be pleased to hear, and retains a high opinion of you.'

Korolev nodded, not at all pleased that the People's Commissar for Internal Affairs was even aware of his existence. Something in his expression must have amused Rodinov because the brief smile that crossed his face appeared genuine enough.

'So high an opinion,' Rodinov went on, 'that he even wondered whether your temporary assignment to the NKVD shouldn't be made permanent.'

Korolev's immediate reaction must have shown because Rodinov laughed.

'Don't worry, Korolev. I can think of few people less suited to the kind of work we generally do. And that's not to speak ill of you. No, Korolev, you're an excellent Militia detective – it's just we're specialists in our field; and you don't use a hammer to cut wood, or a saw to hammer nails – that's all there is to it.'

Korolev did his best to keep his relief to himself.

'Very good,' Rodinov said, picking up a piece of paper from the desk. 'Dubinkin will meet you at Shtange's apartment at eight o'clock. This is the address. I'll expect daily reports. You may go.'

Korolev stood and walked towards the door. He was just about to open it when the colonel interrupted him.

'Korolev, just so you're aware – those weren't my department's men who came for you this evening. And they weren't my orders either. I think you've met Colonel Zaitsev – it seems he wanted to meet you again. Luckily for you, I took the matter over before he did.'

Chapter Fifteen

KOROLEV WAS ABLE to persuade the garage at Petrovka to send a car to the Militia post across the square and occupied himself during the time it took to arrive by calling Yasimov. His old friend looked grim-faced when he pulled up outside his building not fifteen minutes later.

'This better be important – I've had half the *kommunalka* threatening to kill me over you disturbing their sleep with your phone call,' Yasimov said, opening the car door. His eyes widened when he saw the state Korolev was in.

'A long story,' Korolev said, 'and not all of which I can tell you.'

But he told him what he could – and the fact that Yuri was alone somewhere out near Babel's summer house and how he was back on the Azarov case. Yasimov didn't ask any questions, only nodded.

'We'll find him – don't worry.'

§

Korolev drove as if the devil himself were snapping at the rear bumper of the Packard. He threw the heavy car round one corner so hard that its chassis rose onto two wheels, teetering for a moment on the point of turning over before it crashed back down.

'Lyoshka,' Yasimov said. 'We'll never get there if we're dead.'

Korolev took his point and slowed to a more reasonable speed – but even so, he barely lifted his foot from the accelerator the whole journey. By the time he'd reached Peredelkino he was drenched in sweat from the heat of the engine and the effort of bullying the car to do his will. But he at least retained enough good sense to coast down the slope towards the dacha, rolling to a silent stop about fifty metres away.

By now the darkness had given way to a shadowy half-light. Not the slightest breeze moved through the silent trees but the birds must already be stretching themselves in their nests to greet the day. Korolev and Yasimov walked along the gravel drive that led towards the house, their footsteps the only sound, and Korolev hoped his hunch that Yuri would have stayed close to the house – at least until dawn – was right. After all, this was the only spot he knew apart from the river. They moved as quietly as they could, but they must have been making more noise than he thought, because a white face appeared at the caretaker's window. Not long afterwards, Lipski opened the door to his small house, looking at Korolev with sympathy.

'They let you go?'

'They really did just want to talk to me.'

Lipski's glance took in Korolev's battered face but he said nothing.

'I see,' Lipski ran fingers through his thick beard. 'I've kept an eye out but there's been no sign of him – I'm sorry.'

§

They searched the woods, calling Yuri's name, until the sun came up and it was time for Korolev to leave.

'Mitya,' Korolev said to his friend, 'I have to go – if he's still in the locality, my guess is he'll try to take a train to Moscow.'

'I'd better get down to the station, then.'

'If he manages to get that far, he'll try and make his way to

Bolshoi Nikolo-Vorobinsky – can you call Valentina Nikolay-evna? Just in case. Tell her what's happened and ask her to make sure people keep an eye out for him?'

Yasimov nodded, then put a hand on Korolev's arm.

'Don't worry, brother. We'll find him for you – see if we don't.'

But Korolev couldn't shake the fear he felt for his son, despite the reassurance Yasimov offered him.

Chapter Sixteen

THE BUILDING Shtange had lived in was familiar to Korolev. It overlooked Chistye Prudy – a small green area with a pond on the Boulevard Ring that wasn't far – about a mile or so – from Bolshoi Nikolo-Vorobinsky. It was the decoration on the apartment building's external walls which made it a landmark for Muscovites, however. Strange abstract animals and weird elongated plants twisted and turned up its white walls – carved in relief and highlighted with black paint. It reassured him, for some reason – a familiar location was always a good starting point for an investigation.

A baby-faced uniform was standing in front of the building, his summer jacket too tight for him and not as white as it should be. As Korolev approached, he noticed the boy's gaze kept shifting as if he wasn't sure what to do with himself or where to look. One moment, he was staring at the ground, then he was peering into the holster that hung from his belt to check his revolver was still there, then he was examining each of his boots in turn, then rubbing them against the back of his trousers to try and make them look as though they remembered what it felt like to be polished. Yet for all his looking, the boy didn't spot Korolev until he was within a few feet of him – which didn't say much for his abilities as a guard. When he finally noticed his visitor, the boy's eyes widened in a mixture of alarm and suspicion and his hand reached towards the holster.

'Korolev – from Petrovka,' Korolev said, holding out his identification card. The boy took it with relief. This, at last, was something the fellow felt comfortable with – Korolev would be surprised if the boy had come top of his class when it came to examining papers.

'Captain Korolev?' he said, reading from the card and then looking up at him, doubt twisting his mouth. Korolev hadn't had time to change his clothes or clean himself up. Not that there would have been much he could have done about his face anyway.

'I walked into a door,' Korolev said. 'It's me, all right. It's who *you* are I'd like to know.'

'Militiaman Kuznetsky, Comrade Captain,' the boy said, straightening to attention. 'My apologies – it's just you look . . .'

'I know what I look like, believe me – I don't feel much better. So what are you doing here?'

'I was guarding the apartment inside, Comrade Captain, but when they came this morning they told me to wait down here.' He looked up at the apartment building. 'I suppose I'm guarding the whole place now.'

'They?'

'You know, Comrade Captain. *Them.* They were here yesterday as well. And the day before that.'

'I see,' Korolev said. 'When did *they* arrive today?'

Kuznetsky looked at his watch.

'Twenty minutes ago. There are two of our people in there as well. Two forensics men – they came about ten minutes ago – with all their bags and things.'

'What about the body?'

'The doctor took it away the day before yesterday. Not long after it was found.'

'I see,' Korolev said, looking up at the facade once again. 'Which doctor would that have been?'

'A lady doctor, Comrade Captain – I didn't catch her name. She was a well-proportioned lady, not to be disrespectful.'

That would be Chestnova.

'Did you see the body before it was moved?'

'Oh yes, Comrade Captain. I was one of those that found him. His blood went through to the ceiling of the flat below, you see, and they didn't like the look of the stain it made and called us out.'

'Us?'

'Sergeant Bukov and me. From the station. We broke the door in and there he was – like a pin cushion without the pins. I didn't know a fellow had that much blood inside him.'

'He was stabbed then?'

'Stabbed? About a hundred times, he was stabbed.'

'So who's been handling the investigation since?'

Kuznetsky glanced down at his boots, as if they might offer him some assistance in handling a question he clearly didn't want to answer.

'Them,' he said once again. 'Well, only one of them now. It was a different lot before. He's upstairs. The new one, that is.'

Korolev nodded, guessing that this must be Dubinkin. 'I suppose I'd better go and see him then.'

Kuznetsky looked sympathetic.

'He's up on the second floor – you'll find it easily enough. I'd best stay here and guard the building.' Then, remembering who he was talking to, he added 'Comrade Captain'.

'Do that, Kuznetsky. But first call Sergeant Bukov and tell him I want to see him. The Militia will be taking a more active role in the investigation from now on – and I'll need his, and your, assistance.'

Korolev patted the boy on the shoulder as he passed.

He was just about to enter the building when he heard his name being called and turned to find Slivka holding her watch to her ear.

'I'm not late, am I? Damned thing. It's telling the time all right, just not the right time.'

Her glance took in the state of him and she came to a sudden halt.

'What the hell happened to you, Chief?'

'A misunderstanding – I had some visitors last night. They got the wrong end of the stick.'

'It looks like they beat you with it all the same. Why would someone come to your house in the middle of the night? Were they drunk?'

'No,' Korolev said. 'You know the sort of night-time visitor – they come unannounced.'

'Oh. That sort,' Slivka said and ran a hand back through her hair, a gesture which pulled the skin on her forehead tight, but didn't quite obscure her worried frown. 'And you're here? Not somewhere else? They let you go.'

'They wanted to talk to me about the Azarov case,' Korolev said.

'I'd an idea there might be something more to this,' Slivka looked up at the building and sighed. 'The chief just told me to meet you here.'

'When did he call you?'

'About two in the morning. No gentlemen visitors, though.'

'Be thankful – they also managed to frighten Yuri enough that he's running around the woods somewhere out near Babel's place. Yasimov's trying to find him.'

Slivka took this in, shaking her head in disbelief. 'He'll find him though. Yasimov's like a bloodhound.'

'I hope so. Anyway, here we are – back on the Azarov case.'

Slivka blinked twice then extracted a solitary papirosa from one pocket and a solitary match from the other. She whipped the match down the wall of the building and lit the cigarette.

'The Azarov case,' she said, in a voice that announced to the world that her fate was a dark and gloomy one.

'Another of the professor's colleagues managed to get himself killed. We're to handle both investigations – and we're going to be working directly for State Security.'

'Well,' Slivka said, her mouth trailing smoke, 'life isn't just a walk across a field. And even if it were, it should be known that sometimes there's mud to wade through.'

She nodded, as if that were all that needed to be said. Korolev found a reluctant smile tugging at his mouth as they entered the building. Things couldn't be that bad if he had Slivka watching his back.

Chapter Seventeen

THEY FOLLOWED the doorman's directions up the stairwell and Korolev had the sense that the building was holding its collective breath – terrified by what had happened. Certainly there was no sound except the echo of their footsteps on the stairs.

When they reached the second-floor landing, yellow light spilled out of an open doorway along with the murmur of conversation. In case there was any doubt they were in the right place, someone had helpfully marked out the shape of a body on the carpet. Korolev couldn't help but notice that the white tape they'd used had been placed directly onto a wide spread of crusted blood. He wasn't surprised it had gone through to the floor below. There was a lot of it.

'Hello,' Korolev called as he carefully stepped over the outline, looking around as he did so at the splattered walls. To judge from one long arc of blood in particular, it seemed whoever had killed the doctor had managed to sever one of his arteries.

'Come in,' called a voice Korolev didn't recognize, and he followed it to its source – a large sitting room painted wheat-field yellow. Most of one wall was taken up by a fitted sideboard with shelves that climbed to the ceiling – shelves that were empty except for a solitary vase of wilting flowers. There was a large circular table with four wooden chairs around it, a daybed upholstered in deep-red velvet and scattered with silk cushions of various sizes and colours, and a pair of leather armchairs that had seen better days – none of them recent. But despite the furniture the place felt empty. Hollow, even. As if no one lived here. Which, he supposed, was now the case.

The two forensics men, Levschinsky and Ushakov, were standing in the centre of the room with their arms folded, bags and equipment at their feet, looking grey against the bright walls. Around them the carpet was marked with brown streaks and what looked like footprints – blood brought into the apartment by the killer? Or by Militiamen and Chekists who hadn't been conscious of the need to protect a crime scene? Korolev nodded to his two colleagues and turned his attention to the man in the NKVD uniform standing beside the window. Dubinkin, he presumed.

'It's Korolev, isn't it?' The Chekist broke the paper tube off a papirosa and put the short tobacco-filled end into a silver holder. 'And this must be Sergeant Slivka. You'll both know these comrades, I presume.'

He waved a hand in the direction of the others and Korolev nodded. A good-looking fellow, he supposed – a narrow face, despite the extra weight he was carrying around his midriff, and clean-shaven, with smoothed-back dark-brown hair that made him look like some jazz musician from the Empire Restaurant. Dubinkin beckoned him towards the window and gestured down at the bustling traffic of a busy Moscow morning.

'It's a beautiful day, isn't it?'

It was said in a friendly way, but Korolev couldn't help but wonder what the hell the question *meant*. But what was a man supposed to do? Disagree with a Chekist?

'A very fine day, Comrade Lieutenant,' he said, looking down at a column of white-shirted children marching behind a female teacher, their red Pioneer scarves bunched round their throats – a reminder that Yuri was still missing. He felt his hands clenching into fists, thinking he'd better things to be doing than looking out of damned windows to amuse Chekists.

'But what about your son, Korolev?' Dubinkin asked, and Korolev wondered, not for the first time in recent days, whether his thoughts were written on his forehead. 'Any news of him?'

'He's still missing.'

Korolev sensed the other Militiamen's eyes on his and he avoided them. Instead he looked down at the children as they were packed onto a tram; thinking how hot it would be for them in there on a day like this. Yuri's age, too. He stopped himself. There was no point in worrying about Yuri – Yasimov would find him – he was sure of it. He caught Slivka's concerned look and took a deep breath, then let it out, feeling some of his anger go with it.

'It seems to be a good-sized apartment,' Korolev said, deciding that moving the conversation away from his missing son would be wise.

'The State looks after such valued contributors to the cause of Soviet science. There are two other rooms and a small kitchen. One of the rooms is used as a study and the other as a bedroom.'

Korolev turned to the forensics men. 'Have you had a look around?'

'A quick look,' Ushakov said. 'I might be able to do something with the blood in the hallway – we've taken samples. We might even be able to give you a rough time of death based on how long it took the blood to go through to the ceiling below.'

Ushakov nodded down at the carpet.

'As you can see, there are footprints all over the place and just by looking at them I can tell you they belong to at least three or four different people, one of them possibly female. But as we can't compare them to footwear worn by the previous investigators,' Ushakov looked at Dubinkin, 'it probably makes trying to track them down and match them up a wild-goose chase. One thing though – there's a lot of dried blood in and around the kitchen sink, so it's possible the killer tried to clean themselves there. To judge from all the blood on the walls in the hallway, I'd say the likelihood is they were covered in the stuff. Anyway, we'll do our best to make something of it.'

Korolev nodded. 'Do what you can; you can't do more than that. What about the Azarov investigation?'

'We still have everything. No one came to pick it up in the end. We'll get back to work on it.'

That was pretty much all that needed to be said – so the forensics men were left to go about their business.

'I have some background files.' The Chekist pointed to a stack of files that sat on the round table beside the window, along with a cardboard box. 'But before you look at them, I'd like to show you something.'

He led them back to the hallway, and into what appeared to have been the dead man's study. A large desk stood in the centre of the room, its surface bare except for a telephone and a pencil that had been snapped in half. On the walls around it, the fitted bookshelves were also bare and, when Dubinkin opened the drawers of the large filing cabinet, one after another, they were empty as well.

'You won't find one scrap of paper in the entire place. Everything's been removed.'

Korolev took a deep breath and looked back into the corridor at the outline of the dead man.

'What about the body?'

'Your Dr Chestnova took him away, but we've photographs of the scene as it was found. She insisted.'

'Insisted?' Korolev's respect for the doctor increased. If he'd been wearing a hat, he'd have taken it off to her.

'And the murder weapon?'

'A knife, presumably.'

'Yes,' Korolev said patiently. 'I guessed that. I meant have we found it.'

Before the comment was out of his mouth Korolev regretted it, but Dubinkin only laughed.

'I see. No, not that I'm aware of.'

'Has anyone spoken to the neighbours?' Korolev asked. 'And what about the doorman downstairs?'

'I don't think so. At least, not that they let us know about.'

'Do you mind me asking a question?' Slivka said, her hands buried in the pockets of the thin leather jacket she was wearing.

'Not at all, Comrade.'

'Who are "they"?'

'"They" are the Twelfth Department. They were handling the case until yesterday.'

'And you, which department are you?'

'I'm with the Fifth Department. I work for Colonel Rodinov.'

Slivka nodded. She'd come across Rodinov before, when they'd handled that business down in Odessa.

'And may I ask another question?'

'Will anything I say stop you?'

That got a smile from Slivka.

'What's the difference between the two departments? Just so we know where we stand.'

'The Twelfth Department looks after special projects. The Fifth Department looks after counter-intelligence and internal security.'

Slivka frowned. 'So does that mean there are foreign spies involved in this?'

Korolev wondered if it was being women that allowed Slivka and Chestnova to venture where he, for one, wouldn't dare to tread.

'You understand these matters are confidential, Comrade Slivka.'

'I understand we're being asked to investigate two murders and it'll be more difficult if we don't know what is what, and what might be what. That's what I'm thinking.'

Dubinkin looked pointedly at Korolev as though it would be better if he answered her questions, and so Korolev repeated exactly what Rodinov had told him about what the institute might or might not have been researching and what he knew about the killings. After all, if Rodinov had told him, he surely must be allowed to tell Slivka. When he finished, there was a lengthy pause as Slivka thought through the ramifications. Eventually she shrugged, as if deciding that, having considered them, they were better forgotten about.

'Both of them killed within a day of each other – were they friends outside of work?'

'Far from it,' Korolev said. 'In fact, Shtange made it clear to me he didn't like the professor. Not at all.'

Slivka asked the obvious question: 'Where was Shtange on the morning of the professor's death?'

'At the institute. The guards verified it – but Shtange did tell me he'd had an argument with the professor that same morning. Not that it gets us any further – his alibi is watertight. No one goes in or out of that place without it being logged. Anyway, let's not jump to conclusions or we'll end up missing something. It's possible the murders aren't connected.'

'That's true,' Slivka said. 'We're going to have to get uniforms involved, a lot of them. We'll have to go door to door here, and over at Leadership House as well – and quickly. People's memories don't get better over time, just fonder.'

Dubinkin didn't look happy at the thought of Militiamen flooding the neighbourhood.

'If you're worried about keeping it secret,' Korolev said, 'I can tell you for a fact there isn't a man, woman or child in the neighbourhood who doesn't know a man was killed here on Tuesday morning. That's the way Moscow works, Comrade.'

Dubinkin considered this for a moment before shrugging. 'Colonel Rodinov will have to approve it. You said it's possible the murders aren't connected. Any reason?'

'The killer may turn out to be the same person, but I think it's best to presume there are two of them until we know more. One's a gunshot to the head, from behind, and the other's a knife attack, from the front. It suggests different personalities, to me at least.'

'Perhaps,' the Chekist said, but Korolev sensed Dubinkin saw the merit in the approach.

'As for who's directing things – let's work in a comradely fashion. Each to our own area of expertise. Although I've no doubt there'll be some matters in which Comrade Dubinkin should take the lead – in fact I'm sure of it.'

Dubinkin smiled his approval and Korolev felt he'd passed a test he hadn't even been aware he'd been taking.

Chapter Eighteen

AS NO ONE was using it, and it had a telephone line, they decided Shtange's apartment would be as good a base as any for their enquiries – and once forensics had been through the study, Korolev and Slivka moved in. With Colonel Rodinov's agreement, the number of Militia involved in the investigation grew considerably over the following hours. Bukov, the sergeant who'd discovered Shtange's body, arrived as instructed, and soon four pairs of uniforms were working their way through the apartment building under his direction. The Militiaman who'd been standing guard outside the building when Korolev had arrived – Kuznetsky – had been assigned to answer the apartment's telephone and relay messages when needed. One short phone call and the mention of Colonel Rodinov's name had been enough to arrange for Sergeant Belinsky to pick up where he'd left off over at Leadership House. And all the while, the forensics men worked their way methodically through the apartment – removing the carpet from the hallway, dusting, swabbing and sampling.

The information-gathering underway, they began to work through what they already had – sharing Dubinkin's files between them, reading each one before passing it on to the next person in the circle.

There were few surprises. They'd already known they were dealing with two Party members – now they knew the awards and decorations they'd been given, the positions they'd held, where they'd studied and where they'd taught. It was clear that there were differences between the two men – Azarov was a Party activist and a scientist and nothing else. Shtange had other interests – music, for example. He was a competent pianist who played at dances for the hospitals he worked at. He'd also been a keen amateur pilot in Leningrad, with Osoaviakhim, the voluntary State organization that trained citizens in aviation and chemical defence. Perhaps that accounted for the cigarette case with the engraved propeller Shtange had offered him at the institute.

'I wonder why Shtange's wife and family didn't come to Moscow?' Slivka asked.

'You can ask her,' Dubinkin said looking up from his reading. 'Madame Shtange's staying at the Moskva – waiting for her husband's body to be released.'

An interesting piece of information, Korolev thought to himself, wondering how many more the lieutenant was keeping up his sleeve.

He returned to his reading and came across another interesting fact – Madame Shtange was French. How had someone married to a foreign citizen ended up working for a secret institute? He considered asking the question and then decided against it. Even if he was temporarily attached to State Security, that sort of thing wasn't his concern.

Slivka passed him the photographs Chestnova had insisted be taken of the doctor's body. Shtange's expression was calm, given the pool of blood that surrounded his body and the torn fabric and skin where he'd been cut at and stabbed. One of his hands, black with blood in the photograph, was held to his neck – as if he'd been trying to stem the flow. The other, thrown back when he'd fallen, was completely clean – the cuff of the shirt a crisp white. He'd been stabbed in the face at least three times – one of the blows shattering the left lens of a pair of what looked like reading glasses. A frenzied attack, it occurred to Korolev. Quite different to the single shot that had brought an end to Professor Azarov's life.

'He was wearing slippers, do you see?' Korolev said, showing the others the photograph. 'And the top three buttons of his shirt are open over his vest. That says to me he wasn't dressed for company. So whoever it was came to visit him unexpectedly, I'd imagine.'

Not that this deduction helped them much, it occurred to him.

'Let's talk about what happened when,' Slivka said, shuffling through a few papers she'd been examining. 'According to this Militia report, the downstairs neighbour notices a dark, damp mark on his ceiling at 11 a.m. – the blood seeping through the floorboards. Shtange was seen alive by his maid at eight when she made him his breakfast before going to see her son in hospital. So the murder took place within that time period. When Shtange doesn't respond to the neighbour's knocking, the neighbour calls for the caretaker, who isn't immediately available. The neighbour doesn't notice the blood on the door at first, because it was dark in the hallway, but the caretaker does notice it, at about 11.20. He immediately calls the local Militia station. Bukov and Kuznetsky arrive at 11.30, break in the door and find the body. The maid returns home at just past twelve.'

'When do we see the maid?' Korolev asked.

'She should be here by now,' Slivka said. 'I'll check.'

When Slivka left the room, Korolev turned to Dubinkin.

'I think we should find out more about this institute, and I'm thinking you and I should pay them a visit. If nothing else I'd like to know what was in this report Shtange and Azarov were arguing about.'

Dubinkin nodded his agreement.

'We also need to look into Professor Azarov's political activities,' Korolev continued. 'It seems he may have denounced a couple by the name of Golovkin over at Leadership House – they were arrested last week. I'd like to know more about that – but there may have been others as well.'

'And you'd like to know who and when, I suppose?'

'It's an avenue of enquiry. One we can't ignore.'

'Then I'd best be on my way,' Dubinkin said, standing. 'These things are best done in person. We have an extensive but efficient filing system – it shouldn't take me too long. If they've been investigated there will be a file on them.'

He smiled, and the smile told Korolev, in a way he couldn't explain, that there was a file on him as well, and that Dubinkin had read it.

Chapter Nineteen

WHEN DUBINKIN LEFT, Korolev put the phone to work, calling Lipski out at Babel's dacha – no news. Then Bolshoi Nikolo-Vorobinsky – no news there either. Finally he'd called Petrovka in case Yasimov had left a message for him – which he hadn't – and asked the operators to give Yasimov Shtange's phone number if he called in. When Korolev hung up, he felt a physical urge to run out the door, jump into the nearest car and drive straight to Peredelkino.

He should be the one out there looking for his son, he knew it. He shouldn't be relying on friends for something like this. He should also be ringing Zhenia to tell her what had happened – if she was in a position to take his call, that was. He put his head in his hands, feeling tiredness and worry starting to overwhelm him – but Slivka's voice in the corridor made him pull himself together.

She opened the door, followed by a small round-faced woman wearing a white kerchief that covered her hair.

'This is Citizen Lilova, Chief. Dr Shtange's maid. She's working across the street now.'

'You were quick to move on,' Korolev said, sounding testier than he intended. He gathered himself, making the effort to smile.

'You can't let the grass grow under your feet these days.'

Lilova sat down – her sharp blue eyes taking in the empty shelves.

'Food costs money, and the dead don't pay,' she continued. 'Not that I'd anything against the late comrade, but it is what it is. What happened to you?'

'I fell out of a window.'

'Two or three times by the look of it.'

'It's not as bad as it seems. Notice anything different in here?'

'All his books are gone. I saw them taking boxes out of the building yesterday. I wondered what they were up to.'

'We need to ask you a few questions.'

'Of course. If I can help, I will – he was a good man.'

Korolev glanced up at her – she meant it, was his guess.

'How long did you work for him?'

'Since he arrived from Leningrad. Three months back. I know all the caretakers around here, Semyon Semyonovich downstairs told me the fellow needed someone to look after him, and I needed the work. The last people I looked after – well – they're not around any more.'

'What happened to them?'

'Husband to the camps, wife and children to her parents.'

Korolev looked at the maid – she must be at least fifty-five, possibly older. She spoke of her former employer's arrest as casually as she might have described a queue for bread. It was just something that had happened, nothing to get upset about. Galina Matkina had been the same over at Azarov's apartment – as far as they were concerned, arrests only happened to the higher-ups.

'Did you live here? When you worked for him?'

'No, I live with my son and his family – two streets away.'

'The son you were visiting in the hospital?'

'No, that's the youngest – but he lives with us as well.'

Korolev imagined a crowded room – two if they were lucky

– in some communal apartment. The Lord knew how many would be crammed in there.

'Dr Shtange was a nice fellow though – I thought I'd get longer out of him.'

'What do you mean?'

'Well, I've had two arrested, one killed himself and one transferred to Vladivostok.' Lilova seemed to think being sent to Vladivostok wasn't that different to being sent to the Zone – or committing suicide, for that matter. 'And now this. It's not unusual, I suppose. The arrests at least. And transfers aren't unheard of. But this was a surprise. Once they start getting themselves murdered – well – you begin to wonder. Still, I always say – you can't get into too much trouble making soup and washing clothes.'

It was a fair point, although the mention of soup made him remember just how hungry he was.

'Did he ever mention Professor Azarov?'

'That fellow who was killed the day before him – his boss?'

'That's the one.'

'He didn't much like him, I could tell that. I heard them arguing on the telephone once or twice, and one time, after he hung up, he called him a devil. And Comrade Shtange was a mild-mannered man.'

'What were they arguing about?'

'Scientific business, I suspect. Nothing of interest to me anyway.'

'I see. Do you know why he disliked Azarov?'

'It seemed he didn't like the way things were done at the institute. His wife came to visit with his children two weeks ago and he said as much to her.'

Slivka raised an eyebrow and Lilova shrugged her shoulders.

'It's a small flat – I know my faults, Comrades.'

'In our profession, Citizen Lilova, we don't consider curiosity a fault.'

Lilova smiled at him demurely, as if she thought he might be flirting with her. He hoped the sudden warmth in his cheeks didn't mean he was blushing.

'Did you,' he continued, in a gruffer tone of voice, 'happen to overhear or notice anything else you might like to tell us?'

'Such as whether he was having an affair, what he argued with his wife about, whether he gambled away the institute's money? That sort of thing?'

'That sort of thing would be very interesting,' Slivka said.

Lilova shook her head, regret apparent in the gesture.

'I tell you he was as honest a man as I ever met, and a model husband with it – he'd go home to see his family every weekend, even if only for a day. And if he didn't go there, they'd come here. They never had a harsh word for each other. A fine wife, foreign but speaks Russian like any one of us. She's also a doctor. And his two boys were good children, very polite. And as for having a wandering eye for other women, he didn't have the time. Between working at the university and the institute and trekking back and forth to Leningrad, he barely had time to sleep. And sometimes not even that – more than once he worked through the night.'

'Do you know why he was at home on Tuesday morning, not at the institute?'

'He worked here often – unless he was doing surgery, that is. In which case he'd spend days and nights there, looking after his patients. Otherwise he liked to work here. Reading, writing, that sort of thing. He'd take the phone off the hook and I was told to keep visitors away. In my opinion, he didn't like that institute one little bit. And it wasn't just the professor he didn't like about it either. The university was different – he seemed happy when he went over there.'

Korolev wondered what kind of operations Shtange had been carrying out, given Kolya's comments at the zoo, but he decided this was a question better left until his visit to the institute.

'You said visitors?'

'Sometimes students would come from the university – he was very friendly with them, encouraged them. But otherwise there weren't many – he hadn't been in Moscow long.'

'Was there a particular reason he was home the morning he was killed? His boss had just died, after all – I'd have thought he'd have had plenty to do.'

'All I know is that the doctor told me on Monday evening that with Professor Azarov dead he'd almost certainly be leaving Moscow – and that I should think about looking for another place to work. I came in at the same time as usual on Tuesday morning – I made him his breakfast at six – and he was in good spirits, I'd say. Said he wasn't going into the institute and he was fine with me going to visit my boy at the hospital. As I said, he was a comradely sort of a man.'

Korolev looked at Slivka, wondering if she could make sense of it. If Azarov was dead then surely Shtange, as his deputy, should have been at his post – and why would he have thought Azarov's death would mean he'd be leaving? Of course, he'd suggested as much when Korolev had met him, but that had just seemed to be proper socialist modesty. Even if someone else had been immediately appointed to take over from Azarov, surely Shtange would have been responsible for some kind of hand-over?

'Did he say why he'd be leaving?' Slivka asked. 'Or when?'

'No. But he was pleased about it. He missed his family being here. It wasn't his choice to come to Moscow – he was asked to. But he was a good man, promised to make sure I'd be all right. Which was kind of him – there's many just look after themselves these days.'

'How did he react to the professor's death?' Slivka went on.

'He didn't like the fellow, he said as much, but he was shocked by it. He said it was sad that anyone should come to such an end. Even a man like him.'

'Even a man like him?'

'Those were his words.'

They went through all the usual questions with the maid – trying to account for her whereabouts, for Shtange's, asking for a list of all the people he might have had contact with – and by the time they'd finished with her they had the beginnings of a picture of the doctor: conscientious, hard-working, a good comrade and yet, for some hidden reason, a man someone decided to kill.

Chapter Twenty

BY ELEVEN O'CLOCK Korolev and Slivka between them had personally interviewed the downstairs neighbour with the blood-soaked ceiling, the caretaker who'd come to his aid, the people who'd lived above, alongside and across from Shtange's flat and a maid from along the corridor who'd sworn she'd heard a woman scream at around 10.30 on the morning of the murder. Korolev had been the one who'd spoken to the maid but, given she'd done nothing about it at the time, not even look out into the corridor, Korolev didn't think her statement could be relied on. Meanwhile Sergeant Bukov's men were continuing to go through the house apartment by apartment and would soon be taking their enquiries out into the neighbouring buildings and streets. Korolev had left Slivka in charge, knowing that that kind of work needed someone who was capable of giving it their full attention and that, with Yuri still missing and very little sleep the night before, he wasn't the man for the job.

Instead Korolev was sitting in the passenger seat of Dubinkin's car and feeling uncomfortable. The Chekist had returned from his visit to the extensive-yet-efficient State Security filing system to say that he had two clerks working on Azarov's denunciations and that they could expect results later in the day. It had seemed logical to ask Dubinkin to drive with him over to Leadership House to see what could be shaken out of the Azarov side of the investigation, but it wasn't turning out to be a happy experience. Not for the first time they'd come to a stop at a crossroads and the pedestrians had reacted to Dubinkin's uniform in an unpleasant way. It seemed people didn't know whether to run, pretend they'd seen nothing or, perhaps, salute. It bothered him.

'About your uniform,' Korolev said eventually, and not without misgivings. 'I think it frightens people.'

Dubinkin nodded but said nothing, and Korolev got the impression that for the Chekist that might be the whole point.

'It's just, when we're asking people questions – well – I feel it's best if they forget we're Militia. Or, in your case . . .'

'A Chekist or, as Lenin called us, the Sword and the Shield of the Party,' Dubinkin said in a neutral voice that made Korolev want to stop the conversation there and then. But he couldn't do that now, could he? He was stuck in it, fool that he was.

'It's just they're more relaxed then, do you see? And if they're more relaxed, we get more out of them.'

'You think so?' Dubinkin said, clearly unconvinced, but then he seemed to reconsider the point – nodding slowly. 'All right, Korolev. I see how people react to the uniform, I'm not unobservant. Of course, it often has its uses – but here I can see why you might think a more subtle approach may be required. I'll get rid of it.'

Korolev was pleased to see their destination approaching on the other side of the river, offering the perfect excuse for a change of subject.

'It's entrance number eight,' Korolev said, thinking he could kiss each square inch of its oak doors in gratitude for hoving into view when it had.

Sergeant Belinsky was just exiting the building when they pulled up.

'Any news for us, Belinsky?' Korolev asked. Unsurprisingly the sergeant couldn't seem to make up his mind which was more distracting – the Chekist's uniform or Korolev's battered face. 'I fell off a tram – it looks worse than it is.'

'I'm pleased to hear it, Comrade Captain,' Belinsky said, with a grave nod – it seemed he'd decided to pretend Dubinkin wasn't there for the moment. 'I'm afraid we haven't turned up anything directly related to the murder, at least so far, but it does seem as if the professor wasn't a popular neighbour. More than one resident has gone so far as to indicate he wouldn't be missed. And something else, which might be more relevant.'

Now Belinsky remembered the Chekist was there all right – his tongue appeared at one corner of his mouth as he considered how to approach a no-doubt delicate subject.

'The Golovkins? The fact that Azarov denounced them?' Dubinkin asked with a smile.

'Yes,' Belinsky said, blinking with surprise. 'And not just the Golovkins, Comrade Lieutenant. They say he acquired his current apartment as a result of information he passed on to State Security, which resulted in the arrest of the former tenant. The man was called Bramson – arrested last year. His wife as well. There's another case too – a factory director by the name of Menchikov, also arrested. His wife and children still live in the building.'

'Good work, Belinsky,' Korolev said. 'I'd like to talk to Menchikov's wife, if she's here.'

'She is, Comrade Captain. I told her you might want a word. Also, you asked me to make sure the doorman Priudski was available for questioning – but I'm afraid that hasn't been possible.'

While they were talking they'd walked towards the entrance and now Korolev could see that Priudski, the small grey man who'd made his presence so unpleasantly felt on Korolev's first visit, had been replaced by a man of about Korolev's age, taller than Priudski, with short grey hair and a drinker's hollow cheeks.

'What happened to Priudski?' Korolev asked, showing the doorman his identity card. He didn't respond immediately, apparently transfixed by the NKVD badge on Dubinkin's *gymnastiorka.*

'He's no longer working here, Comrade Captain,' the doorman said eventually, turning his full attention to Korolev's feet. 'I'm Timinov.'

'Since when?'

'Since birth,' Timinov said.

'Not you. Priudski,'

'I'm sorry, I thought . . .' the doorman began before stopping, straightening himself up and looking Korolev in the eye. 'Since Tuesday,' he said in a firm voice, before his new confidence seemed to wane. 'He – uh.' He looked at Dubinkin then back to Korolev. 'He was arrested.'

'Arrested?' Dubinkin asked. 'What for?'

The doorman blinked and his eyes dropped to the badge on Dubinkin's breast and then back to the rank badges on his collar.

'Well,' Timinov said. 'I wouldn't know what your colleagues wanted him for, Comrade Lieutenant, and I wouldn't ask either.'

Which was fair enough, Korolev thought.

'State Security arrested him?' Dubinkin asked, looking confused.

The doorman nodded his agreement.

'On Tuesday, you say. When on Tuesday?' Korolev wondered if it had something to do with Shtange's death.

'About six in the evening.'

'I know nothing about this, Korolev, but I'll find out, believe me.' Dubinkin turned to Timinov. 'I need a telephone.'

'There's one in here,' the doorman said and gestured to his small office. Dubinkin looked at his watch and then at Korolev.

'I'm going up to talk to Citizeness Menchikova,' Korolev said. 'But we need to speak to Priudski.'

'I understand,' Dubinkin said. 'Leave it to me.'

§

Korolev followed Timinov up the stairs – there was something familiar about the fellow's face.

'So Timinov, have you worked here long?' Korolev said, and the doorman turned to look at Korolev, his eyes unreadable in the half-light of the stairwell.

'It's Captain Korolev – isn't it?'

'So it says on my identification. From Petrovka.'

'I didn't read it – that Chekist had my attention. And then I didn't recognize you, because of your face.'

Korolev nodded, resisting the temptation to invent yet another improbable excuse for his bruises.

'But we've met before – back in twenty-nine. I was working at the Red Flag Tractor factory then.'

Korolev looked at him more closely, subtracting eight years.

'I remember you. The local uniforms had you fixed for that foreman – the one who woke up with his head cracked open.'

'I owe you for that, Comrade Captain.'

Korolev shrugged. 'You didn't kill him – it's not my job to put innocent people against crimes they'd nothing to do with.'

'All the same, I'm in your debt – there's many would have left things as they were.' Timinov extended his hand and Korolev took it. 'So now you're looking into the professor's death?'

'That's right.'

The doorman nodded, as if that made sense to him.

'I've worked here three years, Comrade. A bit of this and a bit of that – whatever needs doing around the place – and I help out at the theatre and the cinema when I'm needed, or I used to anyway. I'm a doorman now. Well, for the moment at least.'

'And you knew the professor?'

'Oh, I knew him – he tried to have me fired once. I don't like to speak ill of the dead but he was a hard man to like.'

'And Priudski?'

'I don't know much about him, Comrade Captain. I stayed well clear.'

'How come?'

'All I can say is he hung himself on his own rope, I shouldn't wonder.'

Korolev nodded – it seemed he wasn't the only one who'd thought that Priudski's ears were working for State Security. He stopped to recover his breath, looking out one of the dusty windows at the street far below.

'How many damned floors are there in this place?'

'Ten altogether.'

'And which of them is this woman Menchikova on?'

'The tenth. It's not what she's used to, I can tell you. You think Professor Azarov's apartment is big? Well, you should have seen theirs. But a cat couldn't swing a mouse in the room they have now. One more flight of stairs is all.'

Korolev reluctantly started climbing again, reconsidering his views on lifts as he went.

'It's just here, will I knock for you?'

'It's all right,' Korolev managed to say, deciding to take a minute to recover before he did anything else. 'If I need anything I'll call for you.'

'Don't you hesitate, Comrade Captain. Not for an instant. If I hear anything, I'll let you know – you can count on it. I pay my debts.'

Chapter Twenty-One

EVEN THOUGH Menchikova's room was on the highest floor, the view wasn't of the Kremlin, or the Moskva River, the southern districts or even over the rooftops to Gorky Park. No, it was of the dusty courtyard, and the sky. But even that view provided relief from the small low-ceilinged room, not much more than half the size of Korolev's. It certainly wasn't big enough for three small children, Citizen Menchikova and her mother. One of the children wasn't much more than a baby. No wonder when Menchikova opened the door she looked exhausted, but the sight of him woke her up all right. He should be used to it by now, but he didn't like to see people step back in fear when they set eyes on him.

'Citizen Menchikova?'

'Yes?' She made an effort and drew herself up straight as she spoke. Behind her, two young boys stopped wrestling on the bed while the wary eyes of Menchikova's mother, sitting at a small table, took in the identification card Korolev produced. It seemed to him her mother held the infant she was cradling in her arms just a little closer as she did so.

'I'm Korolev, a detective from Petrovka. Would you have a few minutes? I want to talk to you about Professor Azarov.'

She looked at the bloodstains on his shirt and the bruises and scrapes.

'I'm sorry about my face – I had an accident. I haven't had time to clean up.'

Menchikova nodded and reluctantly opened the door wider – but there really wasn't space for anyone else in the room and certainly not someone his size.

'Is there somewhere we could talk more privately?'

Menchikova looked around at the box in which she lived. She looked towards her mother, who nodded her agreement.

'We can go up on the roof if you'd like,' Menchikova said. 'It should be open – it normally is when the weather is like this.'

He followed her out and along the corridor, through an unmarked wooden door that looked like any other and then up some steps that led to another door, this time constructed from metal and looking as though it had been welded shut; yet when Menchikova pushed, it swung open soundlessly and there they were, high above the Moskva, looking down on a slow-moving riverboat far below. The city sprawled away from them in all directions until it vanished into the smoky haze of the horizon.

It should have been a view to savour, but instead Korolev, to his surprise, found that the building seemed to be moving beneath his feet – and he had to lean back against the door for a moment until the sensation passed. Fortunately Menchikova's attention had been elsewhere and he was able to quickly wipe the cold sweat from his forehead before she turned to face him once again.

They weren't the only persons up here – the flat roof ran around three sides of the building's internal courtyard and here and there other inhabitants of the building sat or lay, enjoying the morning sun. Some had brought deckchairs up, some cushions. None were within hearing distance however.

'So the door is always open?' Korolev asked. Menchikova's brown arms and freckled face made it seem likely she came up here from time to time – either that or she worked outdoors. But despite her tan, she looked frail in the sunlight.

'The doorman said there were only two ways into this part of the building – through the front door and the courtyard,' Korolev continued.

'It's meant to be kept locked,' Menchikova said, glancing away as if hoping to avoid his examination. 'But the doormen don't want to be running up and down however many flights of stairs every time someone important wants to sunbathe – there are plenty of people they can't say no to in this place, you see. So in the summer they keep the doors open. I only came up here because you asked for a place to talk, of course. I wouldn't otherwise. I know we're not meant to.'

Korolev sighed and made a note – the fact that the roof was accessible multiplied the number of potential suspects for Azarov's murderer, as well as increasing the number of entry points.

'I'm not here to check whether you use the roof or not, Citizen, believe me.'

Menchikova's frown intensified and, although she said nothing, he realized his words might have sounded ominous. He decided to try a different approach.

'I understand your husband was arrested because of Professor Azarov's denunciation,' he began, but got no further – Menchikova put a hand to her chest and glanced quickly round her, as if looking for a means of escape. Korolev reached out to reassure her, but even this gesture was misinterpreted. She took a step back and he found himself having to leave the safety of the door, immediately feeling the roof sway nauseatingly once again.

'The children. Who will look after them? I knew I'd be blamed, I knew it. As soon as I heard he'd been killed, I knew it.'

'Please, Citizen – I've some questions is all. I'm an ordinary detective. Please just stay where you are.'

She didn't seem to have heard him at first, but she did stop moving, which was something. Korolev reached behind him and took a discreet hold of the door handle. He allowed himself to exhale.

'Look,' Korolev said. 'It seems there wasn't always justification for the way the professor approached such matters. I'm considering making a recommendation that any case the professor was involved in should be looked at again.'

It wasn't exactly a lie, but it wasn't the truth either. He didn't feel any better about it when she stared up at him, her eyes bright with hope.

'Sasha was loyal to the Party, to the State, Comrade,' she said. 'He sweated blood to make sure the factory met its targets. Azarov accused Sasha of questioning the Party line and undermining confidence in the State, which was nonsense. What evidence did he have to tell the Chekists my husband was a Trotskyist saboteur? I'll tell you. Sasha mentioned to him that the factory would struggle to meet its obligations if supply issues weren't resolved soon. That the supply situation was bad. That was all he said. There's nothing disloyal in it – it was a fact. It was a fact he was straining every muscle to make not a fact, but there it was – still a fact.'

Korolev nodded unhappily, thinking that now he'd have to ask Dubinkin to look into it – otherwise he wouldn't be able to live with himself.

'I don't know what he said or otherwise, Comrade, but I'll do what I can.'

Menchikova nodded, reaching forward with her hands to take his.

'And I know why he did it. I know why Azarov lied. I know why he told the Chekists my husband was a saboteur.'

'Why?'

'He wanted our apartment – his application was with the

building manager before the Chekists even put my husband in the back of their car. In the end they gave it to the Weisses, but that's what he was after. It's how he came by the apartment he's in now.'

'When you say the Weisses – you mean Dr Weiss?' Korolev asked.

'A good man – one of the few who still acknowledges me. If it had to go to anyone, I'm glad it went to him.'

'And how did he get hold of it?'

'I don't know – someone must have helped him – someone with more influence than whoever helps Azarov. Isn't that how these things work?'

There was no bitterness in her voice, it was just a statement of fact. It contained no expectation that Korolev might want to comment on her description of how these things were arranged, so he didn't. After all, wasn't that how he'd got his own room? He'd still be sleeping on his cousin's floor if Popov hadn't intervened on his behalf with the Housing Committee. Korolev cleared his throat.

'Is there something you'd like to tell me? About his death?'

'I didn't kill him.'

'That's as may be, but I'll need to know where you were on the morning of the professor's murder.'

'I have a job at the Burevestnik shoe factory over in Sokolniki – as a bookkeeper. I work the late shifts, or across shifts. I'm lucky to have the job – I know it. On Tuesday I was working until noon. I'd started at midnight. When I came back there were policemen already outside, blocking the entrance. The factory can tell you – I didn't leave once during the night. We clock in and out – and there's a timekeeper to ensure we do.'

'That sounds like a good alibi, Citizen. If it stands up, you've nothing to worry about.'

He did his best to detach his hand but she wouldn't let go of it. He was stretched now between the door handle and her grip and beginning to feel awkward.

'Everything will be fine, don't worry,' he said.

'I am worried.'

'Don't be. Worry never made things better – things are what they are.' He listened to that again and shook his head. 'I meant, things aren't bad for you, Citizen Menchikova. You couldn't have killed the professor and that's that.'

'Thank you, Comrade Captain. Thank you.'

She let his hand go. She'd been gripping it so hard, he could feel where her nails had dug into his flesh.

'You say he did the same thing with the apartment he's in now?' he asked.

'Yes – Bramson. That was his name anyway. The wife kept her maiden name, although I don't remember it. They'd a son but I don't know what happened to him either, except that he disappeared, the same as them. Azarov said they were spies. That's all I know. You can never ask, you see, when something like that happens. You're just told and that's it. You never speak of them again.'

'I understand, Citizen. Believe me, I understand.'

Chapter Twenty-Two

KOROLEV MADE his way back down the many flights of stairs, still a little shaken, but feeling better with each downwards step he took. It occurred to him he'd never been on top of a building this high before and, if it were up to him, he never would be again.

'Comrade Captain.' Belinsky was climbing the stairs towards him, and seemed slightly out of breath. 'Nothing much to report as yet, I'm afraid.'

'Keep at it,' Korolev said and then, as he was there, asked Belinsky to check up on Menchikova's alibi.

'Of course, Comrade Captain. Consider it done. One other thing, Lieutenant Dubinkin had to leave. He said he'd see you at one o'clock.'

By which Dubinkin meant that they'd meet again at Dr Chestnova's place of business for the results of the autopsies. Unfortunately, it left him without a car. He looked at his watch – eleven-thirty.

'Could you do me a favour?'

'With pleasure.'

'I'm on my way down to see the professor's widow and I need to get across town afterwards. Can you call Petrovka and ask them to send a driver to pick me up in half an hour?'

Which would give him twenty minutes or so to stop off at his apartment and see if there was any sign of Yuri.

§

Korolev knocked twice on the Azarovs' door and didn't have long to wait till Galina Matkina peered out at him. He smiled but she took one look at his face and then concentrated instead on his shoes.

'An accident,' he said wearily. 'Nothing to worry about.'

'Comrade Captain,' she said, or rather the top of her head did, but before she got round to saying anything else a voice came from the sitting room.

'Show the captain in, Galina.'

Galina stood back, making way for him, lifting her eyes now to gaze at him with an intensity that was almost disturbing, as if she could see something in him that was important. He shrugged his shoulders, wondering not for the first time about the strange behaviour of young people.

'Comrade Azarova?' he asked when he found himself face to face with the voice's owner. She was sitting on a soft chair, a book open on her lap, wearing a black blouse and skirt to match her black hair. She was even wearing black gloves. Was this some kind of mourning garb? Her skin, pale despite the season, seemed drawn tight by grief, and her gloved hands slowly twisted and gripped one to the other in a constant movement he doubted she was aware of. She looked brittle to him, as if barely maintaining even this show of calm.

'Before you ask,' he said, 'I apologize for my appearance. An accident – nothing serious, I assure you.'

She looked at him blankly and it seemed here at least was one person who couldn't care less if he'd been beaten half to death. It was a relief, if the truth were told. He took a seat across from her.

'Comrade Azarova?' he asked once again and there was a moment of silence, which he allowed to reach its natural con-clusion, looking around the room as he waited. As in Shtange's apartment, the bookshelves had been stripped of their contents.

'Yes,' she said, her eyes finally focusing on him. With difficulty it seemed.

'I'm sorry about your husband,' Korolev said, 'but I have to ask some questions.'

At first he thought she hadn't heard him but then she spoke in a low voice, barely more than a whisper.

'You're the detective who was here the other day, aren't you?'

'Korolev, Comrade Azarova. I've been reassigned to the matter – although now I'm reporting to State Security rather than Petrovka. Would you like to see my authorization?'

'The other ones took all our books.' Her mouth twisted, as if she were trying not to cry. 'All of them.'

'When did this happen?'

'The day after – I was . . .' She paused, her brow furrowing as if the memory was somehow confusing. 'I was indisposed on the day of his death. The Militia – you – wouldn't allow me to see him, you see. I had to spend some time in the apartment of an acquaintance. I slept for a long time.'

'I remember – Dr Weiss, wasn't it?'

She nodded.

'Do you mind me asking what time on Tuesday they came for the books?'

She looked puzzled, as if trying to work out why he might want that particular piece of information.

'I'm just curious,' he added. 'No particular reason.'

'In the afternoon; they came at about four o'clock. It took them hours – they had to list each book for the receipt and some of the men could barely read and write. They took a book on birds. What could that have to do with his work? They took novels, dictionaries – even a book of recipes. Everything.'

Korolev was equally puzzled – the only reason he could think of for stripping the shelves would be because the books might be confidential. But shouldn't they have sent specialists in that case? What was the point in taking useless material? Unless, of course, it had all been organized in a great rush.

'I presume they took his papers as well?'

'Yes,' she said. 'As I told you – everything.'

'I'd like to look around in a moment, if that's all right.'

'Of course, do whatever you want. Ask whatever you want.'

'If we could go through the events of the morning of his death to start with. That would be very helpful to me.'

She looked away, out the window at the blue sky, and when she spoke he had to lean forward to hear her.

'We rose at six, as we always do.' She hesitated, and her mouth twisted once again. 'Did. The whistle from the Red October chocolate factory woke us. It always – did. We performed our callisthenics. To the radio. And then we washed and dressed.'

There was a programme every morning that took citizens through a series of physical exercises. Sometimes Korolev listened to it himself.

'And so you breakfasted,' Korolev continued for her, when it began to feel as if she'd forgotten he was there.

'Yes,' she said, and sighed. 'My husband went to the institute earlier than usual, at around seven. That was the last time I saw him. I left the apartment at eight.'

He hoped she wouldn't cry – it was always awkward when citizens cried. Perhaps he should have asked Slivka to talk to her.

'How was the professor? I mean, what was his mood?'

'He was concerned about some developments at the institute, I think, but he didn't say what. That was why he wanted to go into work early. He said he wanted to check something.'

'And by concerned you mean worried?'

'Perhaps.'

Korolev made a quick note.

'I understand you're also a doctor.'

'A psychologist,' she said, but the correction was half-hearted.

'At an orphanage, I believe.'

'Yes, I assist the staff with the children's development.'

Korolev took a moment to consider his next question. The fact was that all morning he'd been wondering what the connection was between the professor and Goldstein's orphanage. After all, if Rodinov was to be believed, merely talking to Goldstein had been enough to have him picked up by the Twelfth Department's people. And if he hadn't spoken to Goldstein, then likely as not Yuri wouldn't be missing. He took a deep breath.

'I heard the professor also worked with children – with orphans, in fact.'

It was a shot in the dark but when she looked up he felt he had her full attention for the first time.

'I've been instructed not to discuss my husband's research in any way.' She spoke sharply.

'Which orphanage is it you work with, Comrade?' Korolev asked, and the question hit the mark. 'It's the Vitsin Street orphanage, isn't it?' he said, and she nodded reluctantly. 'What is it you do there, exactly?'

She examined him for a moment and Korolev was sure she was going to tell him nothing, but in the end she merely shrugged.

'You have to understand the type of children we're dealing with. First there are the *besprizorniki* – the street children – who may have had no education at all, let alone a socialist one. Then there are the children of the enemies of the people, who may have been educated incorrectly. While the street children have little concept of their duties to the State and the Party, the children of enemies can be even more resistant. I assist the staff, using scientific techniques, naturally, to educate the children in proper socialist values. And, in the case of the children of enemies, to re-educate them.'

Azarova spoke in a monotone, almost as if she were reading

from a prepared speech. Korolev wondered if this was how she taught at the orphanage – if so, he could understand why the *besprizorniki* fought tooth and nail to stay well clear of such places.

'Scientific techniques?' Korolev asked. 'Such as?'

'What has this to do with the death of my husband?' Azarova asked wearily. Korolev did his best to smile reassuringly.

'You'll have to forgive me, Comrade Azarova. My job is to gather together all available information, whether it seems directly relevant or not. An investigation is like a puzzle – sometimes the insignificant pieces are the ones which show the way to the solution.'

'If you say so.' Azarova looked doubtful.

'So,' Korolev said, returning to the attack, 'what kind of techniques?'

'There are various techniques that can help make children, as well as adults, more receptive to correct mental processes. Mostly, we just encourage good behaviour and right thinking with rewards, and then we discourage bad behaviour and incorrect thinking with . . .' she paused, 'other methods.'

Korolev wished she'd just said 'punishment'. 'Other methods' sounded worse somehow.

'To speak in the most general terms, we indoctrinate the children. We teach them the truth of Marxist–Leninist theory – in an accessible way – and use this as a framework for their future development into right-thinking socialist citizens.'

The look she gave him contained a challenge and Korolev realized he wouldn't get any more from Azarova on this topic without a fight – and he'd other matters he wanted to discuss with her before it got to that. All the same, he made a note to find out more about these so-called techniques – and this orphanage. He'd an idea it wouldn't be time wasted.

'So, you spent the whole morning at this orphanage?'

'Until not long after eleven. And then I came back and – well.' She put a hand to her mouth.

'It must have been a terrible shock – my sympathies again.'

She nodded and then looked away.

'I must ask about your relationship with your husband, I'm afraid,' Korolev said.

A solitary tear rolled down her cheek but then she seemed to gather herself.

'We were each other's support in our struggle for the great aims of the Revolution and Soviet science – what more is there to say?'

'Not much, I'm sure,' Korolev said, thinking it sounded like a strange sort of marriage. But, then again, perhaps that's why he was divorced.

'Did you ever argue?' he asked.

'Argue? We'd no time for arguments. Our union was intended to strengthen our ability to serve the Party, not to undermine it. Did we argue? That question implies a catalogue of concepts that were alien to our marriage and our commitment to the Revolution. No, we didn't argue and, no, I'd nothing to do with his murder.'

Korolev raised an eyebrow. He didn't doubt that she was sincere – there was no emotion in what she'd said, just a bald statement of fact. But still. He decided to change direction.

'Were you aware your husband met with Dr Shtange on the morning of his murder?'

'Met with Shtange?' She repeated his words as if surprised by them.

'They didn't get on, did they? Dr Shtange was unhappy with the way things were done at the institute, wasn't he?'

'Who told you that?' she asked indignantly. 'Was it Shtange? My husband was the director of the institute and Shtange was his deputy, so Shtange had no right to be unhappy with anything and certainly no right to attempt to alter the way things were done. In my husband's opinion he was a saboteur and a wrecker.'

'I see,' Korolev said, a little taken aback by her passion. 'Had they worked together for long?'

'Three months,' she replied, calmer now. 'It wasn't my husband's decision – he was barely consulted. If the decision had been left to him, the man would still be in Leningrad working with his monkeys.'

'His monkeys?' Korolev asked.

'And his dogs,' she said, her eyes sparkling with disdain.

'And dogs as well, you say?'

Did she think he'd worked in a zoo of some kind?

'Dogs. My husband believed it was impossible to make real scientific progress in the study of the human brain using animals. At best they provide indications – but if you want to drink water, you have to go to the river. Shtange's experience was therefore entirely useless for the work he was assigned to.'

'I suppose,' Korolev said, sensing an opportunity, 'Deputy Director Shtange must have found it difficult to adapt to working with humans. Was that where some of the conflict arose?'

'That is exactly where the conflict arose – not only did the fool not understand the processes my husband was developing, he stated that he considered my husband's work to be unscientific. Even unethical. Shtange, the monkey man, considered *my* husband unethical.'

'Which particular aspects did he consider to be unethical?' Korolev asked innocently. Azarova opened her mouth to answer and then stopped herself.

'I've told you I can't discuss the details of my husband's work, not that he told me about it in any detail. His research was highly secret. But he believed Shtange's supposed concerns were in fact attempts to sabotage its success.'

'I see, did your husband perhaps take some action against Comrade Shtange? Inform State Security as to his concerns, perhaps?'

She shrugged, not meeting his gaze, and her reaction was as good as a written confirmation. Well, that was a motive for murder, Korolev thought – if only Shtange hadn't had such a solid alibi.

'You disagree with such an action, Comrade Korolev?' Azarova's question interrupted his thoughts.

'Comrade Azarova, if you think I disagree with citizens bringing their honest concerns about potential enemies of the State to the proper authorities, then you're much mistaken.' He spoke sternly, as he was supposed to. 'One more question – it seems likely that your husband opened the door to whoever killed him. Your maid says she locked it when she left to go shopping and unlocked it when she came back and found him dead. Was he expecting anyone to visit that morning?'

'No one.' She shook her head after a moment's consideration. 'And I can't think who he would have opened the door to either, if he was working. Galina was under strict instructions to admit no one who might interrupt him and he certainly wouldn't have answered the door himself.'

'I see,' Korolev said. 'One last thing – are you aware that Dr Shtange was also murdered? On Tuesday morning?'

'Murdered? Shtange?' She looked at him blankly.

'You're sure you weren't aware he was dead? No one called to tell you? A friend perhaps?'

'No one.'

It amazed him that the Twelfth Department hadn't questioned her about the deputy director – because if Azarova was in the clear for her husband, that wasn't necessarily the case with regard to Shtange's murder.

'May I ask where you were on Tuesday morning?'

'I was at the orphanage. I leave at eight and I would have arrived at eight-fifteen. I departed at twelve-thirty, no earlier.'

'The day after your husband's murder?'

'Of course.' She seemed surprised he should question it. 'I believed my duty to the State required it. We're under siege by our enemies, Comrade Korolev – we might as well be at war. If you were a soldier and your brother was killed beside you in battle, you'd fight on – wouldn't you? This situation is no different. That's what being part of a Revolution means.'

Korolev thought it best to say nothing, just write the information down: 'Tuesday morning left for orphanage at eight', and the time she'd returned. But he did allow himself to add a small exclamation mark and an asterisk. He looked at his watch. He needed to wind this up.

'Do you mind if I ask why you're not there today?'

'Dr Weiss believes I need to rest – he was annoyed with me for going out on Tuesday. He said I must conserve my strength.' She seemed torn between gratitude and irritation.

'And you do what he says?'

She shrugged.

'Perhaps I shouldn't have gone there on Tuesday. I'm not sure I did useful work. Perhaps I made a mistake – it's difficult to tell.' She seemed tired now, her voice becoming quieter each time she spoke.

He shut his notebook. Slivka could talk to her again later – she might get more out of her with a different approach. And for the moment, he'd no good reason to doubt anything Azarova had said.

'Can you understand what my life will be without him?' she said, looking up again through her tears. 'I've lost – so much. And more will be taken. Galina has heard that the neighbours are already jostling amongst themselves to take over this apartment. I'll be lucky if I'm allowed to stay in the building.'

Korolev nodded – he didn't think she was being paranoid. He'd come into his own room because Valentina Nikolayevna's husband had been killed in an accident. In some buildings in Moscow there were two or three families sharing smaller spaces than one of this apartment's bedrooms. If she was looking for sympathy, she'd find none from her fellow Muscovites.

'Thank you for your time, Comrade. May I look around your husband's study once again? I'm afraid it's necessary.'

'Help yourself,' she said turning away to look out the window, and leaning her head onto the back of the armchair.

He nodded and walked out into the hallway. There was no sign of the girl.

'Where's your maid?'

'She's gone for bread,' she said, and Korolev could have sworn she was crying, but he thought it impolite to go back to check. Instead he turned the handle to the professor's study and saw that, as with Shtange's, the bookcases in his study stood bare, cleared of books and papers. His footsteps sounded loud as he walked across the room to the open window.

He leant out, looking around to see if there was any possibility someone could have climbed in from somewhere, but it seemed impossible. Perhaps if they'd been one of Shtange's monkeys – otherwise there was a five-storey drop to the pavement below.

He turned back to look at the room once again, even considering the two small ventilation grilles high on the wall behind the professor's desk – but not even the smallest of monkeys could have got through one of them. And the mice the professor had complained of wouldn't have been firing bullets.

Everything pointed to the killer having been someone Azarov had let into the apartment.

Now all he needed to do was find out who.

Chapter Twenty-Three

KOROLEV LOOKED INTO Timinov's office on his way out – the doorman rising to his feet when he saw him.

'Listen, Timinov,' he said, waving him back down. 'Are there really mice in a building like this? I'm surprised is all.'

'Mice?'

'Or rats – she said she wasn't sure which.'

'Or rats?' Timinov looked appalled. 'Who told you that? I tell you there'll be hell to pay if there are.'

'Azarov's maid told me on Monday. But it wasn't her who heard them – the professor complained about them on the morning of the murder – said they were in the walls.'

'No one else has said anything.' The caretaker seemed to relax a little. 'That was three days ago – if they were in the building, someone would have heard them since.'

'I'm only repeating what the maid, Galina, said.'

'Mice would be more likely – they'll slip through the smallest crack.' The doorman scratched his head. 'I'll look into it though, you can be sure of that.'

Korolev shrugged. What with a missing son and two murders to solve, to the satisfaction of a certain Colonel Rodinov – he couldn't care if the damned place had kangaroos. He said his farewells and left.

§

The car he'd asked Belinsky to arrange for him was parked outside and, to his surprise, Morozov himself, the head of the car pool, was leaning on its bonnet. The one-eyed Cossack glanced over at his approach, and his surprise at Korolev's appearance was evident.

'I didn't know you could drive,' Korolev said drily, ignoring Morozov's look, and getting into the car. 'I thought you were above that sort of thing.'

'I can't.' Morozov opened the door and sat into the driver's seat. He took another good look at Korolev's face and shook his head slowly. 'Where to, then, Alexei Dmitriyevich?'

'Bolshoi Nikolo-Vorobinsky first – I need to clean up – then the Anatomical Institute.'

Morozov, who'd worn an eye patch ever since an encounter with a bullet during the German War, turned his head to nod his agreement then put the car smoothly into gear – pulling away from the kerb without any obvious signs that he'd checked he was clear to do so.

They drove in silence for a while, which suited Korolev – he'd a few things he needed to think through, after all. He opened his notebook, flicking back through the pages.

'Tell me, Pavel Timofeevich,' he asked Morozov, 'what do you know about the Vitsin Street orphanage? You live over that way, don't you?'

Korolev winced as the car squeezed through a tiny gap between an oncoming bus and a construction truck that had pulled out unexpectedly. He shut one of his own eyes as an experiment – the range of vision was much reduced.

'Why should I know anything about an orphanage on Vitsin Street?'

'Come on, Pavel Timofeevich – it's a stone's throw from you. You must know the place.'

'Oh, I know it all right. It used to be the Monastery of the Annunciation – I pass it every day. As for what the place might be like? Well, I'm glad my children are grown and will never see the inside of it.'

'Not good?'

'It's hard to say – I haven't heard it's bad as such. But people think there's something not quite right about the place all the same.'

'I see.'

Korolev thought about Yuri ending up in such a place and found his jaw was clenched so hard it hurt. The boy would show up, he was sure of it. And he'd get himself out of this investigation in one piece as well. Everything would be all right – if only he could keep himself calm.

§

When Morozov stopped the car on Bolshoi Nikolo-Vorobinsky, Korolev took a quick look around the neighbourhood, just in case the boy was somewhere nearby – wary of approaching the house itself in case State Security might still be on his tail. But there was no sign of him – no sign of anyone, as it happened. The laneway, and the courtyards off it, seemed unnaturally still. But perhaps that was just because of the way the bright noon sunshine seemed to press every corner and curve into straight lines, leaving only white surface and crisp shadows. He was relieved when he stepped into the cool shade of the hallway.

'Korolev, a word with you please.' Lobkovskaya, his elderly downstairs neighbour, stood in her half-open doorway, tapping her walking stick on the floor gently, perhaps to get his attention. Most uncharacteristically, she seemed to be trying to keep her voice to a level which could almost be described as a whisper. She gestured for him to come closer. For a moment, he wondered if she'd news of his son.

'Is it about Yuri?' Korolev said, keeping his own voice low.

The only light in the stairwell came from soot-stained windows on the upper landings and as he came closer to her he could see that the imperturbable old lady appeared – well – perturbed.

'No. Something else. You had visitors, an hour ago.' She put a finger to her lips as if that might make her words quieter. 'I heard them in your room, they moved every piece of furniture. Then I heard them move to the next room and the next. They searched the whole apartment. Careful, quiet men. Not the kind of visitors you'd want to have, I think.'

'When did they leave?'

'Half an hour ago.'

Korolev knew Lobkovskaya well enough not to question her story. After all, she lived directly beneath him – and the old house's walls and floors kept few secrets between neighbours. Nor was he surprised that she was telling him something most Muscovites wouldn't admit was happening – even to themselves. Lobkovskaya was a tough old girl at the end of the day.

'Chekists?' he asked.

She shrugged, then nodded – indicating that his suggestion seemed the most likely possibility. She patted his elbow.

'Shura told me about your boy being missing – she had to go out but asked me to keep an eye out for him. If he comes, I'll look after him – don't worry.'

Korolev nodded his thanks and with a smile Lobkovskaya managed to close her door without making the slightest sound.

Korolev began to climb the stairs one slow step at a time, his eyes adjusting to the half-light as he did so. He listened hard to the sounds of the house, wondering if someone might be waiting for him up above, their intentions unfriendly and a weapon in their hand. He allowed his fingers to trail up the banister, aware of each nick and groove they touched. But when he found himself outside his door he wasn't quite sure how he'd reached it or, indeed, how he'd managed to slip his key into its lock. He paused, took a long, deep breath, and reached for the Walther underneath his armpit. He touched the metal of the pistol's handgrip and then stopped. What was he going to do? Shoot it out with State Security? And anyway, the apartment was empty – Lobkovskaya had said so. For all her age, the woman had ears like a bat. He turned the key.

At first glance everything was perfectly normal. Natasha's exercise books were where they should be. The bags he'd left on the chesterfield during his whirlwind visit that morning were in the same position. The small vase of flowers he'd noticed then was in its same spot. Even the dust dancing in the sunlight that streamed through the half-closed curtains appeared to circle and twirl in the same way it always did. He stopped, stood still and looked again and, on closer examination, there were indeed small anomalies – the bags on the chesterfield had an unusual symmetry, not that he could put his finger on why; and, unless he was much mistaken, the exercise books had been piled by hands other than a 10-year-old girl's – hands that liked to organize things, to tie up loose ends, to make sure a confession covered all possible crimes.

The thought that someone had been in here, because of him, reading through Natasha's homework, running his hands down the seams of Valentina's clothing and handling her belongings – well, it took the air out of his chest all of a sudden. He had to make a conscious effort to start breathing again.

He stood, not moving for at least a minute, becoming almost certain he could smell the faintest trace of the searchers – that slight scent of sour sweat and stale cigarettes wasn't coming just from him; they'd been suffering in the heat as much as he was.

He could almost see them, their practised movements as they searched for – what? The thought soon had him reaching for a knife in the small kitchen and making his way into his bedroom, pulling the curtains shut and then rolling up the small carpet near the window. He pushed the blade of the knife into the crack between two boards and levered up one of them to reveal a small cavity. There it was, sitting there, the bible he kept for the insane reason that he believed it protected him – when the opposite was almost certainly the case. As far as he could tell, it hadn't been disturbed, but how could he be sure?

He replaced the board and the carpet and looked around him – scratching at that familiar itch just beneath his left ear and thinking for a moment. Well, whatever was going on, he decided, after considering the situation from a number of different angles, it wasn't good news – but he had to tidy himself up and move on. There wasn't anything to be done about this – it had happened and that was that.

Removing his clothes, he picked up a towel and made his way to the kitchen to wash.

His first thought was that Rodinov might be behind it. But why would Rodinov search his apartment? What would he gain from it? Nothing. Rodinov had him where he wanted him already. Why waste energy on a man you had firmly under your thumb? No, not Rodinov.

That other Chekist, the one who had taken over the case before Korolev had been reinstated – Zaitsev. Now he might have a reason – he'd certainly wanted to talk to him the night before. If a man like him didn't want a person, Korolev for example, poking into the affairs of his institute, what better way to exert pressure than to dig up some dirt on him? And, if they'd found the bible, then they had it.

He looked up to see his face in the mirror over the sink, his stubble like a shadow, his teeth yellow as a carthorse's, his swollen, purpled eye. The tap squirted out brown water before it began to run cleaner. He leant down, feeling his bruised ribs, his stomach complaining as he did so, and allowed the water to splash over his hands before pulling a scoop of it up to his face, rubbing it into his skin. The fact was he'd nowhere to run to. And how could he run anywhere with Yuri still missing? All he could do was hope that, if he did what Rodinov told him to, things would return to normal. That whatever these Chekists were up to, they'd eventually forget about him.

He picked up his shaving soap and reached for his razor.

Chapter Twenty-Four

WHEN KOROLEV came back out of his building Morozov was leaning against the car once again, his arms folded, his good eye shut as he allowed the sun to warm his face.

'It took longer than I thought it would.'

Morozov opened his eye to look him over. 'You look better in some ways, worse in others,' he said. Korolev knew what he meant – he was tidier, for certain – but shaving seemed to have shown up his cuts and bruises all the more. At least the shirt he was wearing was clean and ironed – that must count for something.

They got into the car and Morozov turned the key in the ignition, causing a bark from the exhaust that sent a cat on the other side of the road leaping for the protection of a windowsill.

'Well, I feel better in some ways and worse in others.'

Korolev ran a hand through his still-wet hair and took a deep breath. He had to focus on one thing – the most important thing. He'd a job to do and doing it well might save both Yuri and him from unpleasantness.

§

By now, they were on the Boulevard Ring heading north and he caught Morozov looking in the rear-view mirror – and not for the first time, it occurred to him. He twisted in the seat to look out of the back window, wondering what had caught the old soldier's attention.

'Do you see them?' Morozov asked.

'Who?'

'Those two fellows in the black Emka.'

Korolev saw them all right – they were hard to miss, given that there wasn't much traffic and they were only a short distance behind. Two familiar men, as it turned out – the two fellows from the station in Peredelkino and from the riverbank.

'I have to ask you, Alexei Dmitriyevich, are you in some sort of trouble? They've been behind us since I picked you up in Bersenevka. I thought they'd dropped us when we went to your place, but they were just waiting at the top of the lane.'

Korolev had a quick look at his surroundings.

'Pavel Timofeevich – if we stop at the next corner it's a five minute walk to Petrovka. I'll need the car for the rest of the day and I'm sure you've better things to be doing than driving me around.'

Morozov looked reluctant and began to shake his head in disagreement, but Korolev touched his shoulder.

'There's no point in two of us being in a mess when one will do. If I need a friend, I know I have one and I'm grateful for it.'

Morozov took Korolev's outstretched hand in his own and shook it once. Then with a grunt that seemed to be born of resignation more than anything else, he pulled the car over to the pavement.

Korolev watched his colleague walk away and was pleased that he didn't look back as he did so. Then he turned his attention to the occupants of the Emka. They'd pulled in, not more than twenty metres back, and were sitting there – looking at him. The plump one smiled and touched a finger to his forehead in salute.

Chapter Twenty-Five

KOROLEV FOLLOWED the cobbled drive until the trees opened up to reveal the imposing facade of the Anatomical Institute. Before the Revolution, the building had housed some prince or other and back then it must have been a sight to see. The years since might have left it a little the worse for wear perhaps, but it was holding itself together somehow, and in that respect it reminded him of certain other remnants of the years before the Revolution – himself included.

Chestnova was sitting on the former palace's marble steps, enjoying the sunshine and engaged in desultory conversation with two burly men in white coats while she worked her way through a papirosa cigarette. As the car came to a halt she put a hand up to shade her eyes so she could see who'd arrived.

'Korolev,' Chestnova said, when he opened the car door. 'I was expecting you before this.'

'I had to stop off at home.'

'Don't worry. I found a pleasant way to pass the time.'

She took a step forward, squinting at his face then reaching a finger to pull the lid of his injured eye down. She shook her head slowly.

'I won't ask.'

'That would be best.'

There was the sound of another car coming along the drive and Dubinkin's Packard emerged from the trees. When it came to a halt, the Chekist stepped out wearing a neat grey suit and an open white shirt. Korolev wouldn't necessarily have spotted him as a Chekist, but perhaps the two fellows in the white coats were better judges of that sort of thing. By the time Dubinkin had taken two more steps, they'd disappeared – leaving only the faintest wisp of smoke to show they'd ever been there.

'Comrade Lieutenant,' Chestnova said, glancing at the space where the two men had been. 'It's always a pleasure.'

'And for me, Doctor.'

'You two know each other?' Korolev asked.

'Comrade Dubinkin and I have come across each other once or twice.' Chestnova spoke in a carefully neutral tone.

'On other matters, Korolev,' Dubinkin said, 'but I've never seen the good doctor wield a scalpel. I'm looking forward to it.'

'I'm sorry to disappoint you then. I do the autopsies as soon as possible in the summer – they've both been completed. I informed your Colonel Zaitsev, of course.'

'I see.' Dubinkin looked disappointed.

'Will Colonel Zaitsev be joining us?' she asked.

'No.' Dubinkin's negative was final.

Chestnova turned her gaze to Korolev and he found himself shrugging his shoulders.

'Let's get on with things then,' the doctor said, and flicked away the cardboard tube that was all that was left of her papirosa.

§

Korolev hadn't seen the grand entrance hall of the Anatomical Institute before – he normally came in the back way when he visited – but this time Chestnova pushed open one of the large oak front doors at the top of the steps, and he followed. Inside, he found himself gazing at magnificent decoration that rose to the roof itself. Columns, turrets, alcoves and the Lord knew what else soared upwards, all framed by two magnificent curving staircases. The hospital's management had done its best to adapt the entrance hall to the current regime, however, and a banner exhorting the workers to meet their Five Year Plan in four years was hung across a balustraded landing, while busts of Stalin, Lenin, Engels and the like now filled the delicately crafted alcoves that must once have been filled by the original owner's aristocratic ancestors. They didn't look too out of place.

'Rococo,' Dubinkin said.

'I don't doubt it, Comrade,' Korolev said in a tone that he hoped conveyed his disapproval of everything the old aristocrats had stood for.

Chestnova led them along a corridor towards the back of the building and Korolev kept his eyes fixed on the white cotton of the doctor's coat where it stretched across her broad shoulders, and tried not to think about death and corpses and autopsies. He'd never liked them.

'Certainly instantaneous,' Chestnova said, when she'd ushered them into one of the autopsy rooms and pulled a sheet away to reveal the professor's naked body lying face down, his body sadly mutilated, and not only by the killer.

'He must have been dead before his head hit the desk. The bullet entered here, high on the skull and to the left, and never came out. I found it lodged at the back of the right jawbone.' She rattled a lead slug in a metal receptacle.

By the look of it, she'd found it by cutting off half the professor's head and extracting most of the contents. Korolev felt the familiar flood of saliva at the back of his cheeks and he swallowed several times – his hands in his pockets forming into fists.

'No gunpowder residue on the entry wound, which suggests the muzzle wasn't too close – I would expect to see some scorching or burning if the muzzle was less than three or four feet away. It depends on the weapon, of course. Then again, if something was used to muffle the sound it might have absorbed it – but I haven't found fabric or anything similar inside the wound, so probably not. Did your men come across anything?'

'No.'

'Well the bullet isn't in bad shape. Big. I'd have expected it to make more of a mess. I'd also have expected it to exit – but again, it didn't. And that's consistent with something your forensics man pointed out – that the other bullet barely penetrated the table top. He thought that might mean a low-velocity weapon – I'd tend to agree with him.'

Chestnova handed the slug to Korolev. 'You can take it away with you.'

Korolev put it in his pocket, not really wanting to think about the contents. Meanwhile, Chestnova was pointing to a purple graze on the dead man's white shoulder – close to his neck.

'This is where the other bullet grazed him. I'd guess it was fired after the professor had slumped forward, the wound is across the top of the right shoulder, as you can see. And there's tearing to his jacket as well. You can see the bullet hole on the desk, here.'

Chestnova picked up a file from a side table and took from it a photograph of the professor's upper body lying across his desk.

'Yes,' Korolev said, taking the picture from her.

'Well – that's it, really. I've had his clothes packed up for you in case the forensics men can make something more of them. I'll run you through the report anyway.'

'Thanks,' Korolev said, unpleasantly aware of his entire body being covered with perspiration, as Chestnova ran them through the dead man's age, weight and overall medical condition. All of which came down to this – a man who could have lived for another thirty years had been snuffed out. Instantaneously.

A pause seemed to have developed around him, and Korolev

looked away from the curling white hair on the professor's chest to find Dubinkin and Chestnova's eyes on him.

'Is there anything you'd like to ask?' the doctor asked, her expression kindly.

Korolev forced himself to look back at the body once again. He wasn't going to be sick, he told himself – he was just a little unwell. Things would be better if he could put a handkerchief over his mouth to take away the smell of death. At least in the winter the bodies stayed cold when they were out of the refrigerated cabinets. He swallowed and pointed to the photograph Chestnova had given him.

'You see there's a pen in his right hand – here – and a document onto which his head has fallen – here. I'm thinking if he was writing, which it looks like he was, and sitting upright, which his body position would indicate, and if you say Azarov was five foot nine, so not a small man, and the fatal bullet wound is high on the skull . . .'

'Yes,' Chestnova said patiently.

'And there's no muzzle residue on him either. And no sign of a pillow or anything being used. Well, then the fellow who did it must have been a giant, surely? He must have been about eight feet tall.'

Chestnova shrugged.

'I just give you facts – it's your job to pull them together into what actually happened.'

'Azarov could have been leaning backwards,' Dubinkin said, 'Talking to someone in front of him whose job was to distract him.'

'That's a possibility,' Korolev managed to say, his nausea forgotten, as he wondered whether that was how State Security went about things when they didn't want a fuss made.

'It's only a thought,' Dubinkin said.

The Chekist stroked his moustache and, to cover his unease, Korolev wrote 'Trajectory' in the notebook he'd opened.

'Have you any other questions?' Chestnova asked.

Korolev shook his head. They both looked to Dubinkin, who smiled and shook his head also.

'Very good, I need to find a porter to help me prepare Dr Shtange,' Chestnova said, giving Korolev a sympathetic glance. 'If you'd like to go outside for a few moments, take a walk around, then I'll be ready by the time you've finished. There's no need to wait here in the meantime.'

Such a woman, Korolev thought to himself, such a wonderful woman — as he walked towards the door as quickly as his pride would allow him.

Chapter Twenty-Six

'TELL ME, KOROLEV,' Dubinkin began, when they were standing on the institute's steps once again, with only a haze of tobacco between them and the sun.

'Tell you what?'

'I'm curious, you see. I've been through your file and you must have seen more bodies than most – in the German War. Against the Whites. In Poland. I'm surprised how squeamish you are. Why is it, do you think? You must see plenty of them in this job as well.'

Korolev wasn't sure whether he should be more concerned that Dubinkin had spotted his squeamishness or that there was a file with his name on it somewhere in the bowels of the Lubyanka. But then again, he'd known there must be. The lieutenant was looking at him the way a chess player might after an opponent had made a surprising move.

'I'm not sure . . .' Korolev began.

'Oh, don't worry about the file. Everybody has a file on them,' the Chekist said. 'Everybody who is worth having a file on, at least. Anyway, yours is nothing to worry about, believe me – exemplary, is how I'd describe it. You've never failed in your duty to the State and your abilities are valuable to us. An occasional weakness and the odd bad association aren't so important in those circumstances – after all, no one's perfect.'

'What do you mean by bad associations?' Korolev asked –

not so much because he wanted to but because he had the impression that Dubinkin had used those words for a reason. And, sure enough, the Chekist had an answer for him.

'Your former wife might be such an association.'

'Zhenia?'

'Have you more than one?' Dubinkin asked, pretending to look shocked. Personally, Korolev thought it wasn't a subject for humour.

'No, only Zhenia. Is she in trouble? With you people?'

Dubinkin pulled the cigarette he was smoking from its silver holder and dropped it to the ground. He considered Korolev for a moment, then shrugged.

'She might be. There's a file on her certainly.'

'My son told me her apartment was searched.'

'So I believe.'

'I haven't been able to get through to her on the phone. People have been hanging up when I call her building.'

The Chekist shrugged again.

'She hasn't been arrested yet, not that I know of. But she's being investigated – that does tend to make neighbours nervous.'

It occurred to Korolev that something about the conversation didn't quite make sense.

'Why are you telling me this?'

The Chekist smiled and nodded to himself, as if pleased with the question.

'Let's say that we feel you should know that we know – about your wife, that is.'

'But I know you know,' Korolev said, wondering whether he being made fun of. 'It's you who are investigating her.'

'That's where you're wrong. A different part of State Security is investigating her. But we know they're investigating her and that might be a good thing for you.'

'You might intervene?'

'Colonel Rodinov values you highly,' Dubinkin said – as if

that were answer enough. Korolev realized how a mouse must feel when played with by a cat. Still, if he understood correctly what Dubinkin was saying about this different part of State Security, then there was something he should tell him.

'Well, if you know all that, Comrade – then you should know some people came to my home today and searched it.'

Dubinkin exhaled a narrow stream of smoke.

'What kind of people?'

'Careful people, your kind of people – everything was left almost exactly as it was, but I'm certain they were there. And there's more, I was followed here. But that they didn't bother to hide.'

'You see, this is why we want to be so open with you – so that you're open with us. It would seem the Twelfth Department aren't pleased the investigation has been taken from them. Just so you know, we're pretty much certain they're the ones who took the doorman, Priudski. At least, no one else seems to have. We've been through the records for all the Moscow prisons – nothing. It's possible they've put him in under another name, so we're checking further. But most likely they have him some- where else altogether.'

Korolev sighed – he'd been temporarily assigned to the NKVD, without his having been given much choice in the matter, and now, as a result, he was being investigated by them.

'It feels like I'm a football being kicked around a field.'

'An excellent analogy,' Dubinkin agreed. 'Except one side wants to puncture you while the other want to keep you in play and use you to score a goal. Which side do you hope wins?'

'Christ,' Korolev said.

'He's not playing. He's not even the referee – Ezhov is. It's as well to be clear about things – if we aren't successful in this investigation of ours, things will not go well. Not for you, not for Sergeant Slivka and probably not for me either.'

Dubinkin didn't seem too bothered by the prospect, inhaling a lungful of smoke with a contented expression.

'Chestnova should be ready by now. Shall we see?' he said eventually.

§

She was. They found the doctor hovering over Shtange's pale corpse like a white-coated carrion bird. She looked up at them, nodded her greeting and without further ado began to describe the man's condition. While she did so, Korolev made his own examination – shocked by the number of wounds. They covered his arm, chest, face and shoulders. Deep incisions, a big knife by the look of it.

'There's one particularly interesting thing about the wounds,' Chestnova said.

Korolev waited – he doubted she'd need any encouragement to tell them and, sure enough, she smiled, as if reading his thoughts.

'You see these ones . . .' She flicked a finger back and forth across the blue-lipped cuts that Korolev had been looking at.

'Stab wounds?' he asked.

'Oh yes, I'd say as much. And enough to do the job five times over. A big blade – eight, maybe ten inches. In places it went right through his body.'

'I can see that.'

'But what do you make of this?'

Chestnova pointed to a long thin cut a couple of centimetres in front of the dead man's ear, precise and clean.

'A different weapon?' Korolev asked, comparing it to the other puncture marks.

'Yes, Korolev. And this weapon, I would almost stake my life on it, was a surgical scalpel. What's more, in my opinion, this wound was made some time after Dr Shtange was already dead.'

Chapter Twenty-Seven

KOROLEV APPROACHED the Hotel Moskva from the Teatralnaya Square side, parking at the end of the cab rank on Okhotny Ryad and showing the *babushka* in charge of it his identity card when she gave him the evil eye. The identity card didn't stop her looking at him with a malevolence that felt like it could blister paint – but at least she stopped waving her hands in his direction and insisting he park elsewhere. That was all he asked for. And that the Chekists who had pulled in a few car-lengths behind would go and bother some other poor citizen.

The Hotel Moskva was an enormous building. It had opened two years before and dwarfed the National Hotel and the Metropol – its near neighbours. If the newsreels proclaimed that Moscow was being transformed into a city which the whole world would envy, then the Moskva was the building to prove that they weren't just talking hot air. Its hard lines and brutal simplicity might not be to everyone's taste, but it was certainly impressive.

A warm-looking doorman in a long coat pushed open a door as high as a double-decker tram and Korolev made his way across a lobby as wide and as long as some football fields he'd played on.

'Korolev,' he said when he reached the reception desk, handing his identity card over. He glanced back at the red carpet he'd marched the length of to get there and allowed his gaze to take in the small clusters of foreigners and bosses, huddled together in encampments of leather armchairs, talking in low tones. They looked insignificant in amongst the square marble columns and the wide expanses of space.

'How may we assist you, Comrade Captain?'

He turned back to the receptionist – a fat head above a frock coat with a cravat to round it off, no less. He appeared to be trying to look down his nose at Korolev but, as Korolev was a good six inches taller than him, he was failing. All the same, his nose looked like it was planning to recoil back into that plump face in horror at the fact that an honest cop like Korolev should wander in unannounced. Korolev was about to become annoyed when he remembered what his face must look like. He shrugged inwardly. The fellow probably had a point.

'I'm here to talk to Madame Shtange, Comrade. She's staying here – and I'm expected.'

'Madame Shtange is a Soviet citizen?' The question was as carefully delivered as a ballet dancer's pirouette. But the meaning was clear enough – if she's a foreigner, you can go whistle, flatfoot – she's State Security's business.

Korolev put his elbows on the counter and yawned, then looked at the receptionist with genial menace, pleased to see his reaction change from puzzlement to concern. Korolev let him sweat for a moment or two before he spoke.

'She's a Soviet resident,' Korolev said. 'A Soviet resident that this Soviet Militiaman wants to talk to. Now, how about you do your duty to the Soviet State and tell her I'm here to speak to her? As I said, she's expecting me. And be quick about it – the consequences for you if you don't cooperate fully will not be pleasant, believe me.'

The receptionist blinked twice and then his demeanour was transformed smoothly to one of ingratiation.

'Of course, Comrade Captain, it would be my pleasure. I

always do my duty to the State, of that you can be completely and absolutely certain. Let me see which room she's in.'

Korolev smiled grimly, thinking there were certain advantages to his temporary assignment. The receptionist pulled out a long drawer that was built into the reception desk and let his fingers flicker along the filing cards it contained. The only problem, Korolev thought to himself, was that being able to push citizens round like this would probably make scoundrels out of most men before a week was out.

'Here we are – seven seventeen.' He turned to look at the wall behind him – hundreds of keys were stored in regular rows along with messages and post. The concierge went to the box numbered 717, extracted a piece of paper and opened it.

'Ah – my apologies, Comrade Captain. You are indeed expected. Madame Shtange is waiting for you in the roof-terrace cafe.'

'The roof-terrace cafe? That would be on the roof?'

The receptionist smiled, as if Korolev had made an amusing joke.

'Of course. Where else?'

'How many storeys up would that be? This roof?'

Korolev could hear the disgruntlement in his voice. It was there for a reason.

'Twelve?' The fellow looked uncertain now.

'Twelve,' Korolev said and felt like battering his head against the smooth surface of the reception desk. Not two hours before he'd sworn he'd never venture on to the top of another tall building, and yet here he was, being forced to do it again almost straight away.

'Shall I ask someone to show you up?'

'Thank you,' Korolev sighed.

The receptionist seemed to remember something suddenly. He looked at him quizzically, then reached for a notebook.

'Captain Korolev, wasn't it?'

'Yes.'

'There's a message for you as well.' He went to an unmarked box underneath the rows of keys and extracted a small piece of paper, handing it over.

It said, 'Captain A.D. Korolev. Call Petrovka.'

Korolev turned it over, just in case, but there was nothing else to be read. It must be about Yuri, surely. He felt his knees begin to shake unaccountably. He wasn't sure if it was from fear or anticipation.

'Can you let me use a telephone?'

'Here,' the receptionist said, placing one on the counter.

'It's Korolev here,' he said when he got through.

'Yes, Comrade Captain,' a woman's tinny voice said. 'Captain Yasimov called. He told me to tell you your son was seen catching a train towards Moscow, one station further along the track. At around ten o'clock. He was with two other boys. Captain Yasimov's moved his enquiries to Moscow now. And First Inspector Popov has asked all detectives to keep a look out for your son as well.'

There was a cough and then the voice continued.

'We all hope he will be found soon.'

Korolev didn't say anything for a moment – if Yuri was heading for Moscow then he'd be heading for the apartment, which was good. But who were these two other boys? And Moscow was a damned big place – finding him, if he didn't go to Bolshoi Nikolo-Vorobinsky, would be hard.

'Thank you,' he said. 'I'm grateful for your concern. I'll call in again in an hour or so, and please pass my thanks to everyone – the chief in particular. And tell Yasimov I owe him.'

§

Korolev hung up and handed the telephone back to the receptionist. It was good news, he was sure of it. Yuri would be home before him, with a bit of luck, and they could forget this whole mess had ever happened.

'I'll go up to this roof of yours, then,' he said.

A young lad in a uniform with a round tasselled cap appeared at the click of the receptionist's fingers and directed Korolev toward the lifts. Korolev looked towards the stairs but the Lord knew how many steps there might be, and he was tired enough as it was. So he did his best to relax as the lift climbed higher and higher. He only realized he'd been holding his breath the whole way when they finally reached the top.

'Here we are,' the youngster said, as proud of the colonnaded roof terrace as if he owned it. And the truth was – it wasn't too bad. The best thing about it was that it had a fine parapet standing about four feet high between a fellow and a plunge to the ground below. And not only that, on top of the parapet, between the columns that stretched the length of the building, there was another two feet of solid-looking glass. Korolev congratulated the hotel's architect from the bottom of his heart.

'Madame Shtange?' he asked when he was led to a corner table where a blonde woman of about thirty sat, a cup of coffee in front of her and a lean, hungry-looking fellow who reminded Korolev of a greyhound sitting opposite. For a moment he was torn between the view – which was extraordinary, overlooking the Lenin Library, the Kremlin Arsenal and the southern half of Moscow – and the woman, who was equally extraordinary, fine-featured yet, it seemed to him, strong, determined and damned attractive to boot.

'Captain Korolev,' she said, examining the identity card he offered her and then stubbing her cigarette into an ashtray that was already half-full. Her accent was foreign, but not too foreign. Meanwhile the greyhound had lifted himself languidly from his seat and was offering his hand.

'This is Monsieur Hubert, from the French embassy,' Madame Shtange said.

'I see,' Korolev said, wishing Dubinkin was here. He shook the fellow's hand anyway. What else was he supposed to do?

'Madame Shtange's a French citizen, Comrade Captain,' the greyhound said. 'She's under the personal protection of our ambassador. Her uncle, you should be aware, is a minister in the current government – a government that is friendly towards the Soviet Union. For the moment, at least.'

Hubert spoke slowly, with a sympathetic expression that Korolev decided shouldn't be taken at face value.

'The French Government?'

'Yes.'

'And a minister, you say.' Korolev managed to restrain his instinctive desire to groan. Dubinkin had promised he'd be here in the next half an hour but he couldn't very well wait till then to start asking questions. 'May I sit down?'

Hubert nodded and Korolev lowered himself into the nearest chair, his tired body celebrating at not having to stand for a few minutes at least. He looked between Madame Shtange and the greyhound and wondered where to begin. Hubert returned his gaze with a watchfulness that suggested that the Frenchman wasn't in favour of the meeting, and Korolev hoped that meant Anna Shtange might be more cooperative than he'd first thought.

'Madame Shtange,' he said, after a moment or two, 'I'm sorry about your husband. I'm afraid I've only just been asked to look after the case – I'm not sure what you've been told but I'll be happy to answer any of your questions, as far as I can at this stage.'

She smiled, but it wasn't a smile that had much warmth to it. She didn't look like she'd slept much in the last two days.

'I've been told almost nothing.' Her voice cracked on 'nothing'. 'I've been told that my husband was murdered. That I should come to Moscow. That I should stay in this hotel. I was told that under no circumstances was I to visit his apartment, the university or the institute. Nor was I to contact anyone, in

Moscow or Leningrad, and certainly not in France. That if I failed to comply with any of these instructions it would cause complications – which I took to mean complications for me and my sons. That's all I've been told.'

Korolev found his eyes wandering to the greyhound, who nodded. He didn't bother to smile this time.

'You're wondering why I contacted the French embassy?'

'That's not my business, Madame Shtange. I'm just a Militia detective. I know nothing about these instructions either.'

She lit up another cigarette, her fingers shaking.

'If it weren't for my husband I'd have left this place years ago. I want to go home – I don't want our children to grow up living in fear.'

Korolev, thinking of Yuri, was unable to answer. His throat felt strangely constricted and he was only able to watch as she crushed the barely smoked cigarette into the pile of those she'd already disposed of. Then she reached for yet another.

'So I've been waiting for someone to tell me something about his death and, still, nobody tells me anything. And then this morning, finally, I was told you'd be coming to see me. Not why or when or who you were – just that Captain Korolev would be coming to see me.'

'I only found out you were in Moscow this morning,' Korolev said.

'I believe you,' she said. 'Nothing surprises me about this place any more. If it will help, I'll tell you what I can. But first, did he suffer? Can you at least tell me if he suffered?'

She reached forward and Korolev felt the weight of her fingers as they rested on his.

'It was quick,' he said, deciding she deserved to know this at least. 'The pathologist thinks death happened almost immediately, so there wouldn't have been time for him to have suffered much. Did they tell you how he died?'

She shook her head.

'As far as we can tell he opened his door to his attacker and then was stabbed a number of times. There were very few defensive wounds, so the pathologist believes he probably wasn't fully aware of what was happening. One of the first blows seems to have cut the artery in his throat. He was also stabbed twice in the heart. He was probably dead before he fell.'

Her mouth was a little round circle of shock and Korolev thought he might have said too much.

'I'm sorry, but you can see the body this afternoon if you wish – it's as well to be prepared. It looks bad, but, as I said, if he was aware of anything, it was only for a matter of seconds.'

She looked at him for a long moment and then turned her head to look across the river towards, coincidentally, the very window Professor Azarov had been looking out of when he'd been killed. Korolev wondered if she knew it was where the professor had lived.

'Thank you.' She whispered the words so quietly that Korolev wondered whether he was meant to hear them. 'You're an unusual Chekist.'

'I'm a Militia detective, Madame Shtange.'

She examined him, taking in his shirt, his jacket, his battered face, and while he held her gaze he wished he were able to look away. It was as if she were looking right into his soul, and he liked to keep his soul to himself.

'No, I see that now,' she said eventually. 'Ask me your questions then, Captain Korolev. I'll answer them.'

Korolev took his notebook from the pocket of his jacket and flicked through its pages till he found an empty one.

'Did you know your husband's colleague, Professor Azarov, was also murdered? The day before?'

'Arkady told me. On Monday, when he found out.'

'I interviewed him on Monday – your husband that is. I was sorry to hear of his death. I liked him, if you don't mind my saying.'

'He was a good and honest man whose fate it was to live at a time like this – and in a place like this. That was his tragedy.'

Korolev looked hard at his notebook and decided he hadn't heard her. She might be able to say such things, with someone from the French embassy sitting alongside her and a French passport in her pocket – but he couldn't hear them, not with a Soviet identity card sitting in his.

'We aren't convinced the two murders are connected,' Korolev continued, 'but it certainly isn't something we're ruling out. Now, it was clear from my discussion with him on Monday that your husband didn't like the professor. Not one bit. And I understand the professor felt the same.'

'Arkady despised him, but he'd nothing to do with Azarov's death. He was at work when it happened, he told me so.'

'Yes, we know where he was. But you must understand we have to look into their relationship.'

She nodded. 'I understand, and the truth is if Azarov hadn't been dead at the time of the murder, I'd have been certain he was my husband's killer. Arkady was on the point of exposing him and the professor knew it.'

'Exposing him?' Korolev said.

'Azarov achieved his position by his willingness to condemn as a traitor or saboteur anyone who stood in his way or opposed him. He also lied through his teeth about everything he'd achieved and might achieve. Once he started working for State Security on his so-called breakthroughs he found he'd a receptive audience for his lies and his accusations. And after that, anyone who disagreed with him was sabotaging State Security itself – with predictable consequences. But my husband was appointed to verify Azarov's claims and Azarov couldn't deal with him the way he'd dealt with the others.'

'Who appointed him?'

'Arkady couldn't tell me. Someone senior enough that Azarov couldn't act against him openly without looking like a rogue. Whoever it was, I'm not sure they were bothered about the morality of the research – I suspect all that interested them was why there'd been so little recent progress and, perhaps most importantly, where all the money had gone.'

Korolev looked down at his notes, underlining some points he wanted to come back to.

'Money?'

'A lot of money – there was equipment to be bought, of course, and salaries to be paid but, even so, the amounts didn't make sense. Or so Arkady said. He put it all in his report. That's why, when Azarov died, he thought it was all over – that he could come back to Leningrad.'

'So he'd finished this report of his?'

'Yes.'

'And it was critical of Professor Azarov?'

'Most definitely. I never saw it, you understand, but it couldn't have been any other way, from the conversations I had with Arkady. He couldn't give me details – but he told me the gist of it. I should have told him to drop it, shouldn't I?'

Korolev ignored the question – she already knew the answer.

'Do you know whether this report was delivered to the appropriate person? Or did your husband still have it when he died?'

'I don't know for certain. The last time I spoke to him he thought he would be home with us by the weekend – that it had been confirmed. I presumed that meant he'd delivered it.'

'May I ask what research your husband was engaged in at the institute?'

'Again, he never told me precisely. The work was secret, I know that much, and obviously he had to be very careful about what he said – especially to me. I do know he found it deeply distasteful. In Leningrad his research focused on behavioural modification, and how that might be useful to State Security is something I can understand his not wanting to discuss.'

She looked towards Hubert, but the greyhound said nothing – although if Korolev wasn't much mistaken he saw a flicker of disappointment. Perhaps the French also wanted to know what the Azarov Institute had been researching. Behavioural modification? It sounded like something Militia captains should stay well clear of; but if foreign countries were interested in the professor's research, that might explain why the two apartments had been stripped of paperwork. It also occurred to him that if Shtange's report exposed wrongdoing and financial irregularities at the institute then that would mean the harshest penalties for those involved, as well as for those who'd failed to protect the State. Was that why the scientists might have been killed?

'Did he tell you anything?' Korolev asked. 'About the research he did there? Anything at all that might be helpful?'

After all, she'd be telling Hubert soon enough, he'd no doubt of that. Another cigarette stubbed out. Another cigarette immediately lit. The golden eyes appraised him before she shook her head, as if to disagree with the question itself.

'As I understand it, there *was* no research – not scientific anyway. Or so Arkady said. It seemed to him that whatever was being attempted wasn't much more than a magic trick that Azarov was trying to dress up in a white coat and call science. But what the trick was, I've no idea. I know Azarov had support at the highest levels, however. That was clear.'

Her eyes flicked to the left, inviting him to look in the direct of the Kremlin. It was an invitation Korolev wouldn't be taking up any time soon. Was she suggesting Stalin himself had approved this damned institute of Azarov's? Already there were Chekists everywhere he looked – and now Stalin? He prayed to the good Lord above that his next case, if he survived this one, had nothing to do with the Organs of State Security and certainly not with the General Secretary. A murder or an armed robbery would be fine.

He grunted and then carried on with the interview and, when all was said and done, and she'd told him all she had to tell, it seemed the only person Madame Shtange could conceive of having wanted to kill her husband had been killed the day before him.

§

'Is Captain Korolev here?' a voice enquired loudly, as they were finishing up. Korolev turned to see a familiar face approaching them.

'This is Lieutenant Dubinkin,' Korolev said, rising to his feet. 'He's also working on the investigation.' Korolev made the introductions and hid his surprise when Dubinkin addressed Hubert and Madame Shtange in apparently fluent French. What was more, it seemed Dubinkin and Hubert knew each other already. Korolev wondered if they shared the same profession.

'Are you from Petrovka as well?' Anna Shtange spoke in Russian and Korolev wondered if it was for his benefit.

'Another organization, Madame Shtange. One equally dedicated to uncovering your husband's killer, of course.'

Dubinkin spoke smoothly, with an apparently sincere concern, but Anna Shtange's reaction was to rise to her feet with something close to fury in her eyes. Korolev found himself stepping forward while giving her his warmest smile. She paused, confused, and he took the opportunity to pick his notebook up from the table and nod to Dubinkin.

'We've just finished, Comrade Dubinkin. I've informed Madame Shtange that arrangements will be made for her to view her husband's body this afternoon.' He turned his attention back to Anna Shtange. 'With luck he should be released to you before the day is out.'

Hubert placed a hand on her arm, and Korolev wondered if the Frenchman shared his concerns. Surely she wouldn't pick a fight with a man like Dubinkin in public – important French uncle or not. She must know what kind of organization she was dealing with.

'If we have any further questions?' Korolev asked, trying to keep the conversation moving, sensing that a pause would be dangerous.

'You may contact Madame Shtange through the embassy,' Hubert said, already steering her towards the lift. 'She'll be staying with us until we can arrange her and her children's return to France.'

Anna Shtange turned, caught Korolev's eye and nodded.

'Thank you, Captain Korolev.'

'My pleasure, Madame Shtange. Your husband's killer will face Soviet justice very soon, believe me.'

She gave him a weak smile, then glanced at Dubinkin.

'Good – Soviet justice is famed throughout the world,' she said, before adding after a moment's pause, 'I could wish them no worse fate.'

Chapter Twenty-Eight

WHEN THEY stepped outside, the heat took Korolev by the throat and then did its best to push him down feet-first into the concrete sidewalk – a strange sensation and not at all pleasant. Up above, sitting on that eyrie of a roof terrace, they'd picked up whatever small breeze was whispering its way across Moscow and, slight as it had been, it had relieved some of the swelter from the day. Down here however the heat was a presence that surrounded you – and it seemed to have got even worse in the last hour or so.

'Were you trying to protect her?' Dubinkin asked with an amused smile.

'I'd finished questioning her,' Korolev said gruffly, hoping it would be enough to keep the fellow in check. 'Are you coming with me to the institute?'

He pointed to the car Morozov had provided him with, noticing that the two goons were still parked not far behind it, although now they were leaning against the car, examining them at their leisure.

'You *were* trying to protect her, weren't you? My dear Korolev, she wasn't in any danger. She's the daughter of an important French politician, one sympathetic to us.'

'Yes, I heard that. It would have been helpful if someone had mentioned it to me earlier.'

'Didn't I?'

'You told me she was French,' Korolev said, his attention focused on the State Security men. 'No more than that.'

Dubinkin chuckled.

'You're a surprise in many ways, Korolev. I thought you'd be some aging bull, waiting his turn to be put out to pasture – but there's more to you than that, isn't there?'

Korolev wasn't that interested in what Dubinkin thought of him. If the truth were told, which it seldom was these days, Korolev was beginning to get a little tired of Dubinkin toying with him. If he wanted to find a subject for study, he should go and look into the head of one of his Chekist friends in that car. He turned to Dubinkin.

'Those two likely looking fellows – leaning against the Emka? Recognize them?'

Dubinkin didn't bother to look.

'I saw them on the way in. I believe they are comrades, yes – if that's your question.'

'Comrades?' Korolev considered the word for a moment or two. 'From this Twelfth Department?'

'I believe so. Would you like me to go and check?'

'No need,' Korolev said. 'I'm sure you're right. Not subtle when it comes to following a man, are they?'

'I think they want be seen, Korolev. I think they wouldn't be following orders if they weren't seen. They're trying to distract you. To put pressure on you.'

Korolev thought back – it had been different once, hadn't it? Back at the time of the Revolution there'd been people who'd pushed their weight around, but you could just push right back – and if your heart was in the right place, it all worked out. How had this mess come about? Here he was, an honest-enough policeman, doing his job, and being followed around Moscow by a couple of State Security bruisers for no good reason other than simply that – he was doing his job.

'Let's just go,' Korolev said, with a sigh and, sure enough, the two heavies managed to summon enough energy to get themselves into their car and pull away from the kerb at the same time as he did. Korolev took a quick glance in the mirror and then decided he'd enough on his plate without worrying about them too.

'Madame Shtange told me about her husband's relationship with Azarov. And a few other interesting things as well.'

'Tell me what she said.'

Korolev told him and, despite his best intentions, wasn't able to resist the occasional instinctive glance in the rear-view mirror.

'Yes, I think she may have described it correctly,' Dubinkin said when he'd finished. 'The Azarov Institute was set up with the support of the former head of State Security, the counter-revolutionary Yagoda. I believe Comrade Ezhov wasn't so convinced – perhaps he's the one who commissioned this report. If so, he's not telling us – which may mean something or may not.'

Korolev had given up trying to understand how things worked within the NKVD – it seemed no one trusted anyone else, however. Just like the rest of the population then.

'But the professor came up with some useful insights in the past, or so Colonel Rodinov said?'

'Yes, he did. Are you sure you want to know what they were?'

What choice did he have? If he didn't know what the professor had been up to, how could he know how it might affect the case? Korolev nodded.

'He developed certain interrogation techniques. They've been particularly effective in preparing enemies of the State for public trial. He was able to ensure that they admitted their guilt, which was of course evident, and that any unnecessary justification or defence that might have misled suggestible citizens was avoided.'

Korolev thought back to the newsreels he'd seen of the trials in the cinemas – he was sure he wasn't the only one who'd thought the defendants had seemed remarkably, if not eerily, compliant. He'd certainly never seen anything like it in a criminal trial. Senior Bolsheviks from long before the Revolution, who'd been in exile with Lenin, had pled guilty to incredible treacheries against the very State they'd fought tooth and nail to bring into being. Zinoviev, Kamenev and half a platoon of the oldest Bolsheviks had been in cahoots with the snake Trotsky and, it seemed, nigh on every foreign enemy you could think of. Now, perhaps, that finally made sense.

'I see,' Korolev said, turning the car into the alleyway that led to the institute's entrance.

He couldn't help wondering how Azarov had gone about his research, although, at the same time, he wasn't looking forward to finding out.

Chapter Twenty-Nine

THE GUARDS manning the gates weren't the same as the ones from Monday, but as soon as they saw Dubinkin's identity card, their resentful suspicion changed to alert welcome. The taller of the two lifted the bar that guarded the entrance and the other walked alongside the car until they reached the back door of the main building.

From the street, the Azarov Institute appeared as though it had always been there and always would be there – but to judge from the activity in the courtyard it seemed this was not entirely the case. A number of workmen were loading trucks with cardboard boxes, metal bedsteads, wooden crates of various sizes and even what looked like a dentist's chair.

'What's going on here?' Korolev asked the guard, who shrugged his shoulders

'I'm not the person to ask about such things, Comrade Captain.'

'Well, who is?'

'We just guard the gate, Comrade Captain. Maybe ask inside.'

'Guard it from who?'

'Enemies, I suppose,' although the fellow looked like he was none too sure what an enemy might look like.

'What happened to the men who were guarding the gate on Monday?' Korolev asked, a possibility beginning to occur to him.

'I wouldn't know, Comrade Captain. This is the first time I've ever been here. I hoped the Comrade Lieutenant might be able to tell us what time we'll be relieved.'

When Dubinkin explained he couldn't help them, the guard said his farewells and they saw him open his hands as he approached his comrade, as if to say – the new arrivals know nothing either. Which was true enough, Korolev thought.

One of the workers told them a man called Danilov was in charge and directed them into the main building, where he assured them they'd find him easily enough. They followed the sound of conversation along a long, oak-lined corridor to what must have been an office but which now stood empty, only the shadows on the carpet indicating where furniture had once rested – and now the carpet was itself in the process of being rolled up by three men. One of the men, a broad-shouldered fellow in a blue shirt, damp with sweat, was telling the others what to do.

'Comrade Danilov?'

'What's it to you?' He rose to his feet, looking at them without enthusiasm. But the surly manner disappeared when Dubinkin showed him his identification card.

'I'm sorry, Comrade Lieutenant,' the man said. 'I thought you might be – well – I don't know quite what I thought. I'm Danilov, right enough.'

'What's going on here?' Korolev asked, stepping over the carpet the two other men were continuing to roll up, apparently oblivious to their presence.

'We're moving the place. We're to have it finished by tomorrow – a big task, I can tell you. But we're up to it.'

Korolev looked to Dubinkin, who was nodding his sympathy to the foreman. Behind them the carpet was lifted on to shoulders and then taken from the room, heading for the courtyard. The men's footsteps sounded loud on the now-bare floorboards.

'Where to?' Korolev asked.

Danilov looked to Dubinkin for permission to answer. It seemed he was under the mistaken impression that Dubinkin was one of those who'd ordered the institute's relocation at a moment's notice. Korolev had to hand it to the Chekist, as Dubinkin gave his permission with a measured nod – he thought on his feet.

'We drive the trucks up Leningradsky Chaussée to a warehouse. Other drivers take them from there. As instructed.'

'Other drivers take them from there?' Korolev asked.

'It's secret business. That's all we need to know.' Danilov turned to Dubinkin. 'We're to tell no one what we've seen. Or what we're doing. That's understood, of course, Comrade Lieutenant. That's why I wasn't sure when you came in.'

'And what about the people? The people who worked here?' Korolev asked.

Danilov shrugged his shoulders. 'I can't help you, Comrade. There was no one here when we arrived yesterday.'

Dubinkin glanced at Korolev with a look that could only be described as meaningful. And, Korolev, despite his bemusement, took the hint. Danilov had clearly been told only what he needed to know – which wasn't much. But if anyone was going to get what he knew out of him, it was going to be Dubinkin.

'We'll just look around,' Dubinkin said. 'We're expecting to meet someone here. All the paperwork's gone already, I take it.'

'Paperwork, Comrade? We haven't seen any paperwork – it must have been your lads did that. There were some of them packing up their own trucks when we arrived.'

'Excellent. Remind me which warehouse you're driving to at the moment – we have two up there. We may have to make a change.'

Danilov gave him the address and then Dubinkin delicately questioned the man without seeming to. As it turned out, the location of the warehouse was the only useful piece of information he had.

§

They left Danilov to his work and walked further down the corridor, opening the door to what had once been Azarov's office. Their footsteps echoed on more bare floorboards. Everything had been taken from the room, except a portrait of Stalin. He looked down at them benevolently.

'This is where I met Shtange,' Korolev said. 'His desk was just there.'

Dubinkin walked to the window, looking out as a truck's engine started.

'Where do you think they're taking everything?' Korolev asked him. 'After the warehouse. And what about the people who worked here – where have they gone?'

'Somewhere we're not meant to find them, I suspect. Although we'll do our best, of course. I suspect Colonel Zaitsev was concerned that the security of the institute's work might have been compromised.'

Dubinkin spoke in a resigned monotone that told Korolev the Chekist considered any hope of locating the missing institute forlorn at best.

'But there's an investigation going on into the death of two men. Surely Colonel Rodinov can just order Zaitsev to take us to the people we want to talk to.'

Dubinkin made a noise that might have been a laugh if there'd been any humour in it.

'The only person who might be able to order Zaitsev about is Ezhov. And even then, it might have to go higher. Zaitsev's an important man and dealing with him is a delicate business – I can't say any more than that.'

Korolev looked around him, thinking that if an entire

institute could disappear, just like that, with no explanation required – then where did that leave a Militia detective?

They walked through the building, from offices to meeting rooms, from operating rooms down deserted corridors to what looked like hospital wards, storage rooms, a canteen. Everywhere was empty or being emptied.

'What do you make of these?' Korolev asked, gesturing towards a metal door. He'd noticed that each area was divided from those adjoining it by two sets of metal doors, each with eyeholes and locks so that moving from one side to another would require both sides to cooperate.

'I imagine they segregated each area,' Dubinkin said. 'That way no one knew everything that was going on. Almost like a cell structure, so that infiltration or treachery could only have a limited effect. And perhaps to make sure information wasn't shared – that people only saw what was in front of them and never the bigger picture.'

'Yes,' Korolev said. 'Shtange said something similar. That only the professor had known everything that went on in the institute.'

They walked out into the courtyard, standing silent amongst the busy workers, none of whom paid them much attention. Men were loading one truck with small metal bed frames.

'I understand the professor didn't restrict his research solely to adults,' Dubinkin said.

Korolev said nothing, his attention drawn by the two long concrete buildings he'd seen on his first visit. They looked like massive bunkers more than anything else. Thick iron shutters were bolted into the walls where windows should be.

'Shall we have a look?'

They walked over and Dubinkin pushed at the massive door of the nearest of the two buildings. To Korolev's surprise, it swung inwards smoothly, only the slightest sound coming from its oiled hinges. The Chekist ran a finger along the edge of the door with what seemed to be admiration – it had been heavily sound-proofed with felt on the inside, even though it was already a good six inches thick.

'I've seen this kind of sound-proofing before.'

So had Korolev – he'd made a brief unwilling visit to the Lubyanka the year before and seen just the same felt applied to some of the doors. And when Dubinkin found the electricity switch, he recognized the circular metal light shades that ran along the narrow central passage. It was cool inside the building but, then again, unless he was wrong, it was a place where the sun had never shone.

Korolev said nothing as he followed the Chekist past the heavy cell doors that lined each side of the corridor. All of them were open.

'Look in here,' Dubinkin said, peering into one.

The room was as dark as a pit. There was nothing in it – not a bed, nor a basin, nor a chair. Not even a bucket for a man's necessary activities. The walls were painted black – as was the floor. Korolev looked round for a light fitting inside the cell. But there was none to be found.

'Put a man in here for a few days and he'll tell you whatever you want him to,' Dubinkin said, and to judge from his voice, his view of such measures wasn't necessarily negative. 'But he won't like you for it. Or ever be the same, I shouldn't think.'

The next three cells were identical – but the fifth was a complete contrast. Here the walls and the floor were painted a glossy white and its high ceiling, ten feet up, was thick glass. Korolev flicked a switch and the room lit up like the inside of a light bulb.

'I wonder what they did about the heat – from the lights,' Dubinkin said.

Always the pragmatist, Korolev thought to himself.

'I don't think they cared much about the poor devils' comfort,' he said. 'There's not even a bench for them to lie on, let alone a cot.'

'Yes, I wondered about that. And do you see, in this cell there's an eyehole. Not in the other ones – probably no point, given they'd have been pitch-black.'

They went through the entire building – there were some cells no bigger than a standing coffin, while others had the same dimensions as the others they'd seen, except that the ceiling was so low a prisoner would have to crawl around on his hands and knees. In the basement there were cells that were really sealed swimming pools, with the entry point in the roof and metric measurements on the wall – calibrated to the centimetre. By the time they'd finished their inspection, Korolev was profoundly depressed.

'What do you make of it?' Dubinkin asked.

'I make nothing of it,' Korolev said. 'I've seen nothing.'

He looked along the corridor – they'd cleaned the place up, but there was still that smell of urine, sweat and fear – the acrid tang of a prison.

'It does make you wonder though.' Dubinkin sounded contemplative, as if an interesting thought had occurred to him. 'If they'd wanted to keep us out of here, they could have. Easily. We'd have needed a tank to get through that door if it had been locked. So why was it left open?'

A message, perhaps? Aimed at a Militia detective exhausted past the point of knowing what it was intended to mean? No, that wasn't right. He knew what it meant all right. It meant keep your damned nose out of our business, Korolev, or face the consequences. He took one last look at the consequences and walked back out into the heat of the sun.

Chapter Thirty

KOROLEV'S LEGS FELT tired as he climbed the stairs to Shtange's apartment, but his soul felt wearier still. His visit to the institute had him asking questions he generally tried to avoid. What kind of revolution had it been now that the State had ended up making a science out of breaking its citizens down and building them up again? And for what? So that they could all think the same, feel the same, chant the same name at the same time – Stalin's name, no doubt. How had it happened? He'd thought the Revolution had been intended to give the people freedom from oppression, not build establishments like the institute. Sometimes it was hard to believe that there was any good left in Soviet power, and that was the truth of it.

'Are you all right?' Slivka asked as he entered Shtange's apartment. The blood-stained carpets had been removed and the floorboards creaked underfoot.

'A missing son, no sleep and an investigation that's as likely to end up with me in the cells as the killer. I've had better days. Is there any news?'

'About the case?'

'Yuri first, if you've heard something.'

'Yasimov came by,' she said and then paused. It didn't look as if Yasimov had brought good news.

'What did he have to say?'

'He thinks he picked up Yuri's trail at Kievsky Station – still in the company of the two boys. You know about them?'

'Yes. And?'

'He's pretty sure they got on a tram but he lost track of them after that. He said he was going to go to the depot to talk to the drivers – see if any of them remembers anything. But for the moment, the trail's gone cold.'

Korolev nodded and picked up the phone, asking to be put through to the apartment building in Bolshoi Nikolo-Vorobinsky. The shared phone was in the hallway and the elderly Lobkovskaya, of the bat-like ears, picked it up.

'It's Korolev. Any sign of him?'

There wasn't. He thanked the old lady for her time and wondered where his son could possibly be.

'There was something else,' Slivka said, when he'd hung up. 'Yasimov said he was pretty sure there were other people looking for Yuri. And not our people. Whoever they were, they left some frightened people behind them.'

Korolev sat down, thinking it through. What if the men were Zaitsev's? 'I'm sorry,' Slivka said reaching a hand out to him. He did his best to smile.

'What about you – any progress?' he said, deciding to ignore for the moment the fear for his son that bubbled in his stomach. He'd go out and look for him as soon as he was finished here, and if the Lord was willing, he'd find him.

Slivka smiled back – not a joyful smile but one that said they'd get through this together. He found it comforting.

'I've been chasing round Moscow, and you'll be surprised to hear I haven't met one person yet who's had a good word to say about the dear professor.'

'I don't like him myself,' Korolev said. 'It was inconsiderate of him to be murdered in such an inconvenient way. And, yes, I've been hearing the same things – and that he denounced people to the Organs – a lot of them. What did you find out about him up at the university?'

'All this is reading between the lines, because – well – because people still don't like to talk about him.'

'Go on.'

'One – he wasn't much of a scientist; the implication is he got to where he was by telling bigwigs what they wanted to hear, by blaming his failures on others on the one hand and by taking credit for their achievements on the other. Although no one said that straight out.'

'You should have spoken to Shtange's widow – she said it straight out. But then she has a French passport and a bigwig uncle who happens to be a government minister.'

'A French government minister?'

'Exactly – it seems with an uncle like that you can say what you want in Moscow. She damned nearly called Dubinkin a murderer to his face.'

Slivka shook her head in disbelief. 'No wonder you look like you've been through the mill. But even if the citizens out at the university don't have such esteemed relatives, the message came across, all the same. They made it clear what they thought of him.'

'Go on.'

'Two – Shtange was a different kettle of fish. Popular with staff and students – a real Bolshevik, they said, and they meant that in a good way.'

'What other way is there?' Korolev said, and Slivka looked as if she'd swallowed her tongue.

'I meant . . .'

'Don't worry, I know what you meant. Carry on.'

Slivka took a moment to collect herself.

'Anyway, he was a good fellow, they were all agreed on that. He was only allocated to the university for two days a week but in that time he did a full week's work. And students were welcomed to his flat when they needed extra tuition. Azarov, on the other hand, hadn't taught in three years – not that his lectures were much missed.'

'And?'

'Three is a rumour, only a rumour – but you know how these things are . . .' Her expression was too neutral to be trusted. 'We probably should pay no attention to it.'

'Get to the point, you scoundrel,' Korolev said looking for something to throw at her. Not anything too hard, this cushion in his hand perhaps.

'Well, if you insist, I'll tell you.' Slivka smiled. 'It's said that Comrade Madame Azarova, the widow of the late departed and much unlamented Professor Azarov . . .' she paused for effect and Korolev found himself leaning forward, 'was having an affair with a certain Dr Weiss, member of the same university faculty and resident of Leadership House. Two storeys up from the Azarovs, I believe.'

'The same Dr Weiss who offered comfort to the said Comrade Madame Azarova on the morning of her husband's murder?'

'The very same. Do you want to hear the fourth discovery?'

'I do.'

'Dr Weiss was denounced as a Rightist saboteur by Professor Azarov only last month at the University Works Meeting. Azarov didn't pull any punches either – went for the knockout. But, for a change, someone stood up to him. Told the meeting Azarov had personal reasons for denouncing the good doctor and, if anyone was against the Revolution and damaging the department's efforts to meet its targets, it wasn't Dr Weiss – oh no, it was Professor Azarov himself, and his failure to live up to the teaching commitments that his position as a professor required.'

'And the reaction?'

'Stunned silence, followed by an outbreak of sporadic clapping, then shouts of agreement that turn into applause, stamping of feet and unrestrained cheering. Azarov storms from the room issuing dire threats. Weiss is exonerated to universal acclaim. And who do you think was the brave citizen who defended him?'

'The good Dr Shtange?'

'The very same.'

Korolev looked at the cushion in his hand – to think he'd even thought of throwing it at this splendid woman.

'Did you speak to Weiss?'

'I did – but before I knew about the rumour or how Shtange had defended him.' She flicked back through her notebook. 'What he did say was that he'd known Azarova for many years and that she was misjudged by many. He was also deeply upset by Shtange's death. Kept shaking his head in bewilderment whenever we discussed it.'

'But not Azarov's?'

'He expressed sympathy for Azarova – said that she'd invested her entire adult life in the man. But the implication was it had been a wasted investment. No, he didn't give a damn about Azarov – but Shtange he did care about. Well, it would make sense, given the fellow most likely saved him from a long trip to the Zone.'

Korolev nodded. Imprisonment would be the standard punishment for offences under Article 58 – political offences, in other words. And if the University Works Meeting had upheld Azarov's criticisms that would have been the likely next step.

'What do you think, now you look back on your conversation with him?'

'I think he might well have been having an affair with her. *Be* having an affair with her, for all I know.'

'It's a line of enquiry,' Korolev said, pleased. 'He lives in the same building, he has a motive, he's known to Azarov. The only question is what he was doing at the time of Azarov's murder.

And whether what he was doing was putting a bullet in the professor's head.'

'That's another interesting thing – I asked him what he was doing on Monday morning and he said he couldn't tell me, said he'd have to request authorization before he could. I didn't push it – it seemed sensible to see what he came back with first. He's not going anywhere, after all.'

Korolev found himself frowning – was this really yet more secret business, or just a guilty man trying to evade a reasonable question?

'We need to talk to him first thing.'

'Yes, because I had Belinsky ask quietly whether anyone in Leadership House might have any suspicions of their own about Weiss and the widow Azarova. Anyway, the Azarovs' maid let slip that Azarova and Weiss were very good friends – that he would often come round during the day.'

'Interesting. Does Weiss have a maid?' If anyone knew anything about what went on in an apartment it was the maid – and perhaps the building's doorman. But without the missing Priudski, the maid would have to do.

'He has a maid. And a wife as well,' Slivka added.

'We're going to have a busy day tomorrow,' Korolev said and found himself praying fervently that this might, after all, turn out to be something as simple as a romantic entanglement that had turned murderous. Although where Shtange came into it, he wasn't quite sure.

'And you, Chief? What did you come up with?'

Korolev sighed and told her how the institute effectively no longer existed and about his conversation with Shtange's widow, who might even now be packing her bags for France.

'It makes me wonder,' Korolev said, 'between you and me, whether this report Shtange was writing mightn't be behind at least some of this. As soon as Shtange is killed, within a couple of hours, it seems, the institute's shut down and most of its paperwork and staff put beyond the reach of any immediate investigation. Not only that, every scrap of paperwork here and in Azarov's office is also removed.'

'I should have said, it's the same at the university. Both Shtange's and Azarov's offices completely stripped. Of everything written, anyway.'

Korolev felt his suspicion hardening.

'I'm wondering if all of this activity is intended to make sure that report never sees the light of day. I wonder what it says.'

'You really want to know?' Slivka asked, her expression doubtful – and it occurred to him that she was right. Who in their right mind would want to see a report whose very existence might have led to a man's death? And if it *had* led to his death, then the likely killer was something to do with the NKVD. Anyone in their right mind would run away from that kind of association. But then again.

'Look, if Shtange was killed for that report, or because of what he might have said about the institute –' Korolev didn't feel he had to mention that if this was the case the perpetrators would most probably have been from the Twelfth Department – 'then wouldn't the killing have been more . . . professional? Do you see what I mean? A well-placed bullet would have been enough, just as it was for Azarov. All that stabbing and blood seems a bit amateurish to me. There's too much emotion as well. Chestnova said he was still being stabbed when he was down on the ground, clearly dead. And then there was another wound, made with a different knife – a scalpel probably – on his cheek. Made when he was already dead.'

He traced the line of the cut on his own face.

'A signature, perhaps? A message?'

'To who? Us? He was a surgeon – something to do with that?' Korolev considered what this might mean and was reminded of someone. And the reminder set his tired mind into motion once again.

'I didn't tell you this before but I had a strange encounter on Tuesday morning – at the zoo.' Korolev was almost thinking aloud. 'With your esteemed uncle.'

Korolev did not esteem Count Kolya, although he occasionally found himself respecting the man in a strange sort of way, and even half a year on from the discovery, it still made him shake his head in amazement that Slivka should turn out to be the niece of none other than the Chief Authority of the Moscow Thieves.

'That's strange. I thought I caught a glimpse of a familiar face today as well. He'd a cap pulled low over his face but I'm sure it was little Mishka. I think he might have been keeping an eye on me. Or on this building anyway.'

Korolev was reminded that he'd yet to take off his own cap and so removed it. The gesture wasn't out of deference to Slivka's presence – he didn't really consider her to be female when they were working – but because he wanted to give his head a vigorous scratch in the hope that it might activate a few brain cells.

'I want to talk to him – Kolya that is. Can you get in touch with him?'

'I might be able to, I'll try anyway.'

'Tell them it's urgent – however you go about it. The thing is,' Korolev mused, rubbing away at his bristly top-covering, 'Kolya said that he'd some things to tell me about the institute and what went on there, and that it had something to do with the Azarov case. And this was on Tuesday morning – *before* Shtange was murdered. I said he should go and bother someone else with his story because – well – because back then we were trying to get away from this case as fast as we could. But the reason I'm reminded of Kolya is because of the scalpel wound. Isn't it the sort of thing a Thief would do? He told me men had died there and, now I've seen the cell blocks, I don't doubt he was telling the truth. What if Thieves were held there? And if

Thieves were operated on at the institute in the name of research then I think that scalpel wound is exactly the sort of thing a Thief would do. A message to show why the man was killed. And, there's something else, I think there were other patients there as well . . .'

And then Korolev told her about the smaller beds – the ones that could only have been big enough for a child. And he knew things were bad when a detective like Slivka had to sit down and hold her head in her hands so that he couldn't see her face.

'And the strangest thing of all, Slivka,' Korolev said, putting coincidences together and finding they fitted a little too well for his liking. 'When Yuri and I ran into those orphans out at Peredelkino, young Kim Goldstein had a scar not too dissimilar to the one someone put on Shtange's cheek for him. Now what do you make of that?'

Chapter Thirty-One

WHEN SLIVKA LEFT for the night, Korolev called Rodinov to give him the daily report he'd requested and, to his surprise, he was put straight through. Korolev told the colonel of each twist and turn the day had brought and, because it was Rodinov he was speaking to, he didn't leave too many of them out. It turned out the men looking for Yuri were most certainly not Rodinov's.

When he'd finished, there was silence on the other end of the line. It carried on for so long that Korolev began to wonder if he'd been cut off. 'Comrade Colonel?'

'I'm thinking, Korolev. Just thinking.'

There was another long pause but this time Korolev allowed it to run its natural course.

'This investigation is becoming complicated,' Rodinov said, just as Korolev had resigned himself to waiting on the line for all eternity. 'Well, it's more than just an investigation now – it would be better described as a chess game. You are obviously one of the pieces and it seems the other side has decided you are worth attacking – indirectly, so far. But you should know things may get more difficult for you.'

'More difficult than my son being missing and the Twelfth Department's men looking for him?'

'You're still at liberty, Korolev, and as far as we're aware, so is your ex-wife. And your son, for that matter. And we don't know for certain these men were from the Twelfth Department. Although I'd be surprised if they weren't.'

Korolev held the phone tight in his grip – there were many things he wanted to say, and not one of them he could.

'Do you play chess, Korolev?'

'I've played it, but not for many years. Maybe once or twice with Yuri.'

'That's a shame – I think you'd be a good player. Solid, mostly, but capable of identifying an opportunity when it comes along. More importantly you know how to be brave when you need to be, to risk defeat in order to achieve victory.'

'If you say so, Comrade Colonel.'

But Korolev suspected that in a chess game like this defeat was permanent.

'You're in a difficult situation, Korolev. Your former wife's situation is also precarious. And, it seems to me, your son is in a difficult position as well.'

Korolev felt his hand grip the telephone so hard it seemed possible he would crush it, but he somehow managed to hold his tongue.

'I think I can intervene in your wife's predicament – I'd like to take her off the board, if that were possible.'

Korolev didn't know what the colonel was suggesting and didn't think he could ask either.

'But with regard to your son we must accept it's a strong possibility that they'll find him before we do. And if they do find him first, Korolev, the question is – how will they use him?'

That wasn't a question Korolev much wanted to consider, let alone answer. The colonel was silent again – no doubt thinking. Korolev wondered if the colonel had a son, and just what he'd be thinking if it was his child out there on the streets of Moscow being hunted by Chekists.

'Well, Korolev,' Rodinov said eventually. 'Whatever happens, you must remember that your best chance of coming out of this in one piece is with me. You probably already know too much to be allowed to survive long if Zaitsev wins. Will you remember that?'

'I will, Comrade Colonel,' Korolev said.

'Good. And from now on you'll report to me face-to-face. The telephone isn't ideal for this kind of conversation. Five o'clock tomorrow – at the side entrance to the Lubyanka. In the meantime, carry on as you've done so far – it's having an effect, it seems. I wish you luck, Korolev.'

The colonel hung up and for a moment Korolev sat listening to the hum of the telephone line in his ear and feeling more alone than he ever had.

Except that wasn't entirely the case. There had been one other time. Nineteen sixteen – the summer – he'd been cut off during some pointless battle that had raged for the best part of a week. He'd spent two days in a shell hole between the lines, knowing if he stuck his head above the ground he'd be shot at by both sides. Just him, half a bottle of water and four dead men. Or what was left of them. And German and Russian shells falling around him as each side tried to work out if the other was coming at them.

He sat there for a moment, remembering it – and coming to the conclusion that his current situation was worse. In 1916, his son hadn't been in the shell hole with him.

Chapter Thirty-Two

KOROLEV DIDN'T GO straight home, even though he was exhausted. He stood on the street outside Shtange's apartment building and thought about where Yuri might be. He had a few ideas. He looked back at the two goons in the Emka. They were looking tired now as well – or perhaps just bored. Well, if he did manage to find Yuri, he'd be damned if these two runts were going to take him away. He'd a temporary assignment to the NKVD, signed by Nikolai Ezhov himself. That must make him a colleague to these two – perhaps even their superior. Anyway, he was coming to understand that there might be some unexpected advantages to this temporary assignment of his. He tipped his hat to the men, and received two blank stares in response. Not very comradely, all things considered.

Korolev pointed the car in the direction of Kuznetsky Most, which would be busy even at this time of night, just in case he might spot Yuri there. Nothing. Then he went west to Arbat, where Moscow's youth liked to gather of an evening, but there was no sign of him there either. Finally he went to Kievsky Station, where the train from Peredelkino came in, parked the car and walked through the station, checking each of the platforms and waiting rooms before picking his way through the surrounding streets. Still nothing.

It was getting dark by the time he decided that if Yuri was in Moscow he'd likely have gone to ground completely. With a dull pain in his chest, he turned the car in the direction of home, although his eyes kept searching, hoping against hope for a sign of the boy. And then, by chance perhaps, or more likely because his subconscious had taken over the driving while he scanned his surroundings, he found himself looking at an enamelled street sign. Vitsin Street.

Vitsin Street wasn't on his direct route home. But still, here he was. And what was more, twenty metres further along the street was the orphanage where the professor's wife worked. He parked the car and stepped out. Sure enough, the Emka pulled in thirty metres further back.

'Who is it?' A voice said from inside when he knocked on the heavy wooden door for the second time.

'Militia. Open up.'

'A moment.'

There was the sound of a heavy lock being opened and a bolt being pulled before the door creaked open a few inches and a pair of wary eyes appeared in the narrow gap.

'What do you want, Comrade?' a deep voice asked him.

'I need to talk to the director.'

'He's having his dinner.'

Korolev had had a long day and a longer night. And he'd good reasons for the temper that had been simmering nicely all day.

'I don't care if he's dancing naked to the damned radio.' Korolev pushed hard at the door. 'I need to see him right now.'

The door didn't move. The wary eyes, it seemed, were attached to a hefty amount of muscle. They blinked once when he pushed but otherwise they maintained their steady gaze.

'Ask nicely and I'll let you in. Otherwise it's good night to you.'

Korolev could feel a headache coming on, but he did his best to swallow his irritation.

'Please open this damned door,' he said. 'I would be very grateful.'

'That's better.' The door swung open and Korolev was surprised to discover that, while the cautious eyes were indeed attached to a body that had more bulk than a prize-winning ox, he'd been talking to a woman. But that was probably just as well, he decided – because if she'd been a man he might have felt obliged to throw a punch, and there was every chance, to judge from the way the fabric stretched across those biceps, that this would have been a mistake.

'My name's Korolev. From Petrovka.'

She examined his identity card before handing it back to him, glancing at his face for the briefest of moments. She made no comment on his black eye.

'We have to be careful. Not all the boys want to be in here – and some of them have friends on the outside. I'm Tambova – the boys call me Little Barrel.' She snuck another look at him, perhaps gauging his reaction, and shrugged.

'I prefer Little Barrel. Sit here and I'll knock on the director's door. Korolev, you said.'

'That's me.'

'Don't let anyone in while I'm away.'

She turned to climb up the staircase behind her, her movements surprisingly delicate.

There was a long wooden bench in the hallway where she probably wanted him to sit, but Korolev decided to take a walk along the corridor that led deeper into the building. At one stage the place had been a monastery, of course, and he found traces of its former identity – the outline of a three-fingered hand raised in blessing behind poorly applied whitewash, ancient wooden doors with crosses cut into the nails, and a stone-flagged floor that had been worn smooth by hundreds of years of monks' feet. He followed his nose until he found himself in a chapel, now a dormitory. Ranks of bunk beds were pressed in on top of each other, with only the narrowest of spaces between them for movement. There were no children, however, only rolled-up mattresses resting on the wooden bases of the beds.

'Can I help you?'

Korolev turned to find himself face to face with a stout man dressed in a white shirt, the top three buttons of which were open – a tuft of grey chest hair and the top of a string vest poking out.

'You are?' Korolev asked.

'I'm the director of the orphanage. Spinsky.' He looked none too pleased to be separated from his supper, but Korolev didn't care. If Spinsky thought he had it tough he should walk in Korolev's shoes for half an hour and see how he liked them.

'Captain Korolev, Moscow CID. I've some questions for you.'

'It's late.'

Korolev said nothing and Spinsky, after a brief pause, sighed and nodded.

'All right then. Is this about the missing boys?'

'Which missing boys would these be?' Korolev asked, more than a little curious.

'Two of them absconded from a trip to Peredelkino. We've sent the children out there for the week.'

Korolev said nothing. His heartbeat sounded loud in his ears.

'Are you all right?' Spinsky asked.

'When was this?'

'Last night. Listen, what's all this about?'

'Have you photographs of them?' Korolev said, ignoring the question. 'The boys that ran, that is.'

'I should think so.'

The director led him outside into the corridor and indicated a low door. 'My office.'

'Do you mind my asking – would one of these two runaways be called Goldstein?'

Spinsky looked over his shoulder as he inserted a key into its lock. 'Yes, have you found him?'

Last night – the same night Yuri had disappeared – two orphans make a run for it. This morning, three boys are seen at the next station along from Peredelkino. One of them – perhaps – Yuri; and another – perhaps – Kim Goldstein.

'Not yet,' Korolev said, his voice much calmer than he felt.

'Please, take a seat,' Spinsky said, opening the door.

'Can you tell me the circumstances? How they managed it?'

'I wasn't there, but the children were missing in the morning – they must have slipped over the wall at some stage. It's less secure out there and, well, it's not unusual. We don't run a prison camp.'

'I know Goldstein lived on the streets. What about this other fellow?'

'Yes, Petrov is his name. They came in together in January – the winter's our biggest recruiter amongst street children.'

'Together. Was there a gang of them came in at the same time?'

'I think so, I'd have to check.'

Goldstein's gang. The Razin Street Irregulars, or so he'd once called them.

'Have you reported their running away to the Militia?'

Spinsky glanced up. 'We used to. But it takes a long time to make the report and nothing ever comes of it. I'm sorry if that seems blunt.'

Which would explain why no one had made the connection. Still, if Yuri was with him the chances were they'd be visiting Goldstein's old haunts – and Korolev knew someone who'd know where at least some of those were.

'Could you check who came in with them? It might be useful. I know a bit about Goldstein and his crew.'

The director frowned. 'All right.'

He pulled a heavy ledger from the shelf beside his desk and opened it up, flicking through the pages.

'There were five of them.'

'May I see?'

The director pushed the ledger across and Korolev ran his finger down the column of names until he found Goldstein's. There were four other children admitted the same day. Beside Goldstein's name and that of Petrov someone had written an 'R' in red ink and today's date.

'The "R" means?'

'Run.'

'This is the other fellow, is it? Petrov? You said you might have photographs of them.'

'Yes, of course.' The director stood and walked to a filing cabinet, opening the drawers until he came back with two files.

'Two of these have an "A" beside them and one a "D",' Korolev said, looking at the ledger entries. 'What do they mean?'

'The "D" means deceased – they were in poor shape when they came in and the boy caught influenza, if I remember. He didn't make it. The other two were transferred to the Azarov Institute.'

Korolev nodded calmly, although he felt anything but calm. In fact he could feel energy racing round his body looking for a way out. He reached into his pocket for his cigarettes – it was the only thing he could think of.

'Do you mind if I smoke?'

'Help yourself.'

Korolev looked at the fingers that held the match as he lit his cigarette; they were steady. He wasn't sure how.

'Professor Azarov's wife works here, of course,' he said, somehow managing to speak in a neutral tone of voice.

'Listen, Comrade. What's this all about? I understand you're with Petrovka, but if I knew what you were looking for perhaps I could help you more.'

'I am with Petrovka,' Korolev said. 'But I've also been assigned to State Security on a certain matter. You should know State Security doesn't answer questions, it asks them. I can show you my letter of authority, if you wish.'

Spinsky looked doubtful, but then he seemed to reconsider. He swallowed before nodding slowly.

'Very good. Yes, Comrade Azarova comes three times a week. I'll be honest, some of our boys are resistant to socialism, and she's been of great assistance in our re-education efforts.'

'When exactly? When does she come in, that is?'

'Monday morning, Tuesday morning and Friday morning, I think. She's with us from eight-thirty until about twelve. She works with other orphanages as well though, on other days and in the afternoons.'

'So she was here on Monday and Tuesday of this week?'

'Monday morning certainly – I saw her myself. Tuesday morning – I can't say for sure because I was out with the boys in Peredelkino – but if she was here, she'd have been here on her own, more or less. All the boys that weren't in the infirmary were put on buses first thing.'

Korolev had been looking through the skimpy files on Goldstein and Petrov. He was sure he recognized Petrov – one of the boys who'd been talking to Yuri by the riverbank. He was another one like Goldstein – reserved. Not without confidence, or something similar – stubbornness perhaps.

'When you say these other two were transferred to the Azarov Institute? What does that mean?'

'It means exactly what I say – we've worked alongside the Azarov Institute for three years now. Most of the children spend a few weeks over there from time to time – if the professor identifies children who will be able to serve the State by assisting him further in his scientific research, they are permanently transferred to his establishment. Most come back, however.'

'I didn't know he ran an orphanage over there.'

The director shrugged his shoulders.

'I don't know what he runs over there, Comrade Captain. It isn't the kind of place you ask questions about. While the children are over there they participate in some neurological testing, I believe. Ones that are particularly suitable stay with them. The boys envy the ones that stay, I can tell you.'

'When you say neurological testing . . . ?'

'I don't know for sure. The children who come back – well, sometimes they've got small scars, just here.' The director pointed to his cheek, at exactly the same place as the murdered Shtange had been cut with a scalpel and where Goldstein had a half-healed gash. 'Nothing to worry about. The boys are proud of them.'

'But you have no further contact with them, the ones that stay? You never see them again?'

That seemed to be what Spinsky was saying. The director looked uncomfortable at the bluntness of the question and, for some reason, began to do up the buttons on his shirt, then undo them.

'At first I was a little uncomfortable with the arrangement, Comrade Captain, as I sense you are. Our children can be tough nuts but we try to treat them well. On the other hand, we often lack staff and struggle with resources.'

'Resources?'

'Food, clothing, textbooks, blankets. Not always – but when things run short it seems we're often as not at the back of the queue when it comes to allocations. Shoes are always a problem, but they are for everyone, I suppose. The Azarov Institute has no such problems – the food the children get over there is first class – and the chosen boys, the ones selected for permanent transfer, they get sent brand-new clothing before they even leave, and a suitcase of the finest quality. I've seen them with my own eyes. Such suitcases.'

Suitcases were one of many things it was impossible to obtain these days. Korolev could understand why Spinsky had been impressed.

'So the children want to go – they know it's important work, that the professor is our top man when it comes to brains. And they believe, if what he says is right, that they'll be the leaders of the future, thanks to his efforts. That he'll mould them into little Stalins.'

Korolev didn't think that Spinsky's prodigies would have been so excited if they'd seen the parts of the Azarov Institute Korolev had visited that afternoon.

'How many children have you transferred there?' Korolev asked, turning the pages of the ledger. There seemed to be at least one 'A' on every page – and there were a lot of pages.

'Quite a few, I should think. Over fifty anyway. I haven't added the numbers up.'

When Korolev and Dubinkin had left the Azarov Institute that afternoon, there'd only been two lonely guards still there – and even they'd been asking when they could leave as well.

'I've been to the Azarov Institute, I didn't see any children there.'

'The institute has another facility, just outside of Moscow, I believe. I don't know exactly where – Madame Azarova tells me it's a wonderful place though, out near Lefortovo. I almost wish I could go there myself sometimes. Like a palace, she says.'

But Spinsky's eyes told a different story and Korolev wondered what he knew and what he didn't. He promised himself he'd be paying him a return visit if things turned out to be as bad as Korolev had a feeling they might be.

'Thank you. I need to use your phone now, if you don't mind. In private.'

'Help yourself,' Spinsky said, and Korolev had the impression he was glad the interview was over.

§

Yasimov's family lived right beside the shared *kommunalka* phone and his son answered. Yasimov himself was soon on the other end of the line.

'With Goldstein and a youngster called Petrov, you say? That fits in with the station sighting. Could Yuri have known they were going to leg it from the orphanage in advance?'

'I don't know. Maybe. Maybe he just ran into them by chance – at the station perhaps. And the rest followed on from that.'

'I remember that youngster, Goldstein. Red hair, runt.'

'Bigger now, but still has the red hair. Cut short, of course – they keep the children's hair trim here.'

'Mmmm. And Petrov – taller, brown hair, also with a close-shaved head, you say? It could be them. It sounds like them.'

'I've photographs. And I've a hunch I know where they might be going. This Azarov Institute had a home for children attached to it – two of his gang were transferred there. Somewhere out near Lefortovo, and I half-wonder if Goldstein doesn't plan to spring them.'

He didn't add that there was every chance the place no longer existed, like the institute itself – but Goldstein couldn't know that might be the case.

'Another thing – there's a sergeant called Pushkin over in Razin street.'

'Pushkin?' Korolev could hear the bemusement in Yasimov's voice.

'I think he finds it as odd as you do. Anyway, he knows Goldstein – and probably knows his haunts as well. There was an old stables they used – I don't know if it's still there. Look him up.'

'I'll do it now, brother.' Yasimov said. 'This very minute.'

'Listen, Mitya. I've a problem here, but if I can slip away – I will.'

Korolev thought about the men in the Emka outside. With a bit of luck he might find a way to drop them.

'If you can, you can. If not, don't worry.'

Korolev felt a little glow of optimism – the Goldstein connection was the first real clue they'd had as to where his son might be.

§

The director had left him with the telephone, no doubt planning to reacquaint himself with his dinner as quickly as possible. When Korolev hung up he gathered the boys' files together and opened the door – and was almost crushed by a surprised Little Barrel stumbling into the room.

'What the hell?' he managed to say, startled more than frightened. But almost instinctively, his hand had reached for his gun and there it was, snug in his hand.

'The director told me to stand here.'

But if Korolev was any judge it wasn't just shyness that was preventing her from meeting his eyes.

'You were listening.' It came out as a statement rather than a question.

'I have ears,' the girl said, her head hanging with shame. 'They do the listening.'

Korolev sighed, replacing the Walther in his holster. He found himself patting her elbow.

'Ears do that, they're tricky things. Come on, I need to go home – you'd better let me out.'

'Of course, Comrade Captain. Thank you. You won't tell him, will you?'

'No, of course not. How much did you hear?'

'About your son. About Kim and Petya. About that place.'

Petya must be Petrov.

'What place are you talking about?'

'The place in the woods, the place where they send them – out near Lefortovo. I keep them safe here – no one hurts them.' She looked up at him, her eyes fierce. 'I look after them.'

'But it's different at this other place?'

'Yes.'

And Korolev saw a teardrop, a huge teardrop, form at the corner of her eye.

Chapter Thirty-Three

WHEN KOROLEV came out of the orphanage he found the Emka had been replaced with another car – a Ford – and two new Chekists as well. He looked at them and they looked back – alert and wide awake – and Korolev felt the tiredness drag at him and realized it would be pointless to try to shake them off.

He drove through the still summer-warm streets with fear for his son's wellbeing weighing heavily on him once again – that glimmer of optimism not quite so strong after Little Barrel's warning. He'd tried to get her to tell him more, but then she'd clammed up so tight he might as well have been talking to himself – and so now he found himself worrying over the little she had said, like a dog with a bone, and not much liking the taste of it. Outside the streets were full of Muscovites enjoying the warmth of the evening, some staggering with drink, others just out to stretch their legs rather than stay put in some sweltering little box that had been carved out of an already over-crowded *kommunalka* just for them. But Korolev looked through them all – the only person he had eyes for was Yuri.

§

By the time he'd reached Bolshoi Nikolo-Vorobinsky, his thoughts had turned against himself. What kind of man was he? That he'd managed to put his own son at risk? He'd known for a year now that this job of his came with compromises, yet he'd usually done his best to avoid them. Why? And what was more, he'd known the job itself was a dangerous one – twice in the last twelve months he'd been close to disaster. And he'd known the risks weren't only being taken by him – every morning he saw the queue of ordinary citizens outside Petrovka, waiting to find out from the records office which prison a relative had been sent to. And yet still he carried on trying to bring an antiquated version of justice to a society that thought telling a joke about the leadership a more serious crime than murder. He could have asked to do something else, training youngsters perhaps – he'd earned it, after all. Instead he'd carried on, putting his head deeper and deeper into the lion's mouth. He could see now it had been selfish. If he got Yuri back he'd give it up, work in a factory if need be, and keep his head where it belonged – intact and on his shoulders.

His steps were slow as he climbed the stairs to his apartment – not least because he'd no hope whatsoever that his son would be there waiting for him. It felt as if the very air itself was thick with collective anxiety, and no trace of the joy he'd expect if the boy had returned safe and sound. He wondered what the other inhabitants of the building made of it all – he'd no doubt they'd seen him park the car, watched him cross the road and now were listening to his footsteps as he climbed the stairs. They'd no doubt seen the two Chekists pull in behind him, as well.

Perhaps they'd already come to the conclusion that whatever was going on with Korolev's son, it would be best to avoid the Militiaman until the matter had resolved itself, one way or another. He couldn't blame them. He doubted Lobkovskaya was the only one who knew that Chekists had searched his room. And now he was going to have to tell Valentina what had happened – and he wondered what she might say.

He opened the door to his apartment and walked through to the shared room. Valentina was sitting at the table, Natasha beside her. Lobkovskaya was on the Chesterfield and Shura, Babel's maid, was beside her. He stopped, looking from face to face, thinking what good fortune it was to have friends such as these – and what a responsibility as well. Valentina, meanwhile, had risen to her feet in one graceful movement. She came to him and wrapped her arms around him and held him close, and Korolev, despite himself, felt tears itching the corners of his eyes.

Chapter Thirty-Four

SOMEHOW HE SLEPT. It probably helped that he was tired from the tips of his ears to the soles of his feet but, even so, at first he found himself waking at the slightest sound, wondering if those might be Yuri's footsteps on the staircase or if the argument down the lane might be something to do with his son.

Eventually sleep took him in its firm grasp and the next thing he knew the early dawn was brightening the window. And then he was on his feet and on the move. He wanted to go to Kievsky station again first thing – if Yuri was in Moscow, he might still be in the neighbourhood of the station, and if he went early enough, he wouldn't be missed from the investigation. And he also wanted to find out if Yasimov had tracked down any of Goldstein's lairs and what, if anything, he'd found there.

He was just walking out onto the street when he saw them: the Chekists who'd followed him halfway round Moscow for most of the previous day, it seemed. They were standing under a streetlamp, smoking and, as usual, they didn't avoid his gaze – instead the plump one waved him over. Korolev looked at them, the collar of his shirt suddenly feeling like a noose. He stared, hoping he'd mistaken the gesture, but then it came again, irritated now. The other one tapped his watch, as if to say, 'We haven't all day, Citizen Korolev, we've other people to be arresting as well, you know.'

There was no ceremony when he reached them. They didn't introduce themselves or tell him what they wanted from him – just directed him down the lane, one of them falling in on either side. They didn't seem that interested in him, if the truth were told – in fact one of them yawned loudly. He wondered whether they'd slept, it didn't look like it – they were unshaven and his nose told him they both needed a wash. Perhaps they'd been up all night, doing whatever men like them did. It was really night-time work, their business, after all.

They turned left at the corner, towards the sugar refinery, and Korolev wasn't surprised to see their car parked further along the street. There was also another car, however – a brand new ZIS, its chrome gleaming despite the long early-morning shadows, a driver leaning against it.

'He wants to talk to you,' the plump goon said and, as he spoke, the driver saw them, walked to the rear door of the car and opened it.

'Come in, Korolev,' a familiar voice said from the back seat and Korolev recognized it as Colonel Zaitsev's. It occurred to him that not many citizens had the privilege of so many close encounters with senior Chekists in such a short period of time. He shrugged, took the sort of breath you might take before diving into a cold lake, and found himself squeezing onto what was left of the back seat. It might have helped if Korolev had been a smaller man. Or Colonel Zaitsev, for that matter. As it was, he found himself closer to the Comrade Colonel than was comfortable.

'Close the door, there's a good fellow, and let me have a look at you.'

The colonel spoke softly, his dark eyes examining Korolev with care. Eventually Zaitsev nodded, as if satisfied with his inspection.

'You look nervous, Korolev, and you're right to be. I wouldn't like to be in your shoes. No. Not at all.'

Korolev looked down at the footwear in question, then at the colonel's boots. He knew the colonel didn't mean it literally, but all the same – if he'd a choice between the colonel's boots and his own shoes, then he wouldn't choose his shoes either. The colonel's boots looked shapely as a pair of ballet dancers – the highly polished leather almost seeming to glow in the car's interior.

'Korolev? I'm talking to you.'

'Yes, Comrade Colonel.' Korolev shook his head to clear it. 'I hear you.'

Which he did, but he'd been distracted by the fact that, while the colonel's boots looked as though they'd just been stripped off an imperial hussar, the rest of Zaitsev's clothes were crumpled and untidy, the buttons on his *gymnastiorka* undone as if he'd been exerting himself, and the buckle on his Sam Browne belt unfastened, letting his stomach spread out.

'Well then. What have you to say for yourself?'

To Korolev's surprise he felt an enormous urge to say exactly what he thought of an organization in which one department told him to investigate two murders and another department came along and told him not to. Because he'd no doubt that this was what he was about to be told. But then, suspecting the brown specks on the colonel's tunic might just be blood, he took a deep breath and reminded himself who he was talking to.

'Comrade Colonel, I always attempt to do my duty to the best of my ability. If this is about the Azarov and Shtange murders, I've only ever followed instructions from my superiors. To the best of my ability.'

The colonel snorted. 'To the best of your ability?'

'Perhaps my ability is limited, Comrade Colonel. I've always tried to recognize my limitations.'

'It's as well you do, Korolev. You are, after all, a simple detective – isn't that right? A simple detective who has managed to become involved in matters well beyond his capabilities.'

In not much more than twenty-four hours Korolev had been directly and indirectly threatened by two Chekist colonels, each of whom, he suspected, wanted completely different things from him. Yes, there was no doubt that he'd got in over his head. The colonel was certainly right about that.

'You've even managed to lose your son.'

Korolev was momentarily angry, but more than that he was concerned. Did Zaitsev have the boy? The colonel seemed to follow his thoughts because he smiled, apparently satisfied that he had Korolev's full attention now.

'Korolev, if I wanted to cause you difficulties, we wouldn't be talking about things in such a comradely way. If I wanted to make life awkward for you, those fellows outside would be having the conversation, not me. And they're very efficient at what they do, believe me. The big one, Blanter, looks on it as training for the ring. He's tireless: punch, punch, punch. All night long. The other one, Svalov, looks softer but don't be deceived – he's the more inventive of the two. You can take my word for it, compared to Svalov, Blanter's the soft one.'

'I can believe it,' Korolev said, strangely pleased that he'd spotted Blanter as a boxer, while at the same time feeling his guts trying to make their way down to his toes.

'Korolev, I want to make life easy for you. I've a proposal, a generous proposal. If you accept it – then, believe me, you'll have a new friend. And friends like me can be useful in times like these. Of course, if you decline it – well – that would be a different story.'

The colonel gestured in the direction of the two Chekists on the other side of the street.

'Comrade Colonel?' Korolev said, reaching into his pocket for his cigarettes. 'Do you mind if I smoke?'

It wasn't that he wasn't afraid, he was. But when a man's afraid for a long time, Korolev knew, he begins to treat it as normality. And normality for him involved smoking cigarettes.

'Of course not. We're going to be friends, after all. Aren't we?'

Korolev found himself offering the colonel the packet and, to his surprise, the Chekist took one, beginning to root around in his pockets for something to light it with before Korolev discovered his hand was now offering his matches as well.

'Thank you, Korolev, a busy night – I smoked the last of mine a couple of hours back.'

'I'm pleased to have the opportunity to assist you, Comrade Colonel,' Korolev said, thinking that cigarettes didn't grow on trees.

Perhaps the colonel heard the reservation in his voice because he laughed, smoke coming out of his mouth as he did so – before reaching into the pocket of his tunic for a handkerchief to dab the sweat from his face, a smile still on his lips.

'Do you know why I want to help you find Professor Azarov's killer?'

Korolev decided that the colonel's question wasn't one he could safely answer.

'Because,' the colonel continued, 'it will stop you, and others, digging around in our affairs. Which would be better for everyone, wouldn't it?'

'From where I'm sitting, I'd have to agree with you,' Korolev said – and something about that amused the colonel all over again.

'Well, if that's your sincere wish – then I've something for you. Pass me that briefcase.'

Korolev did as he was asked and Zaitsev pulled from it a sheet of typed paper, which he inspected briefly before handing it over.

'This is a witness statement – evidence that establishes that there's no direct connection between the murders and the institute. It was Shtange who killed the professor, so there's a connection in that regard – but the reasons have more to do with personal animosity than science.'

Korolev found himself struggling to keep his amazement from showing.

'Personal animosity?' he said in a quiet voice.

'The professor denounced Shtange as a saboteur, maliciously, so the good doctor killed him in revenge – or perhaps self-defence, if you consider the likely consequences if he'd been arrested on basis of the professor's accusation. It doesn't matter, either way, now they're both dead.'

Korolev read the first few lines of the document, before glancing back to the top of the page to find out who'd provided this helpful information.

'But this is Priudski, the doorman. What did he have to do with it?'

'Shtange promised him money to let him into the professor's apartment on the morning of the murder. Shtange then refused to pay him, so Priudski went to his apartment to confront him. When the doctor still wouldn't pay up, he stabbed him. It all turns out to be very straightforward.'

Korolev read the statement and it was as exactly as the colonel said. At first glance, there was nothing obviously wrong with it – the signature was clear and firm and it was in the correct format. Of course, it was typed, which was unusual for Militia witness statements – but perhaps not for State Security. And perhaps its coming from the NKVD accounted for the fact that the paper was of surprisingly good quality, white and crisp to the touch. In Korolev's world, statements were written on thin brownish paper that sometimes looked as if it had been an active participant in the interrogation. He'd opened files to find statements that had been smudged by what might have been sweat, or even tears – and sometimes other substances as well. His instincts told him this statement was too well written and too tidy. And then, of course, there were the anomalies in the story – anomalies that couldn't be just winked away, either.

'Where's Priudski now?' Korolev asked.

'Where you would like him to be?' the colonel said, and seemed pleased with Korolev's reaction. 'You seem surprised – why?'

Korolev's hunch, after reading the statement, had been that Priudski was dead. That the doorman was available for questioning was indeed a surprising development.

'No reason in particular. Of course, it would be usual procedure for me to interview any witness whose statement we relied upon.' Korolev spoke carefully – he wanted to sound as if he were going along with Zaitsev's proposal, but he also wanted to give himself some breathing space. Rodinov had been right, he'd have to play this game for himself now – and he needed time to think.

'You see,' he continued, 'Colonel Rodinov won't be satisfied with this statement just on its own. I'll have to present him with a completed file – every full stop in the right place, every page numbered.'

'Priudski will back up the witness statement, and you may question him as you see fit. I'm aware that Rodinov will need to be fully satisfied by your conclusions. I know the colonel well.'

Korolev didn't need to have been involved in Professor Azarov's telepathy experiments to realize Zaitsev didn't have loving feelings towards his Chekist colleague.

'And custody?'

'Priudski will remain in the custody of the Twelfth Department, the two dead men were ours.'

It seemed this was a point that wasn't up for negotiation.

'We still haven't spoken to all the persons we need to,' Korolev said. 'I won't be able to rely on the statement alone.'

'Speak away, as long as we agree on the outcome. You'll need these.' Zaitsev handed him a sheaf of photographs of

Priudski, as well as a fingerprint card. 'I shouldn't be surprised if Priudski's prints show up at Dr Shtange's apartment.'

Korolev looked at the black smudges on the card and read the date beneath them – yesterday's – and the location where the card had been filled out – 'Internal Prison of the NKVD, Moscow – Butyrka'.

'It sounds as if the case is solved,' Korolev said, but he didn't like the sound of it much.

Zaitsev nodded, closed the briefcase then tapped the confession Korolev was still holding.

'You can keep this. Listen to me, Korolev, and listen carefully. You have a reputation and it's an admirable reputation in many ways. It's said you get the job done, no matter what the risks or the obstacles. They tell me you follow the trail to the end. All of that might be very good when you're hunting bandits or hooligans, but this is a different matter. Know your limitations. I want an end to this investigation within forty-eight hours and I don't want any cleverness out of you. Just so you understand me.'

'It should be possible,' Korolev said. 'I'll do my best. But Colonel Rodinov is the one I report to.'

'Forty-eight hours, Korolev,' the colonel said in a voice that was as cold as a snowstorm in Siberia. 'And there's something else.'

'I'm at your command, Comrade Colonel.'

'There is a report, prepared by Dr Shtange. About the institute. I want it.'

Korolev did his best to look as though this was all news to him. It was difficult, under the colonel's intense examination, but he thought he managed it well enough.

'A report? What kind of a report?'

The colonel seemed to consider how to respond – and if the report contained half of what Anna Shtange thought it might, then Korolev understood why. After all, Zaitsev was the man in ultimate charge of the institute – and that meant he would be responsible for any of its failures.

'I haven't read the report myself, Korolev. But I understand it is critical of Professor Azarov – serious allegations that I want to investigate thoroughly, without interference. Do you understand?'

'Yes, Comrade Colonel.'

'There may be more than one copy. I know Azarov had one, but there may be others. Shtange may have kept one for himself. I need all the copies.'

'I'll do my best, Comrade Colonel. Believe it.'

'Do better than that, Korolev. I think if you put your mind to it, you'll find them for me.'

'But—' Korolev began.

'But nothing, Korolev.'

The colonel reached inside his trouser pocket and produced a small pearl-handled pocket knife. A familiar pocket knife. The colonel handed it to him. It felt warm, as if it still held the warmth of Yuri's hand. Korolev closed his fingers around it, remembering the boy whittling at his stick as they'd walked down to the river.

'Yes, Korolev, it belongs to him. Last night he volunteered to assist the State with an important matter, so I know you won't object. Of course, there are risks that come with this task, but like any good Pioneer, he knows that duty comes first. Now, I want you to think about that. I understand you don't like dead bodies – that they make you ill. How would you feel if you were standing over your own son's corpse, Korolev? Can you imagine what that would be like?'

Korolev said nothing – he couldn't say anything.

Zaitsev nodded. 'So you'll close this investigation and you'll find me those reports, won't you?'

Chapter Thirty-Five

'WHAT HAPPENED HERE? In your own words.' Korolev spoke dispassionately. His calm came, strangely, from ice-cold fury. He hadn't wanted any part of this but they'd dragged him into it all the same – and now they'd taken his son. Why shouldn't he be angry?

They'd gone through Priudski's story once already – how he'd opened the door to the Azarovs' apartment for the doctor, heard the sounds of an argument and the pop, pop of a small revolver. How he'd been horrified by the murder, how Shtange had told him he wanted to spring a surprise on Azarov, nothing more than that. And then, to make matters worse, Shtange had refused to pay up – leaving him with a dead tenant and a guilty conscience. He'd described, step by step, his journey across town to have it out with the murderer, and the meeting's fatal result – for the doctor at least. From time to time, Slivka had looked more than a little puzzled – unsurprisingly. The story still had plenty of holes in it and, to complicate matters, Zaitsev had sent along his pet boxer, Blanter, who had spent most of the interview cracking his knuckles, one by one – all the while staring at Korolev with what seemed to be intense hatred. The man looked as though he hadn't slept in a couple of days, his eyes red-rimmed and his stubble a sweaty grey shadow. Perhaps he blamed Korolev. In any event, it wasn't the ideal atmosphere in which to conduct an interrogation.

Now Priudski stood, in the hallway where Shtange had been killed, looking confused.

'Here?' Priudski asked, looking around him. 'You want to know what happened here?'

The carpet had been taken away and the walls cleaned, so that the only sign of the doctor's murder was a dark stain on the floorboards – a stain which could have been caused by anything. Still, Priudski knew this was the doctor's apartment and this was the hallway so he must know this was where the murder had been committed – he'd already told them as much in the study. And yet it seemed he didn't.

'Where are we exactly?' Priudski asked, speaking slowly, as if not wanting to commit himself.

'You're in an apartment building on Chistye Prudy,' Korolev said, casting a wary glance in Slivka's direction. Even if this might all be complete nonsense, it was important he persuade Slivka to play along, even if only temporarily – and for that he needed Priudski to play his part just a little better.

'Chistye Prudy?' Priudski scratched his head, dropping his gaze to the floor as if there might be a clue there – but Shtange's maid had done a good job of making sure that particular clue wasn't as obvious as it had been the day before.

'What did the doctor say to you when he opened the door?' Korolev asked, deciding to give him a clue. Fortunately the word 'doctor' seemed to have the desired effect.

'He didn't say anything at first,' the doorman said, looking to Blanter, who, Korolev noticed, gave him a small nod. 'He just looked at me as if I was dirt. But I wasn't having that – I'd come for my money and told him so. He said we were both going to a camp in Kolyma if I squealed, so why should he pay me anything. Then he threatened to kick me down the stairs. So I pulled out the knife and told him to pay me what I was owed, or else I'd go to Kolyma with him on my conscience. And what do you think he said to that?'

'Tell me,' Korolev said.

'He called me an old fool and told me I was too old to play with knives. So I lost my temper.' Priudski stopped, and did a passable imitation of regret. 'I didn't mean to kill him but – it just happened that way.'

The Shtange Priudski described bore little relationship to the Shtange Korolev had met but, then again, neither did this Priudski bear much relationship to the doorman he'd encountered just four days before. Either Zaitsev had Priudski's son in his care as well as Yuri, or something else was going on. Maybe the professor's research had been more successful than Dr Shtange had given him credit for.

'How many times did you stab him?'

'A great many. I was angry as hell. There was blood all over the place – that much I can tell you. All over the place.'

'What about you? Did you get covered in blood? When it was going all over the place?'

'A bit,' he replied, looking uncertain – as if he were trying to remember. 'I must have, mustn't I?'

'I would have thought so,' Korolev said in a neutral voice. 'Did you clean yourself up?'

'I did.' The doorman seemed uncertain once again. 'In the sink.'

'Come with me, Citizen Priudski.'

Korolev led the former doorman back into Shtange's study, where he placed a photograph of the dead man on the desk – Korolev saw no recognition in the doorman's face. And even though Blanter was glaring at him once again, Korolev couldn't help it. He had to ask questions – Slivka would expect him to.

'You recognize him, don't you?' Korolev asked and Priudski seemed to take the hint once again.

'It's Dr Shtange,' he said.

'Very good.' Korolev pulled photographs of the dead man's blood-drenched body from an envelope. He laid them on the desk one by one. Priudski picked up each one and examined it with a dreamy expression on his face, then placed it carefully back down, before beginning to touch a finger to each of the dead man's wounds, one after another.

'I stabbed him here, and here, and here . . .'

He spoke quietly, as if to himself.

'What kind of weapon did you use?'

'A knife, what else?' Priudski said, his finger still moving from wound to wound, his focus still on the photograph.

'And what did you do with it? This knife of yours?'

'I threw it into the Moskva – at night, off the bridge. Near where I work.'

Of course, by the time night had fallen on the day of Dr Shtange's murder, Priudski had already been picked up by Zaitsev's men. He wished they'd at least bothered to get his story to hang together a little bit better.

'Describe it to me.'

'It was a fold-out knife. I had it open in my pocket, ready, in case there was trouble. I knew the fellow had shot the professor dead so I came prepared.' Priudski began to touch the photograph once again. 'I stabbed him with it here, and here, and here.'

The way he spoke was disturbing. It was almost as if he'd really killed the man and he was lost in the memory of it. But that couldn't be, could it?

'How big was the knife? The blade, that is?'

Priudski hesitated then held his hands apart. No more than four inches.

'Did you have any other weapons with you?' Korolev asked.

'No, just the knife. I didn't need anything else.'

'Can you tell me about this mark here?' Korolev said, directing Priudski's attention to another photograph, this time of the left side of Shtange's face, and pointing to the scar that had been carved into the skin. Priudski examined it for a time before looking up to Blanter, as if for inspiration.

'After I'd killed him,' he said after a pause, 'I was still angry. So I sliced him up a bit. With the knife.'

'With the fold-out knife?'

It was interesting – whenever the fellow seemed to be in doubt, his first instinct was to look to Blanter. Korolev turned to the Chekist to see yet another small nod from him. The boxer seemed almost to be directing Priudski.

'Yes,' Priudski said.

The Chekist looked back at Korolev, less aggressive now, it seemed. Possibly because he was satisfied with Priudski's performance. Well, if he was, maybe Slivka would be too.

'Is that all?' Blanter asked and it occurred to Korolev that the interview might be the last thing keeping the Chekist from a long-awaited bed. Well, he'd have to wait a bit longer – Korolev was more concerned with what Slivka thought, at this moment in time, and Slivka looked troubled. He had to allow her to ask a question or two if she was to be persuaded to go along with Priudski's confession – even temporarily.

'I've no further questions, Comrade Blanter. You can take him away, as far as I'm concerned. Unless Sergeant Slivka has anything to ask him?'

Slivka looked up from her notebook with a quizzical look. 'How did you meet Dr Shtange?'

For a moment Priudski appeared uncertain, but then his expression changed, reminding Korolev of the secret pleasure a man gets when he picks up a winning hand of cards.

'He used to come round to visit the Azarovs – often. I didn't pay much attention to him until he approached me a few weeks ago. He waited for me outside the building.' The answer slipped off Priudski's tongue as smoothly as anything he'd said so far.

'The building?' Slivka asked.

'Leadership House. Where the Azarovs live. Where I work.'

That was enough, Korolev thought.

'Very good,' he said. 'We've no further questions, Comrade Blanter. Thank you for your assistance.'

Slivka looked at him in surprise, but he ignored her. Blanter looked content – which was something.

'Colonel Zaitsev wants it to be known that his cooperation can be absolutely relied upon. He told me to say that to you most specifically. And this is his telephone number – should you require any more of his cooperation.'

Blanter spoke slowly, almost ponderously – but the message was clear enough.

§

'What was all that about?' Slivka said when the two men had left. 'What did he mean by telling you that Zaitsev's cooperation could be relied upon?'

'Who knows?' Korolev said.

He reached his left hand into his pocket, found Yuri's pocket knife and closed his fingers around it. He sighed. The worst thing about life these days was that when things went wrong – when you were being sucked into the whirlpool – other people were sucked in with you, whether you liked it or not. He smiled at her, but suspected it was a poor effort.

'Well then, let's talk about Priudski. What did you make of him?'

'He was lying, wasn't he?' Slivka wasn't beating around the bush, but he hadn't expected her to.

'Certainly at the end – when he said Shtange had visited the Azarovs,' Korolev said, shrugging. 'But there could be an explanation for that.'

'An explanation?'

'Shock – killing someone can do that to people. I've seen it.'

She looked perplexed. 'You don't believe him, do you?'

'That's not what I said.' Korolev ran a hand over a neck that was already damp with sweat. The day was going to be another scorcher.

'But Madame Shtange said they disliked each other,' Slivka said. 'He and Azarov – they *never* met socially. It's in your notes of the conversation.'

'It is,' Korolev agreed, 'and Chestnova thought that there were two knives. One with a very large blade – eight to ten inches – and the other closer to a medical scalpel. Priudski said he used a single knife, which was shorter, to judge from how far he held his hands apart, and one which he seems to have disposed into the Moskva at night, when he should already have been in custody. What to make of that? I'm not sure.'

'And the man barely knew where he was – he didn't seem to even recognize the doctor when he looked at the photographs.'

'There are certainly questions that need answering – but Slivka, on the other hand, I've seen men react to terrible events in similar ways, back in the war. It's the fear, it wipes everything from their mind – he reminded me of them. Even the confusion – some of them were confused in just such a way. They can't remember things, so they make them up.'

He watched Slivka as he spoke. Unless he was mistaken, she was listening to his argument at least. That was good.

'And the first person the professor's wife blamed for his death was none other than Dr Shtange,' Korolev said, finishing up with what wasn't a bad point, even in these circumstances.

'Yes, she did.' Slivka seemed to be thinking it through. 'You think that's what it was? Some kind of shock? Perhaps he did have more than one knife – only he can't remember the second one?'

'It seems to me it might all just about hang together. Obviously we need to look into it properly.'

Korolev didn't lie often, well not this kind of lie – a lie to a friend – and he wasn't sure he was very good at it, but Slivka seemed to be giving him the benefit of the doubt. She looked at him uncertainly.

'I'll be honest, Chief, I'm not entirely convinced – but if you think we can make something of it, then I'm happy to try.'

'It looks a little improbable, but let's not be too cynical here. Let's not look too hard at the gift-horse's teeth.' Even though that was precisely what they were paid to do. 'It still has four legs and it might take us to where we want to go. Let's ask around and see if we can find anyone who saw him here or near here. Get the uniforms to show his smiling face around the locality. He came here by tram and went away by tram. Let's see if any of the conductors remember him.'

'You mean did anyone see a blood-drenched doorman making his way several miles across town on a tram?'

She paused, seeming to consider what she'd said, before she continued, apparently more receptive to the possibility.

'Of course, this is Moscow. People can be blind when it suits them.'

Korolev didn't like to say that that was because Muscovites were sensible people, by and large.

'Exactly,' he said. 'So ask around – I'll carry on with the other leads, but I want you to focus on this.'

What he meant, of course, was that he wanted her to stay safely away from the things he might or might not have to do to get both Yuri and himself out of this mess in one piece. Or as safely away as possible, anyway.

'All right,' she agreed and if she was still reluctant about Priudski's story, he appreciated the fact that she made some effort to hide it. 'I'll do it, but there's another matter we have to attend to in the meantime.'

'What?'

'Kolya. He'll meet us at Gorky Park. At two. On the embankment – there's a statue of a diver about two hundred metres along from the Krimsky Bridge.'

'I know it. Well done.'

'He'll find us,' Slivka said. 'We just go to the statue and walk on from there – he'll pick us up when he thinks it's safe.'

Korolev made a show of considering this, before shaking his head.

'No, Slivka, I'll see him on my own. You need to keep on at this.'

Slivka gave him a strange glance, and Korolev found it difficult to hold her gaze.

Chapter Thirty-Six

KOROLEV SAT AT Shtange's desk. Dubinkin would be walking through the door in a few minutes and he wanted to spend some time considering his situation before the Chekist arrived. Korolev's fury was still smouldering, but other emotions were making themselves felt now, not least of which was severe anxiety for Yuri's safety. If he allowed it to, he knew fear could slow him down, knew it was essential he kept moving forward on this most perilous of paths. To panic would be fatal for them both. All he could do was pray that the good Lord would preserve Yuri until he could, with luck, rescue him from the dangers the boy now faced.

At least Slivka had been dealt with, more or less. It had been unpleasant to lie to her and he'd been prepared for her to dig her heels in more. But instead she'd been surprisingly compliant – perhaps even suspiciously so. He considered that for a moment – no, she'd gone along with it because she trusted him. He'd have to explain the deception to her at some stage, no doubt, but he hoped she'd forgive him. If she didn't – well – that was just the way things would be. After all, he couldn't take any risks with this – the stakes were too high.

Korolev picked up a couple of the photographs of Priudski. They'd been taken in the last day or so. Korolev presumed they were the arrest photographs. One was taken from the side and in the other the doorman was looking straight at the camera.

The curious thing was, the Priudski who he'd spoken to only a few minutes ago looked quite different to the man who'd stood against a wall in some Chekist building to have his photograph taken. Korolev examined the face carefully. The old Priudski had a sly look about him – and a pursed, down-turned mouth, both of which, to Korolev's mind at least, had been signposts to the malevolence he'd detected when he'd first met him.

This morning, however, it had seemed to him that a lot of the doorman's character had been – well – smoothed from his face. His features seemed more or less the same, but his face was like one of those you might see in a newspaper – the ones that blurred the things you weren't meant to see. Korolev had seen Stalin at close quarters twice, and knew that the General Secretary's face was pitted with small-pox scars. It was a rare newspaper photograph that showed them, however. Korolev half-wondered whether something similar might be going on with Priudski, but how could that possibly be? Could Priudski's entire personality have been rubbed away by someone using Azarov's methods, whatever they were? Had they really managed to convince the doorman of his own guilt? Or had they some other hold over him?

He shook his head slowly. He was pretty sure Priudski hadn't killed Shtange, and it concerned him that his going along with Zaitsev's deception might result in the doorman's imprisonment or execution. He'd never framed an innocent man, or a guilty one for that matter – he'd always let the evidence take him where it needed to take him. And whoever he found at the other end of the trail was the guilty man and that was that. He was doing something damned close to framing Priudski here – but what choice did he have? None. Not at the moment at least. If things changed he'd do his best to get the fellow off the hook – but for now he was going to have to do his level best to convince everyone necessary that Priudski had perpetrated the most vicious of knife attacks, and that was that.

Which brought him back to Dubinkin. It was, of course, essential that the Chekist went along with the idea that Priudski's confession had some substance to it. And, unless Korolev was mistaken, it was in Dubinkin's interests as much as his that this case was put behind them speedily and efficiently. After all, Dubinkin wanted to get out of this business with his hide intact, just as he did – and this was as good a way as any. But there was also something that Zaitsev had let slip which made Korolev wonder if Dubinkin might not have another reason for agreeing to his version of events.

'Good morning, Korolev,' the Chekist said as he came into Shtange's study, interrupting Korolev's chain of thought. Which was just as well – sometimes thinking about things for too long made them seem more difficult than they were. All he had to do now was convince an intelligent, experienced Chekist that a lie was a truth. He wouldn't want that to seem any more difficult than it already was.

'You don't look happy, Korolev – but I hope you've had more success than I have. No Priudski, I'm afraid, but I do have the files of three residents of Leadership House that the late Professor Azarov felt obliged to bring to the attention of State Security. They make interesting reading.'

Dubinkin placed a pile of thick files on the desk. It looked like there were many more than three.

'Menchikov and Bramson we knew about. Let me guess, the third one is Weiss?' Korolev said, keeping his eyes steady on the Chekist.

'I'm impressed.'

'Slivka did some poking around over at the university.'

'I've another five from there and six more from the Azarov Institute.'

Dubinkin took the top five files from the stack and spread them out in a fan shape. These were the university 'traitors', Korolev presumed. He contemplated them for a moment before looking up at Dubinkin. The Chekist seemed to be waiting for him to speak, perhaps to congratulate him. Or was he anticipating something else?

'I've good news for you, Comrade Lieutenant,' Korolev said, picking the doorman's statement up from the table in front of him and passing it over to the Chekist. 'Priudski's shown up after all and, it seems, solved the murders for us at the same time.'

Dubinkin took the sheet of paper, reading through it quickly – his face a moving picture that went from surprise to what looked a lot like irritation. Korolev was persuaded – almost.

'Priudski?' the Chekist said, when he'd finished. 'Where did he appear from? I've had men going cell to cell in every damned prison in Moscow looking for him.'

Korolev filled him in on how the guilty man had been delivered in a nicely wrapped package with a pretty ribbon round it – a ribbon that had been tied by Colonel Zaitsev himself. When he'd finished, Dubinkin let out a long, low whistle. He seemed at a loss for words but after a moment he took Priudski's statement and walked to the window, reading it over once again. Korolev watched him as he did so, unsure if he'd correctly predicted the Chekist's reaction.

'This is extraordinary reading, Korolev,' Dubinkin said, returning to take a seat in front of the desk and pushing the statement towards him. 'I can see a few inconsistencies, however.'

'Which in particular?'

'Wasn't Shtange meant to have been at the institute at the time of Azarov's death?'

'We don't have the records for that – they've disappeared. We only have Shtange's word for it – who is dead – and that of the two guards – who have disappeared.'

'And the murder weapon? This only mentions a knife – it says nothing about a scalpel.'

'Yes,' Korolev said, 'but remember that the scalpel wound

was inconsistent with the others and inflicted after death. It could have been made by someone else. Or it could have been made by him – we think he may be in shock of some form. I've questioned him – and well – I don't think we can rule his story out straight away. It's a strange tale and I wouldn't have picked him as a killer, but then not many people set out to be murderers – it's more often a result of circumstances than character.'

'Very philosophical.'

'Perhaps. But we need to look into his story, one way or the other.'

'And you're not concerned that Colonel Zaitsev might have his own agenda?'

Korolev shrugged. 'I sat in this room not half an hour ago with a man who told me he killed Dr Shtange and conspired to kill Professor Azarov. It's my job to be sceptical, but it's also my job to investigate likely perpetrators. This fellow is a likely perpetrator.'

'And what will you tell Colonel Rodinov?'

'Exactly what I've told you. I didn't much like being followed around Moscow by Zaitsev's men, but maybe he had good reasons. It's not my job to second-guess State Security.'

Dubinkin considered this for a moment, seemingly amused at the idea that someone like Korolev should even contemplate such a possibility.

'No, that's true.'

'I've a question though. People have been telling us that Priudski might have been in close touch with State Security all along. Did you ever look for a file on him?'

Dubinkin shook his head before looking at Korolev suspiciously.

'You're sending me back to look for more files?'

'We need to find out everything we can about the fellow.' Korolev picked up the photograph of Priudski and slid it across the table. 'That's why Slivka and the uniforms are out showing his pretty face around the locality. And it's why I'm making my way over to Leadership House to see what else of his story I can confirm.'

'I can't wait to see the joy on the filing clerks' faces,' Dubinkin said drily as he rose.

'They'll forgive you, I'm sure,' Korolev said. 'But if things happened the way Priudski tells it, then it's a neat ending for us. That's what we want, isn't it?'

He wondered if he'd overplayed his hand for a moment, but Dubinkin, after a brief pause, nodded.

'Yes, Korolev,' Dubinkin said. 'That's exactly what we want.'

§

After Dubinkin left, Korolev walked over to the window and considered the Chekist. There were certainly other ways that Zaitsev could have known about Korolev's squeamishness – it was well known in Petrovka, he was sure, and most of the pathologists he dealt with knew he disliked the way they poked and sawed at dead citizens. But the coincidence of Zaitsev referring to his squeamishness the very day after Dubinkin had observed it made him wonder. Could Dubinkin, Rodinov's man, also be reporting to Zaitsev?

He saw the Chekist appear from the shadow of the building and wait for a tram to pass by – and then out of the shadows cast by the overhanging trees he noticed someone approaching Dubinkin, shaking hands with him. At first he couldn't be sure who it was, but he thought there was something familiar about the man. They discussed something briefly before going their separate ways.

Korolev let Dubinkin go about his business but kept his eye on the other one, hoping to get a clear view of him. The figure disappeared back into the trees and Korolev thought that was it

– that he'd missed him. Then, quite by chance, he caught the briefest of half-glimpses of the fellow through the branches.

He couldn't be absolutely certain, but it seemed to him it was none other than Svalov, the chubbier of Zaitsev's watchers.

'Well, well, well,' Korolev found himself muttering.

Chapter Thirty-Seven

THIRTY MINUTES later a pensive Korolev parked outside Leadership House and found Priudski's replacement, Timinov, standing at the entrance wearing a short-sleeved shirt, open at the neck, his face shaded by a flat cap. Korolev envied him, as he sweated, once again, under a gun-covering outer layer.

The doorman tipped the brim of his cap.

'Enjoying the weather, Comrade?' Korolev asked him, offering him a cigarette.

'We'll miss it in a few months, don't think we won't.' The doorman gave him a cheery smile.

'Listen,' Korolev said, lighting their cigarettes. 'That fellow Priudski – exactly when was he arrested again?'

'On Tuesday afternoon. At close to six.'

'I thought so. The thing is – I need to know if he was here all that day, before he was arrested.'

'I would think so – I can check.'

'Can you check in a quiet fashion?'

'The schedules are there for us all to see – nothing easier. Are you around for long?'

'An hour or so, maybe longer – I need to talk to one or two of the tenants.'

'I'll know by then.' He looked around, lowering his voice. 'And I've something to show you – it may be nothing, but you can be the judge.'

'No better time than now,' Korolev said and followed him to his office, where the doorman handed him a heavy-looking metal torch.

'You'll need this.'

'What for? To hit someone with?' Korolev asked, taking it from him and hefting it in his hand.

'No,' Timinov answered with an enigmatic air. 'You'll need it to see what isn't often seen.'

Korolev followed him, curious now, as they climbed the stairs to the sixth floor. Alongside the lift there was a small, almost invisible door, painted the same colour as the wall. Timinov opened it with a key from a large ring.

'What's this?'

'It's an access door to the lift shaft. Have a look.'

Korolev peered down into the dark shaft then upwards. What light there was came through the gaps between the lift doors on each floor – just enough to show thick cables running the height of the building. Beside the door, in a separate, much smaller space that ran alongside the main lift shaft, there was a narrow ladder.

'What am I looking for?' Korolev asked and, for an answer, Timinov put the torch into his hand.

Sighing, Korolev squeezed through the small door, took a firm hold of a ladder rung with his left hand and with his left foot sought out another, lower rung. His stomach felt hollow, but after he'd tested both rungs and was sure they were secure, he persuaded himself to swing his weight out. And there he was – suspended above a drop that was all the more worrying because of the darkness.

He turned the torch on, pointed it upwards and saw a similar door quite a way up and, on each floor in between, a series of grilles that were each about eighteen inches square. There was one just above his head – which meant they probably led into the ceiling spaces between each floor.

'What are those grilles? Some kind of ventilation system?'

'Correct, Comrade Captain,' said Timinov from the open door. For some reason they were both whispering.

Korolev took a deep breath and pointed his torch downwards, feeling a lurch of nausea as the beam revealed the drop to the bottom. Or *was* it the bottom? No, the cables dropped down to a series of heavy wheels, fixed to what must be the roof of the lift. He angled the torch so that it was directed at the fifth floor and saw that the small grille that marked the entrance to the ventilation system was standing slightly ajar.

'You see it?'

'I see it.' Korolev spoke grimly, realizing he'd have to go down and look at it.

'Think that's where your rats got in?'

'I wonder.'

He ducked back out onto the landing and took off his jacket. There was no point in ruining it. He slipped the torch into his trouser pocket and squeezed himself back into the tiny ladder space. It was tight and, not for the first time, he considered whether it might not be time to lose a few pounds. At least he could only fall to the left, he supposed – there was damn-all space in any other direction. He sighed, made a brief acknowledgement of the infinite power and holiness of the Lord above, and began to move downwards, lowering his entire weight with his arms, feeling for the next rung beneath him with both feet. If only Slivka were here – she was the right size for a job like this. Although if he found what he suspected he was going to find, then it was just as well she wasn't.

Rung by rung he descended – it was slow going and, despite his fear of heights, he found that all he could think about was his almost-new shirt and how hard shirts were to come by these days. Perhaps he should have taken it off altogether. If it was ruined he might never find another.

Now he could hear voices in the gloom – a couple were

arguing somewhere beneath him and, by the sound of it, someone on a floor above was shouting at a subordinate down the telephone, threatening the direst consequences if a delivery of piping wasn't made immediately. The ventilation system seemed to be funnelling the sounds of the apartments into the lift shaft.

Then he felt the top of the open grille under his foot. Good. He nudged it shut and carried on until he was just beneath it, reached for the torch and turned it on. There was a lock that should have held the grille shut – he examined it closely. There were small scratch marks around the mechanism and if it hadn't been picked, then he'd be very surprised. If this had been an ordinary investigation he'd have stopped at this point and had the forensics men take over. But this wasn't an ordinary investigation.

He opened the grille and pulled himself up till he was on the same level. The torch lit up a long square-shaped crawl space, off which more passages ran. If every floor was the same then, by the look of it, if you were small enough you could access any room in the building. There was a fair amount of dust, as you'd expect, but it had been heavily disturbed – and not by rats, or even mice. Well, well, well.

Korolev examined a small hand-shaped mark – an adult would be cramped in such a space, and this looked too small to have been made by a grown man or woman. Had children been scurrying around the ventilation system? But why had only this grille's lock been picked? Korolev considered what it might mean. One thing was for certain – it opened up new possibilities. It most certainly did.

Korolev lowered himself back down and pushed the grille shut above his head, then began the slow, hard work of dragging his body back up the ladder. He'd only gone up six rungs when there was a noise from beneath him. He stopped, unsure what it might be, and then heard the unmistakable bang and judder of a cable connecting to the weight of the lift below. It occurred to him in an instant that there was more of him than would fit inside the ladder's narrow shaft.

'The Lord have mercy upon me,' Korolev muttered over and over again as he began swinging himself up from rung to rung.

He caught a glimpse of Timinov's face above him and thought about shouting out to him, but he had to concentrate on damned well climbing because that damned lift was still coming.

The doorway was tantalizingly close now, but the lift catching up with him and it was travelling at remorseless speed. He wasn't going to make it. He looked down in horror as it glided upwards past his feet, past his knees. He tried to suck himself in but he was just too wide – and then the lift stopped. If he'd wanted to he could have leant down and touched the roof – it was only centimetres away from crushing him.

There was a moment of silence then he heard the lift doors open and Timinov speaking directly beneath him.

'Good morning, Comrade Shepkin. Which floor are you going to?'

'The eighth, of course,' a bad tempered voice answered. 'And why weren't you downstairs when I came in?'

But before the irritated resident had finished berating Timinov for his failure to keep the building secure only days after a 'serious murder' had been committed on the premises, Korolev had made it to the tiny door. He glanced down as he arrived, and was struck by the incongruous sight of three shrunken apple cores on the roof of the lift, almost invisible against its dark surface. He blinked, looked again to check he'd seen what he thought he had, and then swung himself through the tiny door, struggling for breath and dripping sweat.

He was still there, leaning against the wall, considering being sick and thinking better of it, when Timinov came up behind him.

'A close call,' the doorman whispered.

'Why didn't you just tell him I was in the damned lift shaft?' Korolev asked, moving from relief to irritation.

'Because the ventilation shafts are State Security business.'

§

There was a sink in the basement and Korolev allowed the doorman to lead him to it. He did his best to clean himself up with the towel Timinov provided, while listening to him whisper about the ventilation system.

'Can you say that again?'

It seemed his having nearly been crushed by a lift had affected his concentration. Korolev placed his face into the cool water he'd scooped up with both hands and savoured it, before letting it run through his fingers back into the sink.

'I was just telling you,' Timinov's whisper wasn't much louder than an exhaled breath, 'how, although you can't tell when you're in the apartments, there's room enough for a small man to crawl around right above you. And they do crawl. I've had to climb down to a few lifts that have got stuck between floors and I've seen things I wasn't meant to see. Devices.'

'Listening devices?' Korolev whispered back and immediately regretted it. Although the basement should be safe enough, shouldn't it? Or perhaps that was why he wasn't a Chekist – perhaps basements were the very place State Security would want to listen in on. Where better to overhear a whispered conspiracy?

'What else would they be for? One of the other men told me the building was built this way on purpose – that the plans were altered by the Chekists – and it's true they come here so often these days they should run a shuttle service. There's barely a week goes by that they don't arrest four or five of the residents.'

Korolev considered this for a moment. If the Chekists had

wanted Azarov out of the way, surely they'd more efficient methods than shooting him from the ventilation system – they could just have added him to the list of those who were to be arrested that week. Not that he'd had any indication they had wanted him out of the way. And how to account for the small hand-print? Certainly it seemed unlikely that State Security employed a pygmy assassin – but could it belong to a woman? If he were able to ask Ushakov to look at it, perhaps he'd be able to tell him something – but that would put Yuri at risk. In fact, this whole line of enquiry was putting Yuri at risk. On the other hand, if what Rodinov had said about him was right, then Zaitsev wasn't to be trusted when it came to Yuri's safety anyway. At least if he worked out who'd killed the scientists he'd have a bargaining chip – whether it would be worth anything was another question.

'You look troubled,' Timinov said.

'I'm thinking – it takes a lot out of me. I've a question though.'

'Ask me.'

'Who knows about the ventilation shafts – apart from the doormen?'

'Building management, and the men who come to fix the lifts when they stop working. Otherwise no one. The keys to the lift shaft are held in the building manager's office – I only got them today because I said someone had been complaining about mice in the ventilation shafts.'

Korolev wasn't so sure about that – in his experience humans tended to know their surroundings better than even they themselves suspected. And if someone had been in the ventilation shaft, it would explain why there'd been no gunpowder residue found on the professor. It would also explain how he'd been shot from such a high angle.

Korolev looked at his watch.

'How many ways into the lift shaft are there?'

'There are access doors on every other floor, five altogether, and there's a trap-door in the lift itself.'

'I'd like to have a look at them – the lock on the fifth-floor grille seems to have been picked, so maybe that's how they got in. If they had a key, then that points us in a different direction.'

'I see,' Timinov said, and Korolev wondered if he realized that the likely direction was towards State Security – because the doorman still looked quite cheerful.

'Is Comrade Madame Azarova in?' Korolev continued.

'I don't think so.'

'And her maid?'

'She went out an hour ago.'

'Can you get me into the apartment? I'd like to have a quick look at this ventilation space from the other side.'

'Of course,' Timinov said and gave him a conspiratorial smile.

It was strange, Korolev thought, how some people seemed to think playing at detective was an adventure, an amusing diversion from their daily existence. Well, if Timinov wanted to share in the excitement, why not let him?

'Another thing – there are three apple cores on the roof of the lift. Can you get them for me?'

Because nothing would persuade Korolev to step back inside that lift shaft himself.

Chapter Thirty-Eight

TEN MINUTES LATER, Korolev was standing outside Dr Weiss's apartment, three dusty apple cores in his pocket, and more than a few questions and scenarios buzzing around his head.

He was about to knock for a second time when the door was opened by a middle-aged woman in an apron, a mop in her hand and a bucket of soapy water beside her bare feet – her hair covered with a white cotton headscarf.

She seemed surprised to see him at first, then suspicious. Her eyes examined him from head to toe as she rolled something around in her mouth that might have been a ball of spit.

'I'm Korolev, from Moscow CID.'

The woman appeared to reconsider discharging whatever was in her mouth onto the ground in front of him – instead turning to shout back into the apartment.

'Mikhail Nikolayevich, there's another *Ment* at the door. What do you want me to do with him?'

She turned back to Korolev, making a small upward gesture with the mop that seemed to indicate she might have a suggestion of her own.

'Let the Comrade Militiaman in, Tasha. For the sake of kindness, let him in.'

The sound of approaching footsteps brought a tall, well-proportioned man to the door. He pushed a pair of reading glasses back onto his greying hair to examine Korolev more closely, squinting as he did so.

'I was expecting your colleague, Sergeant Slivka.'

'I'm Korolev. I'd like a few moments of your time, Dr Weiss – if you don't mind.'

'She mentioned you. Of course, come through to the sitting room.'

Weiss wasn't exactly good-looking – it appeared his nose had been punched flat once or twice – but he had the sort of benevolent confidence that Korolev suspected women found attractive. And if the clear blue eyes which were calmly appraising him were anything to go by, the fellow was clever too.

'I'll be mopping down the staircase then, Mikhail Nikolayevich,' Tasha growled. 'You shout if you need me. I'll be listening, don't you worry about that.'

She placed a hand on Korolev's arm to move him sideways, revealing a surprising strength, before picking up her bucket. She gave him a threatening look as she passed.

Korolev caught Weiss's small smile.

'Tasha's been with me a long time,' the doctor said, waving him along the short corridor. 'She can be a little – well – abrupt, but she's a loyal soul. A glass of tea? Or something else?'

Weiss picked up a toy aeroplane from an armchair and invited Korolev to sit down. Timinov was right, it *was* a big place.

'How many children do you have, Dr Weiss?'

Weiss looked down at the plane he was holding, smiled and placed it on a small table beside him.

'Ah – yes, the toy. Three – all boys. Eight, eleven and fourteen. They've gone to the park with my wife. I thought it would be better if we spoke without interruption. You know how boys can be – especially when it comes to matters such as this.'

Yes, Korolev thought, thinking that he also knew how wives

could be when an affair came to light during an investigation – not very happy, nine times out of ten.

'I know you spoke to Sergeant Slivka yesterday,' Korolev began, opening his notebook.

'I presumed you'd want to talk to me again, but may I ask what happened to you?'

Korolev looked down at his clothes. His trousers and shirt suggested he'd been – well – nearly killed in a lift shaft. On top of which, his face – well – the bruising probably didn't look any better than it had the day before.

'It goes with the job, I'm afraid.'

'I never knew it was such tough work.'

Korolev remembered the whirr of the cable as the lift came up towards him.

'Sometimes we find ourselves in unfortunate situations, but perhaps this week has been – exceptional.'

Korolev could feel the hair on the back of his neck quivering at the memory of the lift shaft. Anyway, enough of the pleasantries.

'I have to ask about Professor Azarov's wife. About your relationship with her.'

'You're very direct,' Weiss said.

'I don't have time to be otherwise.'

'No, I'm sure you don't.' Weiss rested his hands on his knees and nodded, perhaps to himself. 'I suspect some kind soul has told you that I'm having an affair with Irina Azarova? Is that the case?'

Korolev nodded.

'Then let me try and be just as direct in turn, Comrade Captain. The rumour's true. Unless I'm wrong, your next question will be where I was on the morning of the murder.'

'If you ever want to change professions,' Korolev said drily, 'you can always try mine.'

Weiss smiled and pointed to a sheet of paper that was lying on a low table beside Korolev's chair.

'That tells you where I was and who I was with. When you read it, you'll understand why I couldn't be more frank with Sergeant Slivka.'

The letter was brief and to the point and, curiously, addressed to Captain A.D. Korolev, 38 Petrovka Street. When he'd finished it, Korolev decided he'd have been happier if it had been addressed to someone else. He found himself trying to swallow on a dry mouth and, as a result, making a strange sound not dissimilar to the beginnings of a death rattle.

'You were in a meeting with the General Secretary? Himself?'

Four people had attended the meeting. Two of them were from the Ministry of Health – a man and a woman he'd never heard of. Dr Weiss had been the third, and the fourth was a man he knew all too well, seeing as he was the General Secretary of the Central Committee of the Communist Party of the Soviet Union.

'Comrade Stalin values my advice from time to time,' Weiss explained.

Honestly, Korolev thought to himself, he should move to a different city – some place where people couldn't possibly have meetings with people like Stalin or be connected with State Security or have mysterious benefactors who could land them apartments as big as a metro station. Omsk, perhaps.

'The meeting was from ten until twelve,' Weiss continued. 'Before that I was, as the letter says, waiting. I was waiting from eight o'clock that morning. So I couldn't possibly have had anything to do with the professor's murder.'

As Dr Weiss was pleased to point out, by the time he'd returned from advising the General Secretary on the need for a new children's hospital in Moscow, Belinsky's Militiamen had been on the scene, trying to calm a distraught Irina Azarova. He'd stepped in to assist – as any good physician would.

'I'm sorry I couldn't be more frank yesterday. But it's best to be careful with such a personage.'

'Of course,' Korolev said, wondering where he went with an interview that seemed to have ended before it had begun.

'You wanted to ask me about my relationship with Irina?'

Korolev felt his cheeks redden from a mixture of embarrassment and irritation. This Weiss fellow was making fun of him now.

'Yes.'

'We've known each other for a long time – since we were children. Her mother and mine grew up beside each other on Bolshaya Sadovaya Street, so they were very old friends as well. The family came to live with us during the German War while her father was at the front. I've always been very fond of her – and so has my wife. She knows about Irina, incidentally. That's not the reason why she isn't here, in case you're wondering. I told her when it started.'

Korolev felt disbelief manifesting itself on his face.

'We have that kind of marriage, Korolev,' Weiss said, picking up the toy aeroplane once again and turning it over in his hand absent-mindedly.

'It's unusual, that kind of marriage.'

'You think so? All we are is honest with each other.'

'Your lover wasn't quite so honest when I asked her about her relationship with her husband.'

'But you see, even when we were lovers – and no, we no longer are – I had the sensation she never fully admitted to herself what we were doing. It was a strange feeling – as if the Irina who I spent time with was a completely separate person. It was as if she had a public persona and then a private one – the one I saw when we were together. Although perhaps that isn't so unusual these days. I can tell you that, on many levels, Irina was always loyal to Azarov – to a fault, in my opinion. I know she didn't approve of certain of his actions – but she believed in him. And when, in recent months, she began to uncover some unpleasant truths about her husband, I think that, rather than blaming him, she blamed herself. Her grief isn't feigned, that much I can tell you. She loved him deeply. Much more than he deserved, in my opinion.'

'And you as well?'

'Perhaps – these things happen. Love never follows a predictable path. The heart isn't an organ that has the capacity for logic.' Weiss smiled, and Korolev could have sworn it was with satisfaction at his own nicely turned phrase.

'What was your personal opinion of the professor, if you don't mind?' Korolev asked.

'I thought he was a bully and a braggart.' Weiss's eyes were less kindly than they had been. Much less kindly.

'His area isn't something I have great expertise in, but colleagues who know better than me had reservations. Serious reservations, which they were careful to keep to themselves – because he had considerable support in certain circles.'

'So I hear,' Korolev said, wondering if 'certain circles' was a euphemism for State Security that he hadn't heard before.

'Azarov used that support to his advantage, of course. People say that Irina was as bad as he was – that husband and wife were the same Satan – but it wasn't like that. She was a loyal, dedicated follower. She followed Azarov the same way she follows the Party. She didn't question, she obeyed. Even when she had to hold her nose.'

Korolev found the comparison of Azarov to the Party worrying, particularly as he now knew that the walls of the building were riddled with secret tunnels in which listening devices lurked as well as, possibly, diminutive killers. But Weiss was oblivious to his reaction, moving on to tell Korolev how Azarov had denounced him – and how, with the way things were these days, he'd thought things would go badly. And they probably would have, if Shtange hadn't intervened.

Korolev was surprised.

'If you don't mind my saying, Comrade Weiss. I'd have thought you'd have been secure against such criticism – being an adviser to – well – to *him*.' Korolev nodded in the general direction of the Kremlin.

Weiss smiled but it wasn't a smile with much joy in it.

'I work with senior people, but that can be a problem in itself these days. Such people might think that my being denounced reflects on them – support is therefore the last thing I could expect. No, the fact is I was out on a limb and Shtange's intervention was remarkably brave. Believe me, Korolev, it may not be like this within the Militia – but elsewhere people are like starving wolves – always searching for the weakest to hunt, always trying to show *they* aren't the weakest. I sometimes wonder where it will end, or even if it can end. It has taken on a momentum of its own.'

'Did you know Shtange well?' Korolev asked, finding himself casting a nervous glance at the ventilation grilles.

'Beforehand?' Weiss seemed to consider his answer for a moment or two. 'No, I barely knew him. I'd met him at faculty meetings, knew of him professionally, of course, but not much socially. Of course, he was a person of some importance amongst the students. Even before he came to Moscow, he was known to them through his work with the university flying club in Leningrad – he organized joint exercises, not just in flying but other activities as well. He was much respected and admired for it. He never usually intervened in Works Meetings; he'd only recently joined us, after all, so when he did so on my behalf, I think everyone took note – and the students were inclined to support him. And perhaps most of the Party activists knew what Azarov was up to by then. Not all of them are blind to that sort of thing.'

Weiss smiled at Korolev's reaction – but it was unusual to hear someone even implicitly criticize Party activists these days. A fellow could be excused a raised eyebrow.

'Do you know why Azarov denounced you?'

'I suspect he must have heard the same story you did – about Irina. I can't think of any other reason. Shtange told me afterwards that our affair was often hinted at in the medical faculty – I think it was one of the reasons he decided to intervene. I can only imagine how the rumour started – people draw conclusions from the smallest things. So someone drew a conclusion and then someone, maybe even that same someone, must have told Azarov. Shtange saw the Works Meeting being used to settle a personal score and said as much. The fact that he didn't like Azarov one little bit probably influenced him as well.'

'Did he dislike him enough to kill him?' Korolev asked.

'No, absolutely not. Shtange was less than impressed with him and his institute but he'd never have killed the man.'

'He told you that? About the institute?'

'He knew I had advisory responsibilities at the Ministry of Health, particularly in relation to Moscow. He'd reservations about the way the institute approached its research and the plausibility of some of its aims. He wondered whether action shouldn't be taken.' Weiss spoke carefully, as if weighing each word. And given his surprising openness up until this point, Korolev wondered why the doctor had suddenly had a change of heart.

'Did he give details?'

'Yes, but – well – it was State Security business. I knew nothing could be done, except at the highest level.' He pointed a finger at the ceiling, and Korolev wasn't sure whether he was referring to God, Stalin, the devices in the ventilation system – or perhaps just the person who lived upstairs. It was that kind of building.

They sat there for a moment, looking at each other. Both of them, Korolev suspected, uncomfortable with the direction the conversation had taken. Korolev prayed it wasn't being listened to.

Weiss sighed. 'Look, Korolev, the fact is there are too many scientists taking short cuts these days. It's one of the problems with Five Year Plans – science doesn't develop according to a strict schedule or a set objective. It meanders along, finds its own path. It helps if you think you know where you're going, but sometimes it's what you see on the way that turns out to be the key that unlocks the door to an important discovery. And what you thought you were looking for turns out to be irrelevant, as often as not. Science is full of happy accidents. As for what was being researched at the institute – if what I've heard is true, I doubt it's possible, or desirable.'

'I'd treat any information you gave me with complete discretion,' Korolev said, more in hope than expectation.

Weiss gave a short laugh – not one of amusement.

'Discretion? For all my talk, I know the limits of discretion these days, particularly when matters such as this are concerned. Still, I'd like to help.'

Weiss seemed to consider how this might be done, and Korolev had to restrain himself from pressing him.

'The thing is,' Weiss said eventually, 'you never know these days whether certain information is dangerous to disclose, or whether it's perfectly safe to do so. I'm not just talking about myself, of course, but my family. And others as well. Then there's the institute itself. Vasin, a fellow who worked in the office next to mine at the university until a few months back, also worked at Azarov's institute. But then you see he was arrested, and I didn't ask why; no one does these days. Shtange worked there and he's dead. Azarov himself is dead. So all that doesn't reassure me. And who is to say that any information I have, or any suggestion I've heard, is true. Even if it were, the Party takes a wider view of these things than I can – rightly so.

May I consider this for a little while, discuss it with someone I trust, and – how can I put it – review what I may or may not know, and the information I may or may not have? I want to be cooperative. I feel it's my duty to be cooperative, but I can't rush into this. I have responsibilities to others – you know the way things are.'

He picked up the toy plane again and Korolev knew what he meant by 'responsibilities'. If Korolev was in his shoes he'd have the same misgivings about passing on sensitive information concerning the institute. But Korolev had his own responsibilities. He might not be able to force Weiss, but he could at least remind him of his obligation to the dead man.

'I'd be grateful if you could have your discussions as soon as possible,' he said. 'Dr Shtange helped you out of a tight spot. I think you should remember that.'

Chapter Thirty-Nine

THE FORMER Ivanovsky Convent had been a place of religious worship for several centuries before it had become home to the Moscow Militia's Central Forensics and Technical Department. The bookcases and filing cabinets that surrounded the desks where Sergei Ushakov and his team worked were weighed down with microscopes, piles of reference manuals, mysterious machines with foreign lettering that ticked ominously, plaster casts of various dimensions, boxes, bags, and the Lord alone knew what else — but behind the shelving and the drawers and their multifarious contents, a very different world was represented in the murals that adorned the walls. Here, small scurrying figures ran either towards salvation, or from damnation, while angels watched calmly from the sky. Over there an ancient city was surrounded by high walls from which mail-coated soldiers stared out at a white-flecked sea. What were they waiting for, Korolev wondered. If his mother had still been alive and standing there beside him, she could have told him — no doubt of it. Most likely she'd also have been able to put a name to each of the bearded saints, one alongside another, row upon row of them, their haloed heads stretching up to the domed ceiling.

'I wonder why they never repainted this place?' Korolev asked, surprised the decoration had lasted the twenty years since the Revolution.

'Culturally significant, so they said. We had to ask permission to put electric lighting in.' Ushakov pointed to the three large lights that dangled from the ceiling. 'The electricians had to be watched over by some art historian. I can't remember who painted it all, someone who knew what they were doing, no doubt.'

Korolev nodded, feeling comforted by the hundreds of sympathetic eyes gazing down at him, following his every movement. Fearing for his eternal soul, most likely.

'You got my message?' Ushakov said, and Korolev saw that his expression was unusually grave.

They were the only two in the room and Korolev had the sense that this was deliberate on Ushakov's part. He took a seat.

'Yes, the new doorman at Leadership House passed it on. Here, I have some fingerprints I need you to look at for me. If you lifted them from Shtange's apartment, then we have a winner. At least for Dr Shtange.'

Ushakov took the fingerprint card Zaitsev had provided and read the name.

'Priudski? That fellow who was hanging around the professor's place? He's in NKVD custody?'

'It seems so.'

'I see. We had these already, you know.'

'State Security were kind enough to give me a copy to pass on again, just in case.'

'That's kind of them, I have a few things for you, as well,' Ushakov said, but Korolev hadn't finished. He pulled out Chestnova's small receptacle, with the bullet rattling inside it, and the brown paper bag containing the three apple cores.

'This is the bullet Chestnova pulled from Azarov's head,' he said, handing it over.

'Is it, now?' Ushakov took it from him and unscrewed the lid. Then he pulled a small set of weighing scales across the desk and decanted the bullet onto a small brass plate before adding tiny weights to the other side.

'It's an unusual bullet. We don't produce ammunition like it in the Soviet Union – but your Sergeant Belinsky sent over the firearms certificates they had in their files for the building yesterday. One of the guns is a match – an up-and-under Derringer, owned by one A.A. Bramson. Two barrels – two shots.'

'Bramson? A Bramson lived in Azarov's apartment?'

'A coincidence, isn't it?'

More than a coincidence, thought Korolev, given that Azarov had apparently denounced the former occupant in order to obtain the apartment. But Bramson and his wife had been arrested over a year before.

Ushakov picked up the firearms certificate from a small pile of papers and passed it to Korolev.

'A Derringer isn't much good at a shooting range – its muzzle velocity is less than half of a Nagant's, for example. Also these bullets most probably were manufactured before the Revolution – or maybe even before the German War. That's why such a large-calibre bullet barely dented the table.'

'Yes, Chestnova said she was surprised by how little damage the bullet did. Inside his head, that is.'

'It will kill a man if it hits him in the right place from close up – which, of course, Professor Azarov is proof of.'

Korolev considered the evil-looking piece of lead, small enough to get lost in a man's pocket, but not it seemed in his head.

'The low velocity – might it also explain the miss?'

'It might do. These guns aren't completely inaccurate at short range – and the killer can't have been more than a few feet away, given the size of the room; but, as I said, it's not a precision weapon. Of course, I can't be certain the weapon was

Bramson's Derringer, but it's the only gun we know of connected to the building that takes bullets of this size.'

'I'm sure it's the gun – it has to be. But Bramson was arrested by State Security – his wife as well. I'd have thought any weapon they'd owned would have been confiscated. If it wasn't, however – perhaps it came into Azarov's possession. Priudski's fingerprints come with a confession, you see.' Korolev paused, collecting himself – remembering the script he had to keep to. 'It indicates Shtange was the killer – perhaps he took the Derringer from Azarov and then used it on him.'

Ushakov gave him a quick glance and Korolev wondered, for the briefest of moments, whether the forensics man had spotted his scepticism about the Shtange story.

'I can't tell you anything more without the gun itself, Korolev – that's the fact of the matter. If you find it, I might be able to tell you something else – certainly I could tell you whether the bullet came from that gun. Might Shtange have hidden it somewhere?'

'Maybe,' Korolev said, while his mind focused, not for the first time that day, on whoever had been in the cramped ventilation space, one of the grilles to which had been at the precise angle that the bullet must have come from. That same grille, it had emerged when he'd examined it in Azarov's apartment, had been unscrewed at some stage from the professor's side, so that it could easily be opened from within the ventilation space. Korolev indicated the paper bag.

'What do you make of those?'

Ushakov opened the bag. 'I make of it three former apples, mostly consumed. Should I make anything else of them?'

'I found them in a place the professor's murderer may or may not have been hiding. Therefore I think these apples may or may not have been eaten by the killer.'

Ushakov picked up one of the apples by its stem.

'I can't even tell you what size it was for certain, Korolev. Maybe if I knew exactly where it was found and could recreate the environment over a long enough period and had a sufficient number of different-sized apple cores, each eaten in exactly the same way, then I could tell. Maybe. If not, at least I'd have eaten a lot of apples.'

Korolev took the core from Ushakov and returned it to the bag, sighing. Then he tossed it into the nearby bin.

'I'm sorry, Korolev.'

'I thought it was a long shot.'

Ushakov pulled a glass box down from a shelf.

'I have something else however. Levschinsky spent a happy couple of hours putting this little work of art together for you.'

'What the hell is it?' Korolev asked, playing along – he had a good idea what it was.

'Your Dr Shtange's floor. This is the carpet, these the floor-boards.' He indicated the layers of fabric and wood. 'The blood goes through the gap between the boards, of course. Then there's a layer of dust and rubble. Then the plaster ceiling. We cut that from the flat below so it's probably accurate enough. Strangely the neighbour was quite keen to get rid of that part of his ceiling, and the building management committee was happy enough to arrange its replacement.'

The layers were balanced on a wooden frame that matched the distances between them. Much of the construction was caked with a dark-red, almost black crust.

'It's not something he can be too precise on, but he reckons a minimum of thirty minutes for the blood to go through. If anything, the summer heat would have made it take longer.'

Korolev leant down to look more closely and, as he did so, caught a whiff of the caked blood that made him think better of the idea.

'That reduces the timings for us, thank you,' he managed to

say, his stomach rolling as he straightened. Ushakov glanced up at him.

'Yes, it's beginning to get a bit pungent, isn't it?'

'A little.'

'Pig's blood. Well, it's going into the incinerator in about five minutes' time, unless you want me to keep it.'

Korolev shook his head.

Ushakov smiled and returned the glass box to the shelf, then opened a small wooden box with brass corner fittings – inside was a rack of sample slides.

'As it happens, we came across something else interesting about the blood – not the stuff on the carpet, but where the murderer cleaned themselves – in the sink in the kitchen. We took some samples and not all the blood there was Shtange's. Not, at least, unless he was a miracle of modern medicine and possessed two different blood groups.'

Korolev looked at the slide Ushakov was holding towards him. 'I'll take your word for it,' he said. 'Tricky things, knives, particularly when you're stabbing someone and there's blood all over the handle. Easy to lose your grip and cut yourself.'

'Indeed. Find me the knife, of course . . .'

'And you could tell me more?'

'Yes, and if you have a suspect – I might be able to tell you something more again.'

Ushakov's demeanour had been becoming increasingly serious as the conversation had progressed, and now it was close to funereal. He opened a drawer in his desk to remove from it a thick brown envelope. He put it on the table top and tapped it, as though considering something.

'You said you thought Dr Shtange may have had something to do with the professor's murder?'

'It seems that way.'

'But you're not sure?'

'There are some inconsistencies.' Korolev chose his words

carefully. 'But it seems the story isn't impossible. The doorman, Priudski, let Shtange into the apartment, it seems.'

'That's interesting – because we've got one of Priudski's fingerprints in Azarov's study. On the door handle.'

Korolev shook his head sadly. 'There's an explanation, I'm afraid – he was in the apartment when the Militia arrived. The maid called him up.'

'We didn't think to check if Priudski had been in Shtange's apartment, of course.'

'Why would you?'

Ushakov tapped the envelope once again and Korolev wondered what the hell was in it.

'I can tell you half of Moscow had trundled in and out of that place by the time we got there. I'm presuming the blood in the sink belongs to the murderer, but who knows what our colleagues got up to in there over two whole days?'

'Nothing untoward, I'm sure,' Korolev said when the momentary pause lengthened.

'Of course not,' Ushakov said quickly.

'And the maid mentioned the blood in the sink,' Korolev said. 'I'm sure it's as you say.'

Ushakov finally picked up the envelope again, and sighed.

'Well, we had better luck with the crime scene in Professor Azarov's study. We picked up prints for the maid, the wife, the professor and this Priudski fellow. And one other person's.'

'Go on,' Korolev said, taking the envelope that was now offered to him and looking inside. There was a blood-browned document – about fifty pages thick, he guessed.

'I've written everything up for you, Korolev – but I've left this bit out. It's the document the professor was reading at the time he was shot.'

'I remember it now,' Korolev said. 'I'd forgotten we had it. I think I'd presumed our colleagues would have taken it.'

'I suspect it was an oversight on their part. And you're not the only one who forgot about it. I'd put it in a box in our freezer – blood doesn't do well in this kind of heat, as you know. I only came across it this morning.'

'So no one else knows about it?'

'I don't think so. It's not on the evidence list. And I won't be putting it on it either.'

'Not in the report, not on the evidence list. Why?' Korolev asked, although he'd a hunch he knew the answer.

'If those Chekists took every piece of paper from the dead men's apartments to look for something, I think this might have been what they were looking for.'

'You read it.'

'Enough of it to know I didn't want to read any more, or have it in my possession.'

Korolev sighed. 'And the other person's fingerprints? Shtange's?'

Ushakov nodded. 'All over it.'

Korolev pulled out the document and flicked through the pages that weren't stuck together very quickly. The briefest of glances was enough to tell him it was Shtange's report. And by the time he'd reached the end, he could see it was damning. A report that would have finished Azarov's career for certain. As for anyone else's – that would be something he'd see about later.

'So,' Ushakov said, scratching at his beard with his thumbnail. 'What do we do with this?'

'You do nothing,' Korolev said, putting the report back into its envelope. 'As far as you're concerned this never existed.'

Ushakov managed a weak smile. 'That's what I hoped you'd say.'

'I've something to ask you in exchange though.'

'Ask.'

'I need a positive finding for those fingerprints. I suspect they're there anyway.'

Ushakov paused for an instant, then nodded.

'And this gun certificate?' Korolev said, picking it up. 'You might want to rewrite your report – this Derringer never existed as far as you're concerned, and you certainly never made any connection between it and the bullet. For both our sakes. Things might change but, for the moment, the Shtange–Priudski story is the one that happened.'

Ushakov sighed and Korolev could have sworn he looked ten years older than when he'd first come into the room.

'I understand.'

Chapter Forty

IT WASN'T JUST the heat that made Korolev sweat as he walked to the car – it was also the presence of the envelope hidden under his jacket. He hadn't seen any of Zaitsev's goons since Dubinkin's encounter with Svalov in the park – but that didn't mean they weren't there. Yesterday they'd been open about following him, but today they might have decided to be invisible, and Korolev had tailed enough people to know if the job was done well he wouldn't spot them until it was too late. With that in mind, the report felt like a ticking bomb; he needed to put it somewhere safe – fast.

It was only when he had the car moving that he allowed himself to take a quick look in the mirror. No one was visibly following him and the street seemed empty enough. He should have been reassured – but instead he felt as though an invisible band were tightening around his chest, making each breath a battle. He found himself moving his shoulders, trying to shake some of the tension from them, trying to breathe more slowly as he did so, remembering that Yuri's life was at stake. It wasn't often that anger calmed him, but today seemed to be the exception.

As he drove, he ran over the events of the previous week, trying to put everything in its right place and to make sense of it all. A pattern was forming, most certainly. Of course, a few pieces of the puzzle were still missing, but the shape of the thing was becoming clear. And when, or rather if, he came up with the full picture, his guess was he'd know which of the two colonels was most likely to provide him and Yuri with a way out of this mess.

§

He parked at the back of Shtange's building. He hadn't bothered to look at this man Bramson's file earlier, but he needed to now. And he wanted to see if he could find a safe place to leave the report while he was at it.

'Comrade Captain,' Kuznetsky said, when he opened the door to Shtange's apartment.

'Is Sergeant Slivka here?'

'She called in half an hour ago – she's been at the tram depot talking to drivers. To see if anyone had come across that Priudski fellow.'

Korolev handed him the keys to the car. 'Go and find her – I need to talk to her. Take the car. I parked it around the back.'

'At your command, Comrade Captain.' The Militiaman hesitated.

'Well?' A thought occurred to Korolev. 'You can't drive?'

'No, Comrade Captain, I can drive all right. I just thought you'd want to know, the doctor's wife came with some French gentlemen – not long after you left. They took most of the doctor's belongings away with them. Lieutenant Dubinkin said it was all right, but I thought I'd tell you anyway.'

'Everything?'

'There wasn't much. His books were already gone, of course, but she took what was left – they'd a car. The Comrade Lieutenant said the books were currently under investigation by another department, but that he'd put in a request for her. She wasn't happy about that, I can tell you. Also there was a coat of hers missing. She wasn't happy about that either.'

'A coat?' Korolev said, curious. 'Did she say what kind of coat?'

Kuznetsky took his notebook out of his pocket. 'I made a note. A long black overcoat. French. Large padded shoulders. Four buttons. Why would they only pad the shoulders? You'd get no warmth from padded shoulders on their own.'

'Decadent capitalist fashion, Kuznetsky. Not something that should bother the likes of us. What was Comrade Dubinkin doing here? I thought he'd gone about some business for us.'

He was supposed to be at the Lubyanka, as it happened, searching out Priudski's file.

'He came back about ten minutes after you left. He was looking through the files.'

Which he was entitled to do – but why? What had he been looking for?

'Thank you, Kuznetsky,' Korolev said, expecting him to leave, but the Militiaman showed no inclination to do so.

'Something else as well?'

'That thing you asked me to do, Comrade Captain.'

Korolev had almost forgotten that earlier he'd asked Kuznetsky to talk to the local telephone switchboard and the one for Leadership House.

'I remember – the telephone exchanges.'

'I'd a bit of trouble there, I have to tell you. So, in the end – well – I had to pretend to be someone I wasn't.'

The Militiaman looked remorseful, guilty and frightened all at the same time.

'Someone you shouldn't have?'

'I don't know what came over me, Comrade Captain.'

'You pretended to be me?'

'No, Comrade Captain. Worse still.'

Perhaps it was his nerves, but the logical answer left him trying to suppress appalled hilarity.

'Not Dubinkin?'

Kuznetsky nodded, his head dropping.

'Anyway, the thing is, Comrade Captain, both Dr Shtange's number and Professor Azarov's are restricted – as in, not all operators are permitted to connect them and there's a procedure when they do. If I hadn't pretended to be the Comrade Lieutenant then how would I have found out what calls they'd made?'

'You could have asked him to make the call himself.'

This seemed to be something Kuznetsky hadn't considered – he put a hand to his forehead as if he'd been struck. Korolev felt like shaking him – this was the last thing he wanted to deal with on this of all days.

'What do you think the Comrade Lieutenant would make of you pretending to be him?'

'I think he wouldn't be happy,' Kuznetsky said, his face looking as if it had been whitewashed.

Korolev forced himself to relax. 'I suspect you're right. So we'd best forget about this little enquiry of yours then – people might misconstrue your intentions. Understood?'

'Yes, Comrade Captain.'

'But Kuznetsky, before we forget completely, who did they call?'

Kuznetsky swallowed and his eyes managed to focus on Korolev. He took his notebook from his pocket.

'Professor Azarov made two calls on the morning of his death. The first to a Colonel Zaitsev at the Lubyanka just after nine o'clock and a second to the Bersenevka Militia Station at 11.05.'

The second phone call would have been Galina Matkina calling to report the professor's murder. As for the first, Korolev opened his mouth to say something and then thought better of it. There were times when it was best to think carefully before you said or did anything and this was one of them.

'Also, someone telephoned Dr Shtange from the Azarov apartment on Tuesday morning – at eight o'clock.'

Korolev decided not to say anything about this piece of information either. Colonel Zaitsev and his men were still investigating the Azarov murder at that stage, but they'd left the apartment by then, hadn't they? Or had they?

'What about Priudski's phone?'

'Four outgoing calls to the same number at a quarter past eleven, a quarter past twelve, at twenty to two and at three-thirty. Also a call to Petrovka at half past one.'

Korolev had made the 1.30 call – to talk to Popov.

'Do we know whose number the other one is?'

Kuznetsky's misery seemed to deepen. 'I called the number and asked who it belonged to, but they told me to mind my own business.'

'Did you say who you were?'

'No. But they'll only have to call the operator to find out where the call came from.'

'I see. The Comrade Lieutenant's friends, do you think?'

Kuznetsky really did look as if he were having the worst of days.

'Kuznetsky, we'll keep quiet about this. If it blows up, which I don't think it will – well, I asked you to make the calls and I'll square it with the powers that be, all right? As it happens, this is very useful information. Just keep quiet about it for the present.'

'Of course, Comrade Captain.'

Kuznetsky looked relieved. He tore the pages from his notebook and handed them to him.

'You asked about calls from this number as well.' Kuznetsky nodded to the telephone on Shtange's desk.

'Go on.'

'Two – one to the doctor's wife in Leningrad on Monday evening and one to the Commissariat for Health on Monday afternoon.'

Nothing odd there at least.

'Thanks, Kuznetsky. Now, go and find Slivka.'

Korolev followed the youngster to the door, thinking about the professor's call to Zaitsev and wondering what might have been said in it. As for Priudski's calls – they'd no doubt been to his NKVD handler, whoever that was. Maybe he'd worked for Zaitsev's Twelfth Department – which would explain Korolev's reception at the institute, as well as the colonel's showing up at Azarov's apartment later that afternoon.

§

When Kuznetsky had left, Korolev locked the apartment's newly repaired door, took the report from under his arm and walked through to the study. He sat down at Shtange's desk and placed the envelope in front of him. He looked at it for a moment, reached forward to open it, then paused, pushed back his chair and pulled out the bottom drawer of the desk. There was a cavity beneath it. It would do. Temporarily at least.

Satisfied he had somewhere to hide the document quickly if needed, he slipped the report out of the envelope and ran his finger along its edge – some of the blood-browned pages were stuck together and couldn't be unstuck, at least not without ripping them, but they were relatively few – and mainly at the beginning, where it seemed Dr Shtange had written an introduction. The name of the person to whom that introduction was addressed was obscured, but it was someone familiar with the institute – 'as you indicated', 'as you are aware' . . . It seemed clear from its blunt findings that the report had never been intended for general circulation.

The report was divided into four parts. The first section concerned the scientific basis of the research being undertaken by the institute and, to judge by the notes in the margin, Azarov had taken exception to many of the points made. The next was entitled 'Procedural Failures and Inconsistencies' and Azarov had scribbled on much of this as well. The third part, by far the shortest, was entitled 'Ethical Considerations', while the fourth and last of the main sections covered 'Financial Irregularities'.

Finally there was a brief conclusion. In Shtange's opinion, Korolev read, Azarov should be replaced and the institute's research restricted to the few areas where progress was achievable – and even then a complete overhaul of the research methodology would be necessary. It seemed Shtange considered that nearly all the work done up until this point had been an expensive waste of time.

Korolev turned back to the beginning and began to discover exactly what the institute had been up to. Telepathy, it seemed, had indeed been one area of research – although Shtange considered that there was no scientific basis for it and the results, so far, had produced nothing to change his mind. Korolev was curious as to what 're-education and mental manipulation of enemies' might be, and discovered the aim was to scrub enemies' minds of counter-revolutionary bias and to replace it with pro-Soviet thinking. Shtange set out the means by which Azarov had attempted to cleanse the subjects' minds and it was a disturbing list – surgery, electricity, a surprising variety of drugs, sensory deprivation, fear – the list went on and on.

Some of Shtange's summaries set Korolev's hair on end:

Surgery has certainly succeeded in erasing counter-revolutionary thinking, but only by erasing all mental processes permanently. In other cases, surgical intervention left subjects physically or mentally incapacitated – sometimes both. On several occasions surgical experimentation has resulted in the death of the subject on the operating table. There is no evidence that any of the professor's surgical techniques have resulted in material progress, despite claims to the contrary.

Electrical treatment had been more effective in Shtange's view – 'Subjects' memories have been erased, along with preconceptions of behaviour and thought, when repeated high-voltage electrical shocks to the cortex have been administered for sustained periods.' The problem was putting the correct thinking back in, it seemed, and Shtange recommended this as one of the few areas where further research might be undertaken – although he referred the reader to reservations that he would address later on in the report.

By this time, however, Korolev was feeling sick to his stomach. It was clear to him that, in amongst all the medical jargon and bureaucratic dodging, these brain doctors had been doing things that human beings shouldn't damned well do to other human beings. And what was more, he couldn't help but remember the small beds he'd seen at the institute. Had these rats been opening up the heads of youngsters? Electrocuting children? The orphanage director had said many of the boys had come back from the institute with small scars on their cheeks – was this the explanation? He thought of the scar on Goldstein's face and the terrible thought occurred to him that his Yuri was, likely as not, in the hands of people who'd something to do with this. He gritted his teeth and read on.

Now Shtange was talking about new methods for recovering information from 'reluctant' sources. All those methods that had been attempted for 're-education' had also been tried for this purpose, as well as more traditional methods of torture. Because that's what they'd been doing – torturing those who'd been held there. Korolev remembered the strange cells and their prison stench. If he'd ever had any doubt as to what the place had been for, this report explained it to him in detail. And alongside each of Shtange's negative comments, Azarov had written a defence. In some places his writing was illegible – written with a hand so heavy it had torn the paper. But in others some sort of logic was apparent – if logic was possible from such a man.

And so it went on, and on, and on. Anything that could be

done to mine a man's mind, to change it, stretch it or compress it – had been tried. Thankfully the scientific basis of most of what the professor had attempted had been questioned by the doctor. The section that covered research irregularities was almost unreadable, as the professor – at least, Korolev presumed it was the professor – had scribbled out entire paragraphs. But from what Korolev could make of it, there was an established way of doing these things, and the professor had done it the wrong way – stumbling around looking for a quick solution, rather than taking it step by step. When Shtange had moved on to ethical irregularities, the professor's notes had seemed calmer – 'Bourgeois morality!' he'd written beside a paragraph in which Shtange had questioned the use of humans for such research. 'Necessary sacrifices for the greater cause of socialism,' had been his comment when Shtange had questioned the deaths of so many of the subjects. And beside the paragraph that had confirmed Korolev's worst fears – children had indeed been used and in nearly every aspect of the research – Azarov had written a brief defence in the margin: 'Children have proved the most pliant research subjects – great progress has been made thanks to their inclusion in experimental activities.'

Korolev put his hand over his mouth when he read this, his stomach plummeting. He swore to himself that if the professor hadn't already been dead then he himself would have done the job. Cheerfully.

But it was the section that dealt with financial irregularities that caught Korolev's particular attention – unaccounted-for expenditures, inflated prices paid for basic equipment, salaries paid to non-existent employees. In Shtange's opinion, the institute's budget had been stripped of large quantities of the foreign currency allocated to it for the purchase of equipment, books, periodicals and any number of other items from abroad – and irregularities were apparent in every aspect of the finances. Shtange had no idea who was stealing from the NKVD on such a scale, but considered it imperative that it was investigated immediately.

But the professor knew, because he'd written one name, over and over again, beside each allegation.

Zaitsev.

Zaitsev.

Zaitsev.

Chapter Forty-One

KOROLEV PUT the report back into its envelope and then dropped it into the waiting cavity and replaced the bottom drawer. He now had a good idea what might have been said during one of those phone calls Kuznetsky had found out about.

He stood and walked to the window, looking down on the children playing in the small park, before changing his focus to see the grim, merciless anger that showed in his reflection. He reached into his pocket for cigarettes and lit one up, thinking it all through, and when he'd finished he stubbed the butt out on the glass before opening the window and flicking it out. It was uncultured, the act of a hooligan. But then he'd just read what cultured men had got up to in the name of science. Maybe being uncultured wasn't such a bad thing, if you knew what was right and what was wrong. It might be 'bourgeois morality' to a wretch like the professor, but in Korolev's opinion knowing the difference between right and wrong was what separated humans from wolves.

The stack of files was still on the table and Korolev walked over to it, going through them until he found the Bramson file. He picked it up and stopped when he saw the other name on the file. Goldstein. Varvara Goldstein. Bramson's wife. She'd been arrested on 1 March 1936 – three days after a husband whose surname she hadn't taken. And the couple had a son named after the acronym for the Komsomol International Movement: Kim. Age at the time of the arrest of both his parents – eleven. Korolev swallowed drily. The same Kim Goldstein who was now on the run from the Vitsin Street Orphanage turned out to be the son of the former occupants of Azarov's apartment. People who owed their arrests to the professor. Korolev felt the band around his chest tighten another notch or two and reached for another cigarette. If he came through this alive he'd give the damned things up, he swore it – but for the moment he needed all the help he could get.

Korolev reached for the telephone, tapping for the operator. When she came on the line he asked to be put through to the director of the Vitsin Street Orphanage.

'Comrade Spinsky? Korolev here, from Petrovka. I came to see you last night.'

'I remember.' The tinny voice sounded wary.

'It's about those two boys – the ones that went missing on Wednesday night. I wanted to know where they might have been earlier in the week.'

'Earlier in the week?'

'Monday and Tuesday in particular.'

'Goldstein and Petrov? They'd have been here on the Monday – it was Tuesday morning that we bussed the boys out to Peredelkino.'

'What are the chances one or both of them could have slipped away at some stage?'

'From the orphanage? We keep a close eye on them, but it's not a prison,' Spinsky said, and there was no mistaking the director's concern now.

'So they could have? Do children often leave the Vitsin grounds on their own?'

'Very rarely. Only the older children, even then. As for Goldstein and Petrov – it's not impossible. Unlikely, but not impossible. You'd have to ask Comrade Tambova or one of the others, to be certain.'

'Tambova? Little Barrel?'

'That's what the children call her, yes.' The director sounded as though he didn't approve of such familiarity, either from Korolev or the boys.

'Can I speak to her?'

There was a pause.

'She's out.'

'Doesn't she live at the orphanage?'

'She has time off the same as any other citizen. Today is her day off. I've no idea where she might be.'

'I want to talk to her.'

'I'll tell her you called.'

To Korolev's ears, the director sounded rattled. Korolev wondered if someone might have come to visit him after he'd left the night before. Cartainly Zaitsev would have wanted to know what they'd been talking about, wouldn't he?

'Last night you mentioned a facility out near Lefortovo where the children who were chosen by Professor Azarov were taken – have you remembered where that facility might be?'

There was a lengthy pause. 'I've no idea. As I told you yesterday – the institute takes over responsibility for the children once they are transferred.'

'Yes, so you said. So you said. And you've heard nothing from the either Goldstein or Petrov since last night?' Korolev asked.

'Not a thing. We'll give them a few more days and then we presume they've gone back on the streets. It's not unusual, Comrade Captain. Not unusual at all.'

Korolev smiled grimly. Someone had got to Spinsky, he was sure of it. The man was doing a good impression of being offhand, but Korolev could almost smell his fear down the telephone line.

'One last question, Comrade Director – I can tell you're busy. You remember that there were three other children who came in with Goldstein and Petrov back in January. One of them died and the other two were transferred to Professor Azarov's care. Can you give me the names of the two boys who were transferred?'

'I'm not sure,' Spinsky began.

'Let me remind you who I'm working for on this investigation.'

'One moment,' the director said after a pause, and Korolev heard footsteps and then a drawer squealing open.

'I have them,' the director said. 'Vitaly Petrov and Mikhail Kudrin.'

'Petrov? The runner's brother?'

'Yes, Aleksandr Petrov's younger brother.'

'Thank you.'

The director seemed to be about to ask a question but Korolev hung up. He finished his cigarette – wondering about Vitaly Petrov and Mikhail Kudrin. And where they might be.

Chapter Forty-Two

KOROLEV LEFT the car beside the Gorky Park Metro station. It was a glorious day and men had balled their shirtsleeves high above their sun-browned forearms while women walked beside them, their laughter light and easy. He'd been to Gorky Park before, of course, but every time he came nowadays it seemed there was some new feature designed to entertain and impress the citizens of Moscow. The parachute tower that dominated this end of the park had been in place for a year or two now – a tall structure, bollard-shaped, with an exterior walkway that spiralled round and up it like the stripe on a barber's pole. The queue stretched a hundred metres along the central promenade – these days it seemed you even had to stand in line to throw yourself off a building.

Korolev made his way to the meeting spot down by the river – a band was playing somewhere nearby and he found that he was walking in time with the music. No matter what his feet were up to, however, Korolev's thoughts were focused on Yuri, where the boy might be and whether he was safe – although he kept his eyes moving, scanning the crowd, allowing his gaze to slowly wander around the park. He wasn't even sure who he was looking for – Zaitsev's men or Kolya's Thieves or someone else entirely – but his senses were telling him he was being watched. And he didn't like the feeling.

'Watch your step, Comrade.'

Startled, Korolev stopped, turned, and found himself looking up into the nostrils of a ten-foot-tall drunk. His surprise must have shown because a laugh came from inside the giant's stomach. There were eight of them – huge, crude, papier-mâché representations of the evils of drink. The one he'd nearly walked into was a broad-chested peasant with an unnaturally pink face and two glass eyes that dangled out on springs as it walked. In one hand he clutched a bottle of vodka and the other was just a red-painted stump. The sign around his neck told the full story – 'Drunk at work! He cut off his fist! What a fool! Reduced to a wrist!'

He supposed a subtle approach didn't work with drunks – but all the same.

Ranks of grave-faced *komsomol* youngsters followed behind the giants, chanting advice to the citizenry – 'Drink in moderation – for the good of the Nation!' and 'Behave like a cultured Soviet guy – not like a pig in a filthy sty'.

But some in the crowd chanted right back at them: 'Stop all the singing, and let's have a drink.' And more salty advice directed towards the female marchers, one or two of whom couldn't help but look uncomfortable. And to judge from the raucous laughter, at least some of the crowd were several glasses past heeding any advice on drinking from a squad of teenage activists – and certainly not on their day off. Still, it wasn't any of Korolev's business and the statue of the diver was only a short distance ahead – and there he did have business. Important business.

'Insanity, isn't it?'

It was a deep voice, calm – possessed of a certainty that most could only wish for. Kolya.

Korolev turned, thinking the Thief must be looking at the Komsomol agitators, but his gaze was fixed well past them – up at the parachute tower, where a brave soul threw himself outwards, falling fast until the parachute jerked his body back and he descended the rest of the way at a more survivable pace.

'Don't you think? To throw yourself from such a height and trust in something so flimsy to make sure you land safely.'

Korolev shrugged his shoulders. 'It has its purpose.'

Korolev couldn't help but let his eyes drop to the finger and hand tattoos that turned Kolya's fists blue. Each tattoo had a meaning and there'd be more under his clothes – on his chest, his arms and legs. Kolya's tattoos, like medals, told of deeds he'd performed, battles he'd won and the sentences he'd served. Still others signalled Kolya's rank amongst the Thieves as clearly as the stars or stripes on a soldier's collar. And Kolya was a Field Marshal amongst Thieves – as decorated, in their terms, as any Hero of the Soviet Union.

'Its purpose? To train youngsters for war?' Kolya answered, as he watched another parachute descend. 'Yes, I can see the point of that. We'll need young blood for the Motherland soon enough.'

Korolev looked around him, wondering where Kolya's men were.

'Don't tell me you came alone?'

Kolya pointed an inked finger further along the path in the direction of the big wheel and, sure enough, there was Mishka – eating ice cream from a paper cup while the big fellow he'd seen at the zoo pushed one hand against another.

'Ice cream?' Korolev asked, surprised.

'He's fond of it.'

'It's the weather for it, I suppose.'

Kolya smiled but it seemed to Korolev there was something on his mind – and Korolev couldn't help but wonder what it might be. Was it his imagination or did the Thief look as if he'd aged since he last saw him? He certainly seemed weary.

'But you, Korolev,' the Thief said. 'You came on your own, didn't you?'

'I'd good reason to.'

'I thought as much.' And they began, by unspoken agreement, to walk away from the river towards the central pond, where the statue of a female rower stood surrounded by fountains, her long oar leaning against her shoulder like a rifle.

'So you're investigating the Azarov killing after all,' Kolya said, looking up at the rower's naked buttocks.

Korolev had the strangest sensation of cold, even on this warmest of days – and he wondered if it wasn't a premonition of some kind.

'I was given a choice – but it wasn't much of one.'

'I heard.'

He'd heard, had he? Either the man had a source in the most unlikely of places or he was playing games with him. He'd two NKVD colonels and now a senior Thief trying to twist his mind into a shape that suited them – and frankly he'd had enough of it.

'I'd like to know how you come by information like that, Kolya.'

'What I know and what I don't know won't change if I tell you how I know it.'

Korolev nearly took the bait, but he reminded himself why they were there.

'We didn't come here just to banter back and forth, did we?'

'No.'

'A question?'

'Willingly.'

'When we spoke about the institute out at the zoo, you said you hoped my son never ended up in such a place. What did you mean by it? You see, you don't strike me as the kind of man who'd come and tell me something like that just out of the blue. You'll forgive me – but it seems to me you must have had a reason for it. It's been bothering me.'

It occurred to Korolev that, to other people in the park, they probably looked like two old friends out for a walk in the afternoon sun – the thought made him uncomfortable. They stopped to watch two groups of students battling an enormous ball backwards and forwards across a net – some new sort of game, it seemed.

'I've a boy of my own, Korolev – that's why I came to see you that day.'

The Thief's voice seemed to have lost some of its usual force. Korolev turned and saw that Kolya was pale – his face narrow with concern.

'Two boys, as it happens,' Kolya continued. 'One of them is safe and I'll keep him that way – until it's time for him to stand on his own two feet of course. The other I don't know about for certain. His name is Anton and I haven't seen him since five weeks ago – when I was picked up by your lot over a little misunderstanding.'

'You were arrested?' It was news to Korolev.

'Not exactly. But the person whose name I gave them spent time staring at the sky through crossed bars. Or at least that's what the records show. I won't deny it was my friends' persuasive skills saw that person released and that I was pleased to be out in the fresh air when he was. Fortunately not everyone's as honest as you are, you see. Many are open to persuasion.'

Korolev wasn't surprised – Militiamen did well compared to the general populace, but that didn't mean money wasn't tight and small mouths didn't need feeding.

'It took two weeks for the matter to resolve itself. At the time my wife was down in the south with her people. When I got myself out, I discovered Anton had been taken by some well-meaning folk and placed in a certain orphanage. I wonder if you can guess which one?'

'Vitsin Street.'

'The very same. From the orphanage he was sent somewhere else, and for a while no one was able to tell me where. I've a talent for persuasion, as I've said, and know many people, but none of them could find out – except that he might have been sent to the Azarov Institute. When I heard that, I became concerned, because I'd already heard things about the place. People I know – strong men, clever men, men of authority amongst us – you know the kind – men who'd earned their tattoos and stood by them – they'd ended up there and hadn't fared well. Not one of them will ever be the same, those that survived, that is.'

'You think your boy ended up there?'

'He *was* there – I know that much. But they moved him somewhere else again – somewhere outside Moscow. Some secret establishment.'

'I'm sorry for it, Kolya. I didn't know anything about the institute when we met. Except that it was a place to avoid.'

'I thought as much, Korolev – you wouldn't have walked away if you had. I think I know that much about you.'

Korolev wasn't sure this was the case, but he said nothing in response.

'And I know I won't be grieving for Professor Azarov or that fellow Shtange,' Kolya said. 'They got what they deserved.'

'But you didn't kill them.' Korolev spoke quietly – there were citizens close by after all.

'No,' Kolya said, and Korolev thought he detected regret. 'Their blood isn't on my hands.'

'From the little I know, most of the children who went to the Azarov Institute went back to the orphanage, sooner or later.' Korolev wanted to reassure the Thief, although he wasn't entirely convinced by his own words.

'So I believe, but some stayed on – and no one's quite sure what happen to them. Even the ones that came back – the things they'd had done to them weren't pleasant. They treated them like animals, Korolev, and I'm not just saying that. They did what that fellow Pavlov did with dogs, only with children.

That's Soviet progress, for you. They cut holes in the boys' cheeks, then showed them biscuits and rang a bell or something. The holes were there so they could see if they salivated.'

Korolev found he couldn't say anything at first. His hands, though, were itching to smack the hell out of someone.

'Kim Goldstein?' he managed to say eventually.

Kolya glanced at him. 'Why do you ask about Goldstein?'

'He's your source for this, isn't he? He was at the institute – I need to speak to him.'

'About your son?'

Well, Korolev thought to himself, he'd been fooling himself if he'd thought Kolya wouldn't know that much at least.

'About him, of course. And other things.'

'You know your boy was picked up by Chekists yesterday evening.'

'Not just any Chekists, Kolya.' Korolev hesitated a moment, then told Kolya all that he knew about the Azarov Institute and its relationship to Colonel Zaitsev's Twelfth Department – and how the Vitsin Street Orphanage fitted into the picture. The Thief listened carefully but Korolev had the sense that most of what he was telling him, he already knew.

'There are times, Kolya,' Korolev said in conclusion, 'when I wonder if we haven't been joined together by fate in some way.'

'It's a possibility,' Kolya agreed.

He didn't look too happy at the idea, but then again, nor was Korolev. He found himself kicking a small stone, more to avoid the Thief's gaze than anything else. There was sympathy there, perhaps even kindness, and that wasn't what he wanted to see. It seemed they'd a common interest, and perhaps, as he'd said, they might even have a shared fate. But there could be no question of friendship. Kolya might talk about his code and the Thieves' honour but there wasn't a crime thought up by human-kind that Kolya wouldn't commit if it suited him.

'So the question is – where have they moved this institute to?' Kolya asked.

'We're trying to find out – but this "house in the woods" that Little Barrel at the orphanage mentioned, the place out near Lefortovo – that seems our best bet. My guess is it's the same secret establishment your sources told you about. And, of course, it's under Zaitsev's sole control. It seems to me there's a chance both our boys could be there. A good chance. If we knew where it was.'

'Perhaps. What would you suggest?'

Kolya wasn't pulling his punches today, it seemed, and so Korolev told him the plan he'd come up with, half-amazed to hear what he was suggesting and equally amazed that the Thief seemed to be taking him seriously – even nodding his agreement.

'And unless I'm wrong,' Korolev said in conclusion, 'young Kim Goldstein knows the exact location of this facility.'

'No,' Kolya said, shaking his head. 'He doesn't.'

'You've asked him?'

'Of course I asked him. You're right to think he and his friend were looking for it, same as us. Two of his crew ended up out there, it seems. But where exactly, he has no idea. I've sent people to look for it, of course, but nothing.'

They stood there, two glum-looking, middle-aged men in amongst the summer-swarthy Muscovites.

'Kolya,' Korolev said, after he'd thought it through. 'There's someone I can get to tell us what we need to know, I think. If I can – are we agreed?'

'Yes,' the Thief said, holding out his hand – his eyes bright once again. Korolev, not entirely happily, took it.

'Then I'll get them to tell us. But Kolya, we can't wait around on this – you must understand that. It has to be tonight.'

'It's my son. I'm ready.'

'Then tonight it is.'

'And Slivka?' Kolya asked. 'It's her cousin in the hands of these people. Her flesh and blood.'

'I don't want her involved, Kolya. I'm sick of taking risks with other people's lives.'

Kolya shook his head slowly. 'What you have to understand, Korolev, is that there's no safe place in these times. She's already at risk. And it's not your fault – or your responsibility.'

Chapter Forty-Three

THE CAR'S ENGINE grumbled to a stop and it occurred to Korolev that if he continued to visit Leadership House this often he might eventually acquire some sort of right of residency. The thought appealed to him for a moment as he recalled the size of the apartments and their views over Moscow – but then he remembered State Security's habit of taking residents for early morning drives. On balance, he decided he was fine where he was.

'Comrade Captain.' Timinov nodded a greeting, then looked around him and, satisfied there was no one nearby, nodded once again – more significantly this time.

'You looked at the schedule?'

'Priudski was on duty. Until six. And he was arrested just before he finished for the day.'

'So he was here all that morning. Could he have left for an hour or so – or even longer? Say if he needed to go up to one of the apartments, or something else perhaps?'

'If a doorman leaves his post for any length of time, he has to get cover. He had half an hour for lunch at twelve-thirty and he was covered for that. But I had a look at the book in the canteen, he signed in there at twelve forty – so that's where he went. I even looked at the log for the building, where we sign visitors in and out. If he slipped off during the morning, I don't know how he could have managed it – none of the visitors are more than twenty minutes apart and he has to counter-sign each one of them in and out – which he did.'

'I see,' Korolev said, grasping Timinov's arm in gratitude. 'This has to be kept between us. Understood?'

'Understood.'

'Is the professor's wife in?'

'I'm not sure, Comrade Captain, but the maid, Galina, just went up.'

'I'll pay a visit, I think.'

Korolev looked at the lift's doors for a long moment, felt sweat prickling at the back of his neck, and found his experience earlier in the day had made him even less keen to take it. He started up the stairs, looking at his watch as he did so. He'd two hours before he was due to meet Rodinov, but that should be enough – at least, it would be if Comrade Madame Azarova was at home. If not? Well, he'd solve that problem if it came to pass.

Galina came to the door when he knocked, and her eyes widened at the sight of him.

'Comrade Azarova isn't here,' she said with an urgency that came close to vehemence.

She made to push the door closed, but Korolev put his foot against it, and then a hand. He could feel her try to close it all the same, but that wasn't going to happen. She might have been a farm girl and still have a farm girl's biceps, but Korolev was a solid man, a few too many pounds solid, as it happened. The door swung open under his weight and Galina stepped back.

'Where is she?' Korolev could feel disappointment in his throat like a physical object, but he swallowed it, just about.

'I'm sorry,' Galina said, and there was a break in her voice.

Korolev examined her. He thought back to the last time she'd been here, her strange behaviour. Now more strange behaviour. But then, of course – there *should* be strange behaviour. She must know most of it – she was bright enough.

'You're sorry?' he said. 'You think that's enough?'

The words came out just as bluntly as he intended and Galina's head dropped. Meanwhile Korolev recalled the various pieces of information he'd discovered, dusted them off and lined them up in a row.

'I think you'd better tell me everything, Citizeness Matkina. I think it's about damned time.'

'I don't know what you're talking about – I don't.'

It came out almost like a wail. Her hand went to her throat and, avoiding his eyes, she turned away from him.

'I think you do, Citizeness. Stand aside.'

Korolev walked past her without bothering to wait for permission and she didn't resist him. He made his way into the Azarovs' sitting room and heard the apartment's front door shut and her footsteps following him. He looked around the room. It was as before – the empty shelves, the plush furniture, the panoramic view over the capital city of the Soviet Union. Madame Azarova had sat just there, wearing her black gloves, only yesterday. Black gloves in summer. In a country that didn't mourn that way these days.

'She cut herself, didn't she, Galina? She cut her hand.'

He heard movement – as if Galina were walking in a circle, looking for a way out perhaps. He didn't turn around. If he turned she might be able to tell that he was half-bluffing.

'She came back early on Tuesday morning, didn't she? You weren't expecting her. She came back in a stranger's coat.'

He tried to remember the respective size difference between Azarova and Madame Shtange's wife. Azarova would have been taller, possibly broader in the shoulder as well.

'A coat that was too small for her,' he continued. 'Black, with large shoulders. Four buttons, if I remember.'

'How do you—?' Galina began to say, but Korolev held up a hand to stop her.

'Her hand was bleeding. No, she'd bandaged it with something – hadn't she? And, of course,' Korolev remembered back to the small footprints the forensics men had told him about in Shtange's apartment, 'there was blood on her shoes as well – not her blood. And her clothes underneath the coat – they must have been covered as well. That's why you were so nervous when I came to see her yesterday. And that's why you were sent out immediately. She'd sworn you to secrecy but you're no fool, you knew keeping a secret like that could mean ten years in a mine. So she had something over you. Let me think . . . Ah – the residency permit. Of course. Did she promise she'd get you one? Or did she tell you if you opened your mouth that at best you'd be on a train back home before the week was out? That, more likely, you'd end up in the mine just the same.'

There was silence behind him, before a quiet sobbing began.

'The doorman told me what happened to Dr Shtange,' she said.

Galina's voice was almost drowned out by a sudden hammering from the direction of the bridge. The windows rattled and for a moment it was all Korolev could do just to think. The hammering ended, and Korolev turned to find Galina, tear tracks running down her face.

And behind her, standing in the doorway, face as pale as a sheet of freshly milled paper, was the professor's wife. In the gloved hand that was pointed at him was a small silver automatic.

'You can go into the kitchen, Galina,' Azarova said, calm as death itself.

'I tried to keep him out.'

'I know you did.'

Galina cast Korolev a quick glance and he nodded his agreement. 'Go on, go into the kitchen. Don't worry about anything. This will all be agreed in a sensible fashion or it will go hard with everyone. Harder than anyone can imagine.'

'We'll see about that, Comrade Captain Korolev,' the professor's wife said and, when Galina had made her way back into the corridor, Azarova closed the door behind the girl and turned a key in the lock.

'You overheard our conversation?'

'Enough of it.'

'Well?'

'He killed Boris. I killed him. I'm not going to let you take me to prison for it. I'll shoot myself before that happens.' She spoke matter-of-factly, but Korolev thought back to Shtange's body, stabbed twenty or thirty times. He looked into her eyes and saw something like madness there, but he thought he also saw uncertainty.

'Shtange didn't kill your husband,' he said. 'Someone else killed your husband.'

She appeared to consider this – then shrugged.

'Who?' she asked – as if such a possibility could matter less to her.

'If it's who I think it was, someone who'd a reason to kill him and an opportunity to do it. Anyway, Shtange was at the institute at the time of your husband's death. Whoever it was, it wasn't him.'

Azarova considered this for a moment, before shaking her head in the negative.

'No, it was Shtange. He might not have pulled the trigger himself, but he as good as did so with that report of his. Boris meant well, but Shtange couldn't see that – couldn't see that everything Boris did, every hard decision he made, every necessary brutality, they were all done with the best interests of the State as their basis. We're a country of two hundred million – a few convicted criminals don't count for anything against that. He had to make progress – and quickly. We're in a war already, Korolev. An internal war that each Soviet citizen wages against an enemy that is within themselves. Boris was going to help Soviet citizens defeat that enemy – to allow us to become fully one with the Revolution, completely loyal, completely dedicated.

There would have been no more doubt, no more backsliding – we would all be perfect citizens of a socialist utopia built in Lenin's image.'

Her voice rose as she spoke and by the time she'd finished it wasn't far off the level at which you might address a small crowd – but it seemed she was trying to persuade herself as much as him. Korolev was past persuasion – he was too close to the Revolution as it was, and reluctant to get any closer, given its habit of putting him in dangerous situations. Situations like this one.

'You knew about Shtange's report then?' Korolev said, wishing she'd hold the gun steady at least. He wanted to forget it was there – but the way she was waving it about made that difficult.

'Boris told me about it.'

'Then you know it wasn't just convicted criminals he operated on. There were others as well, children. Children who were once under your care.'

'Minor operations, Korolev. Basic Pavlovian research. The children didn't suffer. What's more they were proud to help drive Soviet science into the future. And they were treated well. I made sure of it. Each one of them was a willing volunteer. When they came back to the orphanage they were envied.'

Her voice rose once again as she spoke, before she seemed to collect herself.

'What my husband did with the men was different, of course. And in another situation – well, if it hadn't been necessary, it wouldn't have been done. The work he did with them was difficult, but vital – for the Revolution. My husband didn't enjoy what he did, believe me, but he knew his duty.'

Korolev couldn't help but glance down again at the gun in Azarova's hand. She followed his gaze, looking back up at him with an expression that was difficult to read.

'What about the children who didn't go back to the orphanage?' Korolev said. 'The ones who went to this other place, this house in the woods? The ones chosen by your husband for their "special aptitude". They didn't have such a pleasant time, did they?'

Azarova frowned. She looked confused.

'They weren't treated well, Comrade Madame Azarova, now were they?'

She shook her head and again her gun began to waver in her grasp.

'The work out there was purely educational. It was more Pavlovian theory, but this time applied in an educational context – he was training the Bolsheviks of the future. Through encouragement, no more than that. It was educational, nothing more.'

'Your husband lied to you, Comrade Azarova, and he used you. What went on out there was barbarism. But you knew that, didn't you?'

She took a step backwards, her face shrinking in on itself. 'I've been out there,' she managed. 'The children are happy. Yes, they are perfectly happy. I talked to them. I looked at the progress they'd made. Such loyalty, such devotion to the Party – it was heartening. Those children will be enormous assets to the State in due course, of that you can rest assured. There was nothing wrong. Nothing at all.'

'Do you know what "repeated high-voltage electrical shocks to the cortex administered for sustained periods" means? I won't forget those words in a hurry. Shtange may not have been an angel but at least he was trying to put a stop to your husband's playing God with poor, orphaned children.'

'That isn't true. It simply isn't true.'

Korolev paused and examined Azarova dispassionately. Her arm had dropped down now, so that the gun pointed at the floor – which was something. From the kitchen he could hear Galina weeping. When Azarova put a gloved hand to her face, Korolev changed his approach.

'Your husband was the monster, not you,' he said in a gentle voice. 'I didn't come here to arrest you, Comrade Madame Azarova. I know you killed Shtange, but you were confused – you were insane with grief. I can understand that.'

She looked confused now. 'But you can't forget about Shtange, you'll have to take me to prison.'

The gun straightened, the barrel's dark circle rising once again. He hoped she'd left the safety catch on.

'You made one mistake,' Korolev said, 'don't make another. Give me the gun. If you tell me where this place is, out in Lefortovo, I'll walk away, and forget everything I've worked out. I don't care about Shtange – as far as I'm concerned, he deserved to die for what he did to those prisoners.'

The hammer, hammer, hammer of the bridge's pile driver came again, rattling the windows once more. A long moment passed. Then, to his relief, Azarova put a hand to her head, placed the gun on the sideboard, and sat down. She looked around her, at him, at the gun, at the room she was in, as if seeing everything for the first time. The hammering stopped and in the silence that followed he could hear a tram pass by on the street below.

'Why do you want to know about that place?'

'I think my son's being held out there.'

She looked at him in disbelief – but then she saw his expression.

'I don't know how this all happened,' she said in a weak voice.

He walked across the room and picked up the gun, made sure the safety was on, then put it in his pocket.

'Now, let's talk.'

Chapter Forty-Four

THERE WAS an atmosphere in Shtange's study it would have taken a mechanical saw a week to cut through – Dubinkin kept glancing at him with a curiosity that Korolev found unnerving, Slivka appeared to have been subsisting on a diet of lemons since breakfast, while poor Kuznetsky looked like a nervous child caught in the middle of an argument he knew nothing about.

Well, Korolev could get rid of one of them, at least.

'Go outside and guard the building, Kuznetsky.'

He immediately regretted the tone in his voice. Not that the young Militiaman seemed to notice.

'Of course, Comrade Captain. From who?'

'From you, for all I care.'

'And the telephone? Who will answer the telephone?'

Korolev looked at him, wondering if the scamp was daring to be cheeky, but it wasn't that – the boy was just confused. Korolev's glance, murderous as it must have been, soon shifted him.

'I'll be outside, Comrade Captain,' Kuznetsky said, and the door was shutting behind him almost before he'd finished speaking. Korolev turned his attention to Dubinkin.

'What did you find out about our friend, Priudski?'

Korolev still had Azarova's small automatic in his pocket and was surprised to discover that his hand had gripped the butt of the weapon – his finger inside the trigger guard and the muzzle pointing at Dubinkin. He slowly unwrapped his fingers from the gun, and crossed his arms over his chest, so that there was less likelihood of a moment of irritation causing him to inadvertently shoot a Chekist.

'He was as you said. A State Security ear. Interestingly though, he didn't report to the Fifth Department, as I'd expect – instead he reported to the Twelfth Department. It looks as if Zaitsev wanted to keep tabs on the professor and was using Priudski to do it. Zaitsev holds the file so I can't tell you as much as I might like. But the clerks were able to do enough cross-referencing to give a good picture of what he was up to.'

'Just because he reported to Colonel Zaitsev—' Korolev began.

'Of course,' Slivka interrupted him, 'we shouldn't jump to conclusions. That would be wrong. After all, we have a perfectly good solution to these crimes already.'

'That's enough, Slivka.'

Slivka said nothing, but it looked as though the lemons were repeating on her.

'As you know, I visited Leadership House this morning,' Korolev said, conscious that the other two seemed to be examining him as if he were a criminal trying to spin them a tale. 'It seems possible Priudski could have left there on Tuesday morning and made his way here, just about. I also spoke to Dr Weiss and I'm satisfied he had nothing to do with either Azarov's or Shtange's death. So will you be, when you read this letter.'

He passed it to Dubinkin.

The Chekist read it through and nodded – it seemed nothing much fazed him. At least Slivka had the good grace to look impressed.

'What about you, Slivka?'

'Me?' Slivka said. 'I spent the day talking to tram drivers, bus conductors, metro workers, kiosk workers, street sweepers and duck feeders. I even hot-tailed it back here to meet you, although you'd slipped off before I arrived. Not that it made any difference. No one saw Priudski. No one saw anything.'

'We don't need them to have.' Korolev spoke deliberately.

'We don't even need evidence now?' Slivka wasn't so much indignant as mystified.

'We have evidence. His confession.'

'But it's inconsistent with much of what we know.'

'We have other evidence.'

'What evidence?'

'His fingerprints. Forensics found them all over this apartment. He did it all right.'

Slivka's mouth dropped open far enough for Korolev to be able to make out her tonsils quite clearly from where he was sitting.

But it was Dubinkin's quick smile, a smile that he suspected he wasn't meant to see, that really caught his attention.

Chapter Forty-Five

COLONEL RODINOV listened to Korolev's account of the day's events with an impassive face – and it made Korolev nervous, this impassiveness, because Korolev thought it was a story worthy of a little bit of interest.

After all, he'd been threatened by an NKVD colonel – and for a change it hadn't been Rodinov. He'd nearly been crushed by a lift. He'd had a gun held on him by a murderess. He'd done his level best to muddy the waters in two murder cases. He'd even produced a blood-stained report into the activities of the Azarov Institute, which now sat on the desk in front of the colonel. Of course, he hadn't mentioned his meeting with the Chief Authority of the Moscow Thieves, but the report alone deserved some excitement – given it was sitting, caked in blood, right in front of him. But Rodinov showed no reaction to a word he said.

The colonel was listening, however – he was listening so hard that Korolev felt as if his words were being sucked right out of his mouth.

'So, you see – I've made some progress, not all of it in the right direction, perhaps, but definitely progress.'

Rodinov's gaze remained remorseless, but Korolev had nothing left to say. He was empty of words and very nearly empty of emotion. It was like that sometimes, when too much happened in too short a period – you just had nothing left, and anything he did have was reserved for Yuri.

'Let's have a look at this report of Shtange's, shall we?'
Rodinov said eventually, after a pause so lengthy that if
they'd been at the theatre the management would have opened
the buffet and called it an intermission. He pulled the document closer to him, opened up the stiff pages and began to
read.

It seemed to Korolev that the colonel was scanning the
report at first – picking up the gist of it without absorbing
details – but when he got to the last few pages, the ones that
dealt with the alleged financial irregularities, the colonel seemed
to take his time. And when he finished and looked up at
Korolev, it was his impression that the colonel could have
recited those pages line by line.

'This part is interesting, Korolev. Very interesting.'

'The part that deals with financial indiscretions?'

The question got him a raised eyebrow, and Korolev wondered whether it hadn't been better when the Chekist had stayed
stony-faced. Rodinov picked up a pen from the desk and twirled
it around – an incongruous gesture from a man who held the
power of life and death over him.

'You're correct, Korolev. Scientific-procedural concerns and
ethical dilemmas are all well and good. It doesn't mean I approve
of what went on there – but I live in the real world. On such
matters there will be opinions either way. In other words, it
would be difficult to act on.'

Rodinov began to tap the pen gently on the table, before
continuing.

'But financial indiscretions such as these are different. If they
can be proved and laid at the door of Zaitsev – well, then that
would be something. Yes, indeed – it would be something, all
right. And it would explain Colonel Zaitsev's actions over the
last few days. Looked at in the light of this report, those actions
would appear to indicate an attempt to cover up serious wrongdoing on his part.'

The thought did not appear to displease Rodinov – but he was still frowning.

'There's a problem, isn't there, Comrade Colonel?'

It didn't look as though the colonel much liked the question, but Korolev didn't much like the answer either – he'd thought through his role in this little chess game between Zaitsev and Rodinov, and he'd thought about the report as well. From where he was sitting, there appeared to be only one obvious result for Korolev – and when all your routes of escape are closed off to you then there really isn't much point in fear.

'Yes, there's a problem,' Rodinov said. 'This is a report prepared by a dead man. It describes crimes, but doesn't produce evidence for them – the sources it mentions are unavailable to us. The only thing that links anything irregular to Zaitsev is his name written in the margin by another dead man. A dead man who, on the basis of the report, seems the likeliest person to have committed these financial misdeeds. Not that we even know for sure that it was Professor Azarov who wrote Zaitsev's name. For all we know it could have been you. Or me.'

Rodinov placed the pen back onto the table and shook his head slowly from side to side. 'It's not enough.'

'So there's nothing to be done.'

Rodinov looked up at him and Korolev thought he detected something in the colonel's gaze which might amount to sympathy.

'Not at the moment. There may be other ways of authenticating the report's contents, of course. But it may take time. At least now I know what I'm looking for.'

'What you really need is the institute's records.'

'They'll surely have been destroyed by now, Korolev. It would be the sensible thing to do. And Zaitsev is sensible. Look at how he's handled this – the doorman's fingerprints in the apartment? He must have had them placed there before we even took over the case, as a precaution.'

Korolev couldn't deny that, when it came to framing a man, Colonel Zaitsev had talent.

'But if we were able to find out where this "house in the woods" is – this facility near Lefortovo?' Korolev said, getting back to the original point. 'There must be a small chance that there's evidence out there that will make your case.'

The colonel held up the report. 'Even if I knew where the place was, I couldn't send men out there based on this. We're not dealing with an ordinary citizen here. We're dealing with a colonel of the NKVD.'

'I thought as much.' Korolev sighed, then looked the colonel in the eyes. 'Comrade Colonel, I've another twenty-four hours to give Colonel Zaitsev that report, the one there in your hands, or he says he'll kill my son and likely me as well.'

It was best to be straightforward about these things, Korolev thought. After all, he'd come here to find something out.

'Would you like to give him this, Korolev? I can have a copy made – you can say you found it wherever you like.' Rodinov shook his head. 'It won't make any difference. You should know that. Colonel Zaitsev will be covering his tracks.'

'And I'm a track.'

'I'll do what I can, Korolev. The situation may be difficult – I can make no promises – but I should be able to protect you. And, as I said, now that I know what I'm looking for – it's only a matter of time.'

'I'm grateful, Comrade Colonel. But it's my son I'm concerned about.'

Rodinov shrugged. 'I understand that, Korolev – and if I could help you, I would.'

And there it was – the answer he'd expected.

'My advice is to proceed as you have been. I'll accept Priudski as Shtange's killer and I'll accept Shtange as the one who murdered Azarov. I don't give a damn about Azarova or whoever was poking around in this ventilation system. You can have this report too. It suits me to have Zaitsev think he's won. Take my advice though, and drag out the investigation as long as you can – call him tomorrow, tell him I've demanded more evidence. While this case is ongoing, you still have something to bargain with.'

Korolev nodded – it wasn't bad advice, but in truth it was like giving him sugar to sprinkle on horse dung. He'd have to eat it all the same.

'There's one other thing, Comrade Colonel.'

'Go on.'

'I'd prefer if you assigned another of your men to the case – someone other than Lieutenant Dubinkin.'

The colonel's attention seemed to have turned back to his paperwork. He didn't look up.

'You have a reason for this request?'

'I'd rather not give it.'

'You'd rather not give it? Where do you think you are?'

'I just don't feel we work well together.'

'Don't be ridiculous, Korolev. I'll see you at the same time tomorrow.'

Korolev nodded but the colonel didn't see it. Nor did he look up when Korolev stood to leave the room.

Chapter Forty-Six

THE APARTMENT WAS empty when Korolev got there, and it unnerved him – normally Valentina and Natasha would be having their evening meal at around this time. He stood for a moment in the doorway, reassuring himself, waiting for the thudding pulse in his head to slow a little and, as he did so, listened to the sounds of the building – muffled laughter from the floor above, a door closing somewhere. There was nothing wrong, he told himself, he was jumping at shadows. They'd probably just gone for a walk around the Boulevard Ring or down to the river – that was it. They might even have gone as far as the pond at Chistye Prudy, which was no great distance. He stood there for a few more minutes, thinking about what he was about to do, for the hundredth time – and considering the potential consequences.

But what choice did he have? Rodinov had as good as told him he was on his own. It might even be worse than that – it wasn't only Zaitsev who might want to cover his tracks come tomorrow. It might well be just as much in Rodinov's interests to ensure that Korolev's mouth was well and truly shut; at least that way Zaitsev couldn't question him about Rodinov's involvement in the whole business. And, as an indirect consequence, it seemed likely that Valentina and Natasha might well be at risk. Not to mention Slivka and Yasimov.

Korolev sighed, walked through to his bedroom and felt on

the top of the wardrobe for the cleaning kit and box of ammunition he kept there, along with a spare clip for the Walther. There was a chance, a small chance – that all of them would come out of this in one piece. And that chance would be just that little bit better if he had every bullet he could lay his hands on in his pockets. The Lord knew the last thing he wanted to do was go shooting at Chekists and the like, but neither was there any point in taking a feather to plough a field.

He sat down on the bed and pulled out the map he'd drawn on the basis of Azarova's recollections, unfolding it onto the pillow. Then having checked the spare clip, he began to press loose bullets from the box into it automatically as he examined his hastily drawn outline of the location of Little Barrel's 'house in the woods'. It looked like something might just be possible. It all depended how many men they had out there – and how many Kolya could produce.

Korolev turned his attention to the Walther, taking out its clip and beginning to clean the weapon. The metallic scent of gun oil filled his nostrils and he felt the slight tremble of adrenaline that it always brought. The key to success would be swiftness. There'd be a telephone connection and that would have to be cut. And if there were any vehicles that might pursue them – he'd like to make sure they couldn't. But still – swiftness was the best policy. Get in, find what they were looking for, and then get the hell out. It was best to presume that their presence would be discovered at some point. And it was best to be prepared if it came to a fight.

Finished with the Walther, he placed it back in its holster, underneath his arm. Then he took the small automatic he'd taken from the professor's widow out of his pocket, turning it over in his hand. He emptied the bullets and began to strip it. The weapon didn't look as though it had been cleaned since it had left the factory, and that had probably been a quarter of a century in the past. If Irina Azarova had fired it in this condition, she'd likely have killed herself rather than him. Still, a gun was a gun. He might need it later on.

A few minutes later and familiar voices came from the corridor outside the apartment. He looked quickly at his watch. He had to meet with Kolya in just under an hour. He put a handful of bullets and the spare clip in his pockets and walked out to them.

'Alexei.' Valentina smiled when she saw him – but the warmth in the smile slowly dimmed.

'You've had news of Yuri?' Her smile had now turned to concern.

'No.'

'I thought . . .'

Her voice faltered and Korolev realized how he must look, hard-faced and with the weight of the world on his shoulders.

'I've had no bad news.' He stopped and looked from Valentina to her daughter, who was listening to him with an expression of determined concentration. At her throat was the red scarf of the Pioneers.

'Natasha, perhaps your mother and I could talk for a moment.'

Natasha glanced between them, but had enough sense to do as she was asked without asking why. When she'd gone into the room she shared with her mother, Korolev took Valentina by the hand and led her into his. He leant in close to her, whispering so low he could barely hear himself.

'Look, Valentina. I have to do something this evening. The only thing is, if it doesn't work out – it might be a mess.'

'Is there anything I can do?'

She doesn't ask what kind of mess, Korolev thought to himself, she asks what she can do to help. And in times like these as well.

'Nothing. Nothing at all. But if I don't come home tonight – maybe you should go to Peredelkino tomorrow, first thing.

To Babel's Dacha. Stay there for a few days. Out of the way of things. Don't get involved in this. In fact, perhaps you'd both be better off spending the night upstairs with Shura. Just in case.'

'Is this to do with Yuri?'

'I'm answering no questions. You know that's best. And I've thought it through, believe me.'

Valentina shook her head but he squeezed her hand, begged her with his eyes.

'Think of Natasha.' He put a hand to her neck, whispering into her ear. 'It's best if you know nothing, nothing at all. So if someone comes to ask you something, you can tell the truth. You knew nothing. I behaved oddly, and that was that.'

She turned her face to him, and for a moment he thought she was going to disagree with him, but instead she stepped forward into his arms and, to his surprise, her lips met his.

He wasn't sure how long they stayed like that but it seemed as though it might be forever – the moment stretching out around them. Her tears were wet against his face and the salty smell of them filled his nostrils. He held her as tight as he dared and thought how small she seemed as he held her in his arms.

'Be careful,' she said, pulling back to look him in the eyes. 'Be very, very careful. And I know you'll bring him home. I know it.'

Then she kissed him once again, on the cheek, ran the sleeve of her shirt across her face to dry it, smiled a crooked smile and left the room.

Chapter Forty-Seven

KOROLEV WALKED quickly through the long-shadowed streets, squinting against the low-hanging sun. He didn't want to think about what had just happened – but whenever his concentration slipped, there it was, a surge of emotion of a kind that wouldn't be much use to him where he was going. Tomorrow he could think about it, and what the future might hold for them. But today was today and tomorrow might never come.

He turned down a side street and then made his way through an archway that led into a courtyard he knew had another doorway at the far end. He crossed the open space quickly, startling a group of citizenry who were sitting on a circle of upturned logs taking in the last of the sun. And then he was past them, ignoring the hard looks from men who stood to see what stranger had come in amongst them, and before any of them could summon the energy at the end of a hot day to question him on his reasons for being there he'd reached the far end of the courtyard and disappeared through the carriage doors, out into an alleyway. He turned left and left and then slowed his pace as he approached the street he'd originally turned off from. He looked to see if anyone might have been following him, but there was no one, and he found himself exhaling a long breath that he seemed to have been holding in since Bolshoi Nikolo-Vorobinsky. Then he took one more look around and, satisfied, made his way quickly across the street to a small lane that would eventually, with more cut-backs and false trails, take him to Kolya.

Unusually for Moscow, the tree-shadowed courtyard that the Thief had designated as their meeting place was deserted – and the buildings that surrounded it were either boarded up or burnt out. The spot must be intended for some new construction project that had yet to start. Cautious, Korolev walked the length of a crumbling stone wall, looking for the green doors Kolya had mentioned. He found them, half-hidden behind a bush. They looked the worse for wear, paint peeling off them in large curls, and the wood underneath grey and brittle. He pushed one of the doors gently and, to his surprise, it slid open on well-oiled hinges.

'You took your time.'

Little Mishka was standing just inside, half-hidden in the late-evening gloom. Korolev wasn't in the mood to bother with him and nor, it seemed, was the Thief his usual combative self, merely nodding Korolev towards a coach house, barely even bothering to scowl. Behind Mishka, Korolev could see the glowing tips of two cigarettes and the dark shape of a large man leaning against a wall to his right. Korolev ignored them. Again, ancient doors opened easily and in the shadows two cars were parked.

'Greetings Korolev.' Kolya's voice came from the darkness as he entered. 'Did you succeed?'

Korolev reached into this pocket. 'I did,' he said, and took out the map of the estate's location.

There was a movement to his left and Korolev turned to see a youngster standing by the wall. When he saw that Korolev had noticed him, Kim Goldstein stepped forward.

'He could be useful to us,' Kolya said. 'Remember – we'll look out of place there, while he might not.'

Korolev breathed deeply and held the boy's gaze. Goldstein nodded to him, the personification of calm.

'What happened to Yuri?'

'Chekists.'

'I know – how though? And how is it you were with him in the first place?'

'We came across him by chance – he was watching the train station from the trees beside the monastery in Peredelkino and saw us come over the wall. He thought there were men staking the place out, although he wasn't sure who they were, so we went to the next station along the track.'

'And when you got to Moscow?'

'We took a tram into the centre – I don't know if they saw us at Kievsky and followed us, but they were waiting for us when we got off.'

'But you got away, didn't you?'

'I couldn't stop them taking Yuri,' Goldstein said. 'I tried – they gave me this.'

He came further into the light and Korolev saw that someone had hit him a good belt – the skin around his eye was puffy and discoloured.

'And Yuri?'

'They took him, like I said, but he was all right the last time I saw him. I only just managed to get away – they took Petya as well.'

Petya was the friend he'd gone over the wall with.

'It's your damned fault he's in this mess, Goldstein, and it'll take more than that bruise to fix it now.'

Goldstein said nothing but held his gaze sullenly.

'I know everything,' Korolev continued. 'I know your father's name was Bramson and your mother's Goldstein and how you took her name. I know your family lived in Azarov's apartment before he did and, somehow or other, you found out about the ventilation system and how to get into it. I know that when Azarov denounced your parents, you ended up on the streets and your parents – well – elsewhere.'

'Dead,' Goldstein said.

'I see,' Korolev said. The anger in the boy's eyes was such that his instinct was to look away, but Korolev held Goldstein's gaze – and waited.

'Azarov took everything from me. When we were taken to his institute for the research project,' Goldstein said, 'I knew I'd been given a chance to take something from him.'

'Where did you get the Derringer from?'

'I knew where my father kept it and when they came for him, I hid it in the ventilation system where no one would find it – under some rubble, right at the end of one of the tunnels.'

'And so on Monday morning you crept out of the orphanage and shot him while he sat at his desk.'

Goldstein shrugged. 'He deserved it. But we got out the night before. We had to wait until the time was right.'

'Did Shtange deserve it? His murder was a direct result of what you did.'

'We went to do the same to him the next day,' Goldstein said quietly. 'Only someone got there before us.'

'That scalpel-cut. You left your mark on him, all the same.'

Things were finally fitting into place.

'He was as bad as Azarov. He might have spoken kindly to us, but he did the same things.'

But in truth, had Shtange really had a choice? Once he was ordered to Moscow – he had to do what he was told. And he'd at least tried to stop it with his report. On the other hand, weren't the prisoners and Thieves humans too? Didn't they have rights? And Shtange had done nothing for them. Korolev shook his head – all he knew was that right and wrong were slippery commodities these days.

'Where's the gun now?'

'In the river.'

Korolev sighed.

'I haven't time for this now but you can believe me when I say I haven't finished with you yet.'

If Goldstein was alarmed, he hid it well, only nodding.

'Shall we look at this map of yours?' Kolya asked, seeming to decide that the silence needed breaking.

'Why don't we?' Korolev said.

The Thief lit a lantern and Korolev spread it out on the bonnet of the nearest car and they stood over it, looking down at his rough sketch. Korolev began to explain how to get there and where to leave the cars.

'We have a visitor.' Mishka's voice came from behind them and they turned to see who he was talking about. A leather-jacketed female stood beside him, arms folded.

Slivka.

'I knew you were up to something,' she said.

'You followed me?'

Slivka took a step forward and her face became visible. She wasn't smiling – if anything she looked angry.

'I didn't have to – he told me.'

She nodded in Kolya's direction – the Thief shrugged.

'You're supposed to be showing me the ropes,' Slivka continued – more than just angry, it seemed – furious. 'Turning me into a first-class detective – not skulking around behind my back.'

'Slivka, the only rope on this little trip is shaped like a noose. I want your neck kept out of it.'

Kolya was leaning against a car listening, and Korolev was suddenly reminded of a pointless argument he and Zhenia had once had while visiting her parents. Except that her parents had pretended not to notice, whereas Kolya sat watching them as if he were at the cinema.

'Kolya,' he said. 'Tell her we've no room.'

'We've room,' Kolya said. 'And Nadezhda's a cool head in a tight spot. We can use her – I've only four men and Mishka. Another gun might come in useful. Besides, she has the right.'

And Korolev could see there wasn't much point in arguing. After all, blood was blood and family was family. And Kolya's son was her blood and her family.

'On your head be it then,' he said eventually.

And so he began to go through the plan all over again.

§

'And when we get to the house itself?' Kolya said. Korolev turned the piece of paper over, and showed them the rough plan of the buildings that he'd prepared with Azarova's help.

'There are three main buildings surrounded by a wall – it's about eight foot high, so manageable. The children's dormitories are in the house itself. On the first floor. There's a stable yard here, to the rear of the house, which was empty the last time Azarova was there – it might not be now. There's also a newer building over here, to the left of the house – two storeys, with several offices on the ground floor. What's upstairs, she didn't know.'

'Guards?'

'As she remembers it, there was one at the gate. An older man. But she remembers that the men and women who looked after the children looked like they might do more than turn down the beds at night. My suspicion is there will be more of them now.'

Then Korolev took a deep breath and told them his plan.

Chapter Forty-Eight

KOROLEV LEANT against the trunk of a tree, waiting for Goldstein and Mishka to come back from scouting the place, and wishing it were possible to have a cigarette. It was strange, he thought, that in a situation where he should be, at the very least, apprehensive, he was instead consumed with desire for tobacco. He shifted his weight and did his best to keep his mind focused on the fear he should be feeling.

To his left, so close he could hear him breathing, was Kolya; and crouching on the ground in front of them was Slivka. Behind him, sitting on a tree trunk, were two more of Kolya's men – Red Sasha and the Deacon. The other two had been left with the cars, just off the main road, to make sure they all had a way out of the place.

It was a good night for this kind of affair, the moon was more than half-full but there were enough clouds passing overhead so that they could move around unseen. There was a stillness in the air that made the small sounds of the woods behind seem amplified – but Korolev was more concerned about the occasional noise from inside the high walls. What if Goldstein had been discovered?

'There,' Kolya whispered and pointed at a figure slipping over the wall at a point just ahead of them.

The boy dropped silently to the ground, sitting still for a long moment, before moving towards them at a crouch, pausing every now and then to listen and look – probably for them. When he was about twenty metres away Kolya gave a low whistle and the boy changed his course. When Goldstein reached them they retreated into the treeline.

'Well?' Kolya asked.

'The place is quiet enough. There's a guard at the main gate and one that walks around the place every fifteen minutes, but that's it, as far as I can see. The one who walks around is older and stout, he's carrying a pistol. The one at the main gate looks younger and fitter – he's got a pistol as well.'

'In his hand?'

'In his belt. They're both wearing holsters.'

'What about the buildings?' Korolev whispered, covering the torch's beam with his closed fingers so that only a pink glow came through. It was just enough to see Azarova's map and the others crowded in close.

'The map is accurate enough,' the boy said. 'The stable block was open and I had a look inside – it's full of crates and equipment, but empty of people. The main house is a different story, three entrances. The front door is here,' he said, pointing. 'It's well-lit around it so I couldn't check if it's locked or not, but my guess is it is. This is the back door and that's definitely locked, I tried it. This is the side entrance and it's open. It seems to lead down to a kitchen of some sort and it's where the walking guard goes when he isn't walking. I heard voices there so there may be others inside. There are lights on in there anyway. Both downstairs and upstairs.

'This is the new building, which looks like it might be what we're looking for. I heard a boy's voice and there are lights on inside. I tried the doors here and here, but it's locked up tight – and the windows are shuttered and secured as well. The walking guard has a key though – he went in for about five minutes while I was watching. I could hear him speaking to someone.'

'The boy's voice?' Korolev asked, trying to keep his optimism under control.

'I couldn't make out what he said but he was in a downstairs room – on the stable side. A woman was talking to him. I think it was the same woman who spoke to the guard.'

'Do you think he could be Yuri?'

'It's possible.'

Kolya turned to him and Korolev found himself nodding.

'Anything else?'

'There are three trucks parked up by the stable block, there's a car in front of the main house and a bus as well.'

'A bus?' Slivka asked.

'A small one – one of those ZIS ones.'

Korolev knew the model – a fourteen-seater. The number of vehicles concerned him, it could mean that there were more people about the place than he'd bargained for.

'Show us the walking guard's route.'

Goldstein traced a route that ran from the side entrance around the inside of the square wall that guarded the buildings, stopping off at the main gate, the newer building and the stable block before returning back to the side entrance. According to Goldstein his circuit took no more than five minutes.

'You said there are lights.'

'The areas around the buildings are lit up but there are plenty of shadows around the walls to move about in. And the stables are only lit at this end.'

Goldstein pointed to the end of the stable block closest to the new building.

Korolev nodded and looked at his watch – it was coming up to midnight. He prayed the voice was Yuri's.

§

They returned to the edge of the trees and didn't have to wait long before Mishka's crouched figure came into view, making its way carefully through the undergrowth. Again Kolya gave his low whistle and the Thief came towards them, one hand moving to his pocket – and Korolev didn't doubt it had wrapped itself around a pistol.

Once Mishka was sure it was them he relaxed and swung the small rucksack he was wearing from his shoulder down onto the ground and squatted beside them. The wall, it turned out, continued right the way around the buildings and at no point was it lower than the part they were currently closest to; in fact in some places it was higher. There were two gates other than the main gate but both were locked, and apart from rough lanes that led into the woods, the metalled drive that led from the main road was the only way in and out – for cars at least. As for the phone line, he'd dealt with it.

'We're best to go in where the kid went – just there.'

Mishka gestured towards the tree Goldstein had used to clamber over the wall.

'Well then,' Korolev said. 'This is how we'll do it.'

He spoke quietly, pointing out who was to go where and when. They had ten minutes, from the moment the walking guard went back into the house, to secure the front gate, search the new building and deal with whoever was in it, and disable the vehicles. Then five minutes from when the walking guard started his next round, in which to take him out of action.

'After that,' he said, 'we go into the main house. But remember the time – no dawdling. And try not to kill anyone – there's no point making this worse than it already is.'

There was silence, but he could see heads nodding in the gloom.

Kolya leant across and pushed something into his hand – a cosh. 'I brought a couple. Just in case.'

Slivka stood up and stretched.

'There's no time like the present,' she said.

'Remember,' Korolev whispered as they began to make their way towards the wall. 'No guns, unless it's life or death.'

Chapter Forty-Nine

KOROLEV WAS CROUCHED in the shadow of the bus — hidden, he hoped, from the main house, yet with a good view over the rest of the area inside the walls. About five minutes previously, there'd been the faintest of sounds from the main gate, then nothing — Kolya's two bruisers must have dealt with the guard. Not long after that, Korolev had seen Goldstein slip across the lit area heading up towards the trucks; then he'd watched as Mishka and Kolya crouched beside the side door to the new building for no more than fifteen seconds, before it opened and they were in. Someone must have found a set of keys on the main gate guard — which meant they were ahead of schedule.

He looked across at Slivka, standing under a low tree, invisible unless you were looking straight at her, except for perhaps the slightest reflection of light from the shoulders of her jacket. If the walking guard kept to the route Goldstein had described, he'd pass between them. All they could do now was wait — and perhaps pray. Korolev found his hand halfway to his shoulder to cross himself when he stopped, remembering that Slivka was probably looking over at him. His hand hung there for a moment before it occurred to him that he'd more to be worried about than Slivka seeing him bless himself.

No, Slivka wasn't someone he needed to fret about. He'd told her everything on the way out about the report, about how

Madame Azarova had killed Shtange. He'd even told her about his meeting with Rodinov and the dead end the report had turned out to be. The one thing he hadn't told her about was Goldstein's part in the business – but that had hardly seemed polite, what with Goldstein sitting in the car beside her. Now he looked across at her and finished what he'd started, his fingers touching his shoulders, his forehead, his lips, praying she made it out of this in one piece. He'd certainly do his best to see to it.

His mind had wandered a little perhaps, so that when a door shut somewhere inside the house he was surprised. He breathed deeply, pulled the cosh from his pocket, hefted it and reminded himself exactly what he had to do.

Now there came the sound of voices. A man's and a woman's. He looked across at Slivka and thought he saw her hand move – but if she meant to tell him something, he couldn't make it out. He prepared himself, bending his knees slightly – imagining the blow and exactly where it would land.

'I'll come with you – I could do with a breath of fresh air.'

A woman's voice. Korolev cursed under his breath, feeling a surge of alarm, but he calmed himself, thought it through. They couldn't let the guard go past – there was no choice. Not with his friend gagged, tied and out for the count at the main gate. Not with the door to the new building open and Mishka and Kolya busy at work. He beckoned Slivka to come forward, to distract them, and she nodded her agreement.

The footsteps were almost upon them now, one heavier, one lighter. Korolev held his breath as the pair came into view, both of them smoking, their pace slow and companionable.

'Comrades, have you a light?' Slivka asked as she stepped out from the shadow of the tree, calm as you like, and the guard was actually holding out his cigarette to her when Korolev's blow hit him between the neck and the ear, exactly where he'd envisaged it. The fellow went down faster than a drunk on an icy pavement.

The woman turned towards him, her mouth opening to scream and he was already swinging the cosh back to deal with her, God forgive him, when Slivka took a hold of her, pulling her back, one hand over her mouth, while with the other hand she showed the woman her pistol.

'Quiet now, Comrade,' Slivka whispered in her ear, her voice gentle, 'and all will be well. Make one noise though – and you won't make another. Understand?'

The woman's eyes were fixed on Korolev and it occurred to him that his face must be clearly visible in the light that was spilling over the top of the bus. It seemed her eyes were begging him for something.

'I asked whether you understood,' Slivka whispered again, pressing the barrel of her gun against the woman's cheek. The woman nodded, once.

'Take her over to the trees,' Korolev managed to say, wondering for the first time why the hell he hadn't had enough sense to make sure he and Slivka had covered their faces. If they did manage to rescue Yuri from this place – who would Zaitsev first suspect? Korolev. And now there was a witness as well. He felt sick to the pit of his stomach.

He leant down and checked the guard's pulse. There was one – which was good. The last thing they wanted was a fatality during the course of the evening. He took the guard under the arms, pulled him up and then swung him over his shoulder, stumbling as he did so. The fellow was no featherweight and Korolev, it seemed, wasn't as young and strong as he'd once been – but he made it as far as the bushes, where he dropped the guard down as softly as he could, searching him quickly and finding a bunch of keys and a packet of cigarettes. He took both – and the Nagant revolver from the fellow's holster for good measure. Then he tied the guard's hands behind his back and lashed his feet together. Finally he gagged him, leaving him on his side, curled up like a child – still out for the count.

Chapter Fifty

KOROLEV MADE his way as quietly and quickly as he could down the slight slope that led to the new building. The door Kolya and Mishka had gone through stood slightly open and he slipped through it, pulling it closed behind him. Ahead of him was a wide central corridor, along either side of which doors stood ajar. At the end of the corridor there was a stairwell with steps leading upwards.

It seemed Kolya and Mishka had been busy – in an office halfway along the corridor, two female nurses were sitting tied to chairs with gags in their mouth. One of them, with red hair, was slumped unconscious against the wall, but the other looked up as he passed. Her eyes were wide with fear. He was about to reassure her when there came a muffled crash from the floor above.

Despite his own instructions about avoiding the use of guns, he found he had the guard's pistol in his hand, with the business end leading the way up the stairs as he climbed them. Suddenly, there was a crash and the sound of feet moving rapidly back and forth.

Korolev opened the door to the upper corridor to find Kolya halfway along it, doing his best to dodge the wild, swinging blows of a huge man in a sleeveless vest. They fought in total silence. Mishka was lying against a wall, trying to push himself back to his feet, blood trickling from a nose that had

been unsympathetically rearranged. The little Thief looked confused.

When Kolya saw him, he went on the attack, landing two
sharp blows, and Korolev took his cue, racing as silently as
he could along the corridor. The giant shrugged off Kolya's
punches and began to turn, but too late – Korolev was already
swinging the butt of the Nagant down with every ounce of his
strength. For a moment, Korolev thought it hadn't been enough,
but the big man slowly fell to his knees, shaking his head as did
so. He knelt for a moment before trying to stand again. Korolev
and Kolya looked at each other, before Korolev, shrugging his
shoulders, hit the giant one more time – even harder, if that
were possible.

Like a felled tree, the big man quivered for a moment than
collapsed to the ground – out for the count, blood pulsing from
his injured head.

'What took you so long?' Kolya said, his voice distorted by
a fat lip and ragged breath. 'I think I broke a finger on that
ape's ear. His ear, mind you, not his jaw or anything solid like
that.'

Korolev found he was also out of breath – either from
running up the stairs or the adrenaline. He wasn't sure which.

'If I'd known you were going to go toe-to-toe with this
fellow I'd have come earlier, just for the show.'

'Did you get the other guard's keys?' Kolya asked.

'I have them.'

'There's a door downstairs we couldn't open. Mishka found
this fellow in there.' Kolya pointed to what seemed to be
some kind of an operating room. Korolev stepped inside. A
long bed fitted with leather straps stood in the centre, its head
almost touching a large black machine covered with dials and
levers – from which a worrying-looking wire skullcap dangled.
Korolev stepped back out to find Kolya helping Mishka to his
feet.

'It looks like he found the fellow with his face. Is he all right?'

'What's it to you?' Mishka growled, holding himself up with one hand against the wall. Then he was sick over his shoes.

'Not too bad then,' Korolev said. 'Mishka, keep an eye on your friend here while we check the rest of the floor.'

They moved quickly from room to room, finding another of the strange machines but otherwise nothing. It seemed the giant had been alone on the upper floor. Korolev looked at his watch. They had to get moving.

'What do we do with that lump in the corridor?' Kolya asked and Korolev, for an answer, pointed to the leather restraining straps on one of the beds.

It took all three of them to drag the giant back into the room he'd emerged from and lift him up on to the bed. They had to pull the straps as tight as they could in order to be able to buckle them onto the last notch, so huge was the man's frame.

Perhaps it was Mishka's swearing as he tried to push his nose back into shape but the giant woke just as they'd finished, his eyes meeting Korolev's for a moment in surprise before they flicked left and right. At the sight of the machine above him however, his eyes went wide with terror and he began to buck and rear on the bed. Even with a gag in place he still managed to make an animal mewling that had the hairs at the back of Korolev's neck standing to attention.

'What the hell's up with him?' Mishka asked.

Korolev saw the rubber skullcap that hung down from the machine – a number of small wires dangling from it. On a hunch, he pulled the thing out and held it directly over the man's head, the wires dangling down to touch his face. The struggling ceased and the giant's body went rigid. Korolev leant down to whisper in his ear.

'I have questions for you. Will you answer them?'

The big man nodded and Korolev undid the buckle of the

gag. There was silence as he did so and Korolev glanced up to see Kolya watching with interest.

'How many are in the main house?'

'The children?' The man had a voice like pouring gravel.

'Them first.'

'Twenty-two'.

'Where?'

'Upstairs. Two dormitories. At the end of the long corridor.'

'And apart from the children?'

There was a slight hesitation, until Korolev made as if to lower the skull cap.

'Eight guards, four nurses and a doctor,' the man said in a rush. 'The guards sleep on the ground floor. It's the big room beside the front door. The nurses and the doctor are upstairs. The rooms off the landing.'

'It's past midnight – who will be up and about?'

'A nurse for the children, the guard who does regular rounds and the guard at the gate. No more than that.'

'And you? What are you up for? And the nurses downstairs?'

'There's an operation later – we're getting ready.'

'In the middle of the night?'

'It's when they do them.'

Korolev wanted to ask why, but he had a more pressing concern.

'There was a boy brought in. Yesterday. Where is he?'

'Blonde hair?'

Korolev's stomach seemed to contract. 'Yes.'

'Downstairs.'

'The locked room? Where's the key?'

Again, hesitation, but Korolev knew how to deal with it now.

'The guard up at the house has it.'

Korolev pulled the keys from his pocket and held them up.

'Which one?'

'The brass one.'

'If you're lying about any of this . . .'

'On my mother's life.'

Korolev looked at the size of the man and pitied the woman who'd had to give birth to him. 'If you even think of trying to escape, we'll make an omelette out of that tiny brain of yours. Just so you know. If you stay where you are – you'll likely come out of this in one piece.'

Korolev motioned Kolya and Mishka to the door.

'Do we trust him?' Kolya asked, when they were halfway down the stairs.

'Well here's the first test,' Korolev said and put the key the big man had indicated into the locked door. It opened easily and there Yuri was – backed into a corner of the room, his knees drawn up in front of him, his arms holding them tightly and his terrified face looking in amazement as Korolev ran the three steps to him and swung him up into his arms.

Chapter Fifty-One

KOROLEV CARRIED his son as they made their way towards the main house, not because Yuri couldn't walk but because he wanted to hold the boy tight to him.

'Did they do anything to you?' Korolev asked him in a whisper.

'No. But the red-haired nurse –' Korolev remembered the one, she'd been out for the count in the corridor – 'she said they were going to fix me, make me loyal to the State. I kept telling her I *was* loyal. But she kept saying it all the same.'

'There's no one more loyal, Yuri,' Korolev said, feeling the boy was rigid with indignation. 'The Party knows that.'

'Yes,' Yuri said. 'Yes, they do. They know everything.'

God help them both if they did, thought Korolev, and nodded to Slivka as she stepped out of the bushes. Korolev was pleased to see Goldstein and the Deacon had joined her.

'Kim,' he said in a quiet voice. 'Take Yuri to the woods. Wait for us there. If there's a problem, head for the cars and go.'

Goldstein nodded, smiled at Yuri and held out a hand to show him the way.

'Yuri,' Korolev said, leaning down to place him on the ground, kissing his head as he did so. 'We'll catch up with you as soon as we can – but don't wait if there's trouble. Kim will get you to the apartment and I'll meet you there. Understood?'

Korolev pushed him towards Goldstein and watched until they disappeared into the shrubbery.

§

They entered the main house through the side door that the guard and the nurse had come out of. They all had their guns out now – six guards could be problematic, and if the giant had been lying and there were more then they really could be in trouble.

Once in, they took the rooms one by one – Korolev and Slivka first making sure the kitchen was clear, while Kolya and the others covered the corridor. There was no need to talk – they worked their way from kitchen, to pantry, to a strongroom with a massive metal door, then into some kind of storage room. They moved quickly and they moved smoothly. Everywhere was empty.

On the ground floor they repeated the exercise, working their way through an incongruously opulent dining room, the table set for twelve, then what seemed to be classrooms, then an office, another office, a sitting room, a toilet. They found the guards just where they'd been told they would be and, with gun barrels pushing into the napes of their necks, bundled them down to the strongroom and locked the half-naked, panicked-looking men inside. Then they started up to the first floor.

Perhaps they'd made too much noise with the guards, and certainly one or two of the stairs creaked as they'd made their way up them, but whether they'd woken him or he'd wandered out onto the landing by chance, Korolev looked up to see a half-dressed man wearing round-rimmed spectacles, staring down at them in surprise, and then fear.

God knew what they must have seemed like to him. Mishka with his broken nose, Kolya with his bumps and bruises and Korolev's two-day-old battering probably not looking pretty either. And if Korolev's face reflected his mood then the fellow was right to look panicked – because a certain Captain of the Workers' and Peasants' Militia had been thinking something through during the last few minutes and had just worked out the answer. If there'd been an operation intended for this very night – then the probable patient had been his son. And if that was true, and if this wretch was a doctor – then Korolev would lay a handsome bet this fellow was the most likely would-be perpetrator of that so-called operation.

'Move one damned inch and I'll put a slug right between your damned eyes and then I'll spit in the hole.'

It was only when he'd finished speaking that Korolev realized the voice was his own. What was more, he was surprised to discover that a large part of him was praying the devil would move that damned inch. Korolev's aim didn't waver until Slivka reached the doctor and turned him until he was facing the wall, pressing her gun into his spine.

'Are you the doctor?' Slivka asked in a quiet voice and the fellow nodded. And it didn't take much prompting for him to tell them where to find the nurses. They were broad-shouldered women – hard-faced even in slumber, and hard to wake as well, but wake them they did, and then Slivka and Mishka pushed them downstairs to join the guards.

Korolev kept the doctor though, and pushed him at gunpoint to the first of the children's dormitories.

'Open it and turn on the light.'

There were twelve metal beds, six on either side of the room. Two of them were empty but the remainder contained boys of around Yuri's age in various states between sleep and bleary awakening, as they reacted to the three men walking into the room.

'Is he here?' Korolev asked, turning to Kolya who was close behind.

Kolya looked at each boy then shook his head.

'No.'

It was curious that the boys didn't seem surprised to find armed men walking amongst them. As they woke, they looked at them with calm disinterest. Korolev was about to reassure them when he realized they didn't need it.

'The next room,' Kolya said, and there was anger in his voice as he pushed the doctor towards the door.

The second dormitory was the same as the first – a dozen beds – and, this time, a dozen boys. As the light went on they stirred, eyes opening, heads lifting from pillows, and suddenly Kolya pushed the doctor out of his way, going straight to a bed at the other end of the room, pulling the boy in it close to his chest, whispering to him, stroking his hair.

'I only did what I was told,' the doctor said to Korolev. 'I only followed orders, no more than that.'

Korolev looked back to Kolya's son and there it was again, that look of serene calm. The boy didn't seem surprised that Kolya was stroking his hair, far from it – he seemed barely to notice.

'What did you do to them?'

'It wasn't me. It was the professor and the others – they set everything up. I just do as I'm told.'

'We'll see about that.'

'I swear it.'

Korolev took a step closer to him and pushed his gun into the doctor's stomach.

'Tell me where the files are – the ones they brought out from Moscow.'

The doctor looked nonplussed.

'What files?'

'In the trucks. They started coming out on Tuesday.'

He looked terrified. 'I've been here all week, there have been no trucks. The only visitors we've had are the ones who came last night, with a boy.'

'And that's the boy you were going to operate on this evening.'

'I told you, Comrade. I only do what I'm told to do.'

'That boy's my son,' Korolev growled.

The doctor took a step back, looking around him as if for a means of escape.

Kolya approached them. 'What did you do to them? These children.' There wasn't anger in his voice; if anything he looked lost. The doctor looked from him to Korolev and back again but he didn't answer. Korolev lifted his gun. The doctor flinched back as the barrel tracked up the length of his body.

'Tell him,' Korolev said, his voice hoarse.

'They have machines,' he told them. 'In the other house. They clean minds with electricity. So there's nothing left.'

'So he doesn't know who I am.'

Kolya wasn't asking a question. He was stating a fact.

'He doesn't know anything. They only know what the political teachers tell them,' the doctor said. And then the whispering began, the children getting out of their beds and moving towards them, pointing at Kolya.

'It's him, I swear it's him.' This, from a brown-haired tyke, who was looking at Kolya as if he were the Lord himself come down to walk amongst them.

Korolev had noticed Kolya's similarity to the General Secretary of the Party before – it had made him wonder sometimes, in fact; and now it seemed he wasn't the only one to notice the resemblance.

'Comrade Stalin?' a boy asked.

'It's all they know,' the doctor said. 'It's all they've been taught.'

And Kolya's son broke through the group and lifted his hand to touch his father's face, his eyes wet with adoration.

Chapter Fifty-Two

THEY LEFT THE other boys in the house. There wasn't any choice – they couldn't bring them all with them and, anyway, they didn't seem to want to leave – the damage had been done. They'd be made into perfect little Party activists, no doubt, who worshipped Stalin and loved Lenin. And who was to say they wouldn't be happier for it? Certainly having a mind that thought for itself hadn't made Korolev content – far from it.

Korolev and Slivka took the doctor down the stairs, and even though he kept asking them what they were going to do with him, they said nothing – just let the man sweat and then pushed the fellow into the strongroom with the others.

Korolev stood in the doorway, looking in at the frightened faces in the small space, and lit the cigarette that every fibre in his body was crying out for. He thought he saw guilt in their expressions and possibly remorse. He hoped he did. He hoped they realized that if you did the kind of things to a person that they'd done – well then – you should expect that something similar might be done to you down the road.

Korolev could feel the heat of Kolya's anger from where he stood behind him

'We said no killing, Kolya.'

'Not here, maybe. But I'm remembering faces.'

Korolev, as it happened, was doing the same. Folk seldom turned the other cheek completely, in his experience, they just waited for an opportunity. It might never come – but if it did, they'd take it. And so he looked at the rats in the strongroom, at each one of their faces, and he memorized them. Then he slowly shut the door and locked it. And left them in the dark.

He turned to Kolya.

'Chances are Zaitsev will hand out their punishment for us, anyway. They failed him.'

'Let's get out of here,' Kolya said. The Thief's eyes looked as if they were glowing with a dark, volcanic rage.

'You go ahead – there's something I have to do.' Korolev's voice sounded tired, even to him.

Slivka stepped forward. 'It's not worth it, Chief. Stick to the plan – in and out. It's the best way.'

'Not them.'

'What then?'

'There might be papers here that back up Shtange's report. Somewhere.'

'We should go,' Slivka said in a flat tone.

'Where to, Slivka? You think they won't know this is our work? Do you think we can hide? There are other people involved in this – Valentina, Yasimov, our friends, our families. You know how these things work. If there's something that backs up what Shtange wrote, we've a chance.'

Slivka looked at him in silence for a moment, then nodded to Kolya.

'Give us ten minutes – we'll see you at the cars.'

Chapter Fifty-Three

KOROLEV COULD hear the boys moving around upstairs as they worked their way through the first of the offices. Meanwhile, file after file dropped to the floor as he and Slivka went through the cabinet drawers one by one.

'What are we looking for?' Slivka said.

'Anything financial. Accounts, invoices, receipts, estimates, orders, payslips – I don't know. Anything with a number and a rouble.'

He left Slivka and went on to the other office – the desk was locked and so he went to the dining room and grabbed a handful of cutlery from the table. Two knives lay bent and broken on the floor by the time he got into the drawers, but he found nothing of use in them – just writing paper and some pencils.

He moved onto the cabinets and then the shelves, throwing books and paper around him, so that anyone walking in would have thought there'd been an explosion. But still he came across nothing which looked like it might be remotely relevant.

'Are there offices in the new building?' Slivka asked, coming in.

'There are, but we don't have time.'

Korolev was finding it difficult to concentrate on anything except the plan they'd made.

'We do, if we're quick.'

Korolev considered this, then considered the alternative. They'd have to make time.

'Well then, let's hurry.'

Perhaps it was his tiredness, or the constant fear he'd been living with for days now – but it felt as though he were moving through water as they ran down to the new building. And even though his eyes were telling him he was moving fast, he'd the strong impression that he'd never reach the door he was heading for. He could barely hear the crunch and slide of his shoes on the gravel over the roaring in his ears. Then he was standing inside the doorway, trying to catch his breath.

'You take the doors on the left. I'll take the right. Let's be quick, but let's be careful.'

The first office yielded nothing – patient files, manuals, an entire drawer full of political lectures, a folder full of photographs of Stalin, charts – everything, it seemed, except what he was looking for. He could hear drawers being emptied by Slivka across the corridor.

'Anything?' he called in to her as he moved onto the second door.

'Nothing,' was her reply.

There was a desk in this room, again locked. He looked round for something to open it with and, for a moment, considered using his gun. Then he saw a coat hook on the back of the door and, using all his weight, wrenched it out of the wood that held it. He wedged it into the desk and then used the heavy chair to hammer out the drawer. Pens. A bar of Three Piglets chocolate.

He took the chocolate for Yuri.

The third office had the two terrified nurses in it, both conscious now. These women in their crisp white dresses – if he hadn't come here tonight it would be his son upstairs looking at them in terror.

'Witches. Devils. Wretches.' He spat each word at them,

flinging useless paper to the floor from the drawers as he did so.

'Chief.'

It was Slivka, standing in the doorway. And there was something wrong. She looked as if the breath had been knocked out of her.

'Chief, two cars have just arrived. They've found the guard at the front gate. He's talking to them. They're closing the place off – they must know we're here.'

He stood, the sweat turning cold on his skin.

Chapter Fifty-Four

IT WAS ALWAYS going to end this way, he supposed.

Korolev stood beside Slivka in a darkened room on the upper floor, watching another carload of men arrive. Svalov, Zaitsev's tubby assistant, sent them up to the main house with Blanter – the boxer. Korolev closed his eyes and felt every last drop of energy drain away from him. Svalov had already surrounded the building they were in and was now looking up at it. It seemed to Korolev that he was staring at the very window they were standing at.

'We could try and run for it.' Slivka's voice sounded tired.

'We're surrounded and they know we're here. They'd shoot us down.'

'That might be better.'

'For us, perhaps.'

Another car pulled in through the gates and Svalov went over to it, leaning down to speak to someone in the front passenger seat.

'Come on, let's go and meet our fate. Leave the guns here.'

Korolev took the guard's Nagant from his pocket and then slipped the Walther from his underarm holster. Was it fifteen years he'd had it? More. He placed Azarova's little pea-shooter beside it. He patted the Walther farewell.

'Slivka,' he said, turning to her, 'for what it's worth, you've been the best of comrades.'

'And you, Chief, have been the best of chiefs.'

They walked down the stairs, shoulder to shoulder, and then along the corridor to the half-open door that led outside.

'I'll go first,' Korolev said.

'I—' Slivka began.

'This once, Nadezhda Andreyevna, let me have my way.'

Slivka looked as though she thought he might be taking advantage of the situation, but she nodded.

One of the cars had a searchlight and as he came out with his hands held high he had to turn his eyes from the glare.

'Take off the jacket, slowly.'

The voice sounded as if it meant business and he complied.

'Who are you?'

'Korolev, captain in the Militia. From Petrovka.' And then, because he thought it couldn't do any harm. 'On temporary assignment to State Security.'

He heard the sound of a car door opening and footsteps approaching, but it was as if the searchlight had mesmerized him, he couldn't look away from it.

'Korolev, it seems you're one step ahead of us.'

Korolev turned to confirm the voice belonged to the man he thought it did.

'Dubinkin?'

'The very same – but you look as though you've seen a ghost, Korolev. Are you all right?'

Dubinkin had that irritating smile on his face once again – the one that told you he knew just that little bit more about you than you did yourself. And Korolev was damned if he'd play along with it.

'We've been worried about you,' the Chekist continued. 'We wondered if you mightn't have bitten off more than you could chew.'

Dubinkin had a cheek to feign concern, and Korolev found

his irritation turning to anger. He'd face the consequences of his actions. But he was damned if he'd be made fun of.

'Did your boss Zaitsev send you here to do his dirty work?' he said, and could hear the bitterness in his voice.

'No,' Dubinkin said, with what appeared to be genuine amusement. 'I've only ever had one boss. And Comrade Colonel Rodinov is a very pleased man this evening. Your investigation has turned from defeat to triumph. How did you know Dr Weiss had a copy of Shtange's report?'

'I didn't,' Korolev said.

'Well,' Dubinkin said, smiling, 'then you're the luckiest man alive.'

Chapter Fifty-Five

IN ALL THE excitement, no one had bothered to ask how Slivka and Korolev had made their way out this far from Moscow, at night, on their own. Nor had anyone questioned how the two of them, again on their own, had managed to secure the entire facility. And as no one asked, Korolev decided not to mention that the Chief Authority of the Moscow Thieves and his right-hand man were waiting for them in the woods – or had been, until the NKVD cars showed up at least. No, he'd kept his mouth shut and thanked the all-merciful Lord above him that, for the moment at least, things seemed to have taken a surprising turn for the better.

During the drive back to Moscow in a car full of large men, however, the reality of his situation began to dawn on him. And during two hours waiting in a Lubyanka corridor to talk to Rodinov, the reality had hit home, and hard. The slow passing of each minute made him more and more conscious that certain questions were going to be asked once the colonel called him in. And he knew Rodinov well enough by now to know that when they were asked, there wouldn't be much point in lying.

So by the time a lean, hungry-looking type had come to fetch him to see the colonel – well – it wasn't just the close atmosphere that was making his shirt damp with sweat.

'Korolev.' The colonel looked up from a typed sheet of

paper that he appeared to be signing. He followed Korolev's gaze to the document and, to Korolev's surprise, smiled.

'Do you know what this is, Korolev?'

Korolev shook his head. As far as he was concerned the colonel could sit there naked as God intended, singing 'Kalinka Malinka', and it would be none of his business.

'I've no idea, Comrade Colonel.'

'I'll tell you. My first orders as the head of the Twelfth Department.'

'I congratulate you, Comrade Colonel.' It seemed the thing to say.

The colonel scribbled what might have been a signature, put his pen down and leant back in his chair to examine Korolev.

'It's been a hard evening for you. Dubinkin said you looked like you thought your last hour had come.'

'I thought he was working for Zaitsev.'

'He was, in a manner of speaking. But he's always worked for me. Blanter and Svalov came to me later in the game, when they saw which way the wind was blowing.'

'I see that now. But at the time . . .'

'I can imagine. Dubinkin said you didn't know Weiss had a copy of the report?'

'I knew he had something.'

'Well, whatever you said to Weiss, he felt obliged to pass the report on to Boldyrev.'

'I don't even know who this Boldyrev is.'

'Comrade Boldyrev is the newly appointed People's Commissar for Health. Haven't you read the papers over the last few days?'

Rodinov smiled at his own joke, and opened a metal cigarette case. One that Korolev had seen before somewhere. It had a propeller engraved on its cover.

'Well, you know now – and when Weiss told him about the report, Boldyrev saw an opportunity to prove himself worthy of promotion to People's Commissar. So he showed it to Molotov. And Molotov showed it to Comrade Stalin. And Comrade Stalin decreed that Zaitsev should be arrested. And he has been.'

Rodinov lit a cigarette and pushed the box over to Korolev. 'It was Dr Shtange who gave Weiss his copy of the report, of course. He knew the contents were damning but he felt loyalty to an outdated academic convention which required him to show it to Azarov before he gave it to the person who'd commissioned it – or in this case, his successor. But just in case things went badly, he thought he'd leave a copy of the report with Weiss for safe keeping.'

Korolev nodded as though he understood. But he didn't.

'Shtange must have told Azarov there was another copy in existence,' the colonel continued. 'As a kind of insurance in case Azarov tried anything, I suppose. And Azarov must have told Zaitsev about it – that's how Zaitsev knew there were at least two copies for you to look for.'

Korolev took a cigarette, listening to the colonel but sneaking another quick look at the cigarette box. He'd seen it only days before, he was sure – and it hadn't been in this room.

'Zaitsev didn't know who had the second copy – no one did – and, of course, you inadvertently removed Azarov's copy before he could place his hands on that one. So all Zaitsev knew about the report was what he'd been told by Azarov on the phone – and that was enough to frighten him, but not too much. Until, that is, Azarov showed up with a bullet in his head and his copy wasn't to be found. Then he began to become concerned. And he became very concerned when Shtange was murdered and his copy couldn't be found either. Well, you can only imagine – I shouldn't be surprised if he thought I was behind the whole thing.'

Korolev was tired enough that if he'd been a horse he'd have been put down – but the cigarette case was bothering him. He should remember where he'd seen it.

'So that's why Zaitsev stripped all the paperwork and books from the apartment. To try to find the report before anyone else got their hands on it.'

'Just in case, however, he shut down the institute. He reasoned that without the institute there'd be next to no evidence to back up the allegations contained in the report. And he was right. Comrade Ezhov hasn't fully settled in as Chief of State Security yet and has enough on his plate, believe me, without going after someone like Zaitsev. So Zaitsev must have felt he was safe – until, of course, someone showed the report to Comrade Stalin himself. Which Comrade Molotov did yesterday evening.'

Korolev had never seen the colonel so – well – ebullient.

'And it's all thanks to you.'

'I only did my duty,' Korolev said.

'Well, not quite.' The colonel looked stern for a moment, but the effort seemed too much for him. He shook his head as if Korolev had done something that had amused him.

'Don't worry, Korolev, I'll overlook what happened out in Lefortovo. As far as I'm concerned you were looking for evidence of Colonel Zaitsev's crimes and that's that. The fact you may have had some unorthodox assistance and seem to have made off with two children is – well – neither here nor there, as far as I'm concerned.'

Korolev didn't know what to say.

'Yes.' the colonel nodded, 'that's the way to leave things – as they are. Your son, I hope, is safe?'

'I hope so,' Korolev said, trying to maintain a sombre expression while relief was singing in his veins. 'I'll find out soon.'

'And so, you'll be pleased to hear, is your wife. Your ex-wife rather. But a word of advice for her – she should leave Zagorsk. I can only intervene once. She might be better off moving to the new territories we're opening up in Siberia – they need good engineers there, and a fresh start will do her no harm.'

Korolev thought about that – about Yuri going even further away. And he felt a small part of his pleasure in the boy's safety diminish.

'I'll tell her.'

'Good.' Rodinov considered him for a moment. 'Which brings us to the murders, I suppose. Professor Azarov?'

Korolev thought about Goldstein and his bravery at the institute. If he'd killed the professor hadn't he been administering a higher form of justice? In any normal society, the professor would have been a criminal – at least in Korolev's opinion. But then hadn't Goldstein's action caused this whole chain of events? He needed to think about it.

'We'll have to carry on our investigations,' he said. 'We have a few leads. It wasn't Shtange, that's for sure. I can only think some of the professor's techniques were used on Priudski to make him give that evidence.'

Rodinov considered this for a moment, then shook his head. 'It doesn't matter. Shtange's dead and his wife leaves for France this afternoon with their children. Shtange will do. That's the end of it, Korolev.'

Korolev was about to object and then stopped himself. Yes, Dr Shtange would do. If his wife ever found out, she'd know the truth and she'd know it in Paris or wherever she ended up. Korolev lived in Moscow and if the colonel said, in as many words, that Shtange had killed the professor – then who was he to second-guess the newly appointed head of the Twelfth Department?

'Now what about Shtange's death?' the colonel continued.

'Madame Azarova,' Korolev said. 'Although, I'm not sure she was quite right in the head at the time.'

And perhaps it was the mention of Shtange's death that finally jolted his exhausted brain to remember who that damned cigarette case belonged to. Perhaps the realization showed on his face, because the colonel slid it across the table to him once again.

'You recognize it now? I saw you looking at it. Did you see it when you went to visit Shtange at the institute?'

'Yes,' Korolev said, remembering Shtange offering him a cigarette from the case and how the propeller had caught his attention.

'The dedication is curious. Open it up.'

Korolev picked up the case and looked inside.

'Read it aloud.'

'*With the fondest regards and enormous gratitude for your efforts,*' Korolev read. '*G.N. Kaminsky.*'

'Dubinkin found it in Zaitsev's office. He thought I might like it as a souvenir. Are you wondering why?'

Korolev was confused – as far as he was aware, Kaminsky was the current People's Commissar for Health. It had confused him earlier when Rodinov had been talking about this fellow Boldyrev having taken over the job.

'I'll tell you, Korolev. On Monday evening, not six hours after our Professor Azarov went to meet his maker, Grigory Kaminsky made a speech to the Central Committee. In that speech he denounced the NKVD for making false arrests. By the time he was halfway through it, half his audience had left the room. By the time he'd finished it, our people were waiting for him. That's how come the position of People's Commissar of Health became vacant.'

'I see.'

'I don't know if you do – you see, Shtange's report was intended for Kaminsky. I don't know if Kaminsky ever received his copy, but he certainly made veiled references to the institute in his speech. That's why Zaitsev felt relatively comfortable about it. He knew Kaminsky was discredited and he knew Shtange, because of the sentiments in this cigarette case, could be discredited as well. But the truth will out, Korolev. The truth will out.'

The colonel seemed to consider what that might mean and his expression turned grave, almost melancholy.

'Yes, we must remember that.'

Chapter Fifty-Six

MOSCOW WAS BEGINNING to wake as he walked home. It must have rained because the streets were wet and their reflection of the yellow morning sky had turned them golden. He was tired, certainly – his shoes felt like they were made of lead – but he was alive and he was safe, relative to the last few days anyway. And a citizen couldn't ask for much more these days.

Sometimes a murder was like a pebble thrown into a pond, the ripples from it spreading wide – and that had been the case here. A bullet fired on a Monday had killed the professor in the morning and contributed to the arrest of the People's Commissar for Health in the afternoon. On Tuesday, it had claimed another life – Shtange's – and seen Priudski arrested. And last night the bullet had claimed Colonel Zaitsev – and Korolev could only guess the colonel's fall would lead to many others.

One bullet had wreaked havoc.

Korolev walked slowly, thinking it through, amazed that he and Yuri had somehow been spared.

But then he remembered where he was going and who might be waiting there for him – and he picked up his pace. By the time he turned the corner of Bolshoi Nikolo-Vorobinsky he was almost running. He must have woken half the house as he clattered up the staircase to the apartment.

They *were* waiting for him, and as he entered the shared

room he saw three faces looking up at him. They must have been sleeping on the chesterfield. Valentina stood, rubbing at her eyes, but Yuri was already running towards him, grabbing him around his waist and Natasha, Valentina's little girl, joined him a moment later. And then all four of them were holding each other, not saying anything, and Korolev found that his eyes were damp – and it wasn't from sadness.

Historical Note

The original idea for *The Twelfth Department* came from a BBC documentary series called *The Brain: A Secret History*. The 'Mind Control' episode featured footage of 1930s Soviet experiments demonstrating the conditioned reflexes of children to eating biscuits – a variation on Pavlov's dog experiments, but this time done with hungry-looking teenagers. It also seemed from the clip that some of the young boys had been operated on – although for what purpose remains unknown.

What is known is that the Soviets were very interested in psychological manipulation from the earliest years of the Revolution – and that both they and the Nazis, despite having repressive regimes, achieved genuine loyalty from their populations through propaganda and the careful exploitation of perceived internal and external threats. It's also true that Soviet interrogation methods were very sophisticated by the 1930s and some of their techniques, particularly sensory deprivation, are still being used by American and British intelligence-gatherers today. Indeed the term 'brainwashing' was coined in response to the inexplicable behaviour of American and British prisoners of war captured during the Korean War – who almost overnight appeared to have become devout Communists.

That having been said, the parts of *The Twelfth Department* that deal with Soviet research into mind control are fictional and none of the events portrayed in this novel are based on actual events.

Three real people are mentioned in *The Twelfth Department* –

Nikolai Ezhov, Isaac Babel and Grigoriy Kaminsky – and it's probably worth saying a little bit about each of them.

Nikolai Ezhov became People's Commissar for Internal Security in September 1936, taking over from his predecessor, Genrikh Yagoda. Yagoda was later arrested and sentenced to death and, on Ezhov's orders, was severely beaten before his execution. Ezhov kept the bullet that killed Yagoda in his office. While the Great Terror began under Yagoda, it reached its peak under Ezhov's direction and, in the brief period he held his post, millions were arrested, many of whom were executed. By 1938 Ezhov had eliminated all internal opposition to Stalin – as well as countless innocents – and become a threat himself in the process. As a result, he was replaced by Lavrenti Beria in late 1938 and, after a few months awaiting a certain fate, was arrested. He was severely beaten before his execution in early 1940.

Isaac Babel wrote some brilliant short stories in the 1920s, before, like many other Soviet writers, becoming relatively unproductive during the 1930s – a time when the State viewed all forms of artistic expression with suspicion. Babel's situation wasn't helped by his having had an affair with Ezhov's wife, and when Ezhov fell from power, the NKVD chief took the opportunity to denounce Babel as a French spy. The writer was arrested not long afterwards and in January 1940 joined a long list of Soviet writers who perished during the Great Terror. It's said he and Ezhov are buried in the same unmarked grave in Moscow's Donskoi cemetery.

Grigory Kaminsky, a lifelong Bolshevik, had reached the rank of People's Commissar for Health in 1937. He was arrested after making a speech at a Central Committee plenum in June of that year during which he criticized the NKVD's indiscriminate arrest of innocent Party activists. Reportedly he also clashed with Stalin, saying, 'If we go on like this we'll shoot the whole Party', to which Stalin replied, 'You wouldn't by chance be friends of these enemies – well, then, you're birds of a feather.' Kaminsky was executed by firing squad at the beginning of 1938 but rehabilitated under Khrushchev in 1955.

Kaminsky's brave action is mentioned in Khrushchev's famous Secret Speech of 1956, which revealed the full extent of Stalin's crimes.

I based the building which houses the completely fictional Azarov Institute on the Igumnov House, which is located at 43 Bolshoi Yakimanka Street. The Igumnov House was built in the 1890s for a wealthy merchant but, by 1937, it had become home to the Moscow Brain Institute, an establishment which investigated Lenin's brain, among others. I'm confident the Brain Institute never engaged in any of the research which occupies the Azarov Institute in these pages. The building was allocated to the French embassy in 1938 and currently serves as the French ambassador's residence in Moscow.

The Hotel Moskva, where Korolev meets Madame Shtange in chapter 27, opened in 1935 and was designed by the architect Alexei Shchusev, who was also responsible for Lenin's mausoleum on nearby Red Square. The Hotel Moskva was one of the most prominent of the new Stalinist-style buildings that replaced so much of the old Moscow during the 1930s and 1940s. The hotel was knocked down in 2004 and replaced with a modern reproduction, but both feature mismatched wings to the facade that faces on to Okhotny Ryad – one wing having larger windows and a more ornate design, while the other is simpler and with smaller windows. The story that Muscovites tell to explain this lack of symmetry is that Stalin mistakenly authorized two alternative plans for the hotel and, rather than ask for clarification, those responsible for the construction implemented one design for each wing, giving the hotel its unbalanced appearance. I've posted some photographs of the original hotel on my website (www.william-ryan.com), including some of the roof terrace where Korolev and Madame Shtange have their conversation.

Gorky Park, where Korolev meets Count Kolya in chapter forty-two, was opened in 1928 and named for Maxim Gorky, the writer much admired by Stalin – and also probably murdered on his orders in 1936. The parachute tower and the statue of the oarswoman that they notice during their conversation were iconic images of 1930s

Moscow and feature in numerous propaganda posters. The parachute tower has long gone but the oarswoman, who has been moved around a bit over the last eighty-odd years, has finally come to rest down on the embankment, calmly overlooking the Moskva. I've posted a number of photographs of the park on my website, both as it was in its heyday and how it is today.

Leadership House, where Professor Azarov lives and is murdered, is closely based on the massive Government House – built in 1931 on the same spot as my fictional recreation and featured in Yuri Trifonov's novel *House on the Embankment*. Aside from over 500 apartments, the building also housed shops, cinemas, theatres and canteens. The residents of Government House suffered disproportionately during the Terror, probably because so many of them were senior Party members and held important positions within Soviet society. Hundreds of tenants were arrested and many of them executed.

For those who are interested in the period and would like to read further, I can recommend the following books – all of which have been of great assistance in trying to recreate the Soviet Union of the 1930s:

Danzig Baldaev (and others), *Russian Criminal Tattoo Encyclopedia*, 3 vols. (Steidl/Fuel, 2003; Fuel, 2006; Fuel, 2008).
Harold Eeman, *Inside Stalin's Russia – Memories of a Diplomat 1936–1941* (Triton, 1977).
Orlando Figes, *The Whisperers* (Allen Lane, 2007).
Sheila Fitzpatrick, *Everyday Stalinism* (Oxford, 1999).
Sheila Fitzpatrick, *Tear off the Masks – Identity and Imposture in Twentieth Century Russia* (Princeton, 2005).
Peter Francis, *I Worked in a Soviet Factory* (Jarrolds, 1939).
Garros, Korenevskaya and Lahusen, *Intimacy and Terror – Soviet Diaries of the 1930s* (New Press, 1995).
Jochen Hellbeck, *Revolution on My Mind – Writing a Diary Under Stalin* (Harvard, 2006).

Christina Kiaer and Eric Naiman, *Everyday Life in Early Soviet Russia* (Indiana University Press, 2006).

Hiroaki Kuromiya, *The Voices of the Dead* (Yale, 2007).

Nina Lugovskaya, *The Diary of a Soviet Schoolgirl 1932–1937* (Glas, 2003).

Nadezhda Mandelstam, *Hope Against Hope* and *Hope Abandoned* (Collins and Harvill, 1971).

Catherine Merridale, *Night of Stone – Death and Memory in Russia* (Granta, 2000).

Simon Sebag Montefiore, *Stalin – The Court of the Red Tsar* (Weidenfeld & Nicolson, 2003).

Peter Pringle, *The Murder of Nikolai Vavilov* (Simon & Schuster, 2008).

Donald Rayfield, *Stalin and His Hangmen* (Viking, 2004).

Lewis Siegelbaum and Andrei Sokolov, *Stalinism as a Way of Life* (Yale, 2004).

Andrew Smith, *I Was a Soviet Worker* (Robert Hale, 1937).

Dominic Streatfield, *The Secret History of Mind Control* (Thomas Dunne Books, 2007).

Kathleen Taylor, *Brainwashing: The Science of Thought Control* (Oxford University Press, 2006).

Guide to the City of Moscow (Co-operative Publishing Society of Foreign Workers in the USSR, 1937).

Any historical errors in *The Twelfth Department* are my responsibility, although they are occasionally deliberate – fiction does, after all, involve quite a lot of making things up. I do like to hear about them, though, so please feel free to get in contact via my website.

There are a number of people who contributed to the writing of *The Twelfth Department* and to whom I'm very grateful.

Alistair Duncan, who worked on the BBC series *The Brain: A Secret History*, gave me very helpful research suggestions that pointed me in the right direction at an early stage.

Daniel Petrov managed to get me into places in Moscow I wouldn't otherwise have been able to visit.

Johnny O'Reilly, the Moscow-based film director, who lives in the House on the Embankment, kindly showed me around his apartment and told me a story or two about the building that made their way into these pages.

Paul Richardson, publisher of the magazine *Russian Life*, read a late draft of *The Twelfth Department* and prevented me from making several embarrassing mistakes.

Barney Spender, Jackie Farrant, Ed Murray and my wife Joanne were all careful and very helpful readers of early drafts of *The Twelfth Department* – their enthusiasm was generous and welcome.

My agent, Andrew Gordon, of David Higham Associates, always reads the earliest drafts of my novels and manages to be both an incisive and an enthusiastic critic – exactly what a writer needs. I'm very fortunate to have him looking after me, not least because he and his colleagues, particularly Tine Nielsen, Ania Corless and Stella Giatrakou, have ensured the Korolev novels have been published in seventeen countries and counting. I'm particularly grateful to Kelley Ragland of Minotaur and Nina Salter of Editions des Deux Terres, who have been very generous in their support and encouragement.

George Lucas of Inkwell Management in New York has also been a careful reader of the Korolev novels, an enthusiastic advocate and a source of sound advice.

I knew before I began writing that having a good editor and a good publisher was important to an author – I now know just how important. I'm always aware of the many people at Mantle and Pan Macmillan who contribute to the success of the Korolev novels, in particular Katie James, who handles publicity, Will Atkins who did a great copy-edit on *The Twelfth Department* and the wonderful Sophie Orme, who does, it seems, just about everything. However, my editor, and publisher, Maria Rejt is – well – Maria. With each novel I understand that little bit more how lucky I am to be both edited and published by her.

extracts reading groups
competitions books new
discounts extracts extracts discounts
competitions reading groups
books new extracts discounts events
events books reading groups
new extracts
books reading groups
new titles reading groups
interviews
reading groups events extracts extracts
discounts events
books
new books events interviews
events new events
books
discounts extracts discounts
www.panmacmillan.com
extracts events reading groups books
competitions books extracts new